John D. Lang

The Coming Event!

Freedom and Independence for the Seven United Provinces of Australia

John D. Lang

The Coming Event!
Freedom and Independence for the Seven United Provinces of Australia

ISBN/EAN: 9783337335557

Printed in Europe, USA, Canada, Australia, Japan

Cover: Foto ©Andreas Hilbeck / pixelio.de

More available books at **www.hansebooks.com**

THE COMING EVENT!

OR

FREEDOM AND INDEPENDENCE

FOR

THE SEVEN UNITED PROVINCES OF AUSTRALIA.

BY

JOHN DUNMORE LANG, D.D., A.M.,

SENIOR MINISTER OF THE SCOTS CHURCH, SYDNEY,
AND RECENTLY ONE OF THE REPRESENTATIVES OF THE CITY OF SYDNEY IN THE
PARLIAMENT OF NEW SOUTH WALES;
HONORARY MEMBER OF THE AFRICAN INSTITUTE OF FRANCE, OF THE AMERICAN
ORIENTAL SOCIETY, AND OF THE LITERARY INSTITUTE OF
OLINDA, IN THE BRAZILS.

ENGLAND WAS NEVER SO RICH, SO GREAT, SO FORMIDABLE TO
FOREIGN POWERS, SO ABSOLUTELY MISTRESS OF THE SEA, AS SINCE THE
LOSS OF HER AMERICAN COLONIES.—*Lord Macaulay's Essays*, II. 62.

SYDNEY:
JOHN L. SHERRIFF, PUBLISHER,
18, WYNYARD SQUARE.

1870.

TO THE ELECTORS OF THE CITY OF SYDNEY.

FELLOW-CITIZENS AND FRIENDS,

In the year 1850, you did me the honour to elect me one of the two representatives of your city in the Colonial Legislature, after I had previously served a sort of apprenticeship in the work of legislation, as one of the six members for the District of Port Phillip, now the great Colony of Victoria, from the year 1843. And in the following year, 1851, when Sydney had been allowed a third member, you did me the honour to elect me again one of the three, and to place me, as you have done so often since, at the head of the poll.

In the year 1853, when I happened to be absent in England, a so-called Constitution Act was passed for the Colony, which was ratified and confirmed by the Imperial Parliament in 1855 ; but as that Act, which had been concocted by the enemies of popular freedom, contained a clause for my special benefit, rendering ministers of religion ineligible for a seat in the future Provincial Parliament, I was precluded from entering the Legislature on the inauguration of Responsible Government in 1856. But as soon as a really popular government had got into power, under the auspices of our present Premier, in the year 1857, the clause in question was repealed, and I was again returned one of your representatives at the next General Election in 1859—an office which I continued to hold, in all the succeeding Parliaments, till the close of the past year, when I deemed it expedient to retire from the Parliamentary arena altogether.

Permit me then, Fellow-citizens and Friends, to inscribe to you this volume, as a memorial of the political connection that has thus so long and so harmoniously subsisted between us, in the hope that you will not be unwilling, when the proper time comes, to take the initiative, as it is alike your interest and your duty to do, for the settlement of the great question that is now virtually submitted for our decision, viz. :—as to whether we and the colonies to the northward are to remain for an indefinite period mere colonies of Britain, or to assume the noble position of a Sovereign and Independent State on the Pacific Ocean, with a territory extending from Cape Howe to Cape York, and the city of Sydney for its capital, as the Queen of the Isles of the Western Pacific.

You will see from this volume that it is the law of nature and the ordinance of God, that full-grown colonies, like ourselves, should assume such a position as I have indicated, at the earliest possible period, *for the benefit of their mother-country, as well as for their own.*

You will also see that from Great Britain's ignoring, or rather wilfully shutting her eyes to this great fact, her colonization system for the last two hundred and fifty years, —so far from meriting the praise which ignorance and self-glorification have so often bestowed upon it—has been nothing less than an enormous political blunder, an offence of very serious magnitude in the eyes of Heaven, and a loss of incalculable amount, not only to herself and her colonies, but to the human race.

You will likewise see that the mother-country, tacitly recognizing this great political blunder of the past, has at length expressed her willingness that we should at once assume such a position as I have indicated, and has in-timated her meaning in the matter in the most significant manner, by the withdrawal of her troops from all these Australian colonies.

You will see moreover that there is an urgent necessity at present for our immediately taking the step I have recommended, from the critical state of things in the rich and beautiful Isles of the Western Pacific, that naturally look to us as their Guide and Protector.

And you will see finally that by assuming the high and highly influential position that thus awaits us—by taking our place at once in the family of nations, with the entire concurrence of Her Majesty's Government—we may be the means of relieving our beloved mother-country, in a comparatively short period, of not less perhaps than half a million of her redundant population, without expense either to herself or to us, and planting them as British colonists in the multitude of the Isles.

Trusting then that you will recognize your present duty in this matter—to yourselves, to Great Britain and to the world—and that you will act accordingly,

I have the honour to be,

Fellow-citizens and Friends,

Your fellow-colonist and well-wisher,

JOHN DUNMORE LANG.

Sydney, New South Wales,
    21st July, 1870.

PREFACE.

THERE is no great public question in which the British nation has so deep an interest, or in regard to which a large proportion of the intelligence of the country is so profoundly and fatally ignorant, as the Colonial question, or the proper relation of a mother-country to her colonies. A system of government for the British colonies has accordingly been suffered to grow up, as if by sheer accident, and to subsist in great measure unquestioned, as far at least as its fundamental principles are concerned, to the present day—a system, however, wholly unwarranted by the laws of nature and the ordinance of God, and not less unjust and oppressive towards its more immediate objects than disastrous and suicidal in its tendencies and results to those who uphold it.

In such circumstances, it is equally desirable and necessary that all intelligent colonists should make themselves well-acquainted with the real bearings of this peculiarly colonial question, the mutual relations of the mother-country and the colonies, and especially with their *own* rights and interests as British Colonists. This is doubtless the more needful, on the part of all right-minded Colonists, as, under the bad system of government that has universally prevailed, till very recently, in the British colonies, from the earliest times of British Colonization—neglected as the colonies always were on the one hand, and regularly thwarted in their every effort for their own social and political advancement on the other—British Colonists, as a class, have in too many instances become apathetic and indifferent in regard to their own rights and interests, and have sunk down into a condition of social, moral, and political degradation. To use the language of an eminent New England patriot, who flourished shortly before the commencement of the American troubles of last century, "There has been a most profound, and I think a shameful silence till it seems almost too late to assert our indisputable rights as men and as citizens."* There has also prevailed among colonists generally, perhaps as the natural consequence of this state of things, a very exorbitant idea of the rights of the mother-country in regard to the colonies. "Many," says the celebrated Dr. Benjamin Franklin, in the preface to his *Considerations on the Nature and the Extent of the Authority of the British Parliament*—" Many will perhaps be surprised to see the legislative authority of the British Parliament over the colonies denied *in every instance*. These the writer informs, that, when he began this piece, he would probably have been surprised at such an opinion himself. For it was the result, not the occasion, of his disquisitions. He entered upon them with a view and expectation of being able to trace some constitutional line between those cases in which we ought, and those in which we ought not, to acknowledge the power of Parliament over us. In the prosecution of his inquiries he became fully convinced that *such a line doth not exist*; and that there can be no medium between acknowledging and denying that power in ALL CASES."†

There is no subject also on which the literature of Great Britain presents so complete a blank. Of the many books on the Colonies with which the British press perpetually teems, where are there any that go to the root of the matter, and discuss with manly freedom the first principles

---

* *The Rights of the British Colonies asserted and proved*, by James Otis, Esq., Boston, New England, 1765, page 63.

† *Considerations on the Nature and the Extent of the Authority of the British Parliament*, by Dr. Benjamin Franklin. Rivington's New York Gazetteer, Oct. 30th, 1774.

of colonization? For my own part I know of none. A few sparks or glimmerings of light were, doubtless, struck out on the subject during the great struggle for freedom and independence in America; but these were soon trodden out again under the iron hoof of irresponsible power, and as far at least as colonization in the Southern Hemisphere has been concerned, the last state of the British colonies— till the advent of Responsible Government in the year 1856 —has been worse than the first: for instead of going forward in the right direction, since the days of the Charleses, we have actually been going back!

It is the primary object of the following work to point out the right principles of colonization, and to confirm the theory thus advanced by an appeal to the principles and practice of those nations, both in ancient and modern times, whose efforts in the work of colonization have not only been successful, but have, notwithstanding all our boasting on the subject, presented a perfect contrast with our own. In short, it is the object of the writer to show, that Great Britain has hitherto been all wrong in her principles and practice in the matter of colonization, and to point out, in accordance with the laws of nature and the ordinance of God, *a more excellent way*; that way being the way of entire freedom and independence for the colonies.

The main object of the work, as its title implies, is therefore to recommend to all parties concerned, both at home and abroad, the speedy and entire political Separation of the United Colonies of Australia from the mother country, and their erection into a Sovereign and Independent State.

While this volume was passing through the Press, an Intercolonial Conference was held in Melbourne, with a view to take into consideration the practicability and the propriety of establishing a General Customs' League and a Uniform Tariff for all the Australian colonies—preparatory,

as such a measure was conceived to be, to a general
federation of the colonies. In the prospect of this most
desirable consummation, the writer had perhaps too
confidently urged the claim for Freedom and Independence
for the Seven United Provinces of Australia. But the
result of that Conference has shewn that it is hopeless to
expect an incorporating union of all the Seven Provinces
at present; the three colonies on Bass' Straits and the Great
Southern Ocean, viz., Victoria, Tasmania, and South Australia, being banded together in favour of Protective Duties,
while New South Wales, the oldest of the group and
the mother of all the rest, adheres firmly to the system of
Free Trade. It has, therefore, become necessary to leave
out of the programme the three Southern Colonies, for the
present at least, and to confine the claim of Freedom and
Independence to the colonies, both present and prospective,
on the Pacific Ocean, from Cape Howe to Cape York, viz.,
New South Wales, Queensland, Capricornia and Carpentaria.

The principal reason for urging the immediate accomplishment of the great object in view is the absolute necessity
for the erection of a Sovereign and Independent Power on
the Pacific, in view of the actual state of things in the
Fiji Islands. On this transcendently important subject,
however, it is pitiful to think that the Conference could
only come to the following impotent conclusion :—

BRITISH PROTECTORATE OVER FIJI.

"This Conference, being of opinion that the geographical
position of the Fiji Islands renders their protection of the
very highest consideration as regards Australia and both
British and Australian commerce;

"Resolves—That it is of the utmost importance to
British interests that these islands should not form part of
or be under the guardianship of any other country than

Great Britain, and that a respectful address to this effect be prepared for transmission to the Imperial authorities."

Did the Conference really suppose that, after their recent declaration in behalf of Colonial Freedom, and their recent and still more significant proceedings, in withdrawing the Imperial troops from the Australian Colonies and New Zealand, Her Majesty's Government could possibly stultify itself by assuming the responsibility of establishing a British Protectorate over the Fiji Islands, and thereby incurring the risk of another war with savages in the Pacific Ocean? There are at present upwards of two thousand white men chiefly British, with about one third Americans and Germans, in the Fiji Islands; and the native population is estimated at two hundred thousand. There is actually at this moment also a requisition in Sydney from the Islands to prohibit the export of firearms for the use of the natives—which, however, cannot be done without an Act of Parliament, and the report of which will certainly not induce Her Majesty's Government to change their minds or to move in the matter, after their bitter recollections of New Zealand. On the other hand, there are people in these Islands actually talking still about annexation to the United States or to the North German Confederation. In such circumstances, there is an evident and urgent necessity for action of some kind in the matter; and earnestly desirous as the writer is, in common with the Intercolonial Conference, that the Fiji Islands may never fall under the guardianship of any foreign power, it must be evident that the only way in which this can be prevented, and a really British Protectorate over these Islands established, is the one recommended in this volume—that of erecting a Sovereign and Independent State on the Pacific. A Government for New Zealand, as a dependency of New South Wales, was successfully established in Sydney, at the instance and *on the recommendation of the writer*, in the year 1840, although a Bill for the Colonization of that Island had been rejected by the House of Commons in 1838, while the Colonial Office was dead against it in 1839. Why then may not a Protectorate for Fiji, under somewhat different auspices, be established in Sydney also?

Sydney, 27th July, 1870.

CONTENTS.

CHAPTER I.

THE RIGHTS OF COLONIES.

CHAPTER II.

ANCIENT AND MODERN COLONIZATION COMPARED AND CONTRASTED.

CHAPTER III.

THE FUTURE AUSTRALIAN EMPIRE.

THE COMING EVENT!

OR

FREEDOM AND INDEPENDENCE

FOR THE

SEVEN UNITED PROVINCES OF AUSTRALIA.

CHAPTER I.

THE RIGHTS OF COLONIES.

SECTION I.—DEFINITIONS AND LIMITATIONS.

A COLONY is a body of people who have gone forth from the Parent State, either simultaneously or progressively, and formed a permanent settlement in some remote territory, whether that territory has been already occupied by an inferior race or not.

There are therefore two things necessary to constitute a colony properly so called; viz. 1st. Emigration from the Parent State; and, 2nd. Permanent settlement in the occupied territory: and if any dependent community is deficient in either of these essentials, it cannot with propriety be designated a colony of the country to which it is subject or on which it is dependent.*

* Of colonization, the principal elements are emigration and the permanent settlement of the emigrants on unoccupied land. A colony, therefore, is a country wholly or partially unoccupied, which receives

B

A British colony is therefore a community of Britons, however formed, permanently settled in some country or territory beyond seas.*   It is a gross abuse of language to apply the designation to any community constituted otherwise; and the prevalence of this abuse serves only to maintain the palpable delusion that the colonies of Britain, or British colonies properly so called, either are, or ever were either numerous or extensive, as compared with the population and resources of the Parent State.   This delusion serves to foster our national pride, while it blinds us to our national danger: it feeds our national vanity, and prevents us from doing our national duty.

Agreeably to this definition, we must exclude from the list of British colonies all such foreign possessions of the British empire as India, Ceylon, and Malta; for the Ionian Islands, which were recently in the same category, have since, on the very judicious advice of their late Lord High Commissioner, the Right Honorable Sir John Young, been happily transferred to the Kingdom of Greece.   These countries are all doubtless dependencies of the British empire, but they are in no respect British colonies.   Ninety-nine out of every hundred of their inhabitants, or rather perhaps nine hundred and ninety-nine out of every thousand, neither are nor ever have been Britons; and the mere handful of Britons who go to any of these countries never think of forming permanent settlements in them, and

emigrants from a distance; and it is a colony of the country from which the emigrants proceed, which is therefore called the mother country.—*A View of the Art of Colonization, &c.* By Edward Gibbon Wakefield, Esq.   London, 1849, p. 16.

* The primary meaning of the word *colonist* is obvious from the maxim of the Roman law, " *Colonus est qui alienum agrum colit.*"   He is a person who cultivates *other people's* land, whether as a mere employé or as a tenant.   The secondary meaning we attach to it is that of a person who cultivates land of his own, or who merely resides, in a colony.

of thereby identifying themselves, "for better, for worse," with their inhabitants. They go to them either to make money or to get honour and glory in the world, and *to return* to spend the evening of their days in their native land. They have none of the peculiar feelings, desires, or prospects of colonists, properly so called, and never can have.

Our definition must also exclude all such dependencies of the British empire as Lower Canada, the Mauritius, St. Lucia, the Cape of Good Hope, Demerara, and Trinidad. Not one of these dependencies is a British colony properly so called. The first three—Lower Canada, the Mauritius, and St. Lucia—were French colonies, conquered and appropriated by Great Britain. The Cape of Good Hope and Demerara were Dutch colonies acquired in a similar way; and Trinidad is merely a conquered colony of Spain. In short, in regard to not a few of the transmarine possessions or dependencies of the empire, which we are in the habit of designating, with great self-complacency, *our colonies*, we have been realizing pretty much the popular idea of the cuckoo, which, it is said, builds no nest of her own, but lays her solitary egg in that of some other bird and forthwith takes possession. In all the instances enumerated—and the list might be somewhat extended if it were necessary—we have merely seized the colonies of other weaker people; and after depositing our solitary egg in them, we have called them *ours*, as if we had planted them from the first. *British colonies*, forsooth! It is a most unwarrantable misnomer. As old Cato well observes—*Jampridem equidem vera nomina rerum amisimus — largiri aliena vocatur liberalitas :* or, in plain English, "We have long lost the proper names for things—for instance, making free with other people's possessions is called *British Colonization !** How many Britons ever go

---

* Cato's Speech in Sallust, De Conjur. Catilin.

to the foreign colonies we have thus appropriated? The merest handful comparatively. How many of these even go to them merely to make money and to return? Almost the whole of them.

Neither are the really British islands of the West Indies —Jamaica, Barbadoes, St. Vincent, &c., including the Bahama Islands—entitled to be called *British* colonies. At least nine out of every ten of the inhabitants of these islands are either Africans, or the descendants of Africans who were originally stolen from their native country, and made slaves of, to grow sugar, cotton, and coffee for Englishmen: and the very few Britons comparatively who ever went to them went merely to make money, and *to return*. These islands are therefore merely British possessions—they are in no respect British colonies, properly so called; both of the essential requisites of a really British colony being wanting: for the negroes, who constitute so large a proportion of the entire population, never emigrated from Great Britain, and the negro-drivers, to use the phraseology of the olden time, regularly return to the mother country whenever they can afford to do so.

Still less are we entitled to profane the designation *British colony*—which I confess I consider a very high and honourable distinction for any community, and one that ought not to be lightly applied or appropriated where it is not deserved—by applying it to any of those numerous posts or stations that are held either for naval and military purposes, or for the furtherance and protection of commerce: such as Heligoland, Gibraltar, Bermuda, Honduras, St. Helena, Ascension, Sierra Leone, the Gambia River, Aden, Malacca, Pulo Penang or Prince of Wales Island, Singapore, Hong Kong, and Labuan. It would be equally absurd to call the Eddystone Lighthouse and Tilbury Fort *British colonies*, as to apply that much abused designation to such places as these. They are all British possessions, and it is doubtless necessary for the purposes of a great maritime and commercial nation that they should always remain so ; but not one of them is a *British colony*, properly so called.

What then are the British colonies, properly so called : as it is evident they must now be reduced to a very small number indeed, as compared with the long list of what are commonly called *British colonies?* They are—

1. The North American colonies of Upper Canada, New-foundland, Nova Scotia, New Brunswick, and Prince Edward's Island, now comprising the Dominion of Canada.

2. The Australian colonies of New South Wales, Victoria, Tasmania, South Australia, Queensland, and Western Australia, or Swan River.

3. The New Zealand group of islands.

4. The Falkland Islands.

5. Vancouver's Island, and Western Columbia.

SECTION II.—OBJECTS OF COLONIZATION.

What then are the proper and legitimate objects which such a country as Great Britain ought to have in view or to propose to herself in forming such colonies as these— British colonies, properly so called? They are—

1. To secure an eligible outlet for her redundant population of all grades and classes.

2. To create a market for her manufactured produce by increasing and multiplying its consumers indefinitely.

3. To open up a field for the growth of raw produce for her trade and manufactures ; and,

4. To sustain and extend her commerce by carrying out all these objects simultaneously.

Now these are noble objects for any nation to pursue; and no wonder that Lord Bacon should designate the peculiar work they indicate *the heroic work* of colonization. Nay, it is something more even than a merely heroic work :

it is the course divinely prescribed in the first commandment given to the human race, *Be fruitful and multiply, and
replenish the earth, and subdue it ;** and it may, therefore, be
inferred that it can never be safe for any nation to neglect
this work, if in the peculiar circumstances to which the
commandment applies.   For, as *God made the earth to be
inhabited*,† he will certainly hold that nation, which he has
specially called in his Providence to carry out this divine
ordinance, responsible for the neglect of its proper duty, if
it has been neglected, and will afflict and punish it accordingly.   For while Divine Providence has peculiar
benefits and advantages in reserve for nations, as well as
for individuals, who pursue the prescribed course, whether
in politics or in anything else, it has pains and penalties of
an endless variety of forms, and of an infinity of degrees of
pressure, for those nations or individuals who act otherwise.

It must be clear therefore as daylight that Great Britain
has been specially called, in the good Providence of God,
to the *heroic* work of colonization.   She has by far the
largest Colonial Empire in the world : she has facilities for
colonization such as no other nation on earth has ever had
since the foundation of the world : and she has a remarkably
redundant, and at the same time a peculiarly energetic,
people, the fittest on earth for this heroic work, and the
most willing to engage in it heartily.   And it must be
equally clear, from our very limited experience on the
subject as a colonizing nation, that a regular and systematic
obedience of the divine commandment, on the part of Great
Britain, would, in such circumstances, enable her to realize
all the objects of colonization enumerated above ; or, in
other words, would infallibly secure an eligible outlet for
her redundant population, of all grades and classes ; create
a market for her manufactured produce by increasing and

* Genesis, i. 28.   † Isaiah. xlv. 12, 18.

multiplying its consumers indefinitely; open up a field for the growth of raw produce for her trade and manufactures to any conceivable extent; and sustain and extend her commerce simultaneously, to a degree hitherto unparalleled in the history of the world.

But from "the beggarly account of empty boxes" which the history of British colonization, properly so called, has hitherto exhibited, as compared with the population and resources of the empire, it must be equally clear and undeniable that Great Britain has utterly failed, both in discharging her proper duty as a nation in this important respect, and in realizing the proper benefits and advantages of colonization to anything like the extent to which they might have been realized; and that she must consequently have incurred the pains and penalties which Divine Providence justly and properly attaches to such neglect. The Condition-of-England question, which is now producing so much anxiety and apprehension throughout the United Kingdom, sufficiently declares what these pains and penalties are. They are, 1st. The extraordinary redundance of the population, of all grades and classes, as compared with the means of comfortable subsistence and eligible employment for these grades and classes respectively; 2nd. The unnatural and enormous competition for employment and subsistence to which this state of things gives rise among what are called the respectable classes of society, of all ranks, occupations, and professions; 3rd. The periodical stagnations of commerce, arising from over-production and the want of outlets, and the frequent ruin of merchants, manufacturers, and traders of all kinds, to which this redundance and competition necessarily lead; 4th. The frequently recurring periods of want of employment for the industrious classes, and the wide-spread destitution which it occasions, together with the normal condition of abject poverty and misery into which whole masses of the humbler classes are constantly sinking; 5th. The fearful increase of pauperism in numerous localities throughout the United Kingdom, in which such a condition of society was quite unknown, within the memory even of the present generation; and, 6th. The frightful increase of crime and of a criminal population, not to speak of the serious and successive shocks which the moral principle of the nation generally must sustain in this downward progress of society.

In the year 1831, during one of those periods of distress, arising from want of employment, among the working classes, which are now of such frequent recurrence throughout the United Kingdom, I happened to be spending an hour or two with the late Rev. Dr. Chalmers, of Edinburgh; and the conversation happening to turn upon the state of the poor and the distress of the times, Dr. C. inveighed, as I thought, somewhat severely, against the improvidence of the humbler classes, and especially their early and imprudent marriages; enlarging upon the necessity of applying the principle of moral restraint somewhat more effectually, to prevent the population from outrunning the means of subsistence. These sentiments, I confess, grated rather harshly upon my ear, as a British colonist; and notwithstanding my habitual veneration for the great and good man, I took the liberty to inform him that I was accustomed to take for my maxim in political economy the divine commandment recorded in the first chapter of the book of Genesis, repeating the passage above cited; and adding, that after riding over millions of acres of as fine land as the sun ever shone on, and in one of the finest climates on the face of the earth, lying utterly waste, I could not help thinking that the divine commandment was a right one after all, and that there must be something radically wrong in our social and political system in not applying the remedy which the case demanded, viz., that of extensive colonization. "Aye," replied Dr. Chalmers, with remarkably good humour, "that may be very sound doctrine in your colony, but it will not do *here*," meaning Edinburgh. I am persuaded, however, that it is *there*, chiefly, and in every place similarly situated in the United Kingdom, that the doctrine is peculiarly applicable.*

SECTION III.—IS THE EXTENSION OF THE EMPIRE OF THE COLONIZING, OR MOTHER COUNTRY, A PROPER AND LEGITIMATE OBJECT OF COLONIZATION.

If the extension of the empire of the mother country were compatible with the attainment of all the proper and legitimate objects of colonization enumerated above, this would be an open question, which I have no hesitation in saying, every rightly constituted mind would be predisposed to answer in the affirmative. But there is *a previous question* to be answered; viz., "Is the extension of the empire of the mother country compatible with the attainment of the other and legitimate ends of colonization?" and this question I have no hesitation in answering in the negative —it is not. Whether empire be made the direct object of colonization, or merely regarded as a necessary inference or corollary from it, the mother country must in either case make up her mind to the sacrifice and loss of all the *other* objects for which colonization is either warrantable or desirable. And this is precisely what has hitherto been

* It was the strong impression which was produced upon my mind, by contemplating the state of things among the working classes of the mother country, as compared with that of persons of the same classes in Australia, at the period referred to above, that induced me to make the important experiment which I was enabled to make at that period, by bringing out a whole shipload of Scotch mechanics, per the *Stirling Castle*, to New South Wales, in the year 1831, *with a view to originate an extensive emigration of the working classes of the United Kingdom to that colony.* This experiment, I may add, was completely successful, and was productive of very important social and economical results in New South Wales.

done by every mother country in Europe, our own not
excepted. Like the foolish dog, in the fable, when swim-
ming across a rapid river with a lump of beef in his mouth
—in order to catch at the shadow, *empire*, we drop the
substance, *beef;* and we then find to our unspeakable
mortification, and perhaps disgrace, that both are gone !
This has been the brief history of European colonization,
without one solitary exception, ever since the discovery of
America. The final result may not indeed have been
arrived at as yet, in certain instances, but we are certainly
hurrying rapidly towards it in all.*

Mr. Wakefield, who has a theory of his own on this
subject, which he puts forth, however, somewhat hesi-
tatingly, would paint the *shadow*, and call it *prestige*, which
he thinks a good equivalent for the solid *beef:* let him
dine upon *prestige* by all means. ·

Mr. Wakefield observes :—

"Regarding colonial government as an essential part

* "It is a most extraordinary feature in the character of the British
Government, that while tho people of England itself are under the
mildest possible laws, and enjoy the largest amount of liberty of any
nation in the world, the colonies of England, which are justly esteemed
her pride and her strength, are subjected to a dominion more assimi-
lated to that of Russia and Turkey than anything else. In the
colonies, the genius of British liberty is no longer to be found. Her
mild sway is exchanged for the iron rod of the despot, and those who
were her children in her native land have become the subjects and the
slaves of petty tyrants. The truth of this will be found in the history
of every colony, and felt in the experience of every colonist; its effects
have been the premature separation of the first American colonies, the
recent rebellion and bloodshed in Canada, the ruin of the present
settlers of New Zealand, the extravagant expenditure of this Government, and the demand upon England for money to support it."—*New
Zealand, in* 1842; *or, the Effects of a Bad Government on a Good Country.
In a letter to the Right Hon. Lord Stanley, Principal Secretary of State
for the Colonies.* By S. M. D. Martin, M.D., President of the New
Zealand Aborigines' Protection Association, and lately a Magistrate of
the Colony. Auckland (New Zealand), 1842.

of colonization, the question remains, whether the government of the colony by the mother country is equally so. Is the subordination of the colony to the mother country, as respects government, an essential condition of colonization? I should say not.*

Another able writer, however,—a member of the parliament of the day, holding office under Lord John Russell's Government,—speaks somewhat more to the point than Mr. Wakefield on this important subject:—

"The contrivance of a subordinate government," observes that writer, "renders the government of a distant territory *possible*, but does not render it *good*."

And again:—

"So great are the disadvantages of dependencies, that it is in general fortunate for a civilized country to be sufficiently powerful to have an independent government, and to be ruled by natives."

And again:—

"The disadvantages in question arise principally from the ignorance and indifference of the dominant country about the position and interests of the dependency."

"The dominant country, in consequence of this ignorance, often abstains from interfering with the concerns of the dependency when its interference would be expedient; and when it does interfere with the concerns of the dependency, its interference, as not being guided by the requisite knowledge of these concerns, is frequently ill-judged and mischievous."†

Sir George Lewis, however, subjoins a very consolatory reflection for all colonists; to whom he administers at the

---

* *A View of the Art of Colonization, &c.*, p. 17. London, 1849.

† *Essay on the Government of Dependencies.* By George (afterwards Sir George) Cornewall Lewis, Esq., M.P. London, 1841, pp. 253, 268, 293.

same time what he doubtless considers very judicious advice :—

"If the inhabitants of dependencies were conscious that many of the inconveniences of their lot are not imputable to the neglect, or ignorance, or selfishness of their rulers, but are the necessary consequences of the form of their government, they would be inclined to submit patiently to *inevitable ills*, which a vain resistance to the authority of a dominant country cannot fail to aggravate."*

Sir George Lewis here admits that there *are* serious "inconveniences" or "ills" in the lot of colonists, and that these are the "necessary consequences of their form of government," or, in other words, of the attempt on the part of the mother country to conjoin *empire* with *colonization*. But whether the ills are "inevitable" is a mere matter of opinion, on which certain colonists will probably take the liberty to differ from Sir George. In the meantime they are extremely obliged to him for his honest opinion as to the utter incompatibility of *empire* with the other legitimate objects of colonization.

"The best customer which a nation can have," observes the same able and honest writer, in further illustration of his views, "is a thriving and industrious community, whether it be dependent or independent. The trade between England and the United States is probably far more profitable to the mother country than it would have been if they had remained in a state of dependence upon her."†

And again :—

"If a state of dependence checks the progress of a community in wealth and prosperity, the consequent limitation of its demand for imported commodities will more than compensate the advantages which the dominant country

---

* Lewis, *Preface.*   † Lewis, p. 225.

can derive from being able to regulate its commercial relations with the dependency."*

But Sir George Lewis is not singular in the views he thus entertains as to the unprofitableness of the mere *domination* which the mother country exercises over her colonies. "What real reason," asks Mr. Merivale, "is there for supposing that the inhabitants of any old and peopled colony, *if severed from the mother country*, would augment their capital less rapidly, would produce a less rapidly increasing amount of goods to exchange for ours, would cultivate our commercial connection less assiduously than they do at present."†

How remarkably different these truly enlightened and patriotic sentiments are from the inflated nonsense and puerilities that have recently been put forth by the *soi disant* representatives of the colonies at their Conferences in London on the subject of the mutual relations of the mother country and the colonies!

But the most important testimony as to the incompatibility of the pursuit of empire with the attainment of the other and legitimate objects of colonization, is that of Professor Heeren, of Göttingen, one of the ablest historical and political writers of the age. Remarking on the universal pursuit of empire in colonization by the different colonizing powers of Europe, that writer observes:—

"Time and experience were required to ascertain the relations in which the colonies might be placed most advantageously for the mother country. Without any consideration of their true value and proper use, the first and prevalent idea was in favour of *an absolute possession,*

* Lewis, p. 231.

† *Lectures on Colonization and Colonies.* Delivered before the University of Oxford in 1839, 1840, and 1841. By Herman Merivale, A.M., Professor of Political Economy, afterwards one of the Under-Secretaries of State for the Colonies. London, 1842: vol. I. p. 228.

and total exclusion of strangers. The propagation of Christianity formed a convenient pretext, and none thought of inquiring either into the justice or the utility of their treatment. In truth, we know not how other views could have been acquired, and yet we must needs lament that *the European system of colonization* should so early have taken a direction as unalterable as it was *destructive to the interests both of the colonies and their mother states.*"*

One of the principal disadvantages of dependencies is their distance from the seat of empire.

"It was an unfortunate circumstance for the British Government," observes the intelligent historian of the United States of America, "during their colonial period, and a strong reason for dissolving its colonial dominion, that it was disabled by distance from adapting its measures to the actual and immediate posture of affairs in America. Months elapsed between the occurrence of events in the colonies, and the arrival of the relative directions from England : and every symptom of the political exigence had frequently undergone a material change before the concerted prescription, good or bad, was applied."†

To the same effect, the celebrated Edmund Burke well observes, "The last cause of this disobedient spirit in the colonies is hardly less powerful than the rest, as it is not merely moral, but laid deep in the natural constitution of things. *Three thousand miles of ocean lie between you and them.* No contrivance can prevent the effect of this distance in weakening government. Seas roll, and months pass, between the order and the execution; and the want of a speedy explanation of a single point is enough to defeat a whole system. . . . . . In large bodies

---

* *Europe and its Colonies,* p. 24.

† Grahame's *History of the United States of America, &c.,* vol. iv. p. 369

the circulation of power must be less vigorous at the extremities."*

Now if even *three thousand miles of ocean* were sufficient to render the pursuit of empire incompatible with the attainment of the other and legitimate objects of colonization, in the case of the original British Colonies of America, how much more strongly must not the increase of that distance to five times this amount—to half the circumference of the globe—render empire and the pursuit of the other objects of colonization utterly incompatible? It is no answer to this argument to tell us that Steam has reduced distances so greatly within the last half century that no part of the world can now be considered remote; for Steam can never give a man residing in London so thorough a knowledge of the state of things, in so remote a colony as New South Wales, as to qualify him to legislate for it: and to pretend to such a qualification, notwithstanding, is virtually laying claim to Omniscience —one of the incommunicable attributes of God.

SECTION IV.—IS THE PROPAGATION OF CHRISTIANITY A PROPER AND LEGITIMATE OBJECT OF COLONIZATION FOR ANY GOVERNMENT?

To this question I would give the unhesitating and direct answer—certainly not, as far as Government is concerned. Governments are instituted for the protection and furtherance of the temporal interests of their subjects: they have nothing to do with the concerns of eternity. A Government is neither a Christian church nor a missionary institution, and can therefore have no right to usurp the proper province of either. All that a Government has to do with the Christian religion is to let it alone—to give it free scope—and to protect its professors, of all denomina-

* Edmund Burke's *Speech on Conciliation with America*, Works, vol. iii. p. 56.

tions, in the enjoyment of their rights and privileges as citizens or subjects. As Professor Heeren well observes, "the propagation of Christianity formed a convenient pretext," with European Powers generally, in seeking to gratify their lust of empire through colonization; but in no instance whatever was it ever more than a mere pretext.

But the case is totally different, as regards *individuals* associating for the promotion of colonization; although, with such associations, the propagation of Christianity has often been a mere pretext also. The able historian of British Colonization in America informs us that letters patent were issued by King James I., in the year 1606, to Sir Thomas Yates, Sir George Somers, Richard Hakluyt, and their associates, granting to them those territories in America lying on the sea coast between the 34th and 45th degrees of North latitude. The design of the patentees was declared to be " to make habitation and plantation, and to deduce a colony of sundry of our people into that part of America commonly called Virginia;" and as the main recommendation of the design, it was announced that " so noble a work may, by the prudence of Almighty God, hereafter tend to the glory of his Divine Majesty, in propagating of Christian religion to such people as yet lie in darkness and miserable ignorance of the true knowledge and worship of God, and may in time bring the infidels and savages living in those parts to human civility, and to a settled and quiet government."*

How the said " Sir Thomas Yates, Sir George Somers, and Richard Hakluyt, and their associates," acquitted themselves of the duties they had thus .voluntarily undertaken "in propagating of Christian religion," and in bringing "the infidels and savages to human civility, and to a settled and quiet government," it is scarcely necessary to

---

* Grahame's *History of the United States of North America, &c.,* vol. i. p. 34. London, 1836.

inquire. It was simply one of those "good intentions" with which, we are told in the Spanish proverb, "hell is paved." But history informs us of an association of private individuals of a somewhat different description, which was formed in England for the purpose of colonization very shortly thereafter, and of which one of the main objects was the propagation of the Christian religion on the continent of America. In a Prospectus which was issued by the projectors of the original Puritan emigration to New England in the year 1620, entitled "General Considerations for the Plantation of New England," the design was recommended to all Christian people on the grounds,—

"That it will be a service unto the Church of great consequence, to carry the Gospel into those parts of the world, and raise a bulwark against the kingdom of Antichrist, which the Jesuits labour to rear up in all parts of the world." "For what," they add, "can be a better or more noble work, and more worthy of a Christian, than to erect and support a reformed particular Church in its infancy, and unite our forces with such a company of faithful people, as by timely assistance may grow stronger and prosper; but for want of it, may be put to great hazard, if not be wholly ruined?"*

Now there has certainly never been any object placed before the Christian world, since the days of the Apostles, of more transcendent importance to the interests of the Christian religion, as well as of mankind generally, than the one declared in this Prospectus; and there has never been any object more remarkably realised. The famous Crusades and their results sink into perfect insignificance when compared with the magnificent results of this comparatively humble project of Christian colonization.

The Puritan emigration consisted altogether of about twenty thousand persons, and extended over a period of

---

* Cotton Mather.

about twenty years, viz., from the year 1620 to the year 1640. These people emigrated, therefore, *professedly*, to raise a bulwark against the progress and prevalence of Romanism in North America; and what has been the result of their emigration in this particular? Why, in the year 1840, when I visited the United States, the original Puritan emigrants had increased and multiplied, in the six New England States, to a nation, perhaps the most thoroughly Protestant in the world, of 2,229,879 souls. But this was a mere nothing, in comparison with what they had effected for the Protestantism of the country generally, in the way of colonization; for as their country is but of limited extent, and naturally poor, they had been obliged to emigrate from time to time, and had thus been the great emigrating and colonizing people of America ever since the War of Independence; spreading themselves over the Middle and Western States, but especially the latter, in numbers, compared with which the largest emigration from any European country has been quite insignificant. For even at the commencement of the present century, when the whole emigration from Europe to the United States was a mere trifle in amount, the emigration to the Western States from New England alone, notwithstanding the comparatively small population which it must have had at that period, amounted to three hundred thousand persons in one year! And these emigrants—these Protestant missionaries—have everywhere carried out with them, to their remotest settlement in the Far West, the grand idea of the original Puritan emigration; constituting themselves, in accordance with that great idea, the "bulwark against the kingdom of Antichrist" wherever they go.

Certain second-rate writers on America, who have views of their own to establish as to the importance of a religious establishment for any country, and who look only at the Romish emigration from Ireland and the Continent of Europe to the United States, are fond of predicting that

that country, and in particular the valley of the Mississippi, will speedily become a Roman Catholic country. But the whole European emigration to the United States is even yet quite insignificant, compared with the internal and thoroughly Protestant emigration from the Eastern to the Western States. In the year 1840, the population of the United States amounted to 17,100,572; and during the previous year Dr. Kenrick, the Roman Catholic Bishop of Philadelphia, who was not likely to under-estimate his own communion, estimated its numbers at somewhat less than a million—*millionem fere pertingimus.* Of that number I ascertained that one-half were located in the Eastern States, and the other half in the valley of the Mississippi; but as the population of that valley was then five millions, the proportion of Roman Catholics could not be more than one in ten. Happening to meet at Philadelphia, in the year 1840, with an intelligent clergyman from the State of Missouri, of which the capital, St. Louis, had once been a French settlement, I asked him what was the estimated proportion of Roman Catholics in that State, and was told *one* in *ten*. This, then, was the general proportion in the valley of the Mississippi at that period; and I do not think it is likely to have altered much since.

It is evident, therefore, that Christian colonization is beyond all comparison, the best means of Christianizing the world; and the subject is surely well worthy of the serious consideration of all Christian communions in the United Kingdom. In advocating and establishing missions to the heathen, they are doubtless doing well; but in neglecting this most effectual means of Christianizing the world, they are committing a species of suicide—they are betraying the citadel of their strength into the hands of the enemy.* Had

---

* The first Article in the Charter of the French Company, formed under Cardinal Richelieu, for the colonization of the West Indies and America, in the year 1635, bound the Compay *D'y faire passer quatre*

the colonizing power of Great Britain been only turned to
account, as it might have been, and as it ought to have
been, for the welfare of the nation, since the Protestant
Reformation, what a vast extent of the earth's surface
might not now have been covered with Protestant Christianity!

Even the ancient Heathen considered the extension of
their own peculiar form of idolatry a worthy object of colonization, and one for which hardships might well be endured.
Virgil speaks of his hero in the following language :—

> "————— Multum ille et terris jactatus et alto,
> Multa quoque et bello passus, *dum conderet urbem,*
> *Inferretque Deos Latio.*"—*Æneid.*
> Vast were the toils he proved, by sea and land,
> And in th' embattled field, *to found a State,*
> *And plant in Italy the Gods of Troy.*

And he represents him elsewhere as saying of Italy—

> "Sacra Deosque dabo."
> Temples and rites and gods I'll give the land.

And again :—

> "Sum pius Æneas, *raptos* qui ex hoste *Penates,*
> *Classe veho mecum,* fama super æthera notus.
> Italiam quæro patriam."—*Æneid.*

Once more :—

> "Litora quum patriæ lacrimans portusque relinquo
> Et campos, ubi Troja fuit. Feror exul in altum
> Cum sociis, natoque, *Penatibus et magnis Dis.*"

Heathen as he was, Virgil had a much higher idea of
the proper objects of colonization than the British people
have hitherto had. Who is there that ever thinks of it
with us, as a means of extending the Christian religion?

mille François Catholiques, pendant l'espace de vingt années. "To convey to these regions 4000 French Catholics during the first twenty
years."—*Droit Public, ou Gouvernement des Colonies Françoises.* Paris,
1771.

SECTION V.—DISTINCTION BETWEEN COLONIZATION, PROPERLY SO
CALLED, AND THE MODES OF SETTLEMENT IN OTHER DEPENDENCIES;
WITH THE NATURAL AND NECESSARY RESULTS OF THAT DIS-
TINCTION.

The families and individuals of the British nation, who
go to any of the long list of British possessions, plantations,
or dependencies which I have enumerated above, but which
are not British colonies properly so called, uniformly go
thither for a temporary *sedes* or settlement only, to remain
there, either longer or shorter, for the accomplishment of
their particular object, and then *to return* to their native
land. They never think of making the place of their
temporary and perhaps reluctant sojourning their *country ;*
they never regard it as their *home.* There is no transference
of affection from Britain to the dependency ; and this is the
uniform burden of their song, *Dulce, dulce domum !* "There
is no place like home !"—meaning England, Scotland, or
Ireland. There are individual exceptions, doubtless ; but
this is the general rule. There are occasional incursions
also of really British colonists into the territory of what
was once a French or Dutch colony, as in Lower Canada
and the Cape of Good Hope ; but these are rare cases, and
the line of demarcation between the colonists of the old and
those of the new *regime* is as strongly marked as if it had
been staked off with a line of palisades.*

But the really British colonist goes to a really British
colony with far different feelings and views and objects.

* " To proceed to a new country in a number sufficiently large to
form *a nation or community within itself*, greatly relieves and moderates
the evils of emigration ; but to abandon our country for another, where
the people have nothing in common with us but the bond of the same
humanity, is to renounce our nationality and our race—*two things
which were not given to man that he may cast them off whenever it pleases
his fantasy.*"—*Count Strzelecki's Physical Description of New South
Wales and Van Diemen's Land, &c.,* p. 381.

He may feel as strongly attached to his native country as the other adventurer, and as loth to leave it; and the better man he is, he will only cherish these generous and manly feelings the more strongly. He may say, with all the deep-toned emotion of the poet—

> " Nos patrios fines, et *dulcia* linquimus arva ;
> Nos patriam fugimus !"*
>
> We leave, alas! our much-loved Father-land,
> To seek a home on some far distant strand.

but Divine Providence has said to him, as plainly as God said to Abraham, *Get thee out of thy country, and from thy kindred, and from thy father's house, unto a land that I will shew thee ;†* and he has made up his mind to the issue. In such circumstances, it is not merely *sedes*—a temporary settlement—which he seeks, but a home and a country, *sedes patriamque*. And as he builds his house in the wilderness, and clears and cultivates the virgin soil; or as his sheep and cattle graze peacefully around him, while his children grow up, perhaps with only the faintest recollections of their native land, the colonist feels that a new object is gradually filling up the *vacuum* in his soul; and without being conscious of any estrangement from the land of his birth, he finds that his affections are gradually and insensibly transferred to the land of his adoption. In short, the colonist is like a tree transplanted from its native soil— it is some time before the shock of transplantation, the tearing up of the tender roots, can be got over; but, by and bye, these wounds are healed ; the tree gets used to the soil; it strikes out fresh roots in every direction, and it probably reaches a far loftier height, exhibits a far more luxuriant growth, and spreads around it a far deeper " continuity of shade," than it would ever have, done in its native soil.

* Virgil, Ecl. 1.   † Genesis, xii. L.

In one word, whether the colonist has had great difficulties to overcome in effecting his settlement in the colonial wilderness, or has experienced a speedy and unexpectedly abundant return for his labours, a strong attachment to his adopted country arises insensibly in his mind; and, as time wears on, and the new interests with which he has become identified are multiplied and strengthened, this feeling gradually ripens into a spirit of what may perhaps be designated *colonial nationality*. His native land gradually fades from his view, and his interest in its peculiar objects becomes fainter and fainter. The particular colony, or group of colonies, to which he belongs, engrosses all his affections, and the idea of the welfare and advancement of his adopted country, like a new passion, takes possession of his soul.

The spirit of colonial nationality, which necessarily arises in the circumstances I have described, is no accidental feeling; it is unquestionably of Divine implantation, and designed, not for evil, but for good. The institution of a family is confessedly a Divine institution, fraught with benefits of inestimable value to mankind; and all the attempts of Robert Owenism, Fourierism, Communism, and Socialism, to set it aside and substitute something better for it, are therefore vain and futile. So also is the institution of *a nation*, or group of many families of kindred origin inhabiting the same country, and separated from the rest of mankind by lofty mountains or vast tracts of ocean. Such a group of families will infallibly have feelings, and interests, and objects, centred in their own country or territory, and differing, in that particular, from those of every other portion of the human race.* In one word, a

* The grouping of mankind into nations is as evidently a divine ordinance, designed for the welfare and advancement of the human race, as the grouping of mankind into families; and the attempt to abrogate the divinely appointed distinction into nations, with a view to the working out of some heartless and perhaps impracticable political theory of centralization, is precisely of the same character as

British colony, properly so called, and especially a group
of such colonies, will infallibly become *a nation,* provided
there is ample room and verge enough for its due development. "Colonies," says the celebrated William Penn,
" are *the seeds of nations,* begun and nourished by the care
of wise and populous countries, conceiving them best
for the increase of human stock, and beneficial for
commerce."*

SECTION VI.—ANALOGY BETWEEN A COLONY AND A CHILD, AND IN-
FERENCES FROM THAT ANALOGY.

As every human being who attains maturity of age must
pass through the three successive states of infancy, of
youth, and of manhood, so must every colony ; and as the
infant must be nourished and cherished, and the youth

the notorious attempt of Robert Owen and others, to abrogate the
divine distinction into families. Divine Providence has of late been
evidently taking into its own hands the work of vindicating this
divine ordinance against the folly, the heartlessness, the injustice, and
the cruel oppression of the whole committee of Royal Incapables, who
have been merely serving their own contemptible ends and mis-
governing Europe these thirty years. The reconstruction of " oppressed nationalities " is the miracle of the age ; and no amount of
physical force that despotism can conjure up for the purpose will
prevent that miracle from being repeated again and again, till
Lombardy, Sicily and Venice, till Hungary and Poland are re-erected
into sovereign and independent states.—*Repeal or Revolution* ; *or, a
Glimpse of the Irish Future.* By the Author of this Work.
London, 1848.

* Speaking of "agricultural colonies, whose object is the cultivation of the soil," Professor Heeren, of Göttingen, observes that
"The colonists, who form them, become landed proprietors, are
formally naturalized, and in process of time become *a nation,* properly
so called."—*Manual of the History of the Political System of Europe
and its Colonies.* By A. H. L. Heeren, Professor of History in the
University of Göttingen, p. 24. London, 1846.

guided and governed by his parents, so must the colony.
But there is a time when the youth is no longer to be
under tutors and governors. He attains his majority at a
certain period fixed by law, and he is thenceforth his own
master; being expected, of course, to support himself, as
well as to guide and govern himself, thenceforward. Now
I maintain that there is, in like manner, a time for every
colony, and especially for every group of colonies, to attain
their majority, so to speak, and to guide and govern themselves thenceforward.

This was the uniform doctrine of the ancients on the
subject of colonization. "The ancients," says an able
French writer, during the protracted struggle between
Great Britain and her American colonies, "The ancients
usually compared the duties of colonies towards their
mother country, to those of children towards their parents.
In the order of nature, the members of a family, scattered
abroad, and each forming a new establishment for himself,
are all in a state of independence, and are no longer bound
to their common parent by any other tie than that of
respect and gratitude. Now if these sentiments are
essentially free in their nature, as is indisputable, they
can never constitute bonds of servitude. Agreeably to
this principle, the ancients were of opinion that the
absolute power pleaded for by the mother countries was
founded neither in natural law nor in truth and justice."*

"Grotius, faithful to this maxim, maintains very properly
that *a colony is a new people that grows up in independence :*
NOVUS POPULUS SUI JURIS NASCITUR."

"The legislative power of the mother country being
unable to repress, either with sufficient celerity or with the

---

* King Tullius (in Dion. Hali.) says :—"We look upon it to be
neither truth nor justice. *that mother cities ought of necessity, and by
the law of nature, to rule over their colonies.*" Grotius, de jure belli,
&c., vol. ii., c. 9, sec. 10.

requisite effect, the abuses of the executive power in her colonies, on account of their remoteness, an equality of condition cannot subsist between the citizens of the mother country and those of the colonies. It becomes, therefore, just and necessary that the latter should have a suitable compensation for the disadvantages of their situation, and for the re-establishment of the equilibrium. Their liberty, therefore, ought to be augmented in proportion to the distance of the countries they inhabit, and the difficulties that stand in the way of their frequent communication with those among whom the legislative body resides."*

And again :—

"Under the yoke of authority, a young colony makes much more rapid progress than if it enjoyed complete independence. The enjoyment of liberty is suitable only for a well

---

* " Les anciens comparoient ordinairement les devoirs des colonies envers leur mère patrie, à ceux des enfans envers leurs pères. Dans l'ordre de la nature, les membres d'une famille, dispersés et formant chacun de nouveaux établissemens, sont tous dans l'indépendance, et ne restent plus liés à leur père commun que par le respect et la reconnaissance. Or, si ces sentimens sont essentiellement libres, ce qui est incontestable, ils ne peuvent donc jamais être des engagemens de servitude. D'après ce principe, l'antiquité pensoit que le pouvoir absolu des métropoles n'étoit par sa nature ni légal, ni vrai, ni juste.

" Grotius, fidèle à cette maxime, prétend avec raison qu'une colonie est un nouveau peuple qui nait dans l'indépendance. *Novus populus sui juris nascitur.*

" La puissance législative de la mère patrie, ne pouvant reprimer assez tôt et toujours éfficacement les abus de la puissance exécutive dans ses colonies, à cause de leur éloignement, l'égalité de sort ne sauroit pas subsister entre les citoyens des métropoles et ceux des colonies. Il devient, alors, juste et nécessaire que ces derniers ayent des prérogatives, qui les dédommagent de leur situation et rétablissent l'équilibre. Leur liberté doit, donc, augmenter à proportion de la distance des payes qu'ils habitent, et des difficultés qui s'opposent à leur fréquente communication avec ceux chez qui réside le corps. législatif."—*De l'Etat et du Sort des Colonies des Anciens Peuples.* Paris, 1777; Philadelphie, 1779, p. 127.

established community, and not for one whose members are
reduced to a feeble and precarious condition. But that very
authority ought necessarily to diminish in proportion as the
number of the colonists increases, or be abrogated when
their wants cease. Everything, then, re-enters into the
imperturbable order of nature; political ties are formed by
new conventions, and the rights of government are established on a new basis."*

"The eagles," said the King of the Ostrogoths, "cease
to feed their young ones, as soon as their wings and talons
are formed; the latter have no need of assistance, when
they are able themselves to seize their prey: it would be a
disgrace, if the young people in our armies were thought to
be of an age unfit for managing their estates, or regulating
the conduct of their lives. It is virtue that constitutes full
age among the Goths.†"

Cocceius, a Dutch commentator, commenting upon the
famous saying of Grotius, quoted above, viz., that, in the
case of a colony, "a new and independent nation is born,"
observes, somewhat strangely and in downright contradiction of his author, as follows:—" *Colonia est* nudum instru-
mentum *populi mittentis, et migrat non ut cives esse desinant,
sed ut alibi habitent; indeque manent sub potestate et imperio
mittentium*."‡

---

* "Sous le joug de l'autorité, une colonie naissante fait des progrès
beaucoup plus rapides que si elle jouissoit d'une entière indépendance.
L'usage de la liberté ne convient qu' à une société bien établie, et non
point à celle dont les membres sont réduits à un état faible et précaire.
Mais cette même autorité doit nécessairement diminuer à mesure que
le nombre des colons augmente, ou être abrogée quand leurs besoins
cessent. Tout rentre alors dans l'ordre imperturbable de la nature ;
les liens de politie se forment par de nouvelles conventions, et les droits
de gouvernment s'établissent sur des nouveaux fondemens."—*De l'
Etat et du Sort des Colonies des Anciens Peuples.* Philadelphie, 1779, p.
216.

† Montesquieu, B. xviii. ch. 26.

‡ Henrici Cocceii *Comment.* t. ii. p. 547.

" A colony is the mere instrument of the colonizing or
mother country: its inhabitants, in emigrating, merely
change their place of abode, but not their citizenship; and,
therefore, they continue under the power and government
of the mother country."

Cocceius was the courtly advocate of their High
Mightinesses the States of Holland, whose government of
their colonies was in the highest degree unjust and
oppressive. His definition of a colony, which is exactly
that of Downing-street under the old regime, was evidently
"made to order," and it simply denies all rights to
colonies.

Singularly enough, there is a perfect parallel to this
impudent Dutch definition of a colony in the Westminster
Review for October, 1852, in an article entitled, " Our
Colonial Empire," but which ought properly to have been
entitled " Milk-pap for Bearded Men !"   The *Radical*
Reviewer, forsooth! would allow of a " Colonial Representative Body," as he calls it, to consist of Delegates from
all the Colonies, to meet in London, but "to be restricted
in its functions to discussion and advice !"   He takes for
granted " the necessity of preserving unity in the central
authority," and admits " the difficulty of separating in all
cases between Imperial and Colonial subjects ;" but he
would make all odds even by " limiting the power of the
Colonial House to the free public discussion of all subjects,
and the recording of its views ! ! !"

I should consider myself degraded by replying to such
drivelling impertinence.   Let the Reviewer know that the
men of progress in the colonies hold, with that great
authority, Dr. Benjamin Franklin, whose opinion on such
subjects is worth that of a hundred Westminster Reviewers,
that such *a constitutional line,* as he supposes, between
Imperial and Colonial interests, *doth not exist;* and that, as
a legitimate corollary from the principles and arguments of

this work, they will go one step further, with the said Benjamin, and simply deny the right of the Imperial Parliament to legislate for them in any case whatsoever.

To return to the parallel between the condition of a colony and that of a child, the period fixed by the law of the land for a young man's reaching his majority is the completion of the twenty-first year of his age; for if an unreasonable or tyrannical parent should refuse to give his son his entire freedom, or to allow him to manage his own affairs, after he has attained that age, the law will at once interfere, on the appeal of the son, and set him free. It will not be received as a valid argument, on the part of the father, to allege that he does not consider his son capable of self-government; for the law can take no cognizance of any such allegation. It simply ascertains the fact that the son has reached the age at which he is legally entitled to entire freedom from all further parental control, and at which therefore the *patria potestas* ceases and determines; and it decides accordingly.

But as there is no positive law, either human or divine, to fix the time when a colony, or a group of colonies, shall be held to have attained their majority, and to be permitted to manage their own affairs, and to guide and govern themselves, it may be alleged, with some shadow of reason, that the analogy fails at this point. Does it do so, however? By no means. For the reason assigned for the decision which the law pronounces, in setting the son who has attained his majority entirely free from the control of his unreasonable and tyrannical parent, is that he is both able and willing to manage his own affairs, and to guide and govern, as well as to maintain, himself. Now, as this reason is equally applicable to both cases, I maintain, without fear of contradiction, that a colony, or group of colonies, attains its political majority, and is thenceforth entitled to entire freedom and

independence, whenever it is both able and willing to
manage its own affairs, and to guide and govern itself,
without either assistance or protection from the parent state.
This is the law of nature, or, in other words, the ordinance
of God; and the parent state, which in such circumstances
refuses to grant entire freedom and independence to any
colony or group of colonies, is resisting the divine ordinance,
and is acting unreasonably and tyrannically. The authority it assumes is usurpation, and the exercise of that
authority is downright tyranny.

There is certainly no law requiring a young man to claim
entire freedom from all parental control when he attains
his majority; and if he chooses to remain in his father's
house, and assist him in his business, that is his own affair,
and is supposed to be matter of private arrangement between
his father and himself, with which no law can interfere.
But it is natural for a young man in such circumstances,
especially if he has learned a business by which he can
maintain a family, and sees a favourable prospect of establishing himself successfully in the world, and has fixed his
affections on some virtuous female of his own class in
society, with whom he can be united in matrimony when
he is his own master—it is natural for a yonng man in
such circumstances not only to desire his entire freedom
and independence, but to assert that freedom and independence, and to act accordingly. By the law of nature,
or, in other words, by the ordinance of God, as well as
by the laws of the land, the young man is constituted the
sole judge as to whether he shall assume and exercise his
entire freedom and independence or not.

In like manner it is not only in accordance with the law
of nature and the ordinance of God that a colony, or group
of colonies, which has attained its political majority, and is
both able and willing to undertake the entire management
of its own affairs, without either assistance or protection

from the parent state, should *desire* its entire freedom and independence with intense earnestness; it is the law of nature and the ordinance of God that it should *have* that freedom and independence. "The desire of independence," observes Professor Heeren, "is natural to agricultural colonies; *because a new nation gradually becomes formed within them.*"* To the same effect, the celebrated Grotius, cited again in the following paragraph by Mr. Ex-Governor Pownall, describes the natural growth of a colony into a new nation :—

"Our colonies and provinces, being each a body politic, and having a right to, and enjoying in fact, a certain legislature, indented rather with the case of the Grecian colonies, as stated by Grotius: Huc referenda est discessio quæ ex consensu fit in colonias, nam *sic* quoque *novus populus sui juris nascitur.*" [To this category is also to be referred the case of the voluntary emigration of people to colonies; for *in this way* too A NEW AND INDEPENDENT NATION IS BORN.]†

The parent state, therefore, is not the judge whether the particular colony or group of colonies, claiming its freedom and independence, is fit for, or ought to be entrusted with such a possession. This is a matter for the colony, or group

* Heeren's *Hist. of the Polit. Syst. of Europe and its Colonies*, p. 272.

† *Administration of the Colonies, by Thomas Pownall, formerly Governor of Massachusetts*, p. 55. London, 1768.—Pownall was a well-meaning man who did his best, as a member of Parliament in England, to reconcile both parties, during the American troubles; but of course without effect. He advocated, what he called, in his own clumsy style, "A grand marine dominion, consisting of our possessions in the Atlantic, and in America, united into one empire, in a one centre, where the seat of Government is." The thing was impracticable: it was contrary to the laws of nature and the ordinance of God, as stated by Grotius in the very passage he cites. And yet this notable expedient has been put forth again within the last few months by those consummate fools who have been constituting themselves a volunteer Parliament in London—for us, the colonists of Australia!

of colonies, to determine for itself. The parent state has as little to say in it as the individual parent in the case of his son.

Nay, it is evident and indisputable that it was on this principle of freedom and independence, as far at least as their own internal government was concerned, that the British colonies in America were originally formed; for, considering the important national interests at stake in the matter, it is not less humiliating than it is melancholy to reflect, that, in the theory and practice of colonization, we have actually been retrograding or going back as a people for the last two hundred and fifty years! "The fundamental idea," observes Mr. Merivale, "of the old or British colonial policy appears to have been, that wherever a man went, he carried with him the rights of an Englishman, whatever these were supposed to be. * * This is remarkably proved by the fact, that representative government was seldom expressly granted in the early charters; it was assumed by the colonists as a matter of right."*

And again :—

"It is curious to observe how notions, which were really as old as the constitution, and had been practically followed out for ages in our colonial administration, became dreaded and stigmatised as dangerous novelties, when they were advanced in the broad form of theories by French and American reformers. The great modern change in political speculation, which has brought us in some respects far on the road towards democracy, has in others led by an obvious course to less liberal sentiments than formerly prevailed."†

And again :—

"We rather shrink from the idea of saddling the first laborious settlers in the wilderness with the duties of self-government. Yet it is worth while to pause, and consider

* Merivale's Lectures, I. 101.   † Merivale I. 103.

in how different a light our ancestors regarded this matter. They never dreamt that the colonist was not fully fitted to enjoy at first whatever measure of liberty was to be ultimately his portion. The people of Massachusetts Bay made their own constitution almost as soon as they arrived there; it was ratified at home; its provisions were transferred not many years afterwards to a royal charter, and continued to exist during the whole period of its dependence. When the enthusiast, Roger Williams, settled Rhode Island, he framed in the very next year a republican polity for his dozen or two of families. It was confirmed by charter in 1662, and continues at this very day to be the constituent law of that flourishing little commonwealth. According to our present ideas Rhode Island would not have been "entitled" to a constitution until a century and a half after its first settlement."

And again :—

"The question remains substantially the same—whether 500 men of ordinary British habits and notions, and not too much scattered over the soil, cannot administer themselves municipally as well as 50,000; whether the size of a community—supposing it protected from external violence—has anything to do with its capacity for self-government."*

The character of the age we live in, and the sentiments it puts forth, whether in the mother country or in the colonies, on such subjects as those under consideration, are very fitly described in the following paragraph by that eminent writer, M. de Tocqueville:—

"The men of the eighteenth century knew little of that passion for comfort which is the mother of servitude—a relaxing passion, though it be tenacious and unalterable, which mingles and intertwines itself with many private

* Merivale's Lectures, II. 289.

D

virtues, such as domestic affections, regularity of life, respect for religion, and even with the lukewarm, though assiduous, practice of public worship, which favours propriety but proscribes heroism, and excels in making decent livers but base citizens."*

SECTION VII.—THE QUESTION, AS TO WHAT IS IMPLIED IN THE TERRITORIAL RIGHTS OF A MOTHER COUNTRY, DISCUSSED AND SETTLED.

It is a common, but an unfounded idea, that the word colony has a territorial meaning, and signifies the tract of country inhabited, or to be inhabited, by any body of colonists, as well as the people who form the colony. It has no such meaning, however. It signifies the people exclusively; as, for instance, when we speak of the colony of Tasmania, we mean simply the body of people inhabiting the island of that name.† Unimportant, however,

---

* M. de Tocqueville. *State of Society in France before the Revolution of* 1789. Page 217.

† The ancients uniformly understood the word colony to signify a regularly organized body of people who had either gone or were going forth from the mother country.to form a settlement in some remote, transmarine or conquered territory. Thus, the historian Tacitus, when reprobating the change of system in the matter of colonization which had taken place in his own time—that of the decline and fall of the Roman Empire—as compared with the practice in the better days of Rome, observes, "Non, ut olim, universae legiones deducebantur cum tribunis, et centurionibus, et sui cujusque ordinis militibus, ut consensu et caritate rempublicam afficerent; sed ignoti inter se, diversis manipulis, sine rectore, sine affectibus mutuis, quasi ex alio genere mortalium, repente in unum collati, *numerus magis quam colonia.*" Tacit. Annal. Lib. 14. Sect. 27. "The ancient practice of colonization—under which entire legions were usually led forth as colonies, with their colonels, captains, and privates, each in his own company, that they might organize a colonial community harmoniously and with mutual affection—this ancient practice was no longer fol-

as it may appear, this mistake, as to the meaning of the word colony, has been rather a serious matter to colonists generally; for by taking it for granted that a particular nation has rights, arising either from discovery or conquest, over a particular unoccupied territory, or colony, in the territorial sense of the word, it has been inferred, without the least shadow of reason, that it has also a right to govern the people who may settle within that territory for all time coming. Now we colonists admit the national right, whether of discovery or of conquest, as a right against any other colonizing nation; but we repudiate the inference of its implying a right to govern the future occupants of the territory, as being altogether unfounded in reason and justice.* For example, we admit the right of Great Britain to the exclusive colonization of the whole east coast of Australia, that coast having been discovered in the interest and on behalf of the British nation by our illustrious fellow countryman, Captain Cook; and we would therefore do our

lowed; but bands of soldiers, totally unknown to each other, and of different legions, without any common head, without mutual affection, as if they were each of a different race of men, were suddenly collected together, *forming rather a mob than a colony.*" By the way, this is very much like Government emigration in our own time.

Dr. Johnson doubtless assigns to the word "colony" the secondary meaning of "The country planted; a plantation;" but it is at least questionable whether the quotation he adduces in proof of this meaning bears it out.

> The rising city, which from far you see,
> Is Carthage; and a Tyrian *colony.—Dryden's Virgil.*

Does this mean a tract of country distinct from its inhabitants? I think not. The word *city* unquestionably suggests people, town's people, and not territory. But even Homer nods occasionally, and so does Dr. Johnson.

* Geography is of no party; Rome and Carthage had no frontiers; Genoa and Venice had no territories. *It is not the soil which determines the constitutions of people.* * * * Waves and mountains are the frontiers of the weak—men are the frontiers of the people —*Lamartine's History of the Girondists*, vol. i. p. 264, Bohn's edition.

best, as Britons, to prevent any other European nation from
forming settlements on that coast.* But we maintain, as
Australian colonists, that this right of discovery, as well as
of exclusive colonization in favour of Great Britain which
it implies, implies no right whatever, on the part of the
British people, to exercise domination over the British
colonists who may settle from time to time on that coast.
The two propositions are totally distinct; although it is the
interest of certain parties to confound them, and thereby to
throw dust in the eyes of the public for the attainment of
their own selfish ends. But to use the language of the
eminent writer, (afterwards, if not now, one of the Under
Secretaries of State in the Colonial Office) whom I have
already quoted repeatedly: "It is impossible to place in

---

* A very important question suggests itself in reference to this
right of discovery, as implying an exclusive right of colonization,
viz. :—How long is it to be supposed to hold good ? And the
common sense of mankind has rightly decided in the case, that if
the right is not exercised within a reasonable period, it lapses and
holds good no longer. Captain Cook, for example, discovered the
Island of New Caledonia in the year 1770, the year of his discovery
of the east coast of Australia, and consequently the exclusive right
of colonizing New Caledonia was vested in Great Britain for a certain period; but as Imperial ignorance' and incapacity, conjoined
with the most culpable neglect of our interests as British colonists,
had allowed the important right to lapse, by doing nothing to confirm
it for the long period of eighty years, the Emperor Louis Napoleon
has, in perfect justice and with great adroitness, stepped into our
shoes and taken possession of the island for the purposes of a French
colony ; thereby availing himself of the wonderful facilities for colonization in that particular locality which the previous colonization of
Australia by Great Britain undoubtedly afforded him. In like
manner, the Dutch were the original discoverers, not only of the
continent of Australia, but of the islands of Van Dieman's Land and
New Zealand; but as they did nothing for more than a century afterwards to confirm the right of exclusive colonization which was
thus undoubtedly vested in them, we stepped into their shoes and
took possession in all the three cases.

too strong a light the errors which our national jealousy and contracted views have imported into our popular theories of colonization."*

We have only to glance at the origin of colonization, to be convinced of the utter baselessness of the alleged right of domination on the part of a mother country, which is gratuitously supposed to result from the acknowledged right of discovery or conquest. Colonization therefore must have been coeval with the first settlements of mankind; originating as it did in the ordinance of God, the laws of nature and the necessities of men. For God made the earth to be inhabited†—not to lie waste, as so much of it has done hitherto, through the folly and perversity of men—and his first command to the human race, even in the Garden of Eden, was *Be fruitful and multiply, and replenish the earth.*‡ Now colonization, with all that leads to it, whether in the laws of nature or the necessities of men, is merely the carrying out of this Divine ordinance. For as soon as the first settlement of mankind had become too confined for the sustenance and comfort of its inhabitants, or, in other words, as soon as the pastures of the neighbourhood had proved too limited for their flocks and herds, or the available arable land not sufficiently extensive for the wants of the community, a portion of their number would necessarily be obliged to separate from the rest, and to form another settlement for themselves at some distance. Besides, the experience of all mankind teaches us that dissensions and quarrels would infallibly arise even in the most limited communities.

---

* Merivale's Lectures on Colonization and Colonies, vol. I. page 244.

† *Thus saith the Lord that created the heavens : God himself that formed the earth and made it ; he hath established it,* HE CREATED IT NOT IN VAIN, HE FORMED IT TO BE INHABITED. Isaiah xlv. 18

‡ Sicuti coelum Diis, ita terras generi mortalium datas ; quæque vacuæ eas publicas esse. Tacit. Annal. Lib. xiii. 55.

and that injustice and oppression would very soon be practised (as sacred history informs us was the case to a frightful
extent in the very first settlement of mankind,) by the
strong and powerful towards the weak and helpless; leaving
the latter no other alternative than that of flight or emigration. But, independently of the motives to emigration, that
would necessarily originate in such circumstances, the mere
desire of change, the restless spirit of adventure and the
hope of bettering their fortunes, would induce many others to
emigrate from the earlier settlements of mankind for the purpose of forming distinct settlements or colonies at a distance.
In short, the redundancy of population, the spirit of adventure, and the evil passions of men would all concur, from
the very earliest period in the history of mankind, in ful-
filling the divine ordinance for the peopling of the earth.

In such circumstances the important question arises,
" Would the remaining inhabitants of the original settlement of mankind, from which the supposed emigration has
emanated, have any right to control the future movements
or procedure of their offshoot or colony, or, in other words,
to govern it ?" And to this question I would unhesitatingly answer, " None whatever." For men, being all
born free and equal, every man—especially in a state of
nature, and antecedently to the formation of regular states
and governments,—has a natural, inherent and absolute
right to consult his own interest, whether real or imaginary,
in all such matters, and to follow his own inclinations, by
settling wherever he pleases, in any unoccupied portion of
the habitable globe; and the community he has left can
thenceforth have no right whatever either to control or to
govern him.*

---

* Under one single government the human race would have been
no more than one extenuated and languishing body, extended without
vigour over the surface of the earth. The different governments are
so many robust and active bodies, which, by mutually assisting each

"It is pretended, indeed," observes a celebrated writer and strenuous advocate of the rights of men, "that the moment we quit a state of nature, as we have given up the control of our actions in return for the superior advantages of law and government, we can never appeal again to any original principles, but must rest content with the advantages that are secured by the terms of the society."* This however, is only a pretence: the Divine command given to mankind to *multiply and replenish the earth* is absolute; and no body of men, no state or government, either has or can have a right to prevent its being obeyed or carried out. The rights of any body of British colonists, going forth to form a settlement within the particular colonial territory over which the British nation has an exclusive right of colonization, are precisely identical, as far as self-government is concerned, with those of the first body of colonists who emigrated from the first settlement of mankind. All that Great Britain can rightly do in the case, as a mother-country, is to secure equal rights, equal privileges, and equal advantages for all British subjects emigrating to the colonial territory; leaving them to settle their civil government thereafter for and by themselves.

SECTION VIII.—THE AUSTRALIAN COLONIES HAVE ATTAINED THEIR POLITICAL MAJORITY, AND ARE CONSEQUENTLY ENTITLED TO THEIR FREEDOM AND INDEPENDENCE.

If, therefore, it is true and cannot be gainsaid, that the desire of freedom and independence is natural to all "agricultural colonies," that is, to all such communities as British colonies, properly so called; if this desire is

other, form one whole, and whose reciprocal action maintains and keeps up motion and life everywhere.—D'Alembert. *Analysis of Montesquieu.*

* Robert Hall.

the natural and necessary result of their peculiar circumstances and situation from the fact that "a nation
becomes formed within them;" if it is divinely implanted,
moreover, and therefore designed for good and not for
evil—for the welfare and advancement of the human
family, and not for its injury or depression; and if such
colonies are entitled to their entire freedom and independence whenever they have attained their political majority,
or are both able and willing to manage their own affairs,
without either assistance or protection from the Parent
State, I maintain that the Australian Colonies, having
attained their political majority, and being both able and
willing to sustain and govern themselves, are fully
entitled to their freedom and independence; and I maintain, moreover, that Great Britain, the Parent State, being
an interested party in the matter, has no more right to
constitute herself a judge in the case, and to put forth
an adverse decision, as certain pretended patriots are now
recommending her to do, than the unreasonable and tyran
nical parent who withholds his freedom from his own
child, after he has reached his majority.

The group of Australian colonies for which I would
claim entire freedom and national independence, as a
matter of right as well as of policy, are those in the
Eastern and South-eastern sections of the Australian Continent, together with the insular colony of Van Dieman's
Land or Tasmania. For as the Eastern and Western portions of the Great South Land are separated from each
other by a central desert, like those of Africa and Arabia,
of many hundred miles in extent, it must be evident that
the eastern and western divisions of that land must each
be, in the first instance at least, if not permanently, under
a separate *regime*. There is as complete a separation of
the eastern and western divisions of the island continent
of Australia as if a wide ocean had rolled between them.

The Eastern and South-eastern colonies of the Australian group are as follows, viz.:—

I. NEW SOUTH WALES, with a coast line of five hundred and forty geographical miles on the Western Pacific Ocean, from Cape Howe, the South-eastern extremity of the land, to Point Danger, or the 28th parallel of South latitude; comprising an estimated area of three hundred and twenty-five thousand square miles, or an extent of country equal to that of Great Britain and France together. A large portion of this territory is doubtless hopelessly sterile; but there is still a vast extent of its superficies equal in quality to any land in the world, and its mineral resources, from gold to coal, are inexhaustible. From the height of its mountains, and the extent of its table-land, it has a great variety of climate, and a corresponding range of productions. Its present population (31st December, 1869) is 485,330.

II. VICTORIA, with a coast line of about five hundred miles along Bass' Straits and the Great Southern Ocean, from Cape Howe, the boundary of New South Wales, to that of South Australia, in the 141st degree of east longitude. It extends, however, only a comparatively small distance inland, and its area is eighty-five thousand square miles, or about the size of Great Britain. A large portion of its surface consists of the finest land in one of the finest climates in the world; and its gold mines are of unequalled richness. Its population, 31st December, 1869, was 710,284.

III. TASMANIA (formerly Van Dieman's Land), a beautiful island, nearly equal in size to Ireland, and in a still milder climate. It possesses agricultural and other capabilities for the sustenance and employment of a dense population, superior to those of most European countries of equal extent. Its population, 31st December, 1868, was 100,706.

IV. SOUTH AUSTRALIA, with a coast line of about four hundred miles along the Great Southern Ocean, and an area of at least three hundred thousand square miles. Only a comparatively small portion, however, of this vast extent of territory is at all fit for the purposes of man,* the rest of it being part of the great central desert of Australia; but the available portion is of superior quality for agriculture, and its copper mines are rich and extensive. Its population, 31st December, 1869, was 181,193.

V. QUEENSLAND, with a coast line of undefined extent, along the Western Pacific, from the Twenty-eighth parallel of latitude northwards. This province will have an area of upwards of two hundred thousand square miles, with several rivers disemboguing in the Pacific, and all available for steam navigation, and a large extent of land of the first quality for all sorts of cultivation suited to the soil and climate. Its mineral resources, including gold, copper, and coal, are inexhaustible. Its present population (31st December, 1869) is about 107,427.

VI. CAPRICORNIA.—There is an agitation now in progress for the separation of the northern portion of Queensland, with a view to its erection into a distinct and independent colony, to which the late Sir Thomas Mitchell assigned by anticipation the very appropriate name of Capricornia. Its separation from Queensland will no doubt be effected in due time, as the population of that part of the territory is already as large as that of Queensland at the period of its separation from New South Wales, in December 1859, while the revenue it yields is much greater. The coast line of this future province would probably extend about five degrees along the Western Pacific from the northern boundary of Queensland. There is already a series of promising towns along its coast-line, as well as in its interior; as for instance Gladstone, Rockhampton, Mackay,

* Vide Captain Sturt's *Discoveries in Central Australia*

Townsville, Bowen, Springsure, and Clermont. Of these, Rockhampton, on the very Tropic, has long since had a population of 4000.

VII. CARPENTARIA.*—The remaining portion of the territory of Eastern Australia, from the northern boundary of Capricornia to Cape York, in a northerly direction, and to the Gulf of Carpentaria in a westerly, would form a sufficient area for a seventh colony, (as the complement of this great group), to be called Carpentaria. There is also a series of towns already founded in this colony of the future, both on the Pacific and on the Gulf; as for example Cardwell and Somerset on the Pacific; Norman, Burketown and Sweer's Island in the Gulf, and Gilberton at the gold mines of the interior.

This three great southern continental provinces of this group—New South Wales, Victoria, and South Australia—are all contiguous to each other, having common boundary lines for many hundreds of miles. They are all intimately connected by means of steam navigation along the coast; and the Murray River, which is navigable for upwards of fourteen hundred miles of its long course from the Australian Alps to the Great Southern Ocean, binds them together still more strongly in the interior. New South Wales has also a common boundary with Queensland, the southernmost of the three Northern colonies; while steam navigation not only connects Tasmania with all the six, but binds them together into one great body politic. In one word, with such bonds of union, these Australian colonies will, doubtless, all eventually form one great community, having common interests and common objects, and

---

* I have no doubt that both of these names—Capricornia, suggested by the late Sir Thomas Mitchell, and Carpentaria, by myself, will meet with the cordial approval of every intelligent reader. They tell at once every sensible person throughout the civilised world where the places they designate are.

mutually striving together in an honourable rivalry for the welfare and advancement of their common country. Their population, which is rapidly increasing, already exceeds a million and a half; and the material resources of that population, in point of wealth and revenue, are unquestionably superior to those of any other community of equal extent on the face of the earth.

I have already stated that there is an agitation now in progress for a Customs' League, and a uniform tariff for all these colonies; and there is also a very general desire for a federal and incorporating union to bind them all up into one great volume. It is felt, however, that this very desirable consummation can scarcely be realized without some such adjustment of the boundaries of the conterminous colonies, as would place them somewhat more on terms of equality with each other than they now are. But as this is a matter that will require considerable discussion, I shall leave it for another section.

SECTION IX.—THE AUSTRALIAN GROUP; WITH THE MODIFICATIONS REQUIRED FOR ITS GENERAL FEDERATION AND NATIONAL UNION.

It is deeply to be regretted that Great Britain should, for thirty years past, have virtually abdicated her proper functions as a great colonizing Power, in not fixing authoritatively, for all time coming, the boundaries of the conterminous colonies of Eastern Australia; and in thereby leaving a matter of such transcendent importance to all parties and interests concerned, to be determined as the selfishness of individual colonists, or the caprice of some self-conceited functionary might suggest. An incalculable amount of evil, implying the grossest injustice to whole communities of unoffending colonists, and the complete sacrifice of their material interests, has been the result of this precious instance of Imperial misgovernment.

The colony of New South Wales has an estimated area of 325,000 square miles, that is an extent of territory equal to that of the whole United Kingdom and all France put together; its Southern boundary, at the town of Albury, on the Murray River, being only 190 miles from Melbourne, the capital of Victoria, although nearly 500, by the only practicable route, from Sydney, its own capital; while its Northern boundary is within eighty miles of Brisbane, the capital of Queensland, although upwards of 500 from Sydney! The fact is this Mammoth colony of New South Wales comprises a portion of territory to the southward, as large as the whole of the colony of Tasmania, which it ought never to have possessed, and which happened to be assigned to it, through the apathy and indifference of the Imperial authorities, *on false pretences;* while it comprises another portion to the northward, larger than all England, which it holds merely on the usurped authority of the Governor of the day—Sir William Denison,—*in the face of an Act of the Imperial Parliament directly to the contrary.* The necessary result of these preposterous political arrangements—arrangements worthy of the inmates of a lunatic asylum—is that the trade of the Southern portion of the colony, instead of coming to Sydney, crosses the Border and goes to Melbourne, while that of the northern is fast going to Brisbane. The following remarkably honest statement on the subject has very recently been made by the late Premier of New South Wales—John Robertson, Esq.—in a debate on the Railway System of the Colony in the Legislative Assembly.

"If Hobson's Bay* was the port for Albury, God Almighty made it so, and they could not prevent it. Albury was within two hundred miles of Hobson's Bay; and Sydney, by the way they must go, was five hundred miles. The

* The city of Melbourne is in or rather on Hobson's Bay.

Albury trade, if we had a railway to Albury to-morrow, would never come to us. With regard to Deniliquin, the most productive district in the colony, it was two hundred miles from Melbourne, and seven hundred miles from Sydney. Was any one stupid enough, biassed enough, to suppose that gentlemen would take their produce to this market, over seven hundred miles, when they could reach Melbourne in two hundred miles? If the boundary of New South Wales had been unadvisedly fixed at the Murray, one hundred and seventy miles from Melbourne, on one side, and within eighty miles from Brisbane on the other, we could not help it. But his hon. friend (Mr. Hoskins) asked why was not the business of this country brought to Sydney? The wrong was done in fixing the boundary—on one side eighty miles from Brisbane, and on the other, two hundred miles from Melbourne. *Could any one doubt that at the time of the severance of Victoria and of Queensland, New South Wales had got far more than her share.* Here was Deniliquin, one of the greatest producing districts of the colony: it could not be denied that it would have been a more satisfactory course to the inhabitants of that district to have put Deniliquin in the colony of Victoria. Then Tenterfield and the Tweed River would have been better placed under the control of Brisbane. If the produce of the South went by Victorian railways to Melbourne, and that of the North by Queensland railways to Brisbane, it was to be attributed to the position of the boundary line between the colonies."—*Vide Empire* Newspaper, 13th April, 1870.

The political arrangements in regard to boundaries, which Mr. Robertson characterizes so justly and condemns so strongly in the passage I have just quoted, were effected as follows :—

In a despatch from Lord John Russell, then Principal Secretary of State for the Colonies, to Governor Sir George

Gipps, of 31st May, 1840, his Lordship announced the intention of the Imperial Government to divide the great colony of New South Wales, which then extended from Cape Capricorn to Bass' Straits, into three portions or colonies; the proposed dividing line between New South Wales and the future colony to the Southward (now Victoria), being the Murrumbidgee River, which runs nearly due west for the greater part of its course, and as nearly as possible in the 36th degree of latitude till it joins the Murray, together with a line from the Murrumbidgee in that latitude to the Pacific Ocean.

The portion of this proposed dividing line—from the Murrumbidgee, where it reaches the 36th parallel of latitude, to the Pacific Ocean—would have been a very injudicious boundary line, as it would have taken from New South Wales the portion of territory extending northwards from Cape Howe, and lying between the Pacific Ocean and the Australian Alps or Snowy Mountains. That portion of territory belongs naturally to New South Wales, and lies into Sydney, having no natural connection with Melbourne or Victoria. But the portion of territory lying between the Murrumbidgee and the Murray Rivers lies as naturally into Victoria, and ought from the first to have formed a part of that colony. But no sooner was Lord John Russell's intention of making the Murrumbidgee and not the Murray River the boundary between the two colonies announced than a great effort was made in the Nominee Legislative Council of the period, at the instance of the late Bishop Broughton, to get the Murray substituted, as the common boundary, for the Murrumbidgee. The following is a part of the bishop's speech on the occasion:—

"In support of the proposal that the Murray should be our Southern boundary, let me ask whose river is the Murray? To whom does it naturally appertain, but to its

first discoverers, who have been exclusively inhabitants
of New South Wales? It was first crossed by Mr. Hume
and Mr. Hovell; its course, from the junction of the Murrumbidgee to the sea, was traced by Captain Sturt, and it
has since been further explored by Sir Thomas Mitchell.
And under whose instructions were these expeditions fitted
out. Under those of Sir Ralph Darling and Sir Richard
Bourke, Governors of New South Wales. And by whom
were they conducted? By officers in the service of the
Government of New South Wales. *And at whose expense?
At the expense of the colonists of New South Wales.*"

Now it is not the fact, although so strongly asserted by
the late Bishop Broughton, who, as a legislator, ought to
have known better, that these expeditions of discovery were
either ordered or paid for (from their Ordinary Revenue)
by the colonists of New South Wales. They were ordered
by the Secretary of State, and paid for from the Land
Revenue of the country, which was then one of the *Droits*
of the Crown. But although it had been true, as the
bishop asserts, that these discoveries had been effected at
the expense of the colonists of New South Wales, does that
circumstance constitute a right on the part of these colonists
to the territory intervening between the two rivers, or
warrant their entirely ignoring the interests and the rights
of the future inhabitants of that territory? Unfortunately,
the rights and interests of the people were never taken into
consideration in the case—being compromised and sacrificed
through the apathy and indifference of the Imperial
Government. Instead of leaving the transcendantly important question, as was actually done, to the decision of
one of the interested parties concerned, the proper course
was for the Secretary of State to have appointed, a Royal
Commission to investigate the subject by taking evidence
on the spot, and to fix a proper boundary line between the
two conterminous colonies. And surely the importance of
the question, involving as it did the best interests of

thousands and tens of thousands of future colonists, would have fully warranted all the expenditure which such a Commission would have cost, ten times over.

It is a hopeless attempt, however, for men to counter-work the laws of nature which, in every instance, are the ordinance of God. The tract of country lying between the Murray and Murrumbidgee rivers, which I took the liberty many years since to designate *Riverina*,* is in reality hopelessly disjoined from New South Wales, and must eventually be either annexed to Victoria or formed into a separate and independent colony. It is 18,843 square miles in extent, or about the size of Van Diemen's Land, now Tasmania. I have recently had occasion to traverse a great part of it, and to come in contact with many of its inhabitants; and I can testify, from all I have heard, as well as from my own observation, that almost all its commercial and other relations are now with Victoria, and not with New South Wales; and that although there is no particular desire on the part of the inhabitants for annexation to Victoria, there is a complete alienation of feeling as well as of interest from New South Wales. The political connection still subsists, but every other has ceased.

But the case of the northern boundary of New South Wales presents a still more flagrant instance of misgovern-ment, and exhibits a still greater amount of wrongdoing on the part both of the Colonial and of the Imperial authorities. Being in England, as one of the representatives of the people of New South Wales, in the year 1847, when Earl Grey's Bill for the better government of the Australian

* The idea was suggested by the name of the province or State of *Entre Rios*, (*Anglice*, between the rivers), a tract of country lying between two of the great rivers of South America. It was a complete misnomer, and a manifest absurdity, to extend the name, as was done by the agitators for separation in 1862, to the Saltbush country to the southwestward, where there is no river at all.

E

Colonies was submitted to the House of Lords, I was invited
by Mr. Under-Secretary Hawes, on the part of his lordship,
to offer any suggestions I might deem of importance for
the improvement of the Bill. I did so accordingly—recommending that the Murrumbidgee and not the Murray should
be the boundary of the two conterminous colonies, and that
a clause should be inserted in the Bill authorising her
Majesty to separate from New South Wales, and to erect
into a distinct colony or colonies, whenever she might deem
it expedient to do so, the whole territory to the northward
of the 30th parallel of south latitude, where there is a
natural and strongly defined boundary line, both on the
coast and in the interior. The former of these suggestions
was either overlooked or ignored, and the Murray River
consequently still remains the common boundary of New
South Wales and Victoria; but the latter—the suggestion
of the thirtieth parallel as the northern boundary of New
South Wales—was adopted by the Colonial Office and embodied in the Act, and has since proved a sort of Magna
Charta for Queensland, which would otherwise have had
no existence as a distinct colony.*

* It may doubtless be alleged, in excuse for certain subsequent proceedings, that the boundary I had thus suggested was not the proper one.
In proof, however, of the propriety of my recommendation, I can appeal
to the Hon. E. Deas Thomson, M.L.C., for many years Colonial
Secretary of New South Wales, who, in a letter addressed to the Right
Honorable Sir William Molesworth, Bart., then Principal Secretary of
State for the Colonies, of date, London, 27th September, 1855, thus
writes, in reference to an attempt to get the boundary-line fixed farther
south :—" I should greatly prefer the thirtieth parallel of south latitude as the frontier line between the two colonies; first, because it
was the most southern boundary-line contemplated by the Act of
Parliament, 13 and 14 Victoria, cap. lix.; and secondly, because any
encroachment upon that line would be received with great jealousy
and discontent by the colonists of New South Wales." I only wish
Mr. Thomson had acted upon this opinion, when he returned to the
colony and *voted for a different line in* 1856.

It will scarcely be credited, however, that in the face of this solemn Act of the Imperial Parliament, as well as in defiance of the petitions and remonstrances of the resident inhabitants of the territory to the northward of the thirtieth parallel, a Colonial Governor should have presumed to set aside that Act, and to establish a boundary of his own—the 28th parallel on the coast, and the 29th in the interior. But such has been the fact, and the result is that New South Wales, already larger than all France, has thus had an additional extent of territory added to it, forty square miles larger than all England!*

It is deeply humiliating for a British subject to contrast the apathy and indifference of our Imperial authorities, and the hardship and suffering thereby entailed on whole communities of colonists, with the watchful care exhibited in cases precisely similar by the Government of the United States. For example, when Texas, a country about as large as France, was annexed to the United States, the American Senate, as the guardian of the

---

* Sir William Denison had no personal knowledge on the subject. He had never taken the trouble to visit the remote districts of the colony himself, as he ought to have done, and as Lord Belmore, the present Governor, has been doing all along, so much to his credit. He merely looked at the map and made his decision accordingly, just as the Secretary of State might have done in Downing-street. He occupied himself, it is true, in what he had no doubt considered more important work—in writing Dundreary despatches to the Duke of Newcastle, then Secretary of State for the Colonies, at the rate, as we were once told by one of his subordinates in the Legislative Assembly, when fishing for a compliment for his master, of eleven a week! Perhaps I paid the compliment deserved at the time, by expressing my cordial sympathy with the Duke of Newcastle, under the merciless infliction to which he was thus subjected, of having to read eleven letters a week on all the police incidents of New South Wales. At all events, we never heard of his Excellency's exploits as a dispatch-writer again. He had surely mistaken his proper place in society. Nature never intended him for anything higher than—a Complete Letter-writer for a Ladies' Boarding School.

rights and interests of the people throughout the Union,
would not allow the annexation to be consummated, until
a proviso was inserted in the Act for the division of Texas
into four distinct States, as soon as the progress of settlement and the amount of the population should warrant
such a division. For as the *beau ideal* of the Americans,
in regard to the extent of territory which any State in
their Union should comprise, is forty to fifty thousand
square miles—more or less according to the physical
character of the country—the Senate in this particular
case would not sanction the admission into the union of a
State with so extensive a territory as that of Texas, lest,
from that very extent of territory, it should acquire a pre-
dominating influence over other and smaller States.

The portion of territory to the northward of the thirtieth
parallel of latitude, still included in New South Wales
by the grace of Sir William Denison, comprises the
Clarence and Richmond Rivers District, of which the
northern portion, or the Richmond River, is nearly five
hundred miles from Sydney. How people at so great a
distance from head quarters can be either well or wisely
governed, is a question that seems never to have suggested itself to that self-conceited and pretentious functionary. How they are *actually* governed under such circumstances, I shall shew from a single example. The
people of the Richmond River required a pontoon or punt
to ferry their stock across the river whenever it happened
to be flooded. A punt was accordingly ordered for the
usual crossing place at Casino, about fifty or sixty miles
from the sea; but as the river banks in that locality were
high and precipitous, and as no approaches had been
formed for the punt, it lay unused in the river till it
sank at its moorings. I had in the meantime been instrumental in settling a Presbyterian clergyman, the Rev.
John Thom, A.M., in a central locality on the river; and

as the punt, which had by this time been got up again, but was found to be of no use at Casino, was urgently required in that locality, Mr. Thom applied, through myself, to the Government of the day, for its removal from Casino to that central spot, which was situated about twenty miles farther down the river. But as the place was nearly five hundred miles from Sydney, this trivial operation, which, under a Government at hand, would have required only a few days, actually took three or four years to accomplish. Mr. Thom, meanwhile, finding it necessary, from the want of a punt, to provide himself with such means of conveyance as he could in visiting his parishioners across the river, got a small boat or dingy for the purpose, which unfortunately, when he was performing an act of courtesy and kindness in ferrying a friend across, capsized with him, and he was drowned.*

But Sir William Denison was not allowed to carry out this unwarrantable act of usurpation without protest or remonstrance. On the contrary, the inhabitants of the Clarence and Richmond Rivers district petitioned her Majesty almost unanimously for their being included in Queensland, the capital of which was comparatively close at hand, and remonstrated in the strongest manner against

* Mr. Thom had been an eminently zealous minister and was much and deeply regretted by his attached people, who have since erected a neat pyramidal monument over his grave, adjoining his church, at Coraki, on the Richmond River, with the following epitaph:—

Erected,
By his sorrowing Flock,
To the Memory of the Rev. JOHN THOM, A.M.,
For four years the zealous Presbyterian Minister
Of this District.
He was born in Kincardineshire, Scotland,
Educated at the University of Aberdeen,
And drowned in the Richmond River,
August 3rd., 1869,
Aged XLII. years.

their annexation to New South Wales, whose capital, the city of Sydney, was at least 350 miles from its nearest point. The first of these petitions was forwarded to the Secretary of State for the Colonies, the late Duke of Newcastle, in the year 1857, about two years before the separation of Queensland from New South Wales; and the second almost immediately after the separation had taken place in the year 1860. But the Duke lent himself entirely and without the slightest investigation to Sir William Denison, and the petitions and remonstrances of the people were consequently disregarded.* Petitions for the carrying out of the Imperial Act of 1850, and the establishment of the common boundary at the thirtieth parallel, were also forwarded to her Majesty by the inhabitants of Queensland, but with equally little effect. In short the setting aside of the Imperial Act of 1850 was the result of something like a joint conspiracy on the part of the Secretary of State for the Colonies and the Governor of New South Wales.†

* "The dissensions between the two countries, which afterwards terminated in the dissolution of the British empire in America, were not a little promoted by the pernicious counsels and *erroneous information* transmitted to the English ministry by the governors of those provinces in which the appointment to that office was exercised by the King,"—*Grahame*, vol. 1, page 289.

† The means that were used to effect this change in the northern boundary of New South Wales, as fixed by the Imperial Parliament, were sufficiently discreditable. Mr. Hargrave, a member of the Legislative Assembly of that colony, for the Electoral District of New England, having views and interests of his own in the matter, got up a petition, which was presented to the Assembly in October, 1856, from "certain magistrates, lessees of Crown lands, and residents in the pastoral districts of New England, M'Leay, Gwydir and Clarence, and the various towns therein," praying for the establishment of an Assize Court at Armidale, thirty miles to the southward of the thirtieth parallel—a measure in which the inhabitants of these districts, both north and south, were all deeply interested. In that petition, however, there was artfully inserted a clause, of which very few of the

The result to Queensland, with Sir William Denison's Boundary Line, is that the capital, and all the public buildings of the colony—Government House, the Parliament House, and the other Metropolitan buildings—are all inconveniently and improperly situated at the southern extremity of the colony, instead of being in the centre of its coast line, as they would have been had the Imperial Act of 1850 been honestly carried out. But there is another unhappy result of this most unwarrantable tampering with an act of the Imperial Legislature. With Sir William Denison's boundary line, there is no well-defined natural boundary for Queensland to the northward; but with the thirtieth parallel for the southern boundary of that colony, there is a natural and strongly defined northern boundary in Dawes' Range at the 25th degree of south latitude. Of that natural boundary the late Sir Thomas Mitchell, Surveyor-General of New South Wales, when suggesting a name for that portion of the territory, thus writes:—" Capricornia—to.express the country under the Tropics, from

petitioners would take any cognizance, to the effect that they " did not desire to be included in any section of the northern districts which might be separated from the present colony of New South Wales." A few of the inhabitants of the Clarence and Richmond Rivers district, who were interested in the general object of the Petition, signed it at once without noticing this artful clause; but the great majority of the petitioners consisted of persons who were living far to the southward of the thirtieth parallel, and who had therefore no right whatever to sign any petition affecting the resident inhabitants of the Clarence District. Through this *ruse*, which might almost be designated a regular swindle, Sir William Denison—who, it was alleged, was by no means a disinterested actor in the matter, as he had two brothers holding at the time nearly a quarter of a million of acres of land, as squatters on the northern frontier, at a merely nominal rental of the twentieth of a penny per acre—affected to change the boundary from the thirtieth to the twenty-eighth parallel of latitude. I have already noticed the action that was taken in the matter by the inhabitants of the Clarence district.

the parallel of 25 deg. South, *where Nature has set up her own landmarks, not to be disputed.*"* "In the event, therefore, of the annexation of the Clarence district, from the 30th parallel of latitude, to Queensland, this great natural division would form an appropriate northern terminus to that colony, which would thus have a coast-line of about 350 English miles, and a superficial area of upwards of 200,000 square miles, while the capital at Brisbane, and the metropolitan buildings of the colony, would be equidistant from its northern and southern extremities."†

There is a strong agitation now in progress, on the part of the inhabitants of the northern portion of Queensland, for separation from that colony at Dawes' Range; and the only equitable way in which this could be effected would be by carrying out the Imperial Act of 1850, and re-establishing the 30th parallel as the common boundary between New South Wales and Queensland. It may be alleged indeed that if the boundary fixed by the Imperial Parliament at the 30th parallel of latitude should be re-established, New South Wales would lose all its valuable Clarence River trade. But this would be a great mistake. With a Customs League and a uniform tariff, which, it is expected, will shortly be established for all these colonies, the trade of the Clarence River would still come to Sydney as at present, although the district should be politically separate from New South Wales; and the probability is that, with a railway from Brisbane to the Clarence River, which would be the speedy and certain result of the annexation of the Clarence River district to Queensland, much of the traffic between Sydney and Queensland would take that

---

* "Expedition into Tropical Australia." By Sir Thomas Mitchell. Page 430.

† "Queensland, Australia." By the author of this volume. London, 1861. Page 2.

course; so that instead of a serious loss to New South Wales, political separation at the 30th parallel would be great gain.

The population of the portion of Queensland to the northward of Dawes' Range, or the 25th parallel of latitude, is now as large as that of Queensland itself at the time of its separation from New South Wales; and its ordinary revenue is much greater than that of Queensland in 1859, the era of separation. There cannot therefore be any impropriety in the present demand for separation on the part of the colonists who are now settled in the northern portion of that colony. And when one takes into consideration the notorious fact—so strongly exhibited in the annals both of Victoria and of Queensland, when these great colonies were mere distant appendages of New South Wales—that the revenue derived from such remote districts is almost uniformly expended for the promotion of objects in which the inhabitants can have no possible interest, while their own proper interests and objects are overlooked and neglected, agitation for another act of separation on behalf of the northern colonists of Queensland will appear not merely justifiable but highly expedient and necessary.

Such, then, are the Seven Colonies or Provinces of Eastern Australia—extending, as they do, over not fewer than thirty-three degrees of latitude, from the South Cape of Van Diemen's Land, or Tasmania, to Cape York—for which, as the nucleus of a great empire of the future, I would claim, *in the interest of Britain, not less than in the right of the Colonies*, immediate and entire freedom and independence. These colonies—with the adjustment of the boundaries of New South Wales, both towards Victoria and towards Queensland, which I have shewn to be not only equitable and just but indispensably necessary, before a

federal and incorporating union can be even thought of—
will stand as follows :—

SQUARE MILES.

1. New South Wales, with the Murrumbidgee
   River, and the 30th parallel of latitude as its
   boundaries   225,708

2. Victoria, with the addition of the territory
   between the Murray and Murrumbidgee
   Rivers   103,843

3. South Australia, with a large extent of
   desert country within its limits, perhaps .   300,000

4. Tasmania, about   24,000

5. Queensland, from the 30th to the 25th
   degree of latitude, upwards of   200,000

6. Capricornia, from the 25th parallel northwards, (northern boundary not yet fixed) .

7. Carpentaria, boundaries not yet defined   .

These colonies are now rapidly settling with a British
population, perfectly capable of forming all such political
combinations as the realisation of the great idea of their
political federation and eventual freedom and independence
would imply. And as there is an agitation in progress, on
the part of the mercantile community of the Australian
colonies, for binding them all into one great whole, by a
Customs League and a uniform Tariff, as a necessary preliminary to a political federation, while the mother-country
is withdrawing her troops, and leaving them to defend
themselves as they may in all future emergencies—declaring
at the same time in express terms that if they really desire
their entire freedom and independence she will not stand
in their way—it cannot be doubted that this great consummation of the future will very shortly be realised. What
then are the analogies with which the procedure of Great
Britain herself, and the history of European nations, pre-

sent us, in reference to the question as to whether such a
community as that of these Australian colonies is fitted and
entitled to assume the position of a sovereign and independent nation?

SECTION X.—HOW CERTAIN OTHER STATES AND NATIONS HAVE AT-
TAINED THEIR NATIONAL INDEPENDENCE.

There is no particular number of men, women and
children required, under any law, either human or divine,
to constitute a nation. The Chinese nation is said to
comprise not fewer than from three hundred and fifty to
four hundred millions of people, or about a third of the
whole human race. The Tahitian nation numbered only
about ten thousand souls, when it was swallowed up, and
"annexed," by the late Louis Philippe of France; for
which fraternal act towards his royal sister, Queen Pomare,
certain people in New South Wales, who were deeply interested in the welfare and advancement of the little nation,
with which that colony had been maintaining friendly
intercourse and commercial relations for considerably
upwards of a quarter of a century, are of opinion that the
said Louis Philippe met with condign punishment in due
time. There is another Polynesian nation, the Hawaiian
or Sandwich Island nation, with a king and parliament
recognised, and its freedom and independence guaranteed
by Great Britain, although it has a considerably smaller
population than that even of the smallest of the actual
Australian colonies; the whole population of the Sandwich
Islands being by the latest accounts only about 80,000
souls. And surely we are not to be told that a people
of British origin are less likely to be able to govern
themselves than so much smaller a number of South Sea
Islanders.

In like manner, the African Republic of Liberia, consisting almost exclusively of emancipated negro slaves from the United States, with a population still more limited, has also been recognized by Great Britain, and admitted into the family of Sovereign and Independent States. Nay, the mere handful of Dutch boors, who crossed the Orange River only a few years ago, from the colony of the Cape of Good Hope, and established an Independent Republic in the interior of Africa, under the able leadership of their chief Pretorius, has also been recognized by Great Britain, at the instance of a former Secretary of State for the Colonies, Sir John Pakington, as a Sovereign and Independent State, and admitted as such into diplomatic relations both with England and Holland, although its entire population did not exceed fifty thousand souls! In the face of such instances it would be preposterous to allege that the intelligent British colonists of Australia, who number upwards of 1,500,000 souls, are not able to govern themselves in their respective provinces, or to form a National Government for their entire community, as a Sovereign and Independent State. Great Britain herself would surely never commit herself to such an absurdity as an allegation of this kind would imply, after her own formal recognition of the Sandwich Islands, the Negro Commonwealth of Liberia and the Dutch Republic of Central Africa, as Sovereign and Independent States.

"A state or commonwealth," says Milton, "is a society sufficient in itself in all things conducible to well-being and commodious life:" and I maintain, without fear of contradiction from any quarter, that the community of the Australian colonies forms, at this moment, just such a society—"a society sufficient in itself in all things conducible to well-being and commodious life."

The present population of the Australian colonies is, unquestionably, at least three times greater than that of Her Majesty's ancient kingdom of Scotland, in the year 1314, when King Robert the Bruce gained the famous battle of Bannockburn, and delivered his country from the intolerable yoke of England. And will it be alleged that the intelligent and generally well-educated Britons, from all the three kingdoms, who now form the population of the Australian colonies, are less able to govern themselves than the half-civilized Scotch of the fourteenth century? Surely a community of such extent, especially when separated by half the circumference of the globe from the dominant country, must form, to use the language of Milton, "a society sufficient in itself in all things conducible to well-being and commodious life."

The famous Republic of Switzerland was founded in the year 1315, the year after the battle of Bannockburn, through the equally decisive battle of Morgarten. In that battle, an Austrian army of not fewer than 20,000 men was defeated by a mere handful of mountaineers, consisting of the confederated bands of the three small forest cantons of Uri, Schwytz, and Unterwalden, and not exceeding 1350 men altogether. The whole territory of these united cantons measures only 1055 square miles, which is less than the area of the single county of Cumberland in New South Wales; and their entire population, at the era of the French Revolution, that is 450 years after the founding of their state, did not exceed 72,500 souls,—a population smaller than that of the city of Sydney at the present day. And yet this mere handful of brave men nobly achieved the freedom and independence of their country, situated although it was in the very centre of Europe, and surrounded by the vast and powerful monarchies of Germany, France, Italy, and Spain; transmitting the precious inheritance unimpaired to their posterity to the present day. For the other cantons of Switzerland, stimulated by their example, gradually joined their confederacy; which now comprises twenty-two cantons, with a population and territory nearly equal to those of Scotland. And yet, with this illustrious example before them in the history of the past,.

there are men of some pretensions even to intelligence who
still doubt whether a million and a half of Britons, at the
very ends of the earth, are fit to manage their own affairs,
or could venture upon such a course as freedom and independence implies with safety and propriety!

The facility and success with which representative institutions have been brought into full operation in all
the Australian colonies, since the advent of popular
government in 1856, is surely a sufficient and satisfactory
proof of the fitness of these colonies for complete self-
government, or in other words, for entire freedom and
independence.

As the course of all the Australian colonies under responsible Government has been much the same, I shall merely
enumerate the principal measures of reform that were
passed, after a whole series of protracted struggles in the
oldest of their number, that of New South Wales, during
the first ten years from the period at which this great change
in our Colonial system was effected. The Constitution Act,
which was sanctioned and adopted by the Imperial Parliament in 1855, had been drawn up by the avowed enemies
of free institutions in that colony; and it contained a variety
of enactments that were strongly opposed to the wishes as
well as to the interests of the people. But its authors had
provided, as they conceived, against the possibility of any
change being effected in the Act, by enacting that the consent and concurrence of a majority of two-thirds of the
members of both Houses of Parliament should be indispensably necessary, ere the slightest change could be effected
in the obnoxious statute or any real measure of reform
passed. The first struggle, therefore, was to get the two-
thirds clause of the Constitution Act repealed; and this,
after much debating, was finally accomplished. The progress of Reform was thenceforth sufficiently rapid. For
example, the electoral power had been so artfully distributed under the Constitution Act as in great mea-

sure to throw it completely into the hands of the few against the many. An Electoral Act was accordingly passed, after another long protracted struggle in the year 1858, establishing manhood suffrage, an approximation at least to equal Electoral Districts and the institution of the Ballot, which I am happy to say has ever since wrought most successfully.* The great

* The late Mr. William Nicholson, for some time Premier in the colony of Victoria, has got the entire credit in England of the introduction of the Ballot into all the Australian Colonies. Perhaps this, however, was scarcely merited. Mr. Nicholson, who was a native of the North of England, and had been first a retail and afterwards a wholesale grocer in Melbourne, although a man of good common sense, had received only the commonest education. When a candidate for a seat in the Legislative Assembly of Victoria, his address to his constituents, like those of not a few others about the same time, who had been suddenly elevated by the gold discoveries to a position in society they could never have anticipated, was accordingly written for him by the late Alderman Kerr, then Town Clerk of Melbourne, who told me the circumstance himself when I happened to be in that city some time before Mr. Kerr's death. Mr. Kerr, a fellow-countryman of mine, had arrived in New South Wales in the year 1832, and was long a protegé of mine, residing for years in a literary capacity under my roof. He there imbibed, as he afterwards acknowledged, those liberal political principles which he afterwards did so much to inculcate for a series of years through the press in Victoria, where he had settled in the year 1840. For being then a young man of good education, and of great natural ability, he was enabled to exercise much influence for good, as the Editor and Proprietor of a Weekly Journal, in the young colony. In the draft of Mr. Nicholson's Address, Mr. Kerr had inserted a clause strongly advocating the introduction of the Ballot. To this clause Mr. Nicholson strongly objected in the first instance; but being talked over on the subject by Mr. Kerr, who insisted on retaining the clause, he consented at length, although somewhat reluctantly, to its insertion in his Address; and it was to this fortunate circumstance that he owed all his subsequent fame. I have deemed it due to the memory of my deceased friend, Mr. Kerr, to mention this incident; for it was to *him* in reality, and not to Mr. Nicholson, that the colony of Victoria was indebted for the introduction and establishment of the Ballot.

difficulty in the way of obtaining land, which had greatly impeded and almost completely prevented the progress of settlement under the old system, was at length happily removed by the passing of a series of Land Bills, at the instance of John Robertson, Esq., the late Premier; the effect of which was to throw open the lands of the colony, for the settlement of the people, and the result of which was the actual settlement of upwards of twenty thousand people on its waste lands. Mr. Gladstone's great measure for the disestablishment of the Irish Church in the year 1869, was anticipated by a similar measure in New South Wales 'in the year 1862; and while the system of concurrent endowment, which had previously been in operation in that colony, was discontinued, the actually salaried clergy of all denominations had their salaries secured to them for life. And last, but not least in this series of great reforms was the passing of the Public Schools' Act, which ensures for the youth of the colony a liberal and unsectarian system of education at the expense of the State; which, I may add, had already provided a well endowed University and a system of colleges for higher education. When, I would ask, therefore, has there ever been enacted in so short a period of time, even in England, such a series of reforms as those which this goodly catalogue presents? And all the other colonies of the group have, with slight differences in mere matters of detail, been acting all the while in a precisely similar manner. If, therefore, it is the law of nature and the ordinance of God, that we, the Australian people, who have already attained our political majority, and are both able and willing to govern ourselves, should be forthwith permitted to do so by the Parent State, there cannot be the shadow of a doubt that the longer a measure of such paramount importance is deferred, incalculable evils will, in one form or other, result both to Great Britain and to Australia. It is unsafe in the highest degree to counteract a law of nature: it is positively sinful to resist an ordinance of God.

SECTION XI.—A COMPROMISE PROPOSED AND CONSIDERED—PARLIAMENTARY REPRESENTATION FOR THE COLONIES.

Among the various expedients that were proposed by ingenious speculators, and rejected by both parties, during the American troubles previous to the war of Independence, was that of Parliamentary Representation for the colonies. It has been suggested also, in more recent times, in the House of Commons; and there have occasionally been colonists of talent and standing who have expressed themselves favourably in regard to it. The person who first suggested the idea appears to have been Oldmixon, an American annalist of the era of Queen Anne and George I. It was afterwards put forward with approbation by the celebrated Dr. Adam Smith, and advocated for a time, but afterwards rejected and strongly opposed, by Dr. Benjamin Franklin. Franklin was too keen an observer of passing events, when sojourning in London as a delegate from the colony of Pennsylvania, not to perceive how utterly valueless for his constituents a seat in the House of Commons would be for the Representative of a colony. Only think how the Honourable Member for Botany Bay would be sneered at on the floor of the House, and what small effect anything he could say would be likely to have on the affairs of the nation! Besides, what possible interest can the people of New South Wales, of Victoria or of South Australia have in one even out of every hundred of the questions that are brought before Parliament? It would decidedly be unconstitutional, and therefore wrong, for the people of England to allow a mere colonial member to vote on any question of British taxation or of internal administration; and would it be accordant

F

with the self-respect which the colonists owe themselves to allow their members to sit silent in the House of Commons? We can learn from the public press, without the circuitous and expensive course of having a Parliamentary Representative to report it, how often the House is counted out every session on colonial questions, of whatever importance they may be to the colonies; and we all know already, without a Parliamentary Representative to guarantee the fact, the precise degree of indifference and disgust with which colonial questions are almost uniformly regarded in that House.

Besides, what are we to do for representation for the colonies in the House of Lords; for we are surely quite as much entitled to representation in that House as in the other? Are we to have colonial Peers of Parliament as well as members of the Lower House—the Marquis of Parramatta, for instance, Lord Wollongong, and Viscount Curraducbidgee? We, colonists, are certainly not responsible for the ridiculousness of the thing—it is no proposal of ours.

Again, if we fell into the trap that is thus proposed to be set for us, by accepting Parliamentary Representation for the colonies, we should virtually declare that the British Parliament has a *right* to legislate for the colonies, just as it has for the people of England, and to precisely the same extent; and we should thereby be bartering away the liberties of our country for a thing of no value whatever. We have certainly no desire, as Australian colonists, to legislate for the people of England; and we deny that the people of England can have any right, by the law of nature, which is the ordinance of God, to legislate for us.

It may not be inexpedient, however, to ascertain what opinions were actually entertained and propounded on this subject by the American colonists of last century; for if Parliamentary Representation was deemed unsuitable and undesirable for them, *a fortiori* it must be undesirable and unsuitable for *us* at the extremity of the globe.

" Our Representatives," says Smith, in his History of New York, " agreeably to the general sense of their constituents, are tenacious in the opinion that * * * the session of Assemblies here is wisely substituted instead of a representation in Parliament, which, all things considered, would *at this remote distance* be extremely *inconvenient and dangerous.*"*

At a considerably later period than the one referred to by this historian, viz., in the year 1765, "there assembled in the town of New York a convention composed of twenty-eight delegates from the assemblies of nine of the colonies; one of their resolutions was as follows, viz.: 'That while all the British subjects are entitled to the privilege of being taxed only by their own representatives, *the remote situation of the colonies rendered it impracticable that they should be represented except in their own subordinate legislatures.*'"†

The Assembly of Massachusetts, during the same year, resolved " That the citizens of Massachusetts never had been, and never could be, adequately represented in the British Parliament."‡

The following is a Resolution of the Original American Congress on the same subject:—

" That the foundation of English liberty, and of all free government, is a right in the people to participate in their Legislative Council; *And as the English colonists are not represented, and from their local and other circumstances*

---

* Grahame's *Hist. of the United States of North America*, vol. iii. p. 324.

† Grahame's *Hist. of the United States of North America*, vol iv. p. 217.

‡ *Ibid.* vol. iii. p. 374.

cannot properly be represented, in the British Parliament, they are entitled to a free and exclusive power of legislation in their several provincial legislatures, where their right of representation can alone be preserved in all cases of taxation and internal polity."*

To the same effect Dr. Benjamin Franklin "declared his conviction, that the legislatures of Britain and America were and ought to be distinct from each other, and that the relation between the two countries was precisely analogous to that which had subsisted between England and Scotland previous to their Union."†

Finally, the famous Jeremy Bentham, in his pamphlet, entitled "Emancipate your Colonies," addressed to the National Assembly of France, characterises the scheme of Parliamentary Representation for the Colonies in the following language :—" *Oh, but they will send deputies: and those deputies will govern us as much as we govern them.*" —Illusion !—What is that but doubling the mischief instead of lessening it? To give yourself a pretence for governing a million or two of strangers, you admit half a dozen. To govern a million or two of people you don't care about, you admit half a dozen people that don't care about you. To govern a set of people whose business you know nothing about, you encumber yourselves with half a dozen starers, who know nothing about yours. Is this fraternity? Is this liberty and equality? Open domination would be a less grievance. Were I an American, I had rather not be represented at all than represented thus.‡ If tyranny must come, let it come without a mask.

---

* *Resolutions of the Congress of Philadelphia,* A. D. 1774.

† Grahame's *History of the United States of North America,* vol. iv. p. 221.

‡ Jeremy Bentham did not form an erroneous estimate of the feelings and spirit of British colonists in such circumstances. The Separation of Victoria from New South Wales was conceded by Her Majesty in

Oh, but information! True, it must be had; but to give information, must a man possess a vote?"

"The colonies," says an able writer in the *Edinburgh Review* for July, 1853, in an article on Earl Grey's Colonial Administration,—"The colonies are not, and cannot be, directly represented in Parliament; the number of members who are well-informed upon any colonial question which is the subject of debate, is always very small; and unless the question can be drawn into the party-contests of the day, the debate takes place before a thin and inattentive audience, whose knowledge of the facts is limited and confused. The popular forms of an Imperial Government secure a hearing to the complaints of dependencies, but they afford few securities for correct decision. * * * Political judges may be indifferent as well as impartial. Some interest is desirable to warm the affections, though too much interest may distort the judgment. This is an evil inherent in every form of dependence; whether the power be vested in a Secretary of State or in a House of Commons."

1845, in answer to a Petition to the Queen, which I had suggested and had assisted in getting up, from the six members of the Legislative Council of that colony for Port Phillip (now Victoria) in the year 1844. But during the six dreary years that were allowed to elapse before Separation was actually effected in 1851, the people of Melbourne, to shew their contempt for representation in Sydney, actually elected as their member, the Right Honourable Earl Grey, then Principal Secretary of State for the Colonies; and His Lordship was asked in the House of Peers, by another noble lord, a member of the Opposition of the period, whether he was not going out to take his seat as Member for Melbourne in our Legislative Council in Sydney. In like manner the constituency of the electoral district of Kennedy in Northern Queensland, indignant at the refusal of their Parliament in Brisbane to grant them Separation from that colony, have recently elected the Right Honourable John Bright as their Member in the local Parliament! These things may doubtless excite a smile in both Houses of the Imperial Parliament, but they are matters of life and death to us, the *green frogs* of Australia.

SECTION XII.—ANOTHER COMPROMISE PROPOSED AND CONSIDERED—
MUNICIPAL INDEPENDENCE.

The late Mr. Edward Gibbon Wakefield, a gentleman for whom I had the highest respect, and who laid the colonial world of his day under the strongest obligations for the invaluable services he rendered to society in the cause of colonization, proposes, in common with various other colonial reformers, that the colonial legislatures should have entire freedom and independence in all *subordinate* matters, or in other words, what he calls municipal independence, but that all imperial questions should be left to the *Imperial* Parliament. As it would require some party, however, to decide which were *imperial* and which were *subordinate* questions, and as no such party can exist under the circumstances supposed, this beautiful theory could never be reduced to practice.

" Many," says the celebrated Dr. Benjamin Franklin, in the preface to his pamphlet, entitled *Considerations on the Nature and the Extent of the Authority of the British Parliament*—" Many will perhaps be surprised to see the legislative authority of the British Parliament over the colonies *denied in every instance*. These the writer informs, that, when he began this piece, he would probably have been surprised at such an opinion himself. For it was the result, not the occasion, of his disquisitions. He entered upon them with a view and expectation of being able to trace some constitutional line between those cases in which we ought and those in which we ought not, to acknowledge the power of Parliament over us. In the prosecution of his enquiries he became fully convinced that *such a line doth not exist;* and that there can be no medium between acknowledging and denying that power in ALL CASES."*

* *Considerations on the Nature and the Extent of the Authority of the British Parliament.* By Dr. Benjamin Franklin. Rivington's *New York Gazetteer*, October 30th, 1774.

It is very remarkable how much better the principles of civil liberty were understood, apparently by everybody, in the seventeenth century, than they are at the present day even by professed colonial reformers. In the year 1610 the Virginia Company passed an ordinance to the effect, that "the enactments of the (Colonial) Assembly should not have the force of law till sanctioned by the Court of Proprietors in England; and that *the orders of this Court should have no force in Virginia till ratified by the Virginia Assembly.*"* There was something like reciprocity in this enactment; but I confess I see nothing of the kind in Mr. Wakefield's proposal.

Again, in the year 1636, the colony of Plymouth (in Massachusetts) drew up a body of laws, of which the first is "That no act, imposition, law, ordinance be made or imposed upon us at present, or to come, *but such as has been or shall be enacted by the consent of the body of freemen, or their representatives, legally assembled, which is according to the free liberties of the freeborn people of England.*"†

Then again, in the year 1662, that is, during the reign of Charles the Second, the worst period in our history, "certain of the leading colonists (of Rhode Island), together with all other persons who should in future be admitted freemen of the society, were incorporated by the title of The Governor and Company of the English Colony of Rhode Island and Providence. The supreme or legislative power was invested in an assembly consisting of the Governor and Assistants, and Representatives *elected from their own number by the freemen.* This assembly was empowered to enact ordinances and forms of government and magistracy, with as much conformity to the laws of England as the state of the country and condition of the people would admit; to

* Grahame's *Hist. of the United States of America,* vol. i. p. 70.
† Holmes' *Annals of America,* vol. i.

erect courts of justice; to regulate the manner of appointment to places of trust; to inflict all lawful punishments;
and to exercise their prerogative of pardon. A governor,
deputy-governor, and ten assistants were appointed to be
annually chosen by the assembly; and the first board of
these officers, nominated by the Charter, on the suggestion
of the provincial agent, were authorised to commence the
work of carrying its provisions into execution."*

A charter equally liberal was granted during the same
year to the Colony of Connecticut, by the same monarch—
Charles the Second!

Again, in the year 1775, the assembly of New York declared, in a petition to Parliament for the redress of
grievances, "that exemption from internal taxation, and
the *exclusive* power of providing for their own civil government and the administration of justice in the colony, are
esteemed by them their undoubted and inalienable rights."†

And again, "The birthright of every British subject is,
to have a property of his own, in his estate, person, and
reputation; subject only to laws enacted by his own concurrence, either in person or by his representatives; and
which birthright accompanies him wheresoever he wanders
or rests, so long as he is within the pale of British dominion, and is true to his allegiance."†

One extract more and I have done: "Massachusetts
and New Hampshire—the one enjoying a chartered, the
other an unchartered jurisdiction—were the only two provinces in New England in which the superior officers of
government were appointed by the Crown, and from the
tribunals of which an appeal was admitted to the king in

* Grahame's *Hist. of the United States*, vol. i. p. 316.

† *Ibid.* vol, iv. p. 369.

‡ Dr. Benjamin Franklin's *Historical Review of the Constitution of
Pennsylvania.* Grahame, vol. iv. p. 440.

Council. In Connecticut and Rhode Island, all the officers of government (excepting the members of the Court of Assembly,) were elected by the inhabitants; and so resolutely was this highly-valued privilege defended, that when King William appointed Fletcher, the governor of New York, to command the Connecticut militia, the province refused to acknowledge his authority. The laws of these States were not subject to the negative, nor the judgments of their tribunals to the review of the king. So perfectly democratic were the constitutions of Connecticut and Rhode Island, that in neither of them was the governor suffered to exercise a negative on the resolutions of the assembly. The spirit of liberty was not repressed in Massachusetts by the encroachments of royal prerogative on the ancient privileges of the people, but was vigorously exerted through the remaining and important organ of the provincial assembly. All the patronage that was vested in the Royal Governor was never able to create more than a very inconsiderable royalist party in this State. The functionaries whom he, or whom the Crown appointed, depended on the popular assembly for the emoluments of their officers; and although the most strenuous efforts and the most formidable threats were employed by the British ministers to free the Governor himself from the same dependence, they were never able to prevail with the Assembly to annex a fixed salary to his office. The people and the popular authorities of Massachusetts were always ready to set an example to the other colonies of a determined resistance to the encroachments of Royal prerogative."*

These American colonists would scarcely have thanked Mr. Wakefield for what he designated "municipal independence," highly as he esteemed it. They looked for something of a much more liberal character, and on a

* Grahame's *Hist. of the United States*, vol. i. p. 421.

much firmer basis than that gentleman seemed disposed to allow. For in order to enable the Imperial Government and Parliament to correct any false step which might be made in the way of granting even Municipal Constitutions for the colonies, by giving the colonists too much, Mr. W. proposed that the Charters granting these constitutions should be revocable by the Parliament at pleasure!

"In order to retain for the Imperial Power the most complete general control over the colony, the colonial constitution, instead of being granted immutably and in perpetuity, as our old municipal charters were, should, in the Charter itself, be declared liable to revocation or alteration by the Crown, upon address from both Houses of Parliament."*

And did Mr. Wakefield really suppose that the Australian colonists—now a million and a half of people, at the ends of the earth—would be abject and spiritless enough to accept such a constitution as this? I thought he had known us better. In one word, there is only one way in which the question can be settled definitively, and at the same time satisfactorily for all parties, that is, the way prescribed by the law of nature and the ordinance of God.

But "why," it may be asked—"Why not rest satisfied with a General Government ·for the whole of the Australian provinces, in addition to the Local Government for each, (as proposed by Earl Grey, in the year 1849,) without constituting that General Government a National Government, and without dissolving the existing connection with the British Empire? Why should there not still be a Supreme and controuling authority in the Mother-country?"

* *View of the Art of Colonization, &c.*, By Edward Gibbon Wakefield, Esq., p. 308. London, 1849.

This question, I would observe in reply, although often asked by persons even of the highest intelligence in the Mother-country, betrays so wonderful an ignorance of human nature, as well as of the history of the world, that it would seem a studied insult to the common sense of mankind to propose it, if it were not self-evident that the inordinate vanity and extreme selfishness of men in the possession of power render them blind to its real import. To any man of a rightly constituted mind, there can be no earthly equivalent for freedom or self-government. To a community entitled to the blessing of self-government, there can be no earthly equivalent for national independence. The man who can submit willingly, and without the direst necessity, to the deprivation of his personal freedom is a slave at heart. The community entitled to self-government that can willingly submit to a condition of political dependence, when it might otherwise obtain its entire political freedom and national independence, is utterly unworthy of a place and a name among the nations of the earth.*

Is it not the natural and necessary consequence of a young man's coming of age and being able to do for himself, that he should desire to originate a family and to form an establishment of his own? Does he not gain immensely in self-respect, as well as in the estimation of his fellow-citizens, when he takes up this new position and discharges its duties accordingly? Does he not feel that he is thenceforth a man and not a mere boy, and does

---

* When Caractacus—the noble British prince, who had been betrayed by his own countrymen into the hands of the Romans, after an unsuccessful struggle for the freedom and independence of his country, and been carried as a prisoner to Rome, in the reign of the Emperor Claudius—was asked how he had dared to appear in arms against the Majesty of Rome, he replied by asking indignantly—"Does it follow, because you have a mind to rule over all, that therefore every one must tamely submit?" *Rapin. His. of Eng.* Book I.

he not act or endeavour to act in accordance with the dignity of this new and higher character ? In particular, is not the virtue of self-reliance—the parent of all that is great and noble in humanity—which is then exhibited in his character and procedure, perhaps for the first time, of incalculable advantage to him for the gradual development of his own native energies both of body and mind ? And does not his mind expand with his new circumstances, so that he takes up, as a matter of course, a higher position in society, and forms and executes enterprises which he would never have dreamed of before ?

And is it not precisely the same with a community, which is merely a collection of such individuals ? Is it fitting that such a community should be kept in leading-strings for an indefinite period, at the pleasure or caprice of others ? Is it just and right that such a community should be directed in all its most important concerns, and guided and influenced in all its movements, by people who are individually no better than so many of its own members, and who can know almost nothing about their real circumstances and condition, for this best of all reasons, that they are living on opposite sides of the globe—so far apart that when it is day with the one it is night with the other ? Nay, is it not a blasphemous assumption of the Divine attributes of omniscience and infallibility for any men in such circumstances to pretend to be able to govern a whole series of fullgrown communities at the ends of the earth ? And is it not tantamount to a confession of utter imbecility—of being no better than mere children or idiots—on the part of such a community, to submit patiently to such monstrous usurpation ? If Great Britain has a right to govern the Australian colonies, then ought there never to have been any subordinate government upon earth, since the patriarch Noah came forth from the ark and erected his tent at the foot of Mount Ararat, as the head of his family and the universal sovereign of this habitable globe; for we are all the undoubted colonists of that aboriginal stock—we have all come forth from that first settlement and Head-quarters of the postdiluvian world. What right can Great Britain, one of the mere derivative colonies from this primaeval stock, have to prescribe conditions of obedience to us, who are only a single remove farther from our common father Noah, that venerable king of men, especially when we have the whole solid globe interposed between us and this pretended seat of legitimate authority over us in Downing-street and London? In short, if we, the Australian people, have a natural and inherent right to our freedom and independence, as the great Grotius and a host of other illustrious names assure us we have, what right can either Her Majesty, Queen Victoria, or the Imperial Parliament, have to subject us to their dominion one hour longer than we please ourselves? They may doubtless be of opinion—honestly enough—that we are still greatly in want of a dry-nurse over the water, and that we should otherwise be in danger of soiling our clean pinafores; in short, they may be of opinion that we should be much happier and better off in every way under *their* guidance than if governing ourselves. But we are not bound by their opinion in a matter in which our own interests and happiness are so deeply at stake. We have a right to think and act for ourselves in the case, and this is surely sufficient to incline the balance in our favour, independently of the other and higher considerations I have enumerated above.

To bring the matter to a short issue, let the case be reversed. Supposing then that we, the Australian people, were an old established and colonizing people, as we shall doubtless be some day or other, and that we had at length discovered, through one of our illustrious navigators, a large island called Great Britain, somewhere on the other side of the world; and supposing that shortly after this discovery was made, that is, nearly a century ago, we had planted a colony in the said island and given great grants of land and plenty of slave-labour to the settlers, to induce respectable people to take up their abode in the new colony ; and supposing that this colony had increased and multiplied in the interval till it had become a flourishing community of a million and a half of souls : would it be right and proper for us, the Senate and people of Australia, to insist that these Australian colonists of Britain should refrain from asserting their freedom and independence, when both able and willing to achieve it for themselves, in deference to us, their lords and masters at Botany Bay, and because their rejection of our yoke would diminish the glory of the Australian Empire in the eyes of those respectable neighbours of ours, the people of China and Japan ? This is what logicians call a *reductio ad absurdum,* and I appeal to the common sense of mankind, as to whether it is not sufficient to decide the whole question. The law of the case is simply the Law of Christ, the great Lawgiver for all nations, *Whatsoever ye would that men should do unto you, do ye even so unto them.* This is the Golden Rule for all such cases, and there can be no difficulty in its application.

SECTION XIII.—NATIONALITY A REAL AND NOT AN IMAGINARY GOOD.

If the desire of freedom and independence is natural to colonists, as I have shown it is—if it is the necessary result of the circumstances in which they are placed, inasmuch as "a nation is formed within them"— it must necessarily be implanted in their breasts by the All-wise and Beneficent Creator; and it is doubtless so implanted that it may be gratified. The feeling of nationality is no emanation from the nether regions : it comes down to us from heaven. It is the gift of God for the welfare and advancement of his creature man, and bears no resemblance to *the works of the Devil!*

So far indeed from the feeling of nationality being a mere matter of the imagination, it constitutes a bond of brotherhood of the most influential and salutary character, and forms one of the most powerful principles of virtuous action. Like the main-spring of a watch, it sets the whole machinery in motion. Like the heart, it causes the pulse of life to beat in the farthest extremities of the system. It is the very soul of society, which animates and exalts the whole brother-hood of associated men.

And must the young Australian be debarred from the exercise of that generous and manly feeling, of which every rightly constituted mind is conscious, when he exclaims, with deep emotion,

This is my own, my native land!

And must it be held a crime for the Australian colonist, who has come forth in the vigour of manhood to this far land, to labour earnestly for the freedom and independence of his adopted country, and to identify himself, in reality, as well as in imagination, with the coming glories of that great nation of the future, of which he forms a part?

In one word, nationality, or their entire freedom and independence, is absolutely necessary for the social welfare and political advancement of the Australian colonies. Give us *this*, and you give us everything to enable us to become a great and glorious people. Withhold *this*, and you give us nothing. "Is not dependence, however slight," observes that truly eminent man, the late Sir James Brooke, the Rajah of Sarawak, when contemplating the abject condition of the Malayan race in the Indian Archipelago, under the depressing influence of Dutch domination for three long centuries—"Is not dependence, however slight, a bar [to national advancement ?] I should answer, Yes. *National independence is essential to the first dawn of political institutions.*"*

The value and importance of National Independence may be ascertained and inferred from the estimation in which it has always been held by the wisest, the greatest and the best of men in all countries and ages; from the costly sacrifices and heroic efforts that have been so often made for its achievement, and from the splendid results with which its attainment has been generally, if not uniformly, followed.

"There is a charm and a moral power in the very idea of nationality, that demonstrates alike its divine original and the beneficence of its design. It nerves the arm of the patriot, and renders him irresistible. It is a moral instinct omnipotent for good, and it cannot possibly have been implanted in the breast of man for evil."†

Look at Switzerland, whose national independence dates from the famous battle of Morgarten, in the year 1315, when the three small forest cantons of Uri, Schwytz and Unterwalden—with a territory not so large altogether as the single county of Cumberland in New South Wales, and a population consisting almost entirely of shepherds and neatherds, and so limited withal, that the whole of the male adults capable of bearing arms, did not exceed 1350 men—successfully opposed the whole power of Austria and completely routed an army of 20,000 strong, including a large body of horse and many knights in complete armour.' A second memorable battle—that of Sempach—was fought by the same heroic people, with a similar result, in the year 1386; and from that period

* *Narrative of Events in Borneo and Celebes, &c.,* vol. i. p. 67. London, 1849.

† *Repeal or Revolution; or, a Glimpse of the Irish Future.* By the author of this work. London, 1848.

their confederation has gradually increased, not by conquest, but by voluntary adhesion, from three to twenty-
two cantons. But their whole territory is even yet considerably smaller in extent than Her Majesty's ancient
kingdom of Scotland, and their entire population amounts
at the utmost to three millions. But this mere handful
of people, although situated in the very centre of Europe,
and surrounded by mighty and often hostile empires, have
nobly maintained their freedom and independence for five
centuries and a half; preserving their simple republican
institutions unchanged, and transmitting them unimpaired
from generation to generation, while every country around
them has been convulsed, and has changed its constitution
and its masters, again and again. But the energy and
force of character, which their national independence produced and perpetuated, have hitherto enabled this simple
people to maintain, in the face of all Europe, the noble
position, and to preserve unsullied the illustrious name
which their virtuous and heroic forefathers had thus
bequeathed them.

Not less memorable was the struggle for national
independence in Scotland, against the unprincipled ambition and tyranny of Edward the First of England: not
less illustrious was its successful issue in the famous battle
of Bannockburn, through the long-continued and heroic
exertions of that Royal patriot, king Robert the Bruce,
in the year 1314, the very year before the establishment of
the Swiss Republic.

"The complete independence of Scotland," says the
historian, Tytler, "for which the people of that land had
obstinately sustained a war of thirty-two years' duration,
was at last amply acknowledged, and established on the
firmest basis; and England, with her powerful fleets, and
superb armies, her proud nobility, and her wealthy
exchequer, was, by superior courage and military talent,

G

compelled to renounce for ever her schemes of unjust aggression."*

"Such," observes the same historian.—"Such was the great battle of Bannockburn, interesting above all others which have been fought between the then rival nations, if we consider the issue which hung upon it, and very glorious to Scotland, both in the determined courage with which it was disputed by the troops, the high military talents displayed by the king of Scotland and his leaders, and the amazing disparity between the numbers of the combatants.† Its consequences were in the highest degree important. . It put an end for ever to all hopes on the part of England of accomplishing the conquest of her sister country. The plan, of which we can discover the foundations as far back as the reign of Alexander III., and for the furtherance of which the first Edward was content to throw away so much of treasure, and blood, and character, was put down in the way all such schemes ought to be defeated, by the strong hand of freeborn men, who were determined to remain so ; and the spirit of indignant resistance to foreign power, which had been awakened by Wallace, but crushed for a season by the dissensions of a jealous and an ambitious nobility, was directed and concentrated by the master-spirit of Bruce, and found fully adequate to overwhelm the united military energies of a kingdom, far superior to Scotland in all that constituted military strength. Nor have the consequences of this victory been partial or confined. *Their duration throughout succeeding centuries of*

---

* *Hist. of Scotland.* By Tytler, vol. i. p. 438, Sub Anno 1329.

† The English consisted of upwards of 100,000 men, including 40,000 cavalry, of whom 3000 were in complete armour, both man and horse, and 50,000 archers. The greatest force that Bruce could collect did not amount to 40,000 fighting men. Thirty thousand of the English were left dead upon the field, including 200 knights and 700 esquires,

Scottish history and Scottish liberty, down to the hour in which we now write, cannot be questioned; and without launching out into any inappropriate field of historical speculation, we have only to think of the most obvious consequences which must have resulted from Scotland becoming a conquered province of England; and if we wish for proof, to fix our eyes on the present condition of Ireland, in order to feel the present reality of all that we owe to the victory of Bannockburn, and to the memory of such men as Bruce, Randolph, and Douglass."

Before leaving this subject, I would point out an incident in the history of the great struggle for national independence which was then brought to a successful issue in Scotland, which exhibits in the most interesting manner the estimation in which that great blessing was held by the noble-minded Scotsmen of the 14th century.

In the year 1320, when king Edward II., of England, was pursuing the unprincipled schemes of his father, Edward I., for the subjugation of Scotland, and was using pecuniary and other influence at Rome to get the Scots and their king, the famous Robert Bruce, placed under the ban of the Pope as rebels against their alleged liege lord, the king of England, "the Scottish nobility," as the historian Tytler informs us, "assembled in Parliament at Aberbrothock, and with consent of the king, the barons, freeholders, and whole community of Scotland, directed a letter or manifesto to the Pope," containing, among others, the following noble sentiments. "If he," (that is king Robert Bruce) "should desist from what he has begun, and should shew an inclination to subject us or our kingdom to the king of England, or to his people, then we declare, we will use our utmost effort to expel him from the throne, as our enemy, and the subverter of his own and of our right, and we will choose another king to rule over us, who will be able to

* *Hist. of Scotland.* By P. F. Tytler, Esq. i. 321.

defend us; for *as long as a hundred Scotsmen are left alive we will never be subject to the dominion of England. It is not for glory, riches, or honour, that we fight, but for that liberty which no good man will consent to lose but with his life.*"*

The Seven United Provinces of Holland, which had previously groaned under the intolerable yoke of Spain, declared themselves independent, and formed the Batavian Republic, in the year 1579; their entire population at the time being in all probability considerably less than that of the Australian colonies at the present day † They were then but a paltry collection of insignificant fishing villages at the mouths of the Rhine, just as the founders of Swiss liberty were a mere company of Shepherds and Neatherds on the flanks of the higher Alps. But—so wonderful was the change which was then effected in their whole national character—within twenty-five years from the declaration of their independence, these Dutch fishermen had become the first maritime power of Europe, and were able to keep both Spain and Portugal at bay; establishing a great empire in the East, and discovering *New* Holland, which we trust is destined to follow the same noble example, as far as the attainment of independence is concerned, in the year 1605.

" As soon," says Professor Gervinus, of Heidelberg, one of the ablest historical and political writers of the age— " As soon as this petty nation (Holland) had asserted its independence, when the tree (according to Maurice of Saxony), was yet only a sapling, it made Antwerp, its

---

* *Hist. of Scotland.* By Patrick Fraser Tytler, Esq. i. 368.

† The present population of the kingdom of Holland, exclusive of the duchy of Luxembourg, which formed no part of the Seven United Provinces, does not exceed 3,000,000. My estimate of its amount three centuries ago must therefore be pretty correct, for there was no country in Europe that benifited so much from immigration as Holland, during the seventeenth and eighteenth centuries.

metropolis, the centre of the commerce of the world, and amassed enormous riches by the freight of goods. In a most unequal conflict, it made successful war with Spain. By the activity of its mercantile establishments, it first connected the different quarters of the world with one another, by a constant interchange of goods. It soon commanded the greatest naval force in Europe, precipitated the State, which drained the mines of Peru, into bankruptcy, and shook the power of its immense colonies in the East and in the West."*

"The Greeks," says Professor Heeren, of Göttingen, "had no idea of a commonwealth which did not govern itself."† And the spirit that animated that wonderful people has not yet completely died out in the land which they have rendered so illustrious by their noble deeds. The comparatively recent struggle for the independence of Greece, exhibited a whole series of deeds of self-sacrifice and heroism as illustrious as any that adorn the ancient annals of their nation. Modern Greece, which achieved its independence in the year 1829, and now enjoys that independence under the guarantee of Britain, France, and Russia, has even yet, after the lapse of nearly half a century, a population of not more than a million of souls. In one word, the value of national independence cannot possibly be estimated at too high a rate by those who possess it, and the effort to attain it, in whatever way that effort requires to be made, is the most ennobling in which the human faculties and energies can be engaged. "I hold," says General Santa Anna, for some time President of the Republic of Mexico, a country which we are apt to place at the very bottom of the scale for all that is honourable and ennobling to humanity—"I hold that independence is the greatest of our blessings, and every good citizen should defend it with all his power."‡

---

* Gervinus' *Introduction to the History of the 19th century.*
† Heeren's Greece.   ‡ *Santa Anna. Times,* April 5, 1853.

England has been thrice conquered—first by the Romans, afterwards by the Anglo-Saxons, and last of all by the Normans—and on each of these occasions, the history of the times records numerous and most affecting instances of the desperate struggles of the vanquished for the preservation of their freedom and independence, and the heroic sacrifices and privations to which they voluntarily submitted, rather than bend their necks under the yoke of their heartless and ruthless conquerors. The case of Caractacus, the British prince, who was carried in chains to Rome, under the Emperor Claudius, has been already referred to. A series of struggles of a similar kind characterized the era of the Anglo Saxon invasion in the fifth century; for the Saxons, from being friends and allies, soon became the bitterest enemies of the Britons. "At length," says the historian, "the last ties of amity were broken; the Saxons called in the Picts, against whom they had themselves been called in; and, by favour of this diversion, advanced into the interior of Britain, driving the British population before them, or forcing them to submission. The latter did not yield without great resistance: they once drove back the Saxons to the coast, and compelled them to re-embark; but the Saxons returned with increased numbers and aggravated fury, possessed themselves of many miles of country on the right bank of the Thames, and never afterwards quitted their conquest." And again, when speaking of the final retreat of the Britons into Wales: "This mountainous and unfruitful territory was the dwelling-place of the Cambrians: here they offered a safe though poor asylum to emigrants from every corner of Britain--to men who, say the old historians, chose rather to lead a life of hard liberty than to inhabit a fine country under a foreign yoke."* About five centuries later, the Anglo

---

* *History of the Conquest of England by the Normans.* From the French of A. Thierry, vol. ı. p. 18-26.

Saxons, who were then the people of England, had similar calamities to experience in their turn from their conquerors the Normans; the nobles and wealthier classes being almost uniformly stripped of their possessions, and the mass of the people reduced to slavery. Many of the English of that period had to fly from their country, like the Poles and Hungarians of a recent period, after being again and again defeated in battle; and so numerous were these English refugees even in Greece, that they actually formed a company in the army of the Greek Emperor at Constantinople. "Other chiefs and rich men, who could not, or would not, cross the sea, retired into the forests, with their clients and families. The great roads, along which the Norman convoys passed, were infested by their armed bands, and they took back from the conquerors by stratagem what the conquerors had taken by force; thus recovering the ransom of their inheritances, and avenging by assassination the massacre of their fellow-countrymen." "The north country especially, which had most obstinately resisted the invaders, became the land of vagrancy in arms, the last protection of the vanquished. The forests in the province of York were the haunt of a numerous band who had for their chief a (Saxon) prince. In the central parts and near London, under the walls of the Norman castles, various bands were also formed of these men who, say the old writers, rejecting slavery to the last, made the desert their asylum."*

So strongly devoted were the Anglo Saxons, or the English people generally, of that period, to the cause of their national independence, that for more than a century and a half after the dismal era of the Norman Conquest, whenever any eminent man of the English race, who had distinguished himself, either in Church or

---

* *History of the Conquest of England by the Normans*, vol. II. p. 3-5.

State, in the cause of his oppressed fellow-countrymen,
was at length judicially murdered, as was sure to be the
case in every such instance, by their Norman butchers,
"the native English bestowed on him, as on Waltheof,
the titles of *holy* and *blessed.*" They regarded him
thenceforth as a Saint, and made pilgrimages to his
tomb. "This was the lot of almost all men of any
eminence who had suffered for their resistance to the
power founded upon the conquest." "The great idea
of national independence was revealed to *them* as well as
to us: they assembled around it whatever they could
imagine as noblest and most brilliant: they made it
as religious as we make it poetical; they consecrated
it by immortal life in a world of bliss, as we con-
secrate it by a more infallible immortality in the remembrance of future times and the consciences of upright
men."*

"I suppose," says a talented minister of religion, in
a work of fiction, which, however, contains many lessons
of truth—"I suppose it will be agreed, that if ever mankind do that which claims the name and rank of virtue, it
is when they freely offer up their lives for their country,
and for a cause which, whatever may be their misjudgment
in the case, they believe to be the cause of liberty. Man
is then the greater in his disinterestedness, in the spirit
with which he renounces himself, and offers his neck
to the axe of the executioner, than he can be if clothed
in any robe of honour, or sitting upon any throne of
power."†

---

* *History of the Conquest of England by the Normans.* From the
French of A. Thierry, vol. ii. p. 93-94.

† *Zenobia, or the Fall of Palmyra.* By the Rev. Wm. Ware.

SECTION XIV.—AN OBJECTION URGED AND CONSIDERED—GREAT BRITAIN PLANTED THE AUSTRALIAN COLONIES, AND HAS THEREFORE A RIGHT TO RULE THEM.

This was the notable argument of the celebrated Dr. Johnson, when working as a literary day-labourer for his Government pension, during the discreditable and disastrous struggle with the American Colonies. Forgetting that these colonies had, with the single exception of Georgia, been planted without assistance of any kind from the parent state; and perhaps wilfully forgetting also, that some of the most prominent among them had originated in the fierce intolerance and unnatural and atrocious persecution of the Government of the day, the courtly pensioner put forth the notable argument, in defence of the British taxation of America, that, " as Great Britain had nourished the calf, she had a right to milk the cow." But, to use another of the homely similes of the distinguished moralist, Great Britain soon found to her cost that "it was the bull she was attempting to milk" all the while; for he soon kicked her over, pails and all; a mishap which cost her at least a hundred and fifty millions sterling, besides broken bones and loss of character.*

God forbid that the freedom and independence of the Australian colonies should ever require to be effected in any such way! Happily indeed there is now no apprehension of any such necessity ever recurring. "The people of England," says the leading journal of Europe, " have long ago renounced any wish to retain by force of

* At the commencement of the War of Independence in America the national debt of Great Britain amounted to £128,500,000. On the 5th of January 1786, when the arrears of the War of Independence had all been paid, it amounted to £268,130,000, notwithstanding the extraordinary efforts and exertions of the war period, over and above the national loss indicated by the amount of additional debt incurred.

arms remote settlements, inhabited by people of our own
race, in unwilling and compulsory subjection. Henceforth
the bond of union which unites Britain to her colonies
must be -free."* And the Imperial Government of the
present day have nobly endorsed these enlightened and
patriotic sentiments, by telling us, in so many words, that
if the Australian colonies really desire their entire freedom
and independence, Her Majesty's Government will not
stand in their way.

Great Britain originally planted the colony of New
South Wales, of which that of Van Dieman's Land, or
Tasmania, was a mere off-shoot, as a Penal Settlement;
and it served that purpose accordingly for fifty years; the
expenditure incurred by the mother country during that
period, being fully compensated by the service rendered
her by the colony. As to the moral effects of the system
on the colony generally, it is now thirty years since transportation to New South Wales was finally discontinued;
and of the whole number of the criminals who were
landed in the colony under that system during the previous
fifty years there still survived on the first of January,
1869, only ninety-five persons in all; but it will doubtless
be gratifying to any rightly-constituted mind to learn—
what I can state from my own experience and observation
for the last forty years and upwards—that not a few of the
whole number settled down in all parts of the colony from
time to time, and reared reputable and industrious families;
the different members of which are now engaged in all
manner of industrial pursuits, while some of them are
occupying prominent and influential positions in society.

But Great Britain has also received an ample compensation for her outlay in planting the Australian Colonies,
in another and much more valuable form—in the magnificent outlet she has thereby established for her redundant

* *Times*, July 30th, 1852.

population; in the valuable and indefinitely extending market for her mauufactured goods of all kinds which she has thus created, and in the boundless field she has opened up for the production of the raw material required for her manufactures, and for the employment of her home population. Assuredly, Great Britain has never expended any money for which she will receive an ampler return than she has alrea ly received, and will still continue to receive, for all time coming, from the expenditure she incurred in the establishment of the Australian Colonies.* Independently of the market for goods of all kinds which these colonies afford to the mother-country, to an extent unequalled in any other country of the same population in the world, Great Britain actually received from the Colony of New South Wales alone, during the first ten years from the introduction of the system of selling the waste lands of the colony, and devoting a large portion of the proceeds for the promotion of emigration not less than a million sterling; the whole of which was expended in relieving the mother-country of a serious public burden by paying for the conveyance of persons of the humbler classes from Great Britain and Ireland to New South Wales.

Being in England, duriug the famine in the Highlands and Islands of Scotland, in the year 1837, I learned, accidentally, that a Deputation, at the head of which was the late Rev. Dr. M'Leod, of Glasgow, had been sent up to London to solicit assistance from Government for the poor Highlanders, and especially to ask for aid for their emigration to Canada. The Government of the day gave

* In parting with a portion of our capital for the foundation of colonies, we are, in effect, placing it out at interest. Applied to a new and fertile soil, it produces far more than it could produce at home; and the benefit of that superior productiveness is felt by us in an increased supply of useful commodities, for which we are able to give the produce of our own industry in exchange on favourable terms, from the strength of the demand. *Merivale*, i. 228.

the Deputation a contribution for the Highlanders to the
extent of Ten Thousand Pounds; but Lord Glenelg, who
was then Secretary of State for the Colonies, told them with
regret that Government had no funds at their disposal for
sending any number of the Highlanders to Canada. In
this emergency, I informed the Deputation, to their great gratification, that there was a fund, which was then becoming
of importance, arising from the sale of Waste Land in New
South Wales, which the Government had it completely in
their power to appropriate for the emigration of so many at
least of the Highlanders to that colony. The Deputation
prudently acted upon my information, and applied at once to
Lord Glenelg at the Colonial Office; submitting, in answer
to the usual objections of Government at the suggestion of
any new idea, the public printed documents with which I
had furnished them from the colony. The result was the
complete success of the application, and the emigration at
the expense of the colony of not fewer than four thousand
of the poor Highlanders to New South Wales. This
emigration extended over three years, and was effected in
eighteen different ships, which were chartered for the
purpose by the Emigration Commissioners.

But even, although Great Britain had never received any
pecuniary or other compensation for the expenditure she
incurred in the establishment of the Australian Colonies,
this would in no way have affected the right of these
colonies to their entire freedom and independence, on the attainment of their political majority. The slave has an
absolute right to his freedom, whether his master has cleared
his purchase-money by him or not. The son, who has
completed the twenty-first year of his age, has an *absolute*
right to entire freedom from parental controul, whatever
his father may have expended on his board and education.
It is the law of nature and the ordinance of God, that the
parent should provide for the child during his non-age,
without entering him in his ledger as a debtor for the

expense of his up-bringing. If the parent has discharged his duty in the case, the child will delight to repay the obligation in whatever way he can. *He will honour his father and mother*, from the instinctive feeling of filial affection, as well as *that his days may be long in the land which the Lord his God shall give him;* and so far from this feeling being extinguished by the mere fact of his being legally free from all parental controul, it will still grow with his growth and strengthen with his strength, till, in the course of nature, he is called to deposit the remains of his venerated parent with sorrow in the grave.

SECTION XV.—ANOTHER OBJECTION STARTED AND CONSIDERED—THE COLONIES ARE CLAIMING THEIR FREEDOM AND INDEPENDENCE, BECAUSE THEY HATE THEIR MOTHER COUNTRY, WHICH HAS DONE SO MUCH FOR THEM, AND HER MAJESTY, THE QUEEN, TO WHOM THEY OWE ALL DUE ALLEGIANCE.

Now, as British Colonists, we, the inhabitants of the Australian Colonies, who are earnestly desiring our freedom and independence, repel this peculiarly offensive charge as being equally false and unfounded. From our inmost hearts, we can say, and we do say, with the poet :—

England, with all thy faults, we love thee still !

And we are conscious of no other feeling towards Her Majesty the Queen,—that pattern of every domestic, every royal virtue,—but that of unfeigned respect and reverential admiration. But what has all this to do with the *previous* question, as to whether we, as British Colonists who have attained our political majority, have, or have not, an inherent and indefeasible right, under the law of nature and the ordinance of God, to our entire freedom and independence? We are entitled to have this question considered and answered first; for personal rights have a

much higher claim in the eye of the law than mere con-
ventional rights and reasons of state policy. We insist
then that we *have* such a right—and *that* is the question.

Besides, is the son who has received his education and
learned his business,—both perhaps under his father's
roof,—but who sees a fair prospect of establishing himself in the world, and of rearing and supporting a family
of his own, and who has accordingly fixed his affections
on some suitable helpmeet, and planned out an establishment for himself,—is such a son supposed to hate his
father because he is endeavouring to do the best he can
for himself; and is the future intercourse (or rather no
intercourse whatever) which is to subsist between them
to be characterized by angry criminations and recrimina-
tions, by acts of mutual and unnatural hostility? On the
contrary, when the dutiful son leaves the parental roof,
to take up this new and more important position in the
world, he will leave it with the tear of heartfelt affection
in his eye—he will leave it with his father's blessing and
his mother's prayers.

And such, in the ordinary course of nature, are precisely the feelings that would subsist between a mother-
country and her colonies, if no acts of human folly and
madness were allowed to intervene, even although the
latter were asserting their natural, inherent, and indefeasible right to entire freedom and independence, on the
attainment of their political majority.

And as to the charge of our violating or renouncing
our allegiance to Her Majesty the Queen, in claiming, as
we do, our entire freedom and independence, I repeat it,
there is *a previous question* to be put and answered, ere
this knotty point can be determined, ere this offensive
charge can be substantiated—I mean the question as to
whether we, as British colonists who have attained our
political majority, have, or have not, a right to our
entire freedom and independence. For if we have such

a right, as I have shown we have, the right of Her
Majesty the Queen to reign over us necessarily ceases
and determines. Under the universal government of God
there cannot possibly be two inconsistent and incompatible
rights; and the right to obedience or allegiance on the one
part, is clearly inconsistent and incompatible with the right
to freedom and independence on the other. It is precisely
where and when the one of these rights ends, that the other
begins : they cannot possibly occupy the same place, or extend to the same persons. The alleged right of a sovereign
to reign over a people who, by the law of nature and the
ordinance of God, have a right to their freedom and independence accordingly, is a mere imaginary right, and has
no existence in reality. In plain English, it is downright
usurpation, and its exercise is tyranny and oppression. Let
us hear no more, then, of this pitiful, this contemptible
charge, about our violating or renouncing our allegiance.
The question is, Do we *owe* such allegiance, in the sense in
which the term is used in the charge, as implying that we
have no rights in the case? To which I unhesitatingly
answer, No.

SECTION XVI.—A THIRD OBJECTION STATED AND CONSIDERED.—THE
BRITISH COLONIES ARE PART AND PARCEL OF THE BRITISH EMPIRE
—AN EMPIRE ON WHICH THE SUN NEVER SETS, AND WHICH, FAR
MORE THAN ANY EVEN OF THE SO-CALLED UNIVERSAL EMPIRES OF
ANTIQUITY, EXTENDS ITS SCEPTRE TO ALL THE FOUR QUARTERS
OF THE GLOBE—TO EVERY CONTINENT, WITHOUT EXCEPTION, AND
TO ALMOST EVERY ISLE : IT MUST BE GLORIOUS, THEREFORE, TO
BELONG TO SUCH AN EMPIRE: IT CANNOT BUT BE MONSTROUS,
UNNATURAL, SUICIDAL AND HIGHLY CRIMINAL TO ATTEMPT TO DIS-
MEMBER IT.

There can be no question as to the enormous extent of
the British empire and the colossal character of its power.
Girdling the earth, as it does, in every zone, and covering

the sea, it is as like a universal empire as possible, *and therefore the more likely to be dismembered, as it is called, very shortly.* For Divine Providence has, for the last thirteen hundred and fifty years, that is, ever since the Roman Empire, or fourth universal monarchy, fell, set its face against the establishment of anything like another universal empire or fifth monarchy upon earth; consequently, the more extensive any empire becomes, and the more closely it approaches to universality, we have every reason to believe that it is only the nearer its fall or dismemberment. It is instructive to glance at the past history of the world in connection with this point; as in comparing the present with the past, we may be enabled, with some degree of confidence, to anticipate the future.

The first attempt to establish a universal empire or fifth monarchy upon earth, since the fall of the Roman empire in the West, was made by the Saracens; who, succeeding to a portion at least of the noble inheritance of Rome in the East and West, speedily overran both Asia and Africa, but were finally checked at their entrance into Europe by Charles Martel in the south of France. The Turks, who in later times succeeded the Saracens in their Eastern dominion, also received their final check, when apparently on the highway to universal empire in the West, from John Sobieski, king of Poland, under the walls of Vienna. As to similar attempts among Christian nations, Charlemagne endeavoured, with no small degree of success, for a time, to reunite the scattered fragments of the Roman empire in the West; but the mushroom dominion of that great potentate soon fell to pieces again under the government of his sons. At the era of the Reformation Charles the Fifth made a similar attempt with precisely similar results : and so did Louis the Fourteenth at a later period ; and so also, in our own times, did the renowned Napoleon.

There are two periods in British history very remarkable in relation to this law of Divine Providence. In the year

1756, the famous battle of Plassy gave England the presidency of Bengal and the future empire of India. But as if this was not sufficient, the battle of Quebec, in the year 1759, when the gallant Wolfe fell in the arms of victory on the heights of Abraham, gave England the whole of the French empire in North America, as was afterwards solemnly and definitively determined by the Treaty of Paris in 1763. Never had the British empire been so extensive as at that period; never was its power so resistless; and never was there a fairer prospect of its dominion becoming all but universal.* But Divine Providence had determined many ages before that no other universal monarchy should be established on earth; and, as if in fulfilment of this decree, a spirit of infatuation was sent forth into the counsels of George the Third; a series of arbitrary and oppressive measures was enacted by the Imperial Parliament in reference to the American colonies; and thirteen noble provinces were at length wrested from the British empire, just as ten of the tribes of Israel had been from the family of David, in remarkably similar circumstances—on a question of iniquitous taxation.†

Now it appears to me that we are approaching a somewhat similar crisis in the history of the British empire at the present moment. For a long time past we have been

---

* Her possessions in North America, extending from the Mississippi to the great St. Lawrence, and from the ocean to the Alleghany Mountains, were enlarged at the Peace of Paris, by the acquisition of all Canada and Florida. Never did British authority *seem* more firmly established in these regions; but events soon *proved* that it never was less so.—*Europe and its Colonies, by Professor Heeren*, p. 278.

† THE KING HEARKENED NOT UNTO THE PEOPLE FOR THE CAUSE WAS FROM THE LORD. * * * *So when all Israel saw that the king hearkened not unto them, the people answered the king, saying, What portion have we in David? neither have we inheritance in the son of Jesse: to your tents, O Israel: now see to thine own house, David. So Israel departed unto their tents.*—1 Kings, xii. 15, 16.

H

adding province to province in India, till our empire in that
country now comprises a hundred and eighty millions of
people, about an eighth part of the whole human
race! We have also been adding province to province
in Africa.   We have humbled China, and planted
a colony, as we call it by courtesy, and a line of
posts, on her frontier.   We have annexed New Zealand to our Australasian dominion; and we have added
Aden, Singapore, and Labuan, to our empire in the
East; and certain political enthusiasts in the colonies are
actually promising us the whole multitude of the isles of
the vast Pacific.   In short, never was the British empire
more extensive than it is at present; never was its power
more formidable, in every land and on every sea.   The
Press everywhere is telling us *usque ad nauseam* that the
sun never sets upon it, and a certain idolatrous limner at
the first Great Exhibition, catching the vainglorious spirit
of the age, actually represented the four quarters of the
globe paying homage to Queen Victoria!

Now no man of the slightest discernment can be blind
to these very significant signs of the times.   Such national
pride, accompanied as it is with such national dereliction
of duty towards the poor in the land, for whom this vast
colonial empire is held in trust, necessarily precedes a
fall; for it cannot but be peculiarly offensive in the eyes
of the Great Governor among the nations.   We are evidently hastening to another great crisis in the history of
our country.   We are on the eve of another dismemberment; and I shall be greatly mistaken, if, in a very few
years hence, both the eastern colonies of Australia and
the British colonies of North America shall not have
ceased to belong to the British Empire.   Which of the
two great groups will go first, no man can tell; but it is
certain, at all events, that they are both getting ready.

And why should they not?   And why should a great
nation like ours seek to prevent them?   If it is the right

of these groups of colonies, by the law of nature and the ordinance of God, to form two great nations, instead of a series of miserable and till very lately miserably-governed dependencies, and to assume the prominent and highly influential position they are destined to occupy in that capacity on the face of the earth, why should Englishmen endeavour, in their folly and madness, either to prevent or to postpone " a consummation so devoutly to be wished ?"*

Besides, how can we—Britons and Protestants as we profess to be—how can we pretend to object to the claim of the Pope to govern the whole Christian Church, in all its numerous, diversified, and widely scattered settlements —*on which the Sun never sets*—when we ourselves actually set up, as we have been doing for all our colonies for

---

* Prejudices and prepossessions are stubborn things in all cases ; but in none, more peculiarly obstinate, than in relinquishing detached parts of an unwieldy extended empire; there not being, I believe, a single instance in all history of any nation surrendering a distant province voluntarily, and of free choice, notwithstanding it was greatly their interest to have done it. The English, in particular, have given remarkable proofs of their unwillingness. For though it was undeniably their interest to have abandoned all the provinces which they held in France, yet they never gave up one of them till they were compelled to it by force of arms. Now, indeed, and at this distance of time, we see clearly that our forefathers were wretched politicians in endeavouring to retain any one of the French provinces, which, if it was a little one, would be a continual drain, and perhaps an increasing expense; and if it was a great one, might grow up to be a rival, and become the seat of empire. I say, we can see these things clearly enough at present: yet, alas ! what advantages do we derive from the discovery? And what application do we make of such historical mementos to the business of the present day ? The remotest of our provinces in France were hardly 300 miles distant from our own coasts; the nearest of those in America are about 3000. " *Humble Address and earnest Appeal*" *in favour of Separation from America, by Josiah Tucker, D.D., Dean of Gloucester*, p. 70. Gloucester, 1775.

a century past—until yesterday, as it were—a sort of political Pope in Downing-street, and empower him to govern the whole Colonial Empire of Britain, in all its numerous and endlessly diversified and widely scattered settlements—*on which also the sun never sets?* Reasoning upon Protestant principles, and without reference to points of doctrine, the pretended right to govern is in both cases sheer usurpation —a mere trampling under foot of the sacred and inherent rights of men. In both cases, also, the pretended right is based upon the same blasphemous assumption—an assumption of two of the incommunicable attributes of the Godhead—Omniscience and Infallibility! For example— "the Pope knows everything throughout the Christian Church, as well as everything that is needful for it; and therefore he can never go wrong in governing it "—this is Popery in Religion. "The Secretary of State for the Colonies knows everything throughout the Colonial Empire of Britain, as well as everything that is needful for it; and therefore he can never go wrong in governing it "—this is Popery in Politics: the first cause or moving spring of the two enormities being also precisely the same—an unhallowed lust of empire, on the part of the two bodies which the Pope and the colonial autocrat respectively represent, contrary alike to the ordinance of God and the rights of men.

As to the glory of belonging to such an empire as that of Britain, "I am of opinion," says Mr. Wakefield, in the language of a supposed speaker whose sentiments he adopts, "that the extent and glory of an empire are solid advantages for all its inhabitants, *and especially those who inhabit its centre.* I think that whatever the possession of our colonies may cost us in money, the possession is worth more in money than its money cost, and infinitely more in other respects. For by overawing foreign nations and impressing mankind with a *prestige* of our might, it enables us to keep the peace of the world, which we have no interest in disturbing, as it would enable us to disturb the world if we pleased. The advantage is, that the possession of this immense empire by England causes the mere name of England to be a real and mighty power; the greatest power that now exists in the world."†

I admit that for those who are at "the centre" of the national system, where all its life and heat are concentrated, it may be very pleasant and self-satisfying to look around on their vast domain of colonies of all sorts, of plantations, possessions, and dependencies, and to say, with Robinson Crusoe,

> " We are monarchs of all we survey;"

but the condition of those who are at the extremities of the system may, from that very circumstance, be supremely uncomfortable; and whether the latter are to surrender their natural and inherent rights, merely to gratify the vanity, or to minister to the self-importance of those who are at the centre of the system, is a question which, I conceive, admits but of one answer. It so completely sets aside the golden rule of doing to others as we should wish to be done by, that one can scarcely help feeling ashamed at hearing of such a proposition from any person calling himself an Englishman. Is it either just or right—for that is the question—that the best and dearest interests of any people should be compromised and sacrificed; that their social progress should be impeded and retarded in an endless variety of ways; that they should be refused their proper position among the nations, and degraded to a condition of pitiable and humiliating subserviency—in order to minister to the gratification of this mean contemptible vanity on the part of another people at the ends of the earth? For what, I ask, are the British people better than we— the British colonists of Australia—except that they are

† *View of the Art of Colonization, &c.*, p. 98.

twenty to one of us ?   But does this give them any right,
by the law of nature or the ordinance of God, to govern
us ?   Does this mere numerical superiority demonstrate
that they are

> Born to command ten thousand slaves, like us,

the insignificant dwellers in Australia ?

"Dependence upon a distant government," says an able
writer in the *Edinburgh Review* for July, 1853, in an article
on Earl Grey's Colonial Administration, "Dependence
upon a distant government seems to us a great, an
unceasing, and an inevitable evil. It may, in a certain
state of a given community, be outweighed or compensated
by counter advantages; but a dependency must, from the
necessity of the case, be to a certain extent ill-governed.
The evils of political parties (provided their dissensions do
not end in despotism or civil war) are, in our judgment,
trifling indeed, as compared with the evils of dependence
on the decision of persons living at a distance of thousands
of miles, belonging to a different political community, and
imperfectly informed as to the state and circumstances of
the dependency."

Again, to talk of England keeping the peace of the
world, while she has eight hundred millions of debt of her
own, incurred almost exclusively through her generally
unjust and unnecessary wars, is amusing enough; but it
can surely be no reason why British colonists, who have a
natural and inherent right to nationality, should be forced
to continue in the very subordinate and unsatisfactory
condition of mere dependents and vassals. *If thou mayest
be made free*, says the apostle Paul (and the advice applies
to communities as well as to individuals), *use it rather.**

It would have been supremely ridiculous, as well as ex-

* 1 *Corinth.* vii. 21.

ceedingly heartless and unfeeling, for a cotton-planter in
South Carolina, under the old regime of Slavery, on
learning that his "niggers" were anxious for their freedom,
to tell them that "he considered them very unreasonable
creatures indeed; that the ownership of so many of them
gave *him* a standing and influence in society, an importance
in the country, which he could not otherwise possess; that
he had three votes for a Congress-man for every five or
them, and that in such circumstances it was very ungrateful in them to seek to lessen *his* consequence in
the world by desiring their freedom." It is equally
ridiculous, however, and equally unfeeling and insulting
to British colonists, to tell them that it is necessary for
England, in order to maintain her dignity and importance
in the world, to retain in a state of humiliating vassalage
those to whom God has not only given the desire of freedom and the right to assert it, but the means and ability
to use it for their own welfare and advancement. There
was much sympathy professed a few years ago by men of
all ranks and classes throughout the United Kingdom for
the unhappy condition of the American slave; but if it is
true that "the man who hates his brother is a murderer"
at heart, then I maintain that the man, of whatever rank
or influence in society, who uses his influence to prevent
those British colonists that have attained their political
majority, from obtaining their freedom and independence,
merely because he imagines that the honour and glory of
England would thereby be somewhat impaired, is a slave-
holder at heart; and when he tells me, in the mawkish
language of the day, that "his heart bleeds for the slave,"
I tell him in the plainest English in reply, that "he is a
hypocrite and a liar:" for if he has no sympathy for his
colonial brother whom he *has* seen, how can he sympathise with the poor African slave whom he has never
seen?

Notwithstanding the confident assertions that are sometimes put forth, although without the least shadow of proof, in respectable quarters—as for instance, by Mr. Gilbert Wakefield and Earl Grey—as to the value of Colonies to the mother-country, in the sense of dependencies, or places to be governed from home, I deny that England has anything to lose from the freedom and independence of her Australian Colonies, and I maintain that she has everything to gain. Mr. Wakefield's *prestige* is merely another name for *shadow* : it has no substance in it, no real value. And although Earl Grey, in his elaborate but unsuccessful apology for his own maladministration of the colonies, ostentatiously expresses his opinion that "the British Colonial Empire ought to be maintained, because much of the power and influence of Great Britain depends upon her having large colonial possessions in different parts of the world,"* as if that were anything to us, the question is simply—What solid advantages does England really derive from her possession of such dependencies as the Australian colonies? In answer to this question, the late Sir George Lewis, in his able and singularly honest work, on *the Government of Dependencies*, enumerates the advantages which a parent state or dominant country derives from its supremacy over a dependency as follows, viz. :—

1. *Tribute, or revenue paid by the dependency.* —This, it is well known, was the system in universal practice among

* *The Colonial Policy of Lord John Russell's Administration.* By Earl Grey. 2 vols. 8vo. London, 1853.

the ancients in the government of their dependent provinces ;* but the attempt to enforce it in America led to the War of Independence in that country, and the claim was at length formally renounced by the 18 Geo. III. cap. 12.†

2. *Assistance for military or naval purposes.*—Such assistance was very frequently rendered by the earlier colonists of America, in the wars of the mother country with France, which had then an extensive empire in that country ; but no such assistance could either be expected or would be necessary now. It is worthy of remark that the celebrated Dr. Adam Smith considered the contribution of revenue and military force as so essential to the very idea of a colony that he regarded any dependency as utterly valueless that did not contribute either the one or the other. His words are as follows :—

"Countries which contribute neither revenue nor military force towards the support of the empire cannot be considered as provinces. They may perhaps be considered as appendages, as a sort of splendid and showy equipage of the empire."‡

3. *Advantages to the dominant country from its trade with the dependency.*—Since the commencement of the present Free Trade system, no special advantage can be derived by the mother country from this source.

4. *Facilities afforded by dependencies to the dominant country for the emigration of its surplus population, and for an advantageous employment of its capital.*—Sir George Lewis

---

* *What thinkest thou, Simon ? Of whom do the kings of the earth take custom or tribute ? Of their own children, or of strangers ? Peter saith unto him, of strangers.* Matthew xvii. 25, 26.

† According to the present feelings and opinions of men, no direct benefit, by way of tribute or payment of any sort, can be derived by England from her colonies.—*The Colonies of England, by John Arthur Roebuck, M.P.* London, 1849, p. 11.

‡ *Wealth of Nations*, b. v. c. 3.

admits, however, that in order to secure this advantage to the mother country, it is not necessary that the colony should be a dependency of the parent state; of which abundant proof will be given in the sequel.

5. *Facilities for the transportation of convicts to a dependency.*—These facilities, however, are now at an end in all the Australian colonies of the Eastern group.

6. *The glory of possessing dependencies.*—This, therefore, is the only real advantage, if it is one, that remains. On this point, however, Sir George Lewis very judiciously observes, that " a nation derives no true glory from any possession which produces no assignable advantage to itself or to other communities. If a country possesses a dependency from which it derives no public revenue, no military or naval strength, and no commercial advantages or facilities for emigration which it would not equally enjoy though the dependency were independent, and *if*, moreover, *the dependency suffers the evils which are the almost inevitable consequences of its political condition*, such a possession cannot justly be called glorious."*

"The honour of a nation," says the distinguished American moralist, Dr. Channing, to the same effect,— "The honour of a nation consists, *not in the forced and reluctant submission of other States*, but in equal laws and free institutions, in cultivated fields and prosperous cities, in the development of intellectual and moral power, in the diffusion of knowledge, in magnanimity and justice, in the virtues and blessings of peace."†

Sir George Lewis also enumerates the advantages derivable by a dependency from its dependence on the dominant country under the following heads, viz. :—

1. *Protection by the dominant country.*—This I shall show

---

* *Lewis on the Government of Dependencies*, p. 240.
† *Channing's Essay on War.*

in the sequel is quite unnecessary in the case of the Australian colonies.

2. *Pecuniary assistance by the dominant country.*—Nothing of this kind is required in these colonies.

3. *Commercial advantages.*—But these have all been done away with under the Free Trade system.

There is therefore not one substantial advantage, derivable either by the mother-country on the one hand, or by the Australian colonies on the other, from the continuance of the present connection of domination and dependency. The only advantage remaining to the mother-country is a merely imaginary one—the glory of the thing; which, Sir George Lewis admits, is utterly valueless, and which is surely not to be considered for one moment as an adequate compensation for the loss which the mother-country herself sustains, as well as for the unspeakable evil which is entailed on the colonies, by the continuance of their state of dependency.

The doctrine that a mother-country, and particularly Great Britain, derives no real benefit from the government of distant and full-grown colonies, has obtained the cordial and unqualified support of the most distinguished writers of the age, both British and Foreign. And it is one of the gratifying signs of the times, that the true relation of a colony to its mother-country is thus at length understood and appreciated in the most influential quarters, both at home and abroad.

"Is it a secret to you," asks the celebrated Jeremy Bentham, in his famous address to the French Convention of 1793, recommending them to emancipate their colonies, "Is it a secret to you any more than ourselves, that our colonies cost us much, that they yield us nothing—that our government makes us pay them for suffering it to govern them—and that all the use or purpose of this compact is to make places, and wars that breed more places ?"*

To the same effect that eminent and universally-respected Statesman, the late Sir James Mackintosh, expresses himself as follows:—"Colonial possessions have been so unanswerably demonstrated to be commercially useless, and politically ruinous, that the conviction of philosophers cannot fail of having, in due time, its effect upon the minds of enlightened Europe, and delivering the Empire from this cumbrous and destructive appendage.."†

"With respect to Canada," observes the late Sir Henry Parnell,—"With respect to Canada (including our other possessions on the continent of North America) no case can be made out to show that we should not have *every commercial advantage* we are supposed now to have, if it were made *an independent state.* Neither our manufactures, foreign commerce, nor shipping, would be injured by such a measure. On the other hand, what has the nation lost by Canada? Fifty or sixty millions have already been expended: the annual charge on the British Treasury is now full £600,000 a year; and we learn from the Second Report of the Committee of Finance, that a plan of fortifying Canada has been for two or three years in progress, which is to cost £3,000,000.‡

"The total charge on our revenue," says Mr. Merivale, "on account of the military, naval, and civil establishments of the colonies, amounted to £2,360,000 in 1835."

And again :—

" By the war of 1739," said Lord Sheffield, " which may be truly called an American contest, we incurred a debt of upwards of £31,000,000 ; by the war of 1755, we

---

* *Emancipate your Colonies.* Jeremy Bentham.

† Sir James Mackintosh, *Vindiciae Gallicae.*

‡ *Financial Reform.* By the late Sir Henry Parnell, M. P. for Dundee.

incurred a further debt of £71,500,000; and by the war of the revolt we have added to both these debts nearly £100,000,000 more. And thus we have expended a far larger sum in defending and retaining our colonies than the value of all the merchandise we have ever sent them."*

"A country," says McCulloch, "which founds a colony on the liberal principle of allowing it to trade freely with all the world, necessarily possesses considerable advantages in its market from identity of language, religion, customs, &c. These are natural and legitimate sources of preference of which it cannot be deprived; and these, combined with equal or greater cheapness of the products suitable for the colonial markets, will give its merchants the complete command of them."†

"Under the present system of management," observes the celebrated Dr. Adam Smith, "Great Britain derives nothing but loss from the dominion which she assumes over her colonies.

"To propose that Great Britain should voluntarily give up all authority over her colonies, and leave them to elect their own magistrates, to enact their own laws, and to make peace and war as they might think proper, would be to propose such a measure as never was, and never will be adopted by any nation in the world. No nation ever voluntarily gave up the dominion of any province, how troublesome soever it might be to govern it, and how small soever the revenue which it afforded might be in proportion to the expense which it occasioned. Such sacrifices, though they might frequently be agreeable to the interest, are always mortifying to the pride of every nation. * * * The most visionary enthusiast would scarce be capable of proposing such a measure, with any serious hopes at least of

---

* *Merivale*, vol. I. p. 237.

† McCulloch's *Statistical Account of the British Empire*, vol. I. p. 595.

its ever being adopted. If it was adopted, however, Great Britain would not only be immediately freed from the whole annual expense of the peace establishment of the colonies, but *might settle with them such a treaty of commerce as would effectually secure her a free trade,* more advantageous to the great body of the people, though less so to the merchants, than the monopoly which she at present enjoys. By thus parting good friends, the natural affection of the colonies to the mother-country, which, perhaps, our late dissensions have well nigh extinguished, would quickly revive. It might dispose them not only to respect, for whole centuries together, that treaty of commerce which they had concluded with us at parting, but to favour us in war as well as in trade, and, instead of turbulent and factious subjects, to become our most faithful, affectionate, and generous allies; and the same sort of parental affection on the one side, and filial respect on the other, might revive between Great Britain and her colonies, which used to subsist between the colonies of ancient Greece and the mother-city from which they descended."*

But the world has been making great advances since the days of Adam Smith; for the following generous and enlightened sentiment has appeared, (as I have already had occasion to observe), in an article on Australia in the leading journal of Europe, nearly eighteen years ago.—"The people of England have long ago renounced any wish to retain by force of arms remote settlements, inhabited by people of our own race, in unwilling and compulsory subjection. Henceforth the bond of union which unites Britain to her colonies must be free."†

"Before the American Revolution," observes Mr. Merivale, "we possessed colonies even more extensive and

---

* *Wealth of Nations,* vol. iii. c. 7.
† *Times,* July 30, 1852.

valuable than at present. Yet the trade with those colonies, though a thriving one, never seems to have been in a wholly satisfactory state. And during the latter years of the connection, mutual jealousies and antipathies, more powerful even than self-interest, nearly reduced it to ruin. As soon as the connection was severed, what was the consequence? Was our profitable colonial trade turned into a losing foreign trade? All the world knows, on the contrary, that the commerce between the mother-country and the colonies was but a peddling traffic compared with that vast international intercourse, the greatest the world has ever known, which grew up between them when they had exchanged the tie of subjection for that of equality."

"No one now really doubts that the separation of our North American colonies has been, in an economical sense, advantageous to us. And yet precisely the same arguments are current at this very day, respecting the superior profit of colonial commerce, and the wealth arising from colonial domination, which were in every one's mouth before that great event had occurred, and by its results confounded all such calculations. So easily does our reason contrive to forget the strongest lessons, or to evade their force, when prejudice and love of power warp it in the contrary direction."*

"England," observes Professor Gervinus, "was no more weakened by the loss of her colonies (as France had intended), than she was by the closing of the Continent under Napoleon; on the contrary, the full development of her internal strength and her judicious administration, only then began to display itself. That to which she chiefly owed the greatness of her commerce, and the power it communicated to her government, the active energy of the people, no war could vanquish, but on the contrary, was

---

* *Merivale,* vol. I. p. 230.

strengthened by the freedom of the State and of the trade with North America. In these results a sentence of condemnation was pronounced on the old colonial system."

And again :—" Great as England has become by her colonies, she has never received from them an accession of power, since they have been more expense than profit to her, and their occupation by the military has weakened rather than strengthened the mother-country."*

To the same effect, an able writer in the *Edinburgh Review*, well observes :—" The power of England may be attributed by foreign states to a false cause, and may be thought to be owing to the possession of colonies, when it is, in fact, owing to the industry and energy of our native population. But if foreign nations found that the subtraction of a colony did not, in fact, diminish the power of England, they would not treat her with less respect. The independence of the American colonies furnishes an apt illustration; for although the continental nations believed that this change had struck a deadly blow at England, they soon forgot their false theory, when they observed the inexhaustible resources which she displayed during the French war, nothwithstanding the loss of her barren American sovereignty."†

But the benefit resulting from the entire political separation of the mother-country and her colonies, in the case of America, was not entirely on the side of Britain. "In a state of dependence," observes a writer who undoubtedly contributed greatly to this consummation,—" In a state of dependence, and with a fettered commerce, though with all the advantages of peace, her [America's] trade could not balance itself, and she annually ran into debt. But now in a state of independence, though involved in war, she

---

* *Gervinus. Introd. to Hist. of 19th Cent.*

† *Edinburgh Review* for July, 1853. Article on *Earl Grey's Colonial Administration.*   •

requires no credit; her stores are full of merchandise, and gold and silver become the currency of the country."*

There are still, indeed, individuals, both in our own and in other mother-countries of Europe, who cling to the old fallacy of empire, and regard either the actual or the possible loss of dominion over distant colonies as an event in the highest degree to be deprecated and deplored. And it is singular enough that one should have to include among such persons—the adherents of an exploded system—so eminent a writer as Mr. Carlyle. But while that distinguished writer, like the celebrated Dr. Johnson, devoutly believes in the right of Great Britain to ride the colonies at her pleasure, and to use them for her own purposes exclusively, he admits that the public opinion, including that of British Statesmen, is very much against him.

"Constitutions for the Colonies," says Mr. Carlyle, "are now on the anvil; the discontented colonies are all to be cured of their miseries by Constitutions. Whether that will cure their miseries, or only operate as a Godfrey's Cordial to stop their whimpering, and in the end worsen all their miseries, may be a sad doubt to us. One thing strikes a remote spectator in these Colonial questions; the singular placidity with which the British Statesman at this time, *backed by the British monied classes*, is prepared to surrender whatsoever interest Britain, as foundress of these establishments, might pretend to have in the decision."†

. In like manner, the late M. de Chateaubriand, in his "Travels in North America," laments over the loss of the French empire in that country with the most piteous ululations. But another Frenchman, of less brilliancy of genius indeed, but of far keener discernment in matters of

* *Letter to the Abbé Raynal on the affairs of North America.* By Thomas Paine, M.A. Philadelphia, 1782, page 29.

† T. Carlyle, *Latter Day Pamphlets.*

I

every-day life, passes a very different judgment on that event, in regard to its real bearings on the material interests and social welfare of France.

"It is high time," says M. Say, the eminent French political economist, who wrote much about the same period as M. de Chateaubriand, "to drop our absurd lamentations for the loss of our colonies, considered as a source of national prosperity. For, in the first place, France now enjoys a greater degree of prosperity than while she retained her colonies; witness the increase of her population. Before the Revolution, her revenues could maintain but twenty-five millions of people; they now (1819) support thirty millions. In the second place, the first principles of political economy will teach us, that *the loss of colonies by no means implies a loss of the trade with them.* With what did France buy colonial products before? With her own domestic products, to be sure. Has she not continued to buy them since in the same way, though sometimes of a neutral, or even of an enemy?"

And again:—

"The ancients, by their system of colonization, made themselves friends all over the known world; the moderns have sought to make subjects, and *therefore* have made enemies. Governors, deputed by the mother-country, feel not the slightest interest in the diffusion of happiness and real wealth amongst a people, with whom they do not propose to spend their lives, to sink into privacy and retirement, or to conciliate popularity. They know their consideration in the mother-country will depend upon the fortune they return with, not upon their behaviour in office. Add to this the large discretionary power, that must unavoidably be vested in the deputed rulers of distant possessions, and there will be every ingredient towards the composition of *a truly detestable government.*"*

*M. Say, *Political Economy*. Paris, 1820.

Many thanks, M. Say, for the correct definition you have thus given us of colonial government—such as it was, previous to the year 1856, when responsible government was established, by Act of the Imperial Parliament, in all these Australian Colonies. For I have no hesitation in acknowledging it as the general result of my own observation and experience for more than thirty years previous to that great event, that the British government of the Australian colonies was, in comparison, with what the government of such communities ought to have been in the present age of free institutions and general enlightenment, during the whole of that period, "detestable government"—suicidal for Great Britain herself as a great manufacturing and commercial country, with a redundant but peculiarly energetic population, and ruinous for the best interests of the colonies, both morally and materially, in an endless variety of ways.

Besides, all the great names in the literature, both of our own and of foreign countries, are decidedly in favour of the entire freedom and independence of colonies as the best possible condition, both for the mother-country and for the dependency. I have already enumerated Grotius, Heeren, Milton, Franklin, Dr. Adam Smith, Sir George Lewis, Professor Gervinus, M. Say, and Jeremy Bentham I may add Turgot, Talleyrand, Storch, Chardoza, Dr. Thomas Cooper, of America, Malthus, Brougham, Huskisson, Baring, Ricardo, Torrens, Senior; and last, but not least, the eminent political writer, Mr. James Mill. These distinguished men are unanimously of opinion that dominion over colonies is of no real use to a mother-country in increasing her commercial prosperity, and that its actual and never-failing tendency is to produce or to perpetuate bad government for the colonies.

"A word of recapitulation," says Jeremy Bentham to the French Convention, in summing up his argument, which is equally applicable to the case of Great Britain and her Australian colonies, " and I have done—you will, I say, give up your colonies—because you have no right to govern them ; because they had rather not be governed by you ; because it is against their interest to be governed by you ; because you get nothing by governing them ; because you can't keep them ; because the expense of trying to keep them would be ruinous ; because your Constitution would suffer by your keeping them; because your principles forbid your keeping them ; and because you would do good to all the world by parting with them."*

It is difficult indeed to say which of the two parties, the mother-country or the colonies, suffered the most under the monstrous system that uniformly characterised the government of the Colonies of Great Britain, till the advent of popular government in the year 1856—that system which for two centuries and a half sacrificed more or less all the legitimate objects of colonization for the gratification of an unhallowed lust of empire, unwarranted by the laws of God, and trampling under foot the rights of men.

There has recently indeed been a singular outburst of pseudo-patriotism, if not rather of absolute folly, on this subject, on the part of a few returned colonists in England, who would fain be esteemed authorities in matters of Colonial policy and government. It has been occasioned by the orders that have recently been issued from the Colonial Office for the withdrawal of the Imperial troops from New Zealand and the Australian colonies, and the expression of sentiments and views on the part of Her Majesty's Government, in accordance with those of the constellation of really eminent men I have just enumerated. Leaving therefore the case of New Zealand for further consideration in the sequel, Her Majesty's Government

* *Emancipate your Colonies.* Jeremy Bentham.

have distinctly intimated to the authorities of the colonies generally, on issuing the recent orders for the withdrawal of the troops, (which, it must be confessed, have been stationed in these Australian colonies for years past rather for ornament than for use), that if this or any other group of colonies should desire to be separated from the mother-country, and to become an independent nationality or nationalities, Her Majesty's Government would leave them entire liberty of action in the matter, and would not oppose their desire in any way.

This course of procedure, and the expression of opinion which it implies, on the part of the Imperial authorities, —so entirely in accordance with the opinions of the most eminent statesmen and politicians of the Old World,—has, it seems, excited the apprehensions and aroused the indig-nation of a few very uninfluential Colonial worthies now resident in England to a very great degree; and con-ferences have accordingly been held in London, and meet-ings for discussion organized, and deputations appointed, to ascertain the real intentions of ministers on the subject, as if some great catastrophe, fraught with ruin to the country, were impending. One of these pseudo-patriots, Mr. Edward Wilson, one of the joint-proprietors of the Melbourne *Argus*, daily newspaper, has recently written a letter to the *Times*, in which,—after alleging that the attempt to break up our Colonial Empire, which he imputes of course to Earl Granville, the Minister for the Colonies, is one of the most foolish that has ever been entertained by the Government of a nation—he proceeds as follows:—

"It is simply the most tremendous experiment that the world has ever seen. It might be a success, but what if it turned out a failure? We colonists might find out that we had done wrong; but our sun would shine, our wool would grow, our vines would flourish, and in one way or other we should manage to pull through. But what of England—with all that highly artificial organization which has lifted her from her narrow limits and ungenial climate into the employment of numbers incalculably greater than she can maintain from anything grown within her own bounds—what of her, if she should find that in wantonly parting with her colonies, she had parted with half her trade, and three-fourths of her national *prestige?* How then would your shallow *doctrinaire* be detected as the mere lunatic, who had tampered with the very foundations of a highly elaborate structure, of the delicate constitution of which he had shewn himself absolutely ignorant?"

And to shew that Mr. Wilson is not singular in entertaining the sentiments to which he gives expression in this inflated appeal, the editor of *The Weekly Review*, of date, London, November 13th, 1869, after quoting Mr. Wilson's letter, gives his own comment on it, as follows:

"This language is strong, but it is just. If any one look at the map of England and see what an insignificant country it is compared with its influence in the world, and then think how much its population is dependent upon the demands of other countries, he will see that its *prestige* and power cannot be maintained if its Colonial empire is to be broken to fragments. Our colonies and our Indian empire are our great strength, which bring to us wealth from all parts of the world, and give to us an internal power far beyond our internal resources. They enable us to maintain our overflowing population. If this Colonial empire is broken up, our trade will rapidly diminish. Statistics prove abundantly that colonies carry on immensely more commerce with the mother-country than independent States. If the tie were broken, the demand for British goods would probably soon all but cease. Other connections would be formed, and home manufactures would be protected by prohibitive duties."

Nay, these pseudo-patriots have summoned both Earl Grey and His Grace the Duke of Manchester to the rescue, to prevent if possible the awful consummation they anticipate. Earl Grey, in a letter to one of the patriots, Mr. A. Youl, of date, Howick, Bilton, Northumberland, September 4th, 1869, solemnly declares that " *The breaking up of the great Colonial Empire of England would, in my opinion, be a calamity to the colonies, to this country, and to the world.*" The Duke of Manchester also, in a letter which was read at the annual meeting of the Social Science Congress, iu December last, addressed to Sir Stafford Northcote, M.P., President, expresses himself as follows :—" *If we lose our colonies, our power is gone.* On the other hand, if we amalgamate our colonies with us, if we take them into partnership with us in the government of the Empire, I am convinced we should greatly increase our power. It seems to me that the only practicable plan would be to substitute for the Colonial Office a Council, containing representatives of the United Kingdom and the Colonies in fair proportion according to their wealth and the number of their inhabitants."

Now, (without reverting ;to the subject of Parliamentary Representation for the Colonies, which the Duke of Manchester seems to desiderate), it is particularly worthy of remark that precisely the same fears that are now entertained and the same dismal forebodings that are now put forth by Earl Grey and the Duke in regard to the probable result of the separation of any of our present colonies from the mother-country, were entertained and put forth a century ago by a still greater statesman than either of these noblemen, in regard to the probable result of the separation of the thirteen American colonies from Great Britain. The statesman I refer to was the great Earl of Chatham; and the very interesting fact is thus recorded in his usual graphic style by Lord Macaulay.

" He (William Pitt) had not quite completed his nineteenth year, when, on the 7th April, 1778, he attended his father (the Earl of Chatham) to Westminster. A great debate was expected. It was known that France had recognised the independence of the United States. The Duke of Richmond was about to declare his opinion that all thought of subjugating these States ought to be relinquished. Chatham always maintained that the resistance of the colonists to the mother-country was justifiable. *But he conceived, very erroneously, that on the day on which their independence should be acknowledged, the greatness of England would be at an end.* Though sinking under the weight of years and infirmities, he determined, in spite of the entreaties of his family, to be in his place. His son supported him to a seat. The excitement and exertion were too much for the old man. In the very act of addressing the peers, he fell back in convulsions. A few weeks later his corpse was borne, with gloomy pomp, from the Painted Chamber to the Abbey."*

So far, however, from the gloomy forebodings of the Earl of Chatham, in anticipation of the probable separation and loss of the thirteen American colonies, being realised, it is matter of history that Great Britain arose from that dismal period of defeat and disaster, of national humiliation and disgrace, like a giant refreshed with wine, and entered at once on a career of national greatness and glory such as the great Earl could never have anticipated.† And so would it be *a fortiori*, as I shall shew in the sequel, in the event of the peaceful separation of the Australian Colonies from the mother-country. There is, I firmly believe, a career of national greatness and glory for Great Britain, in friendly alliance and co-operation with Australia—free and indepen-

---

* Lord Macaulay's Sketch of the Life of William Pitt. *Miscellanies*, vol. ii. 312.

† England was never so rich, so great, so formidable to foreign powers, so absolutely mistress of the sea, as since the loss of her American colonies.—Lord Macaulay's *Essays*, vol. ii. p. 62.

dent—such as her most sanguine orators and poets have
never imagined.

SECTION XVIII.—A FOURTH OBJECTION STATED AND CONSIDERED—
THE COLONISTS WHO ARE CALLING OUT FOR THEIR FREEDOM AND IN-
DEPENDENCE ARE A MERE PACK OF REPUBLICANS, AND ARE UNFIT TO
GOVERN THEMSELVES.

After nearly fifty years' experience in the Australian Colonies, and especially after more than fourteen years' experience of the working of such representative institutions as
we have in New South Wales, I have no hesitation in
expressing it as my belief and conviction, that the very
worst government which it is possible to suppose could
ever emanate from popular election in these colonies, in the
event of their attaining their entire freedom and independence, would be incomparably better than the very best we
ever had under their connection with Great Britain previous
to the year 1856. The celebrated Adam Smith informs us
that the thirteen American colonies, containing at the time
a population of nearly three millions, were not only
governed, but well governed, previous to the War of Independence, for the incredibly small amount of £64,760 per
annum, or at the rate of five-pence per head.* But the

* The expense of their own civil government has always been
very moderate. It has generally been confined to what was necessary for paying competent salaries to the governor, to the judges, and
to some other officers of police, and for maintaining a few of the most
useful public works. The expense of the civil establishment of
Massachusetts' Bay, before the commencement of the present disturbances, used to be about £18,000 a-year. That of New Hampshire
and Rhode Island £3,500. That of Connecticut £4,000. That of New
York and Pennsylvania £4,500 each. That of New Jersey £1,200.
That of Virginia and South Carolina £8,000 each. The civil establishments of Nova Scotia and Georgia are partly supported by an annual
grant of parliament. But Nova Scotia pays, besides, about £7,000

government of New South Wales (including the district of
Port Phillip, now the colony of Victoria), containing a
population of not more than 265,503, on the 31st December,
1850—that is, at the close of the year before the gold
discoveries in Australia had intervened to revolutionize the
whole state of society in both colonies—actually cost for
that year £564,487 15s. 1d., or deducting £171,505 6s. 4d.,
expended for immigration, £392,982 8s. 9d.; or at the
rate of £1 9s. 7d. per head!* But colonial government,
under the system in operation previous to the year 1856,
or rather previous to the establishment of semi-repre-
sentative institutions in 1843, was a mere despotism,
under which the people's money was abstracted from them
by men who had no right to take it, and expended in great
measure in the maintenance of unnecessary offices, or in
the payment of extravagant salaries, while the general
improvement of the country in an endless variety of ways
was utterly neglected, and public works of urgent necessity,
for the welfare and advancement of the people, were
indefinitely postponed.

The grand secret of this prodigious difference between
the two cases under comparison is simply *this*, that the
American colonies had in great measure been self-governed
all along, while the Australian colonies were under the

a-year towards the public expenses of the colony ; and Georgia about
£2,500 a-year. All the different civil establishments in North America,
in short, exclusive of those of Maryland and North Carolina, of which
no exact account has been got, did not, before the commencement of
the present disturbances, cost the inhabitants above £64,760 a-year;
an ever memorable example at how small an expense three millions of
people may not only be governed, but well governed.—*Smith's Wealth
of Nations*, vol. ii. p. 372.

* I take the year before the gold discoveries as affording a fair
criterion for Australia generally ; because society has been so completely
revolutionised, since that great event in the gold colonies, as scarcely
to afford a proper ground of comparison in a case like the present.

despotism of the Secretary of State for the Colonies in Downing-street, and his local agents the different Governors of the colonies.

As to the charge, that the Australian colonists are somewhat tinctured with republicanism, I fear it must be admitted. The fact is, there is no other form of government either practicable or possible, in a British colony obtaining its freedom and independence, than that of a republic. Without inquiring, therefore, for the present, as to whether any one form of government is better than another, it is sufficiently obvious that we must be prepared, as British colonists, if we are ever to become free and independent at all, to take that particular form, "for better, for worse."*

And why should we be either unwilling or afraid to do

* Mr. Wakefield seems to have arrived at a somewhat different conclusion on this important point, as will be evident from the following passage of his work :—

"The Imperial Sovereign is a person as well as an institution, and we reverence the one as much as we value the other. To transplant a complete offshoot of the whole is, therefore, simply impossible. The nearest approach to doing so would be by the erection of Canada, for example, into an independent monarchy, and filling its throne with a child of the British sovereign. But *the colonies are intended to be subordinate to the empire,* and though it would, I think, be wise to make the younger branches of a royal family, whose social position here is anything but agreeable, subordinate sovereigns of the more important colonies, yet *subordination requires that the colonial chief magistrate should be appointed and removable by the imperial.—View of the Art of Colonization,* p. 307.

Whether this beautiful theory of subordinate sovereignty would be practicable in Canada, so very near as it is to the United States, 1 have no idea whatever. I can safely state, however, that the thing would be utterly impracticable in the Australian colonies. Besides, I do not think it advisable to put forth theories of this kind, which inexperienced people of all ranks in England would probably unite in admiring, but which would most certainly lead to a civil war, if attempted to be carried out in the colonies generally.

so? It is now seventy years and upwards since the celebrated Charles James Fox characterized the British Government as a disguised republic; and the Reform Acts have since taken away no inconsiderable portion of the disguise. Why then should Englishmen object to a Republic without disguise for their emancipated colonies? Why should they object to a form of government which has given birth, in every department of human excellence, to a series of the greatest and noblest men that have ever trod the earth? Why should they vainly attempt to disparage those glorious republics of antiquity, from which we have inherited so much that exalts and embellishes humanity, and whose invaluable annals are so prolific in the most splendid achievements that the pen of history records?*

No wonder that there should be a wide-spread and deep-rooted, although, in many instances, I believe, an affected prejudice against Republican institutions, among the hangers-on for office both at home and abroad—among the numerous horde of helpless and hungry expectants of a share in the spoils of the people. But that such a prejudice, whether real or affected, should extend to men professing the Christian religion, and receiving the Holy Scriptures of both Testaments as the Word of God, I confess, sur-passes my comprehension. "The Christian religion," says Novalis, an able German writer of the present century, "is the root of all democracy, the highest fact in the rights of man."† Besides, it is matter of sacred history that the only form of human government that was ever divinely established upon earth was the Republican—in the wilder-

* In (*ancient*) Mexico, small colonies (*of Indians*), wearied of tyranny, gave themselves republican constitutions. Now, it is only after long popular struggles that these free constitutions can be formed. The existence of republics does not indicate a very recent civilization.— *Humboldt, New Spain*, book ii. 6.

† Novalis, quoted by Carlyle.

ness of Sinai—and that God himself interposed, in the person of his own accredited minister, to protest against the unwarrantable innovation, when that form of government was at length set aside in the commonwealth of Israel, and monarchy established in its stead.* Monarchy doubtless prevailed for a long period in that country, *by Divine permission,* as many things else do in this lower world, that are certainly not of Divine appointment ; but Republicanism existed from the first *by Divine appointment ;* and it cannot, I submit, be a very bad form of government, which can plead such an authority in its favour.

I shall be told indeed that the Israelitish government was a *theocracy,* and that it therefore forms no precedent for us. But it was evidently quite as much a theocracy under the kings, as during the commonwealth. Nay, in the original *Magna Charta* of Israel—that famous *Constitutional Act* which came down from Heaven, bearing the *Sign Manual* of the Eternal, for the establishment of a Republic, more glorious, and happier far, while it subsisted, than those of either Greece or Rome—there was an express provision for the foreseen contingency of the establishment of a monarchy ; and the theocracy was, therefore, as complete in every part of it, during the reigns of David and Solomon, as under the presidency of Joshua

---

* Then all the elders of Israel gathered themselves together, and came to Samuel unto Ramah, And said unto him, Behold, thou art old and thy sons walk not in thy ways: now make us a king to judge us like all the nations. But the thing displeased Samuel, when they said, Give us a king to judge us. And Samuel prayed unto the Lord, And the Lord said unto Samuel, Hearken unto the voice of the people in all that they say unto thee ; for they have not rejected thee, but they have rejected me, that I should not reign over them. According to all the works which they have done since the day that I brought them up out of Egypt even unto this day, wherewith they have forsaken me, and served other Gods, so do they also unto thee.— 1 *Samuel,* viii. 4-9.

and Samuel.* There was no part of the theocratic government set aside or abrogated on the introduction of
monarchical institutions : the Divine command, in regard
to the outward form of government, was merely set at
nought, just as it was in a thousand other instances ; but
the Divine Constitution subsisted in every other particular
notwithstanding. It is impossible for any man of common
understanding to come to any other conclusion on reading
the beautiful and affecting passage quoted below.

In that ancient Magna Charta, moreover, we find all
the principles of manly freedom established and developed
—universal suffrage, perfect political equality (combined
with one of the most beautiful and affecting devices
imaginable to preserve it) and popular election ; the three
grand fundamental principles of Republican government.
As this, however, may be regarded as an unwarrantable
assertion, I beg to subjoin the proof, which can easily

* When thou art come unto the land which the Lord thy God
giveth thee, and shalt possess it, and shalt dwell therein, and shalt
say, I will set a king over me, like as all the nations that *are* about
me ; Thou shalt in any wise set *him* king over thee, whom the Lord
thy God shall choose : *one* from among thy brethren shalt thou set
king over thee : thou mayest not set a stranger over thee, which *is*
not thy brother. But he shall not multiply horses to himself, nor
cause the people to return to Egypt, to the end that he should
multiply horses : forasmuch as the Lord has said unto you, Ye shall
henceforth return no more that way. Neither shall he multiply wives
to himself, that his heart turn not away : neither shall he greatly
multiply to himself silver and gold. And it shall be, when he sitteth
upon the throne of his kingdom, that he shall write him a copy of
this law in a book of *that which is* before the priests tho Levites :
And it shall be with him, and he shall read therein all the days of his
life : that he may learn to fear the Lord his God, to keep all the words
of this law and these statutes, to do them : That his heart be not
lifted up above his brethren, and that he turn not aside from the
commandment, *to* the right hand, or *to* the left : to the end that he
may prolong *his* days in his kingdom, he, and his children, in the midst
of Israel.—*Deuteronomy*, xvii. 14—20.

be verified, as the authorities are in everybody's hands.

When the congregation of Israel, therefore, were assembled on the plains of Moab, previous to their entrance into the promised land, it had become a matter of necessity to ascertain who were thenceforth to be considered *the nation*, for all political purposes; and among whom, and on what principles, the national domain, which was about to be acquired, was to be parcelled out and divided: for the ancient conquest of Canaan was attended with very different results to the great body of the people who were thenceforth to inhabit the land, from those of the famous Norman Conquest of England. *A Census* was accordingly taken by Divine command—not of all the people, however, but of *all the males, from twenty years old and upwards;* who were thenceforth to be considered for all political purposes *the nation.* For on their number being ascertained to be 601,730 (Six hundred and one thousand, seven hundred and thirty), it was further divinely directed that the land should be equally divided among these males, without partiality and without distinction; the families which had a larger proportion of such males to have a larger extent of land, and those which had fewer to have less.* And in order, as much as possible, to

---

* And it came to pass after the plague, that the Lord spake unto Moses and unto Eleazar the son of Aaron the priest, saying, Take the sum of all the congregation of the children of Israel, from twenty years old and upward, throughout their father's house, all that are able to go to war in Israel. And Moses and Eleazar the priest spake with them in the plains of Moab by Jordan *near* Jericho, saying, *Take the sum of the people,* from twenty years old and upward ; as the Lord commanded Moses and the children of Israel, which went forth out of the land of Egypt. * * These *were* the numbers of the children of Israel, six hundred thousand and a thousand seven hundred and thirty. And the Lord spake unto Moses, saying, Unto these the land shall be divided for an inheritance according to the number of names.

preserve this political equality, and the equality of property which was deemed necessary to maintain it, it was further provided that, every fiftieth year, all those who had in the mean time been *sold off* or *sold out*, whether through mismanagement or misfortune, should return every man to the possession of his family.*

And when these principles had been in so far reduced to practice, we learn, from an interesting incident, that the mode of appointment to public offices was by popular election. For after a portion of the land had been surveyed and settled, under the presidency of Joshua, there still remained seven tribes to be located. In these circumstances, Joshua assembled the people, and directed them to elect whomsoever they might consider "fit and proper persons" to survey and divide the land, and he would appoint them accordingly, by giving them their Commissions and Instructions, as the Head of the Executive.†

To many thou shalt give the more inheritance, to few thou shalt give the less inheritance: to every one shall his inheritance be given according to those that were numbered of him. Notwithstanding the land shall be divided by lot: according to the names of the tribes of their fathers they shall inherit. According to the lot shall the possession thereof be divided between many and few.—*Numbers*, xxvi. 1—4. 51—56.

* And thou shalt number seven sabbaths of years unto thee, seven times seven years; and the space of seven sabbaths of years shall be unto thee forty and nine years. Then thou shalt cause the trumpet of the jubilee to sound on the tenth *day* of the seventh month, in the day of atonement shall ye make the trumpet sound throughout all your land And ye shall hallow the fiftieth year, and proclaim liberty throughout *all* the land unto all the inhabitants thereof: it shall be a jubilee unto you; and ye shall return every man unto his possession, and ye shall return every man unto his family.—*Leviticus*, xxv. 8—10.

† And there remained among the children of Israel seven tribes, which had not yet received their inheritance. And Joshua said unto the children of Israel, How long *are* ye slack to go to possess the land, which the Lord God of your fathers hath given you? Give out from

Here, then, are the three great fundamental principles of Republican government—Universal Suffrage, Perfect Political Equality, and Popular Election—in full operation, under the Divine sanction and appointment, in the commonwealth of ancient Israel. And surely if the God of Heaven deemed it just and necessary to establish such principles of national government for the welfare and advancement of His own chosen people, I appeal, with perfect confidence, to professed Christians of all denominations throughout the United Kingdom, as to whether it can be either wrong or unwarrantable to advocate the establishment of such principles for the government of a community of British origin at the ends of the earth.

In the year 1635, the mere handful of Puritan-settlers who had then but very recently gone forth from England to plant the new colony of Connecticut, on the banks of the beautiful river of that name, in North America, met together, by appointment, *in a barn*, to form a Constitution for the future government of their country, as they were empowered to do under their Charter. They accordingly framed a Constitution, based on the three principles I have indicated as the characteristic features of the Constitution of ancient Israel—Universal Suffrage, Perfect Political Equality and Popular Election—and that Constitution remained unchanged for upwards of one hundred and forty years, or until the Revolution of 1776! It had necessarily to undergo some change on an event of such mighty moment for the whole country; but what was the amount of that

among you three men for *each* tribe: and I will send them, and they shall rise, and go through the land, and describe it according to the inheritance of them; and they shall come *again* to me. And they shall divide it into seven parts: Judah shall abide in their coast on the south, and the house of Joseph shall abide in their coasts on the north. Ye shall therefore describe the land *into* seven parts, and bring the *description* hither to me, that I may cast lots for you here before the Lord our God.—*Joshua*, xviii. 2—6.

J

change ? Why it was simply the substitution of the word *People* for the word *King ;* for, with that necessary altera- tion excepted, the Constitution of Connecticut remains unchanged and in full operation as it was originally framed, to the present day ! In short, these honest men did the right thing at first, and it required no mending afterwards. But where, it may be asked, did they get such objectionable principles, which, till very recently, were so generally re- ferred by political writers and statesmen to *Chartism, Com- munism,* and *Socialism ;* as it is matter of history that none of these *isms* were heard of till a full century and a half after their time ? Why, they got them, as is quite evident from the preceding argument, in precisely the same place in which I have got them; and in which any person may get them still—in that *Word of God which endureth for ever.*

As to the question whether the Australian colonies are fit to be trusted with a government based on such liberal principles, the very proposal of such a question is an insult to the understanding, and an outrage on the rights of British freemen. Let it be remembered, that the people for whom the singularly free constitution of ancient Israel was established, were living under the mere twilight of Judaism, and were oppressed, moreover, with the weight of its burdensome ceremonial, while we, a community of British origin, rejoice in the light and liberty of the Gospel. Let it be remembered, moreover, that only a few years before this free constitution was proclaimed, the whole nation of Israel were a nation of slaves. In short, the only preparation for national freedom is freedom itself.*

---

* Many politicians of our time are in the habit of laying it down as a self-evident proposition that no people ought to be free till they are fit to use their freedom. The maxim is worthy of the fool in the old story, who resolved not to go into the water till he had learned to swim. If men are to wait for liberty till they have become wise and good in slavery, they may indeed wait for ever.—*Macaulay's Essays,* i. 42.

There are, doubtless, people in England who still peck and laugh at the idea of universal suffrage for any community of British origin, on the ground of its alleged injustice in excluding the women and children; who, as they allege, ought also to have votes. Let these "minute philosophers," however, explain, if they can, why the God of Heaven authorised Moses and Eleazar to leave out the women and children of ancient Israel, when they were numbering *the nation* (as it was thenceforth to be considered for all political purposes), and we shall meet them on the point. It is comparatively easy for "iniquity established by law," and rendered venerable by the practice of ages, to make itself merry with the rights of men; but it ought to be remembered, that it is not always perfectly safe in these stirring times.

I cannot allow the subject to pass without directing the attention of the reader to the remarkably different principles on which the two communities of ancient Israel on the one hand, and the British nation on the other, were established in regard to property in land. In the community which, we all admit, God himself set up, there were ascertained, by the census of Moses and Eleazar on the plains of Moab, to be 601,730 six (hundred and one thousand, seven hundred and thirty) proprietors of land, in the Hebrew Commonwealth, that is about one for every five of the entire population, and each of these proprietors having an equal share, for a population not exceeding at the utmost three millions of souls! But in Great Britain and Ireland, under a constitution, doubtless, the most glorious and happy, both in Church and State, that was ever devised by man, there were, according to Mr. D'Israeli,* not more than about 240,000 (two hundred

* In one of his speeches in the House of Commons about twenty

and forty thousand) proprietors of land for a population
of about twenty-eight millions of people; that is about
one to every 116⅔ of the entire population, not to say a
single word for the present on the very different principles
on which the shares have been allotted in the two cases!
Hinc illæ lachrymæ! Hence the enormous competition for
a subsistence among all classes throughout the three kingdoms.   Hence the perpetual recurrence of scenes of
frightful destitution, from the want of employment, and
the want even of the commonest necessaries of life, among
whole masses of the people.   Hence the peculiarly omi-
nous aspect of the condition-of-England question at
present to all concerned !

Let it not be supposed, however, that, in making such a
comparison, I have any wish for a redistribution of the
property of the mother-country.   I am no Communist or
Socialist, although any man who honestly advocates the
cause of the people, whether at home or abroad, will be
sure to be subjected to that reproach.   My object is very
different.   Conceiving, as I do, that colonization is the
grand necessity of the times for the British people, it is
simply to inform the struggling classes of all grades of
society at home, for whom there is evidently no inheritance
provided in the land of their fathers, that there is land
enough and to spare for them all in the noble colonies of
Australia, and the adjacent islands of the vast Pacific.
We *have seen the land ; and behold it is very good! and the
gold of that land is good also.*   Let them come to us in any

years ago ; for the difference of time up to the present date does not
affect the general question.
> A time there was, ere England's griefs began,
> When every rood of ground maintained its man ;
> For him light labour spread her wholesome store,
> Just gave what life required, and gave no more ;
> His best companions, innocence and health ;
> And his best riches, ignorance of wealth.— *Goldsmith.*

numbers, under such able and honest leadership as may easily be found, to assist us in setting up and maintaining a government in these lands somewhat more on God's model than on that of man,—a government based, like that of ancient Israel, on universal suffrage, perfect political equality, and popular election; and under which, moreover, they may all literally *sit, each under his own vine, and under his own fig-tree, and none to make them afraid.*

In regard to the bearing of Republican government on the development of national spirit, national character, and national virtue, I would beg to quote the following remarks of the learned and eloquent historian of Greece on the result of the establishment of popular government in the City and State of Athens, after the subversion of as selfish, effete, and unprincipled an oligarchy as that which prevailed, under the fostering care of the Colonial Office, in the Australian Colonies till the recent changes in our political system.

"The grand and new idea of the Sovereign People, composed of free and equal citizens, or liberty and equality —to use words which so profoundly moved the French nation half a century ago—it was this comprehensive political idea which acted with electric effect upon the Athenians, creating within them a host of sentiments, motives, sympathies, and capacities, to which they had before been strangers. Democracy, in Grecian antiquity, possessed the privilege, not only of kindling an earnest and unanimous attachment to the constitution in the bosoms of the citizens, but also of creating an energy of public and private action, such as could never be obtained under an oligarchy, where the utmost that could be hoped for was a passive acquiescence and obedience. * * * Herodotus, in his comparison of the three sorts of government, puts in the front rank of the advantages of democracy 'its most splendid name and promise,' its power of enlisting the hearts of

the citizens in support of their constitution, and of providing
for all a common bond of union and fraternity. This is
what even democracy did not always do; but it was what
no other government in Greece *could* do : a reason alone
sufficient to stamp it as the best government, and presenting the greatest chance of beneficial results, for a Grecian
community."*

I happened to reach the city of Rio de Janeiro, in the
Brazils, where I remained a fortnight, on my first voyage
to New South Wales, in the month of January, 1823, only
a few days after the country had thrown off the yoke of
Portugal, and proclaimed its national existence and independence. It was a period of extraordinary excitement and
enthusiasm ; and triumphal arches, thrown across the principal streets of the city, bearing in large letters the inscrip-
tion *Independencia ó Morte*, "Independence or Death," proclaimed the new-born liberties and awakened spirit of the
people. Don Pedro, the eldest son of the King of Portugal,
who happened to be in the country at the time, adroitly
placed himself at the head of the movement, and guaranteeing liberal institutions to the people, probably secured the
country for a generation or two for his family. But "the
new idea of the Sovereign People" was evidently working
the same changes at Rio as it had done at Athens, and was
visibly infusing new life into the whole community. I
have twice visited the country since (not at Rio, however,
but at Pernambuco), in the years 1839 and 1846; and it
was impossible, on either of these occasions, not to recognise the transforming influence and beneficial working of
popular freedom and national independence. All public
improvements in the country were dated from the era of
Independence. A National System of Education had been
established on a popular basis, *free from all priestly control ;*
and a bill had been actually under the consideration of the

* *History of Greece.* By George Grote, Esq., vol. iv. p, 241.

Brazilian Senate for the legalising of the marriage of priests. The monasteries were tumbling down, but schools and colleges were rising in their stead. I assisted, by particular desire, in 1846, as a Master of Arts of a European University, at the creation of a Bachelor of Laws in the Brazilian University of Olinda, the most ancient city on the continent of America; and in return for a letter of congratulation and good wishes which I addressed, in the Latin language, to the graduate, I had the honour, some time after my arrival in England, of receiving a diploma of honorary membership from the Literary Institute of that ancient city. .

In regard to the bearing of Republican institutions on public and private morals, and on the prevalence and practice of pure and undefiled religion, I think it must be evident to the readers of Holy Scripture, that notwithstanding their frequent national defections, the morals of the nation of Israel were much purer under the Judges or Presidents of the Hebrew Commonwealth, than under the Kings: and as to the prevalence of that high-toned piety which the law of God enjoins, we have an express testimony on the subject which cannot be gainsaid. In that dark and dismal period which preceded the fall of Jerusalem, and the temporary extinction of the Jewish State, it was natural for the patriot and prophet Jeremiah, when anticipating and lamenting over the approaching ruin of his country, to look back with a melancholy pleasure to those brighter and palmier days of its past history, when Israel walked with God, and God blessed Israel. And to what period in the past history of his nation does he look for these glorious days? Is it to the reigns of Josiah and Hezekiah, those reforming kings of Judah? Is it to the period of the warrior David, the sweet singer of Israel? By no means. The prophet at once overleaps the whole period of the monarchy, and recurs instinctively to the far brighter and palmier period of the infancy of the Hebrew Commonwealth. *I remember thee, the kindness of thy youth, the love of thine espousals, when thou wentest after me in the wilderness, in a land that was not sown. Israel was holiness unto the Lord, the first fruits of his increase.*

There is no reason to fear, therefore, either for morals or for religion, under a popular form of government, established on the ancient and divinely accredited basis of universal suffrage, perfect political equality, and popular election.

SECTION XIX.—A .FIFTH OBJECTION URGED—THE AUSTRALIAN COLONIES WOULD BE UNABLE TO DEFEND AND PROTECT THEMSELVES FROM FOREIGN AGGRESSION, IN THE EVENT OF THEIR OBTAINING THEIR FREEDOM AND INDEPENDENCE, AND WOULD, THEREFORE, IF ABANDONED BY GREAT BRITAIN, VERY SOON FALL INTO THE HANDS OF SOME OTHER POWER.

This is an argument against colonial freedom and independence, which is often put forth triumphantly by those who find it to their personal advantage to keep things as they are, and which is not without considerable weight with timorous and nervous people ; but we only require to look at it for a moment to feel assured of its utter worthlessness. For who, I ask, are the enemies with whom the Australian colonies, if free and independent, would have to contend ? Is it the wretched Aborigines of our own territory ? Alas! most of them have already disappeared from the face of the earth; *the last man* of the Sydney tribe or nation, once a comparatively numerous body of people, having died twenty years ago ? Is it the New Zealanders or the South Sea Islanders ? The very idea is absurd. Is it the Malays of the Indian Archipelago, or the adventurous subjects of the Emperors of China and Japan ? Those inoffensive and unwarlike people could never even find

* *Jerem.* ii. 2, 3.

their way to the Australian colonies without assistance
from ourselves. They have no idea where they lie, and
have probably never heard of them.. It is evident, therefore, that the formidable enemies of free and independent
Australia can be no Aboriginal people within the vast
semicircle, having Australia for its centre, and extending
northwards to the Equator, and eastwards from the Cape
of Good Hope to Cape Horn.

We must therefore look for the future enemies of free
and independent Australia among the civilized and Christian
nations of Europe and America ; and before entertaining
the very idea that any of these nations would commit any
act of unprovoked aggression upon us, we must do them
the honour to suppose that they are no better than the
Scandinavian Sea-kings of the middle ages—mere pirates
and robbers—which they would all doubtless consider a
very high compliment. Away with the unnatural and
anti-Christian policy that would thus proclaim the whole
human race but ourselves "rogues and vagabonds," and
get Acts of Parliament passed, and treaties and alliances
formed, to denounce them, and fleets and armies hired to
put them down ! This was the policy that saddled Great
Britain with her eight hundred millions of debt, and that
has reduced whole masses of her population, in the midst
of all the elements of national wealth and universal prosperity, to a state of suffering and wretchedness utterly
discreditable to any civilized nation.

Considering then that we have nothing to fear from
external aggression in Australia, within the vast semicircle extending northward and eastward from the Cape of
Good Hope to Cape Horn, and that we have all the
substantial protection besides that a three or four months'
voyage, which it takes to reach us, implies, against the
supposed Sea-kings—the pirate and robber States—of
modern Europe and America, we can easily afford to treat

the famous question of *National Defences* very coolly.
Besides Great Britain herself, the only maritime powers
in Christendom that could be supposed capable, even if
they possessed the inclination, of committing acts of aggression upon free and independent Australia, are France, and
Russia, and America; but so far from any of these great
Powers having the slightest inclination to meddle with us
in such circumstances, I appeal to every intelligent reader,
as to whether it would not be a far likelier event, that the
Envoys we should have to send to these countries with the
tidings of our freedom and independence, would be received
at Paris, and Petersburg, and Washington, with the most
cordial welcome, and that we should be admitted at once
into the great family of nations with the liveliest demon-
strations of joy.

As to hostile aggressions, in the shape of predatory or
piratical attacks on our Colonial towns, like those of the
Buccaneers of America on the towns of the Spanish
American Colonies in the seventeenth century, it ought
surely to be borne in mind that the age of the Buccaneers
is long past, and that there are too many powerful flags in
Christendom, in this advanced period of the nineteenth
century, to allow a second edition of the old Buccaneers to
walk the high seas in any part of the civilized world. And
as to a regular invasion of the country, with a view to
conquest and permanent occupation, I would ask, "Has
anything of the kind ever been attempted, by any European
power whatsoever, in the case of the emancipated Spanish
and Portuguese Colonies of South America?" And if no
European Power has ever invaded the Ex-colonies of Spain
and Portugal, in America, is it at all likely that
any such power would invade the Ex-colonies of Britain
in Australia? Is the *prestige* still so much in favour of
Spain and Portugal, and of the once formidable race of the
Peninsula, that there is no virtue in a British descent

to repel an intending invader? Is Great Britain so fallen from her high estate, that her full-grown Australian children are to be treated as the common Pariahs of the world, fit only to become the slaves of the first European master who chooses to flourish the whip over their devoted heads, and to claim possession of them as his "goods and chattels?" Away with such absurdities!

Then as to the Trade of the Australian colonies, on the supposition of their Freedom and Independence, it is preposterous to suppose that it would stand in need of any other protection than could be easily and fully guaranteed to it. With the exception of steamboats and coasting vessels, the Australian colonists have as yet but little shipping of their own. Their trade, which is almost exclusively with the mother-country, is conducted principally by means of British vessels, with a few American, Dutch, German, and French. Now if these nations did not find the Australian trade profitable to themselves, they would certainly not engage in it; but so long as they do engage in it, their respective flags will afford it the requisite protection, for their own sakes, whether Australia be independent or not. It is simply the better market which Australian produce finds in the mother-country, and the British tastes and habits of the Australian colonists, who naturally prefer the produce and manufactures of the old country to those of any other European nation, that give the virtual monopoly of the Australian trade to Great Britain; and it will be entirely her own fault, if Great Britain ever loses that monopoly, whatever be the political condition of Australia. It is by no means the interest of the Australian colonists to create a mercantile navy of their own for their trade with the old world. All they will require for half a century to come will be steam-boats and other vessels of moderate tonnage for their coasting trade. Labour can be much more profitably employed in Australia in raising raw produce for the foreign market than in ship building, and

mariners can be much more easily obtained in the old
world than in Australia. Neither is it the interest of Great
Britain that the carrying trade with Australia should pass
into the hands of the Australian people; and so long as she
enjoys her present monopoly, it will be her own direct
interest to protect that trade, as she is well able and can
well afford to do.

In the event of a general European war, in which Great
Britain should be a principal — whether her opponent
be France, or Russia, or any other European power—she
would be entirely relieved of the cost and trouble of protecting *us*, if we were free and independent, and she would
therefore just have so many more ships of war to protect
her own coasts. But as for us, and our foreign trade, we
should in the meantime be in precisely the same condition
as the United States were in during the long French War.
The Americans then lived at peace with all nations, and
traded with all alike. None of the belligerents ever
thought of invading the United States, or of molesting the
American flag; and the consequence was that the Union
prospered amazingly during the war, and had become so
strong at the close of it as to enforce even from France,
during the energetic presidency of General Jackson, the
payment of a large amount, for certain alleged aggressions
upon American merchantmen during its continuance. Nay,
removed as she is from the field of European strife so much
farther than America, Australia would be still less likely to
suffer in any way from European warfare. Her flag would
be respected by all the belligerents : and the prevalence of
a general European war, during which the flags of these
belligerents would be in constant danger from each other,
would only have the effect of raising Australia, as the long
French war did the United States, in circumstances
precisely similar, into a first-rate Maritime Power. In
such an event, many even of the lovers of peace in the old

world would gladly emigrate to her territory, to enrol themselves among her free people, and thereby to avail themselves of such protection as her flag would afford them, both by sea and land, when Europe had been again transformed into a field of blood. But even, on the supposition that there should be no Australian marine, in the event of a general European war, if Great Britain were no longer able to protect the Australian trade in her own merchant ships, from French or Russian cruizers, our elder brother Jonathan would gladly step in to relieve her of her present monopoly, and to frank our commerce with her Stars and Stripes to all the world. In one word, if the Australian people desire to live at peace with all mankind for a century to come, the sooner they become free and independent the better; for in that event, and in that event alone, would their trade and territory be effectually protected from all hostile aggression whatsoever.

The fact is, the only chance we have of hearing of war in any shape in Australia for a century to come, lies in our connection with Great Britain, as a group of her many dependencies. And considering the warlike propensities of our worthy mother, and the character she has so long sustained of being the prize-fighter and pay-mistress of the world, our chance of peace under her wing is at best but very precarious.* If she chose

* Colonists have generally no predilection for war: they have almost uniformly been dragged into it by the mother-country, for her *own* purposes, and not for *theirs.* Take a case in point: " Three years before this period (anno 1698), King William had concerted a plan for the general defence of the American settlements against the French forces in Canada and their Indian allies; in conformity with which, every colony was required to furnish a pecuniary contingent proportioned to the amount of its population,—to be administered according to the directions of the king. This plan was submitted to all the provincial legislatures, *and disregarded or rejected by every one of them;* the colonies most exposed to attack being desirous of employ-

to go to war, which she may do at any time, and on any question in which we may not have the slightest imaginable interest, with any of the three great Powers I have mentioned, what a noble chance there would be for

ing their forces in the manner most agreeable to their own judgment and immediate exigencies; and those which were more remote from the point of danger, objecting to participate in the expense. Governor Nicholson clearly perceived the utility of King William's plan as a preparative for the ulterior object of a General Government of the colonies: *and though peace had now been established*, he determined to signalize his recent promotion, by reviving the royal project and retrieving its failure. He ventured accordingly to introduce this unwelcome proposition to the assembly of Virginia; and employed all the resources of his address and ingenuity to procure its adoption. He asserted that a fort on the western frontier of New York was essential to the security of Virginia; and insisted that the legislature of this province was consequently engaged by every consideration of prudence, equity, and generosity, to contribute to its erection and support. But his arguments, though backed by all the aid they could desire from reference to the wish and suggestion of the king, proved totally unavailing; and the proposition experienced an unqualified rejection from the Assembly. Nicholson, astonished and provoked at this discomfiture, hastened to transmit a report of the proceeding to the king; in which he strongly reprobated the refractory spirit of the Virginians, and urged the propriety of compelling them yet to acknowledge their duty, and consult their true interests. William was so far moved by this representation, as to recommend to the Provincial Assembly a more deliberate consideration of the governor's proposition; and he even condescended to repeat the arguments which Nicholson had already unsuccessfully employed. But these reasons gained no additional currency from the stamp of royal sanction. The king's project encountered again the most determined rejection from the Assembly ; and his argument elicited from them only a firm but respectful remonstrance, in which they declared their conviction, "that neither the forts then in being, nor any other that might be built in the province of New York, could in the slightest degree avail to the defence and security of Virginia; for that either the French or the northern Indians might invade this colony, and yet not approach within 100 miles of any of those forts.'"—*Graham's History of the United States of America*, vol. iii. p. 14.

a few French, or Russian, or American frigates and privateers to cruise off Cape Leeuwin to pick up the outward-bounders, or off the North and South Capes of New Zealand, to alter the destination and ownership of our ships homeward bound to London and Liverpool, with their valuable cargoes of fine wool and tallow, copper and gold! Besides, we should have the pleasure of such an occasional interlude as the burning of our towns on the coast, and the destruction of our ships in port: which would be enacted from no imaginable hostility to us as Australians, or colonists, but simply to annoy and to punish our pugnacious parent in London!*

"Oh! but that is the very case in point," I shall be told. "Great Britain would defend and protect us in case of war, as she would be bound to do. She would have frigates cruising off Cape Leeuwin; she would have others off both Capes of New Zealand, and others still off this stormy Cape Horn, where you are now writing, and scarce able to guide the pen from the rolling and plunging of the ship in this tempestuous sea.* Besides, she would have ships of war cruizing along our whole line of coast, and occasionally enlivening us with their presence in our harbours; and what is best of all, *she would make her own people pay all the expenses, without asking a farthing from us!*"† Now this is a great deal too much for Great Britain to do for us. We have no desire whatever to put her to the slightest trouble

---

* It will doubtless be recollected that, shortly after the Crimean War, a Russian fleet wintered in the harbour of New York—with what object or for what reason, was not known at the time. It oozed out, however—at least it was so reported on apparently good authority—that the real object of the movement was, that the Russian fleet might be in readiness for a hostile aggression upon the cities of Sydney and Melbourne, in the event of any interference, on the part of England, in the affairs of Poland. This will always be our source of danger so long as we are colonies of England.

† This passage, with much that both precedes and follows it, was

or expense in the matter, or to tax her people a single farthing for our protection and defence—simply because it is quite unnecessary. Let her only give us our freedom and independence, and we promise her we will live at peace with all the world,--for this good reason, if for no better. that we could not afford to go to war; and she will in the meantime save the expense of her proposed naval armament for the protection and defence of Australia in the event of a European war.

It is worthy of remark that a strong recommendation, to . this very effect, was given to the Imperial Government of the day, by an eminent member of the British peerage, sixteen years ago. In a debate, in the House of Lords, on the 15th June, 1854, (reported in the *Times* of the following day), on the Duke of Newcastle's Motion for the Second Reading of the Canada Legislative Council Bill, the EARL OF ELLENBOROUGH spoke as follows :

" We made such progress last year in the work of concession to Canada, that the question now was, not whether we should stop in our career, still less whether we should attempt to go back, but whether we should not, in the most friendly spirit towards Canada and the other North American Colonies, consult with their Legislatures on the expediency of taking measures for the complete release of those colonies from all dependence on the Crown and Parliament of Great Britain. He recollected having a conversation with Mr. Huskisson in 1828, during the time that Statesman held the seals of the Colonial office, in which he intimated most distinctly that the time had already arrived for the separation of Canada from this country ; and

written when actually doubling Cape Horn twenty years since with a strong northwestly gale, and a heavy sea, in latitude 58 ° South.

† Quicquid delirant reges, plectuntur Achivi.

Whether the war be with the Maories or with the Kaffirs, John Bull must pay the expense.—*Free Translation.*

Mr. Huskisson had even so maturely considered the matter that he mentioned the form of government which he thought it would be for our interest to have established in Canada, when our connexion with the colony should cease. * * * What was the use—what the practical advantage of continuing our connexion with the Colonies? The connexion might be of some small use in time of peace; but on the other hand, consider the danger arising from it in matters relating to war. * * It was certain that in the event of war occurring between this country and the United States, on grounds totally unconnected with the Colonies, they must, from their connexion with us, be drawn into the war, and their whole frontier would be exposed to the greatest calamities. Under these circumstances, it was a matter worthy of serious consideration whether we should not endeavour, in the most friendly manner, to divest ourselves of a connexion which must prove equally onerous to both parties. Now, in case of war, could we hope to defend the colonies successfully? * * * Considering the increased strength and appliances at the command of the United States, it would hardly be possible to defend Canada with any hope of success. * * * Under these circumstances, he hoped that, at an early period, the Government would communicate with the leading persons in the Legislative Assemblies of the North American Colonies, with the view of ascertaining their opinion on the subject of separation. We should consult with them in the most friendly spirit, as if they were members of one and the same family in which we felt a deep concern."

After some declamatory observations, of an opposite tendency from the Duke of Newcastle, "LORD BROUGHAM wished to say one word, after the severe rebuke which had been given by the noble Duke. He had the misfortune of coming within the description of persons against whom the

K

noble Duke had so powerfully and indignantly declaimed
—namely, those who, while desiring a separation of
Canada, as a colony, from the mother country, did not wish
to throw the colonists over or to abandon them. And why
should the noble Duke denounce so vehemently this
opinion? It was by no means novel. It had been ,enter-
tained and expressed by many eminent men. It was an
opinion shared in by Lord Ashburton and by Lord St.
Vincent; and those who held the doctrine of separation did
so, not because they were disposed to undervalue the importance of Canada, but rather because they highly
estimated the importance of that country. They believed
that after a certain period of time—after what was called
"passing the youth of nations," that of a colonial life—the
best thing that could happen to a country in colonial connexion with an old State was, that without any quarrel,
without any coldness or alienation of any sort, but with
perfect amity and goodwill, and on purely voluntary
grounds, there should succeed to that colonial connexion a
connexion between two Free and Independent States."

The same idea was also entertained by the celebrated
Dr. Arnold, who seems to have had our Australian Colonies
in his eye when he penned the following observation.
" When the time arrives at which a colony is too great to
be dependent, *distance making union impossible with a mother
country at the end of the earth*, the only alternative is COM-
PLETE SEPARATION."

Now, would it not be greatly preferable for all parties
and interests concerned, if these Australian colonies were
separate and independent, before the mother country becomes
involved in any European war ? What, I ask, would Great
Britain herself lose by such an event? Nothing but an
empty name. Nay, she would be a positive gainer to a
very large amount; for she would thenceforth be relieved
of the enormous cost of protecting the Australian colonies.

in time of war, while their profitable trade would continue
to flow in the old channels, and be rapidly and indefinitely
increased. The colonies, on the other hand, could lose
nothing imaginable by the change. On the contrary, they
would gain immensely in every respect; they would forthwith form a national government for themselves on a
thoroughly popular basis, under which they would at once
take a high place in the family of nations, and live at
peace with all the world, whatever wars might be waged
in Europe.

The notable idea, which has often been put forth by the
press in England, that if great Britain should abandon her
Australian colonies, either America or some other European
power would take them up, scarcely deserves the slightest
notice. From the passage I have quoted above, from
Mr. Grote's History of Greece, the reader will doubtless
infer that *to take* a free and independent country, like
Australia of the future, would be something very different
from the taking of a mere dependency. Even supposing
that the yoke of Britain were galling in the Australian
colonies—which it has never been since the advent of
responsible government—that of France, or Russia, or even
of America, would be a hundred-fold more galling—it would
be absolutely intolerable; for "Britons never can be
slaves." I am utterly astonished, however, that a man of
such high standing in the literary world as Mr. Froude, the
historian, could write as he does in an article on England
and the Colonies, in *Frazer's Magazine* for January last, of
the possibility of our annexation, in any circumstances
whatever, to America. "If we throw off the colonies," says
Mr. Froude, "it is at least possible that they may apply
for admittance into the American Union; and it is equally
possible that the Americans may not refuse them. Canada,
they already calculate on as a certainty. Why may not
the Cape and Australia and New Zealand follow?" Mr.

Froude seems to think that we, the Australian people, are a mere family of helpless children squalling in a nursery. Why then did he not recommend that a Nursery Governess should be sent out to us at once, with a bale of pinafores, bibs and tuckers, and plenty of milk-pap for us all?

SECTION XX.—HOW THE CLAIM OF FREEDOM AND INDEPENDENCE IS LIKELY TO BE RECEIVED BY THE PARENT STATE.

There is no political truth so universally admitted as that certain colonies, or groups of colonies, will ultimately attain their freedom and independence, and become great and powerful nations.* The idea that millions, or even hundreds of thousands, of intelligent and enterprising people, living together in any country whatever, will allow themselves, in this advanced period of the world's history, to be governed by any other people residing at the opposite extremity of the globe, is so preeminently absurd that no person of any pretensions to common sense or common honesty would venture to stake his reputation upon putting it forth. "There must ultimately, therefore," it is universally admitted, "be a time for the separation of the colony, or group of colonies, from the Parent State. But nobody, surely," it will be added, " can suppose that this time has come yet! Wait a while longer by all means,—it is only a question of time."

But this question of time is just the point upon which the whole case turns. For while the colonist maintains that the *present* time is the time fixed by the law of nature

---

* "Every colony ought by us to be looked upon as a country destined, at some period of its existence, to govern itself.—*The Colonies of England*. By John Arthur Roebuck, Esq., M.P., p. 170. "When their numbers are multiplied, and their capital accumulated so as to render manufactures profitable, they will assuredly cease to be colonists.—*Merivale*, i. 218.

and the ordinance of God, as the community to which he belongs has attained its political majority, and is both able and willing to govern itself; "Pooh, pooh!" says one honourable member of the House of Commons after another, although I am happy to say the Right Honourable the Secretary of State for the Colonies maintains a dignified neutrality on the subject, and very prudently leaves the decision of the question to the colonists themselves—"Pooh, pooh! the *future* time can be the only proper time for the consideration of so grave a question. Let us hear no more of it, therefore, for half a century to come."

Thus the very people who will take infinite credit, from all who are simple enough to give it them, for their glorification of Kossuth and Garibaldi for their heroic efforts to establish the freedom and independence of Hungary and Rome, will look as cold as the frigid zone upon those who presume to claim for a whole group of British colonies—that is, for their own countrymen, and friends, and brothers—that freedom and independence to which they are unquestionably entitled by the law of nature and the ordinance of God. "There are instances," says Professor Heeren, "in which individual rulers, weary of power, have freely resigned it; but no *people* ever yet voluntarily surrendered authority over a subject nation."*

But although it were contrary to all experience to suppose that Great Britain will ever spontaneously relinquish the sovereignty of any of her colonies in the absence of pressure from without, it is now universally admitted that she

* *Reflections on the Politics of Ancient Greece.*—Jeremy Bentham expresses a similar idea in regard to an aristocracy, and this is perhaps more directly applicable to the case in question; the power in that case being in the hands of the Imperial Parliament, which can only be regarded as an aristocracy exercising authority over the colonies. "Of voluntary surrenders of *monarchy* into the hands of expectant and monarchical successors, there is no want of examples: not even in

will never repeat the enormous political blunder of the first American war, by attempting to compel their unwilling submission by force of arms. "The people of England," says the leading journal of Europe, in a passage I have already quoted above, "have long ago renounced any wish to retain by force of arms remote settlements, inhabited by people of our own race, in unwilling and compulsory subjection. Henceforth the bond of union which unites Britain to her colonies must be free."*

The Australian Colonies will therefore have no need of a second Washington to achieve their freedom and independence; and still less will they stand in need of another La Fayette to assist him. They will only have to signify their desire to become a free, sovereign and independent State, in real earnest, and the thing will be done without further trouble. Like the extraction of a tooth, the operation may give our dear mother a momentary pang; but it will be all over in a twinkling, and she will then be agreeably surprised to find herself, notwithstanding the recognition of our freedom and independence, much better than ever.

The silent but successful operation of the Free Trade System for the last quarter of a century has already wrought a wonderful change in public opinion in England on the subject of her relations with the Colonies; and I have myself had occasion to observe again and again, during my last visit to the mother country, that when any modest and

modern—not even in European history:—Charles the Fifth of Germany, monarch of so many vast monarchies; Christina of Sweden; Victor Amadeus of Savoy; Philip the Fifth of Spain; here, in so many different nations, we have already four examples. But, on the part of an aristocratical body, where is there as much as any one example to be found of the surrender of the minutest particle of power which they were able to retain?"—Jeremy Bentham, *Plan of Parliamentary Reform.*

* *Times,* July 30, 1852.

moderate advocate of colonial rights addresses an intelligent audience on the subject of colonial freedom in any of
the great cities of the United Kingdom—assuring our
fellow countrymen that, we colonists, honour and respect
her Majesty the Queen, and admire the British Constitution
as cordially as any of themselves; that we cherish the same
strong attachment to the British people we have ever done,
and are unfeignedly desirous to maintain relations of the
strictest friendship with them to the end of time; but that
it is absolutely necessary for our own welfare and advancement in the world, and indeed for *their* best interests as
well as our own, that we should henceforth be left to govern
ourselves as a Sovereign and Independent State—I have
uniformly found on all such occasions, without one solitary
exception—in London, Liverpool and Manchester, in Edinburgh, Glasgow, Dundee and Aberdeen—that the calm
dispassionate proposal of Freedom and Independence for
the Golden Lands of Australia, calls forth an immediate,
warm, hearty, generous and enthusiastic response from the
British People.

CHAPTER II.

ANCIENT AND MODERN COLONIZATION COMPARED AND CONTRASTED.

SECTION I.—CARTHAGINIAN COLONIZATION.

THE principal colonizing nations of antiquity were the Carthaginians, the Greeks, and the Romans.* Like the Phœnicians of their mother country, the famous cities of Tyre and Sidon, the Carthaginians were essentially a trading people, and their colonies were originally small factories, established exclusively for the purposes of trade, in remote countries already occupied by a people less advanced in the arts of civilization, like those of the East India Company at Calcutta, Madras, and Bombay, in the seventeenth century. By degrees, however, as these factories gained strength, through the accession of additional traders and adventurers from the mother country,

---

* King Solomon appears to have done something considerable in the way of colonization. The sacred writer informs us that *Solomon went to Hamath-Zobah, and prevailed against it. And he built Tadmor in the wilderness, and all the store cities, which he built at Hamath.*—2 Chron. viii. 3, 4. In these countries, as well as in the conquests of his father, David, to the eastward, Solomon probably planted one or more colonies of emigrants from the land of Israel, dividing among them the conquered territories. The advice given in Prov. xxiv. 27. *Prepare thy work without, and make it fit for thyself in the field, and afterwards build thine house,* appears to have been intended for these emigrants, to whom it must have proved the best possible advice: for it is difficult to conceive how it could have applied to the circumstances of a long settled country like the land of Israel in the days of Solomon.

who settled in and around the factories, and in many
instances intermarried with the natives, they were able
eventually to take a part in all the quarrels and petty wars
of the neighbouring chiefs, and thereby to subject them
successively to their own authority, until at length each
factory became the capital of a powerful State; which was.
thenceforth tributary to Carthage, and was governed with
despotic authority. by Generals and Governors appointed
by the Carthaginian Senate. In this way the Carthaginians
established trading factories and made extensive territorial
acquisitions and conquests in the North of Africa, in Sicily,.
in Sardinia, in Corsica, and in Spain, thereby creating an
extensive and formidable power, precisely like that of our
own East India Company of the past in Hindostan; the
Carthaginian settlers and traders in these factories being
compensated for their deprivation of all share in the
government of their adopted country, by their general
license to plunder the natives. Carthaginian colonization
was therefore improperly so called, being rather a series of
annexations and conquests than colonization; its main
principles being, like those of our own East India Company, cupidity and usurpation.

Section II.—The Greek Colonies.

One of the most interesting features in the history of the
ancient world, is the remarkable extent to which the mere
handful of people who inhabited "the Isles of Greece"
diffused their singularly beautiful language, their
equitable laws, their "elegant mythology,"* and above
all the spirit of manly freedom that pervaded their
whole political system, over the remotest regions of
the then known world. We know comparatively little.

---

* "The elegant mythology of the Greeks."—*Gibbon*. Be it so—of
course with a few grains of salt !

of Phœnician colonization; and the barbarous and impolitic decree of the Roman Senate, *Delenda est Carthago*,* appears to have extended to the literature as well as to the walls of Carthage, to the archives of her history as well as to the monuments of her power. But the glorious Greeks have left the traces of their presence on every shore to which it was possible to steer their adventurous galleys, from the Pillars of Hercules to the Sea of Azof; and the solitary marble columns of her once splendid, but now fallen, temples, and palaces, and towers, that are still to be found alike, in the midst of surrounding desolation, on the verge of every African desert and every Asiatic coast, proclaim to the admiring traveller how mighty a people must once have lived and reigned in the Central Sea.

And yet the native land of these heroes of the olden time—Greece Proper—was actually smaller than Scotland: the famous Peloponnesus, which occupies so large a space in ancient history, being only about the size of Yorkshire;†

---

* These were the terms of the famous decree of the Roman Senate for the destruction of Carthage, the ancient political rival of Rome.

† The Greek States made such a conspicuous figure in history, that the reader will not easily believe their inhabitants were so few, or their territories so small, as certain circumstances compel us to admit. The whole extent of their country, even when they flourished most, comprehended only the peninsula of Peloponnesus, and the territories stretching northwards from the isthmus of Corinth to the borders of Macedonia, bounded by the Archipelago on the east, and by Epirus and the Ionian Sea on the west. The mean breadth of Peloponnesus from north to south can scarcely be reckoned more than 140 miles, and its mean length from east to west cannot be estimated at more than 210 miles. Yet within this narrow boundary, were contained six independent States, Achaia, Elis, Messenia, Laconia, Argolis, and Arcadia. Admitting, then, that the territories of these States were nearly of equal extent, the dimensions of each particular State will appear to be no more than 23 miles in breadth, and 35 in length.

The country belonging to the Greeks on the north side of the isthmus, I have computed from the best maps, to contain, of mean

for it was not until a comparatively late period, and after all the great works of Grecian colonization had been in some measure completed, that the Macedonians, who were afterwards so celebrated in Grecian history, were admitted into the brotherhood of the Greeks. The climate was doubtless superior to that of England, and the available land of greater fertility; but much of the superficial area of the country consisted of bare rocks and barren hills, and the territory of Attica in particular was very inferior in its agricultural capabilities. But the Greeks, and especially those of the islands, were a maritime people, and a comparatively large proportion of their number preferred living by commerce to the cultivation of the soil. Their foreign trade necessarily extended their knowledge and expanded their minds, whilst it brought them large accessions to their national wealth: and this wealth nourished and sustained literature and science, philosophy and the arts. The consequence was that the Greeks were a cultivated and refined people, while the ruder Romans, who were steadily advancing to universal empire in their

breadth, 153 miles from north to south, and of mean length, 258 miles from east to west. It comprehended no fewer than the following nine independent commonwealths, Thessaly, Locris, Bœotia, Attica, Megaris, Phocis, Ætolia, Acarnania, and Doris. Supposing, then, as in the former case, these commonwealths to have been nearly equal in point of territory, in order to obtain an idea of the mean magnitude of their dominions, we shall find each of them to have possessed lands to the extent only of 17 miles in breadth, and 28 in length. What is still more extraordinary, several of them consisted of cities, which were independent of one another, and were associated only for mutual defence. Both the Locrians and the Achæans afford instances of this case. The former had not even all their territories contiguous, nor did they act always in concert, and the twelve cities of the latter seem to have been connected in no other manner than by alliance.—*History of the Colonization of the Free States of Antiquity, applied to the present Contest between Great Britain and her American Colonies,* (attributed to W. Barron, Esq., F.R.S., Edinburgh,) p. 22. London, 1777.

immediate neighbourhood, could only do two things—bear arms and cultivate the soil.

The political state of Greece, moreover, was most unfortunate, and apparently most unfavourable to national advancement. Instead of forming one great whole, and being thereby enabled to concentrate the national energies upon any one object or series of objects, the country, like Italy in the middle ages, was broken up into almost as many sovereign and independent States as there are counties in England : and these States were in perpetual warfare with each other—Greek everywhere and at all times meeting Greek in mortal strife, and the resources of the country being wasted the meanwhile in fruitless and ruinous wars.

And yet it was under all these disadvantages that, what Lord Bacon very properly designates the "heroic work" of colonization, was commenced among the ancient Greeks, and carried on from time to time with all the native energy and vigour of that wonderful people, till it reached at length to an extent and magnitude that renders the utmost efforts even of Great Britain in modern times, and notwithstanding all the appliances of modern civilization, insignificant in comparison.

The first remote country, to which the colonizing efforts of the ancient Greeks were directed, was Asia Minor ; and each of the three great divisions of their race—the Ionians, the Æolians, and the Dorians—formed a whole series of colonies on the coast of that country; the Ionians and Æolians having each twelve cities or independent sovereignties, and the Dorians six.* It is immaterial whether

* Two hundred and forty years after the Trojan war, the western coast of Asia Minor was planted by the Æolians in the north, the Ionians in the middle, and the Dorians in the south (anno A.C. 944.) *Hist. of Ancient Greece, its Colonies and Conquests.* By John Gillies, L.L.D., vol. i. p. 103.

we refer the great migration, which led to the planting of these colonies or States, to a particular year, as is done by historians of the second class, who are generally dealers in the marvellous, or consider what is commonly called "the Ionian Migration" a legend, with Mr. Grote, and spread it over a long series of years; for the result is in either case precisely the same. The probability indeed is that there were not fewer than thirty different migrations altogether; each having a separate leader, and each founding a distinct city or State.* For as the same national calamity at home would, in all likelihood, either induce or compel a great many families and individuals of the same tribe or people to emigrate simultaneously from their native country, it was absolutely necessary in these times that they should do so, to enable them to effect a settlement in their adopted country at all; for Asia Minor was already inhabited, although but thinly, by a warlike people, when it was colonized by the Greeks, and every distinct colony had consequently to defend itself against "the barbarians."†

---

* There existed at the commencement of historical Greece in 776 B.C. besides the Ionians in Attica and the Cyclades, twelve Ionian cities of note on or near the coasts of Asia Minor, besides a few others less important. Enumerated from south to north, they stand—Milêtus, Myus, Priené, Samos, Ephesus, Kolophon, Lebedus, Teos, Erythræ, Chios, Klazomenæ, Phokæa.

That these cities, the great ornament of the Ionic name, were founded by emigrants from European Greece, there is no reason to doubt. How or when they were founded, we have no history to tell us: the legend gives us a great event called the Ionic migration, referred by chronologists to one special year, 140 years after the Trojan war.—*History of Greece*. By George Grote, Esq., vol. iii. p. 230.

† Not the prosperity, not the policy, but the troubles and misfortunes of the country gave origin to the principal colonies of Greece. The ÆOLIC MIGRATION was an immediate consequence of the conquest of Peloponnesus by the Heracleids. The great IONIC MIGRATION took place somewhat later, but produced colonies still more flourishing. It was led from Athens by Androclus and Nileus, younger sons of Codrus,

In such circumstances, there was no such contemptible word as " protection "—in the sense of a naval or military force from the mother country, which certain timid people consider absolutely necessary for a *British* colony—in the whole colonial Greek vocabulary. Every colony defended and protected itself from the very first.

As these colonial cities or States grew and prospered, they generally became mother countries in their turn, and sent out other colonies, either into the interior, or along the remoter coasts of the adjacent seas. We shall have some idea of the prodigious amount of subsidiary colonization, which was thus originated in all the other twenty nine original cities or colonies of Asia Minor, from what history informs us in regard to the famous city of Milêtus —the first of the Ionian cities, and the city in which the great apostle of the Gentiles held his interesting and affecting interview with the elders of the Church of Ephesus, when driven from that city by a popular commotion.* "Of the Ionic towns," says Mr. Grote, "with which our real knowledge of Asia Minor begins, Milêtus was the most powerful; and its celebrity was derived not merely from its own wealth and population, but also from the extraordinary number of its colonies, established principally in the Propontis and Euxine, and amounting, as we are told by some authors, to not less than seventy-five or eighty."†

In this way, doubtless, the Carian or Dorian province of Lycia, towards the south coast of Asia Minor, was colonized from the old colonies—the Dorian Hexapolis, with its principal city Halicarnassus—on the coast. In that

---

upon the occasion of the determination of the succession to the Archonship in favour of Medon. The Carian colonies in general boasted the DORIAN name.—*History of Greece.* By William Mitford, Esq., vol. i. p. 376.

* Acts, xx., 17-38.

† *History of Greece.* By George Grote, vol. iii. p. 241.

province Sir Charles Fellowes has, within the last forty or
fifty years, discovered a whole series of magnificent remains
of Grecian antiquity; on which Mr. Buckingham, late M.P.,
makes the following judicious remark :—

" In the single province of Lycia—embracing little more
than a degree in latitude and longitude, or not more than
2,000,000 acres, with a large portion of this limited area
occupied by rocky mountains and inaccessible cliffs, with
not a single large navigable river or lake,—were no less
than thirty-six cities, in the time of Herodotus; while over
the 200,000,000 of acres in our Western provinces, we
could not present, in the united public works and edifices
all put together, so much of architectural beauty, cost, and
grandeur, as some single one of these cities of Asia Minor
possesses, even now, in such of their remains as have yet
come down to us after 2000 years or more of time!"†

But Lycia was only one small province of Asia Minor.
The whole country was a series of such provinces—all
colonized successively by the Greeks, and all doubtless
exhibiting the magnificent remains of Grecian architecture
to the present day.

At a somewhat later period in the history of Greece,
Grecian colonization took a westerly direction; and one
of the principal colonizing cities or states of Greece,
which sent out colonies in that direction, was the celebrated
city or State of Corinth. Of the many colonies planted by
that city, I shall mention only three. The first was Locris,
on the north coast of the Gulf of Corinth, to which I shall
have occasion to refer in the sequel, and which in its turn
became a colonizing city also, and planted another city of
its own name, which afterwards became wealthy and
populous, to a far greater extent than the parent city, on
the coast of Italy. The second of the Corinthian colonies

† Buckingham, *Model of a Town, &c.*

I shall mention was the city of Corcyra or Corfu, on the island of that name. This city also soon became a mother-city or State, and planted the colony of Epidamnus on the mainland, about which it was able to go to war, as it actually did, with the Parent State. The third Corinthian colony was the city or State of Syracuse, in the island of Sicily, which very soon far outstripped its Parent State in wealth and splendour and population; being not less than fourteen English miles in circumference, at the period of its greatest glory.

The city of Agrigentum was another Grecian city in Sicily, scarcely, if at all, inferior to Syracuse; and the two insignificant Grecian States of Chalcis and Megara had each also a distinct colony, or city and district, in that island. It would seem, therefore, that Mr. Grote is decidedly in error when he speaks in the following disparaging terms of the Grecian Colonies in Sicily :—

"Such were the chief establishments founded by the Greeks in Sicily during the two centuries after their first settlement in 735 B.C.   *   *   *   *   *Their progress*, though very great, during this most prosperous interval (between the foundation of Naxos in 735 B.C. to the reign of Gelon in Syracuse in 485 B.C.), *is not to be compared to that of the English colonies in America;* but it was nevertheless very great, and appears greater from being concentrated as it was in and around a few cities."*

---

* *History of Greece.* By George Grote, Esq., vol. iii. p. 491. Mr. Grote ought to have recollected that the English colonies in America, whether he refers to the original Thirteen, or to the present British North American provinces, were the colonies of a mighty empire, having an extent of domestic territory, so to speak, probably four or five times larger than that of Greece Proper, with perhaps four times its population; having nothing, moreover, in the shape of internal wars to distract it at home, possessing facilities for colonization incomparably superior to those of ancient Greece, and being able to concentrate its whole force in the way of colonization on any particular

The South of Italy was also another extensive field of Grecian colonization; and so important was it considered in this respect by the Greeks themselves, that it was commonly called *Magna Græcia*, or Greece the Greater. Naples still bears the commonplace name of New Town,[*] which was given it by the original Greek colonists; and, not to exhaust the patience of the reader with more numerous examples, the Greek colonies of Marseilles and Lyons in the South of France, and of Cyrene on the coast of Africa, were evidences of the presence and energy of the Greeks in these comparatively remote lands.

"The colony of Sybaris, called afterwards Thurii, in Italy, was settled by the Achæans. It was powerful and successful, had under its jurisdiction four adjacent States, possessed twenty-five cities, and could bring into the field 300,000 men, which it did in the war with its neighbours the Crotoniatæ, or inhabitants of Croton also a colony of Achæa, by whom they were completely routed, and their city destroyed."[†]

Such were the mighty and magnificent results of Grecian colonization. Considering the limited extent, and comparatively small population of Greece, and especially considering the unfortunately divided state of the country, and the constant prevalence of intestine wars, it is altogether one of the most remarkable phenomena in the history of man. But even all this was comparatively nothing to the mighty influence which this wonderful people acquired throughout the civilised world, after the subversion of the Persian

point; whereas the Greek colonies of Sicily were each the colony of a small insignificant State, no bigger than a second or third rate town in England, while Sicily itself was only one of the many fields of Grecian colonization. A comparison, in such cases, Mr. Grote will surely allow, is scarcely warrantable. ·

[*] Neapolis, Naples, or New Town.

[†] *History of the Colonization of the Free States of Antiquity. London,* 1777.

L

empire by Alexander the Great.   Their language then
became the universal tongue of the civilised world; dis--
placing alike the Coptic in Egypt and the Syriac in Antioch
and Palmyra, while the influence of their laws and learning
was felt to the utmost bounds of civilization.

The amazing extent and influence of Grecian colonisation
is proclaimed, in the most unmistakable manner, by the
fact that the Greek, and not the Latin, language was the
language of by far the greater portion of the civilised world,
even when the Roman empire was at the height of its
glory; for notwithstanding the universal triumph of the
Roman arms, the language of the conquerors never made
any progress in any country which the Greeks had colonized.*   The field of Grecian colonisation was the scene of
the earliest and greatest triumphs of christianity.   The
seven apostolic churches were all planted in Grecian colonies; and the New Testament, including even the epistle
addressed to the Romans themselves, was written in the
Greek language, because Grecian colonisation had made
that language the language of the civilised world.

SECTION III.—THE BENEFICIAL RESULTS OF GRECIAN COLONIZATION
TO GREECE PROPER.

In a passage quoted by Dr. M'Culloch, in his valuable
Dictionary of Commerce, the philosopher Seneca assigns
three different causes for emigration in the ancient world,
and particularly in ancient Greece.†   The first was

---

* Greek, and not Latin, was the language of the Lower Empire,
that is the *Roman* Empire in the East : and for upwards of a thousand
years, the throne of the Cæsars was filled by men who spoke Greek.

† Nec omnibus eadem eausa relinquendi quærendique patriam fuit.
Alios domestica seditio submovit: alios nimia superfluentis populi
frequentia, ad exonerandas vires, emisit: quosdam fertilis oræ, et in
majus laudatæ, fama corrupit: alios alia causa excivit domibus suis.—
Seneca, *Consol. ad Helviam*, c. 6.

civil dissensions; the second was redundance of population; and the third was the favourable accounts which
had been received of the capabilities of the particular
colony to which the emigration was to be directed. As
Seneca was a much better judge than we can be of the
comparative influence of these causes respectively in the
ancient world, we shall take them in the order in which he
gives them, beginning with *civil dissensions*.

It is a remarkable fact that kingly government appears
to have been generally subverted in ancient Greece, and
to have been as generally succeeded by some popular
form of government before the age of Grecian colonization began. The traditional leaders of the great
Ionian migration, and the founders of the city of
Miletus, the first of the twelve cities of the Ionian confederation of Asia Minor, were Nileus and Androclus the
sons of Codrus, the last king of Athens. Now, it
must be evident that, under the ill-balanced republics that
succeeded the overthrow of monarchy, or, as the Greeks
called it, *tyranny*, in the numerous petty States of that
country, a state of things would speedily arise, of which
we can have no experience, under our comparatively well-
balanced representative institutions, and our more permanent forms of government. There must necessarily, under
so imperfect a system, have been a perpetual struggle for
place and power between the *ins* and the *outs;* and that
struggle would give rise to a far more rancorous hostility
between these two classes than we can have any idea of.
Society would everywhere resolve itself into two formidable
factions, of which the mutual hostility would only become
the more rancorous as wealth and population increased,
and of which the party in opposition would not always be
the only uneasy class of the two. In order to maintain
their own authority, the party in power would naturally
endeavour to make the yoke of their political opponents as
grievous as possible, and to attach as large a portion as

possible of the general population to their persons and interests. Such a state of things would at length become intolerable to the weaker party, who, with their friends and adherents, would seek refuge from the insufferable evils of their condition in emigration. We find accordingly that the party in the ascendant in a Grecian colony was generally opposed to the party in power in the mother city or State; if the Tories were *in* at Corinth, the Whigs had their turn at Corcyra.

We have a somewhat remarkable, and at the same time instructive and amusing instance of this in the case to which I have just alluded—that of the famous city or State of Corinth, and the colonial cities of Corcyra, and Epidamnus. The aristocrats, it seems, were long in the ascendant at Corinth, and the democratic party accordingly resolved to emigrate, and founded the city or colony of Corcyra in the neighbouring island of Corfu. But the Corcyræans themselves, who very soon became a powerful maritime people, having eventually carried matters with too high a hand in their own city, a party of the citizens emigrated in like manner with their friends and adherents, and founded the city and State of Epidamnus on the mainland of Greece. In process of time the party who had the upper hand in Epidamnus deemed it expedient and necessary, doubtless for the public welfare, to banish certain of their own citizens who happened unfortunately to be in the political minority, and who naturally threw themselves upon the sympathies of Corcyra, their mother-city. The Whigs of Corcyra at once espoused the cause of these unoffending and deeply injured people, and accordingly insisted upon the Tories of Epidamnus, their own colony, replacing them bodily in their offices, their honours, and their estates. This, however, the Epidamnians were by no means disposed to do; but being unable to protect their city against the powerful fleet of Corcyra, they appealed, for assistance in their distress, to the old Tories of their grand-mother-city of Corinth, who at once declared for Epidamnus; and hence originated a regular Greek war! It cannot be denied, however, that in at once relieving any great mother-city or State of a number of unquiet spirits, with all their discontented and disaffected friends and adherents, the process of colonization, which was thus rapid and universal all over the country, was of unspeakable advantage to the different States of Greece; as it served, in numerous instances, to preserve the public peace when there would otherwise have been fierce commotions and civil wars.

But in far more numerous instances emigration and colonization in ancient Greece must have originated in a redundancy of population. With a fine climate, a fertile soil, a flourishing colonial trade, and a popular government, population would doubtless increase, on the mainland and in the isles of Greece, with prodigious rapidity; and an outlet for that population would soon come to be considered one of the first necessities of every Grecian State. Certain portions of their territory also, as for instance Attica, and certain of the islands, being naturally sterile and unproductive, the inhabitants necessarily became a maritime and commercial people; who soon obtained a sufficient acquaintance with the capabilities of remote countries for the settlement of colonies, and to whom therefore emigration would be a far less formidable affair than to the plodding agriculturist. Grecian colonies were thus formed successively in all the distant localities enumerated above: some adventurous individual of standing and talent putting himself at the head of the movement, and organizing a numerous party among his fellow-citizens to form a settlement in some new-found-land; or the State assuming the initiative in the matter, by a decree of the Sovereign People, and sending forth the colonists with the best wishes of their mother-country, and with all the solemnities of religion. The Grecian colony was thus formed and organized before it embarked; and it went forth, like a swarm of bees from the parent hive, to reproduce the whole framework of society, according to the pattern of their native land, in the place of their appointed settlement, far, far away.

And what a difference there must have been in any great effort of colonization in such circumstances as these, from the miserable affair that we call colonization ! In the case of the Greeks, men of all ranks in society, of all professions and occupations, went forth on the great undertaking, and staked their character and their fortunes on the issue ; but they all went forth from the same mother-city or State, and they were all perfectly acquainted with each other before they started on their noble undertaking. As an embryo community, they had all from the first the same interesting associations, and the same endearing recollections of the land they had left; they had all the same objects and interests, the same feelings and views in the land of their adoption. The sprightly and enterprising Ionian from Athens was not incommoded with the presence of the dull Bœotian from Thebes, or the plodding Dorian from the plain of Argos. Ionians, Æolians, and Dorians had all their separate colonies ; and every Greek emigrant found himself on his arrival in his adopted country in the midst of his old neighbours, and countrymen, and friends. They all left the same locality in the *old* country, and they all settled together in the *new*.

Under our colonization system, people of a certain class only—people who have somehow lost their way in the world—people who have tried everything at home and have uniformly failed—people who have already reached, or are fast verging towards the lower walks of life—people of this kind assemble from all quarters of the three kingdoms, and meet together for the first time in some great shipping port, as for instance, Liverpool. Unlike the companions of Æneas, they require no long navigation to carry them to the land of the Harpies; for, in all likelihood, they find them *there;* and they suffer far more from the *sharks* on land than they are ever likely to do from the sharks at sea. They pay their fare at length, as Jonah did when *he went to go unto Tarshish;* and they go down into the sides of the vessel, with hearts perhaps too full either for sleep or for tears, each as utterly unacquainted with his numerous fellow-passengers as they are with him. On arriving in their adopted country, after a few weeks' intercourse and acquaintance on board ship, they again separate for ever, one going to the north and another to the south, and a third to the west; and falling, as they now do, among utter strangers, the moral restraints of their native vicinage are gradually weakened, and perhaps completely lost.

What is termed *Government Emigration* is something equally exceptional with all this—equally heartless. Instead of directing the emigrant ships to proceed successively to different ports in the United Kingdom—as for instance to the east and west coasts of England and Scotland, respectively, and to the north and south of Ireland—where there would at least be some chance of people emigrating in considerable numbers from the same locality, the Government Bounty emigrants are collected by a regular staff of whippers-in from all parts of the three kingdoms, and forwarded by steamboat to Plymouth—a place which nineteen out of every twenty of them have probably never heard of before — where the Government commissioners have a depôt, into which these emigrants (many of them sometimes exceptionable enough) are collected from all quarters, like slaves from the interior of Africa in some great *barracoon* on the coast; the sequel being precisely the same as in the Liverpool private ships. And this is what

we presume to call *colonization*, forsooth, and to compare
with that of the ancient Greeks!

The third of the causes of emigration and colonisation in
ancient Greece was, according to Seneca, the favourable
reports that were given of the new or intended colony.
When the settlement was once successfully formed, it would
naturally attract emigrants from the mother-city or State,
in proportion to the tidings of the success of the first adventurers; and thus all the three great divisions of the
Grecian race—the Ionians, the Æolians, and the Dorians,
corresponding to the English, Irish, and Scotch of our own
country,—had each their whole series of colonies, both in
the east and west, which would all serve as favourite
centres of attraction to the adventurous youth of their respective races.

In the meantime the extensive commerce which would
originate in so vast a colonial system would afford a
boundless market for the various products of the national
industry of Greece, and supply her looms, her workshops,
her dockyards, and her furnaces, with raw produce for her
different manufactures; while the lofty fame of her
statesmen and generals, her historians and philosophers,
her orators and poets, her architects and sculptors and
painters, would fill her academies with the ingenious youth of every remote colony, and concentrate
upon her the admiration of the world. In such a
state of things crime would be comparatively rare;
for there would be plenty of employment at remunerating wages for all classes, while all would enjoy
in comparative abundance both the necessaries and the
comforts of life. In short, I can conceive no substantial
advantage of colonization which Greece Proper must not
have enjoyed in a very high degree in the midst of her vast
colonial empire; and it is mortifying to reflect that while
Greece so nobly fulfilled her evident and undoubted

mission in the ancient world, as the great colonizing power of antiquity, that Power which has so evidently been called by Divine Providence to occupy the same distinguished place in the modern world, and which enjoys facilities for the purpose of which the loftiest imaginations of Greece could never have dreamt, should have hitherto neglected in great measure to follow her bright example, and failed for the most part to realize the same magnificent results.

SECTION IV.—BRITISH COLONIZATION BEFORE THE WAR OF AMERICAN INDEPENDENCE.

Without adverting, for the present, to the colonization-practice of Spain, Portugal and Holland, in the sixteenth, seventeenth and eighteenth centuries, it may not be unprofitable to contrast, with this product of the isles of Greece, the vaunted colonization of Britain, both before and since the war of American Independence. To begin then with the colonies of New England in America, these, as I have already observed, were planted during the twenty years that elapsed from the year 1620 to the year 1640 ; the original colonists consisting of about twenty thousand persons, who had fled for liberty of conscience to the American wilderness, from the tyranny of Charles the First, and the relentless intolerance of his minister Laud. The fact of so extensive an emigration having taken place, within so limited a period, and so near to our own times,— without referring to the enormous emigration from the United Kingdom, produced by the Irish Famine of 1847, and the Gold Discoveries in Australia of a still later period —may show that there is no antecedent improbability in the common historical account of the great Ionian migration ; for under a strong impelling power in the mother-country, like the persecution of the Puritans in England, the same effect would doubtless have followed. With a few insignificant exceptions, no further emigration took place from the mother-country to New England till the War of Independence. Bancroft, the American historian, estimates the population of New England, at the Revolution of 1688, at seventy-five thousand.

Virginia was the oldest English colony on the continent of America. It was originally planted during the reign of James I., in the year 1606; but in the year 1642, its population did not exceed 20,000; and according to Bancroft, it amounted only to 50,000 at the Revolution of 1688. At the usual rate of increase in America—doubling in thirty years—this amount of population would give 640,000 in the year 1792; which must have been pretty near the actual amount, for in the year 1800 the population of Virginia amounted to 880,200—of whom, however, about one-half were negroes! How insignificant, therefore, must the whole amount of British emigration to the colony of Virginia—*the old Dominion*, as it used to be called--have been, previous to the era of Independence, when the whole white population of the country, with all its increase, after a hundred and seventy years, amounted only to 320,000!

It is commonly alleged that the original colonists of Virginia were cavaliers, or gentlemen, and not Round Heads, or plebeians, like the Puritan colonists of New England; who differed from the Virginian colonists in this important particular, that they almost uniformly carried their wives and families along with them to that country. Whatever they were, there was so large a number of males, and so serious a want of female population in the young colony, that the Virginian Company in England had to send out whole ship-loads of young women—I presume from the workhouses or other similar establishments of the period, as in the case of the Irish Female Orphan Emigration to New South Wales in the years 1848 and 1849—

to supply the deficiency; and these young women were literally sold to their future husbands, the gentlemen and cavaliers of Virginia (!), at so many pounds of tobacco each, to repay the Company the cost of their passage out. There was another species of emigration to Virginia and the American colonies generally, which had been long in practice before the War of Independence,—it was that of shipmasters carrying out labouring people, or adventurers, who were unable to pay their own passage, and selling their services for a certain period to the colonists, after their arrival, to reimburse themselves for the outlay; people of this class being called *Redemptioners*. But the want of labour was so great in the American colonies, and the flow of voluntary emigration so limited, that the atrocious practice of kidnapping for the colonies was long and systematically had recourse to in the seaport towns of the United Kingdom; unfortunate people, both male and female, from the country chiefly, being allured on board ships ready for sea, and carried off and sold for a time for their passage money, like the Redemptioners. And last of all, there was the convict emigration to Virginia and certain of the other American colonies, which amounted for some time previous to the War of Independence to about two thousand annually. And yet, with all these sources of supply, so little creditable to Great Britain as a great colonizing country, the entire white population of Virginia did not exceed 320,000, even including foreigners and their off-spring, at the era of the American war; that is, at the close of one hundred and seventy years of British colonization! The original amount of British emigration required to produce such a result after so long an interval, must there-fore have been exceedingly small.

The colony of New York was originally a conquest from the Dutch, during the reign of Charles the Second; and the number of its inhabitants, who were consequently all Dutchmen, at the period of its capture, was upwards of ten thousand.* To these there were subsequently added a number of German Protestant refugees from the Palatinate, and also of French Huguenots, who had been driven from their country after the Repeal of the Edict of Nantes. So considerable indeed was this latter infusion that the French language continued to be spoken in certain localities in the neighbourhood of New York till the war of the Revolution.†

The colony of New Jersey was originally settled in great measure by emigrants from Scotland, who had been driven

* This circumstance alone is quite sufficient to account for the extremely limited British emigration to the colony of New York till the War of Independence, when a new order of things commenced. Previous to that period, it was a Dutch colony in reality, although a British in name and in government; and the British people do not like to settle in foreign colonies under any circumstances, as the state of the Cape colony, of Lower Canada, and of the Mauritius, sufficiently proves to the present day.

† Governor Hunter carried out about two thousand Palatines, as they were then called, or German Protestant refugees, to the colony of New York, in the Reign of Queen Anne; for the English emigration of that period was very limited. There was a French Huguenot agricultural settlement at that time about twenty miles from the city; and the emigrants, in writing home to their persecuted friends in France, informed them, that " after their week's labour was over, they regularly walked to New York every Saturday afternoon, to attend divine service with their countrymen, in the French Protestant church there, twice every Sabbath; and rising *a great while before day* on Monday morning, they walked back to their own settlement again, to resume the labours of the week;" adding " What a privilege!"

Quis talia fando,

Temperet a lachrymis ?

It was the extensive prevalence of such principles as these, in the original emigration to that country, that has formed the cement of the Republican Institutions of America : it is the want of such a cement that renders precisely similar institutions a mere wall built with untempered mortar in Mexico and elsewhere. The American has therefore no reason to fear for the stability of his social fabric. *His foundation is in the holy mountains.—Psalm* lxxxvii. 1.

from their country by persecution; with whom were incorporated a body of Polish Protestants whose emigration had had a similar origin. The Polish names are common in this part of America to the present day.

The origin and character of the settlement of Penn is well known; although it is a gross injustice to the memory of many other excellent and Christian men, connected with the original colonisation of America, as well as a very common error, to suppose that he was either the first or the only founder of a colony in that country who purchased the lands he occupied from the Indians. " Not only " observes the American historian, whom I have already quoted so frequently, "' were all the lands occupied by the colonists [of New England] fairly purchased from their Indian owners, but, in some parts of the country, the lands were subject to quitrents to the Indians," " which," says Belknap, in 1784, " are annually paid to their posterity."*

The colony of Pennsylvania absorbed a small colony of Swedes on the bank of the Delaware River; and, in common with all the other States to the South, with the exception of Georgia, it received a comparatively large number of French Huguenots—a people who had unquestionably a much larger share in the colonisation of America than is generally supposed.† In the reign of Queen Anne the

---

* Grahame's *Hist. of the United States of North America.* London, 1836, vol. i. p. 412.

† Charles the Second contributed from his own privy purse a sum sufficient to defray the cost of the passage out to Carolina of two shiploads of French Protestants. Charles is commonly accused of having spent upon his mistresses the money collected at the instance of Cromwell and his secretary Milton for the relief of the Protestants of the Piedmontese Valleys; but I presume part of it went this way, and there is no necessity for making the bad man worse than he was. His sending out these unfortunate French Protestants was unquestionably a good action, even if he never performed another in his life.

French population of Charleston, in South Carolina, was as
large as the English; and it is a remarkable fact, which I
ascertained myself in America, that of the seven Presidents
of the American Congress during the revolutionary war,
and before the adoption of the present Constitution of the
United States, not fewer than four were of French Huguenot descent. The number of Germans also who had settled
from time to time, in the provinces to the southward of
New England, before the War of Independence, was very
great; acts of naturalisation, on behalf of German Protestants, being of constant recurrence in the proceedings
of the legislatures of all these provinces during the
entire colonial period. In short, there is reason to believe
that as large a proportion as one-third of all the original
European settlers in the United States to the southward of
New England, previous to the revolutionary war, consisted
of foreigners; including the ten thousand Dutch, of the
era of Charles the Second, in the State of New York.* .

It is evident, therefore, that, up to the War of American
Independence, the entire amount of emigration from Great
Britain to America had been paltry in the extreme; considering the extent, the population, and the resources of
the mother country.† A few distinguished leaders, such as

* From the following statement of one of the more prominent
actors in the American Revolution, it would appear that the estimate
I have formed of the amount of British emigration to America before
that period, is rather over than under the truth. "Not one-third of
the inhabitants, even of this province (Pennsylvania), are of English
descent." *Common Sense*, by Thomas Paine. M.A., Philadelphia, 1776.

† The whole population of New England, which amounted, in the
year 1790, to 1,009,522, sprung, with only a very few exceptions,
from the twenty thousand Puritan emigrants of the reign of Charles
the First. But the colony of Virginia was an older colony still than
New England, while the Carolinas were settled in the reign of Charles
the Second. Supposing then that the rate of increase was as rapid in
the middle and southern colonies as it was in New England, it would
have required little more than 40,000 emigrants to have been settled

the Puritan chiefs in New England, Lord Baltimore in Maryland, William Penn in Pennsylvania, and a few others, started up indeed, from time to time, with their respective schemes, and either through their personal influence or the peculiar circumstances of the times, gave a slight impulse to the public mind in favour of their particular projects: but under the depressing and deadening influences to be afterwards indicated, this temporary excitement soon died away; the subject of colonization never got hold of the national mind, except in the way of dislike and aversion; it never became a matter of public interest or concernment to any extent; and although a few families and individuals were still emigrating to the different colonies from some part or other of the mother country every year, the total amount of such emigration was at no time so considerable as to affect the condition of the United Kingdoms, either for good or for evil, in any conceivable manner or degree. Instead, therefore, of realizing, to anything like the extent to which they might otherwise have been realized, the proper and legitimate objects of colonization, from the possession of her American

in these colonies before the middle of the seventeenth century to have called into existence the whole remaining American population at the commencement of the War of Independence, or rather at the first census of the United States in 1790. Bancroft estimates the whole population of the American colonies at the Revolution of 1688 at 200,000, which was distributed as follows, viz.:—New England, 75,000; New York, 20,000; New Jersey, 10,000; Pennsylvania and Delaware, 12,000; Maryland, 25,000; Virginia, 50,000; the Carolinas, 8,000. In the year 1790, the population of the United States amounted to 3,921,326, of whom 697,697 were negro slaves; the whole population at the commencement of the war being, according to Mr. McGregor, only 2,500,000. Deducting from this latter estimate half a million of slaves, and an equal number for the descendants of foreigners, there remains at the very utmost only 1,500,000 for British colonization with all its increase for 170 years! How extremely contemptible is such a result!

·colonies, I question whether the condition of the mother country would have been materially affected in any way, ·except perhaps in the temporary stoppage of the usual supply of tobacco, had the whole of the Thirteen Colonies been annihilated, at any period from their first settlement till the War of Independence

It is equally evident that a large proportion of the ·actual amount of British emigration to America, previous to the War of Independence, was the effect of ·religious persecution at home; and it must not be forgotten that another portion of it consisted of persons who had ·been banished from England for their crimes, and who were then sent to America, just as they have been since, in much · larger numbers, to Australia, merely to be got rid of.

All that the British government ever did, with the single exception I shall notice immediately, for the promotion of British colonization in America, previous to the revolutionary war, consisted in giving charters of incorporation to joint stock companies, or to such private proprietors as had interest enough to procure them from the Court, for the planting of colonies. In the case of Georgia, indeed, a ·small Parliamentary grant was conceded for the formation of that colony, about the year 1732, at the instance of its founder, General Oglethorpe; but this I believe was the ·only instance previous to the War of Independence, in which the British Government had ever done anything for the promotion of colonization in the extensive territory ·comprised within the thirteen original colonies of America.

SECTION V.—BRITISH COLONIZATION SINCE THE AMERICAN WAR.

I have already observed that we have no right to consider either Lower Canada or the Cape of Good Hope *British* ·colonies, or to take credit in any way for their colonization.

As well might Gelon, the tyrant of Syracuse, have considered any of the Carthaginian settlements in Sicily, which he had reduced under his dominion, *Greek* colonies. The amount of *British* colonization in these countries is quite insignificant, and can in no respect be considered as a distinct element in the calculation we subjoin. The number of French colonists in Upper Canada is probably as large as that of English, Scotch, and Irish in Lower Canada; and there are probably as many Germans in the Australian colonies as the whole of the British-born inhabitants of the Cape Colony.

In estimating the results of British colonization during the whole period of our national existence as a colonizing power, we are scarcely warranted to take into account the enormous emigration produced by the Irish Famine of 1847, 1848, and 1849, and the Gold Discoveries of a later period in Australia. The emigration originating in these anomalous events is, in no respect, to be placed to the credit of Great Britain as a colonizing power. It should rather be regarded as the result of an extraordinary interposition of Divine Providence, to ensure the accomplishment of a great national work, of unspeakable importance to the whole civilized world, which the British Government and nation had till then neglected. Let us therefore take, as the period of our estimate, that of the Decennial Census of 1841; especially as we shall afterwards have occasion to compare the results of American colonization, with those of our own efforts in this particular department, from the era of American Independence till that period. The following is the Census of the population of the British North American and Australian Colonies respectively at the period referred to.

British North American Colonies.

Upper Canada 486,055
Newfoundland . . . . , ... 75,094

M

Nova Scotia and Cape Breton 178,237
New Brunswick 156,142
Prince Edward's Island 47,034

Total population in 1842 942,562

Australian Colonies.

New South Wales, including Port Phillip, now
    Victoria, in 1841 . . . . . *. 128,718
Van Dieman's Land, 31st December, 1844 . . 57,420
South Australia, 31st December, 1844 . . . 17,366
Western Australia, or Swan River, in 1848 . 4,483
New Zealand, including 1580 soldiers, in 1848 10,483

218,447

Total population of the British Colonies at
    the periods indicated 1,161,009

"The entire population of the Australian group of colonies," according to Mr. Porter, in his *Progress of the Nation*, "amounted, at the end of 1848, to 333,754;" but it would obviously be unfair to compare the amount for that year with the result of American colonization in 1840.

Such then was the amount of British colonization, properly so called, at the periods indicated. How extremely insignificant, when contrasted on the one hand with the population and resources of the mother-country, and the unprecedented facilities for colonization which it possesses beyond any other country on the face of the earth; and on the other with the wonderful and successful efforts of the ancient Greeks in the same field of heroic exertion! I question whether the population of the city of Syracuse alone, which was merely one of the many colonies of the comparatively small City and State of Corinth, was not as large as the whole amount of British colonization properly so called in the year 1848. Again, the entire population of the Australian colonies, including New Zealand, was not greater in that year than that of the single city of Glasgow in our own country. As to the Grecian colonial population of Asia Minor, it was, probably, as early as the days of Herodotus, considerably greater than that of the mother-country. In the days of the apostles, it was doubtless fifty times greater.

Besides, there is a most important point of difference to be observed, in by far the greater portion of the British colonization of the present century, as compared with that of the ancient Greeks. Our colonization, up to the period indicated, consisted for the most part of mere paupers, driven from their native country by sheer want, and importing into their adopted country nothing but labour of the rudest description, with characters often debased in the downward progress of the masses, from comparative comfort to the confines of starvation. It was one of the items of complaint of the late Legislative Council of New South Wales that " Our territorial revenue, diminished as it is by a most mistaken policy, is in a great measure confined to the introduction among us of people unsuited to our wants, and in many instances the outpourings of the poor houses and Unions of the United Kingdom, instead of being applied in directing to this colony a stream of vigorous and efficient labour, calculated to elevate the character of our industrial population." Grecian colonization, on the contrary, consisted of people of all ranks of society; and the humblest of these colonists were, for a reason which I shall state in the sequel, of much higher standing in society than the great majority of ours. There are people even in this age of refinement so low in the social scale, that they cannot be made to rise to a higher level; and it is positively dangerous to any community to allow whole masses of the people, as has been the case in many instances in the United Kingdom, to reach so hopeless a condition. Mere paupers make but very indifferent colonists anywhere; and the Greeks understood the art of colonization so well, that they never attempted it. To tell the real truth, however, they practised that art so successfully, that they escaped both the evil itself and the danger to society which the neglect of it is sure to occasion, and from which the United Kingdom has hitherto suffered so deeply, as it will continue to do till we alter our plan.

Another particular, in which our colonization system differs from that of the Greeks, is the large amount of convict colonization which has characterized our system. Since the year 1787, Great Britain has transported to the Australian colonies upwards of 100,000 convicts. There was nothing of the kind known among the ancient Greeks. Their colonists were always freemen—the freeest of the free and the bravest of the brave. But how did they get such people to colonize with, and in such numbers, too, under a system of morals and religion confessedly so inferior to ours? And how were they not incommoded with that immense accumulation of crime and of a criminal population, which almost compels us to form convict colonies? These are very important questions, which well deserve an answer.

SECTION VI—IS COLONIZATION ONE OF THE LOST ARTS?

Previous to the Gold Discoveries of 1851, when a new and unprecedented impulse was given to society throughout the British Empire, it seemed to be the general impression that, like several others of the useful arts of life, that were long successfully practised by the ancients, but are utterly unknown to the moderns, colonization, that noblest of all the arts, was entirely lost; and the comparative results we have given above of Grecian and British

colonization are surely sufficient to prove that the idea was
well founded. For whole, centuries in succession, colonization served to carry off the redundant population of Greece,
and to secure plenty of employment at remunerating wages,
and abundance of all things for those who remained. Now,
had British colonization previous to the Gold Discoveries
ever had the slightest effect on the enormous redundancy
of the population of Britain, with the single exception of
the comparative depopulation of Ireland in the years 1847-
1849—a fact, taking with it all its attendant circumstances,
in the highest degree discreditable to any civilized country?
Had it done anything to ensure to the myriads of labourers,
and artisans, and operatives of all classes, "a fair day's
wages for a fair day's work?" For the redundant population of the higher and middle classes of society, for whom
an eligible outlet is as prime a necessity of life as it is for
the most unskilled labourers in the land, British colonization had done nothing whatever. And what had it done in
the way of carrying off the dangerous classes of society of
all grades, from the Parliamentary agitator to the humblest
socialist and leveller in the land? Why, with the exception
of those whom the discovery of gold in Australia has
disposed of, they are all there yet, ready for anything that
may present itself in the mysterious future! It had done
something indeed in the way of showing what might be
done under a system at all characterised by common sense
and common honesty, for the creation of a market for the
produce of the mother-country, and for raising raw material
for her manufactures. But the trifle that was actually
done in either way, in comparison with what might have
been done, was perfectly contemptible. It was quite fair,
therefore, to regard colonization on a system at all adequate
to the urgent necessities of the case, as one of "the lost
arts."

It was so regarded at least by some of the ablest writers
of the day. Mr. Edward Gibbon Wakefield, one of these

writers, very justly speaks of our national system of
colonization in the following disparaging terms:—

"To use a heedless expression of the *Quarterly Review*,
it renders the colonies 'unfit abodes for any but convicts,
paupers, and desperate or needy persons.' It cures th'ose
who emigrate in spite of it, of their *maladie du pays*. It is
the one great impediment to the overflow of Britain's
excessive capital and labour. It has placed colonization
itself among *the lost arts*, and is thus a negative cause of
that excessive competition of capital with labour, in a
limited field of employment for both, which is now the
condition of England and the difficulty of her statesmen."

"It is remarkable," observes the Rev. Dr. (afterwards
Bishop) Hinds, late Dean of Carlisle, in a paper embodied
in Mr. Wakefield's work, "that notwithstanding the
greater facilities which modern times afford for the settlement and growth of colonies, the ancients were more successful with theirs than we are with ours. If we look back
on the history of Greek emigration especially, we find many
ruinous enterprises indeed, owing sometimes to the situation
for the new settlement being ill-chosen, sometimes to the
difficulties and dangers of rude and unskilful navigation;
sometimes again, to the imprudence of settlers, or the
jealousy of neighbours embroiling the infant state in
quarrels before it was strong enough to protect itself.
But supposing the colony to escape accidents of this kind,
it was generally so efficient in itself, so well organized and
equipped, as to thrive; and this at far less cost, it would
seem, and with less looking after, on the part of the parent
state, than is usually bestowed (and often bestowed in vain)
on our colonial establishments. After a few years, a colony
was seen, not unfrequently, to rise into a condition of
maturity that afforded support or threatened rivalry to the
state that had lately called it into existence.

"Our colonies are, in fact, far less liable to those accidents

which have been alluded to as occasionally interfering with
the success of those of ancient times, both from the greater
stock of useful knowledge, and from the greater power and
wealth possessed by those who now send out colonies.
And yet how many instances are there of modern European
states, carefully providing for a new plantation of its
people—expending on it ten times as much money and
labour as sufficed in earlier ages; and still this tender
plant of theirs will be stunted and sickly; and, if it does
not die, must be still tended and nursed like an exotic.
At length, after years of anxious looking after, it is found
to have cost the parent state more than it is worth; or,
perhaps, as in the case of the United States, we have
succeeded in rearing a child that disowns its parent—that
has acquired habits and feelings, and a tone and character
incompatible with that political *storge* which colonies
formerly are represented as entertaining, through generations for the mother country."

And again,—

"Want presses a part of the population of an old-
established community such as ours. *Those who are
suffering under this pressure* are encouraged to go and
settle themselves elsewhere, in a country whose soil,
perhaps, has been ascertained to be fertile, its climate
healthy, and its other circumstances favourable for the
enterprise. The protection of our arms, and the benefit of
free commercial intercourse with us and with other nations,
are held out as inducements to emigrate. We are liberal,
perhaps profuse, in our grants of aid from the public purse.
We moreover furnish for our helpless community a government, and perhaps laws; and appoint over them some tried
civil or military servant of the state, to be succeeded by
others of the same high character. Our newspapers are
full of glowing pictures of this land of milk and honey. All
who are needy and discontented—all who seek in vain at

home for independence and comfort and future wealth, are called upon to seize the golden moment, and repair to it.

"'Eja!
Quid statis? Nolint. Atque licet esse beatis!

Those who do go, have, for the most part made a reluctant choice between starvation and exile. They go, often indeed with their imaginations full of vague notions of future riches, for which they are nothing the better: but they go with a consciousness of being *exiled;* and when they arrive at their destination it is an exile."

And again, after alluding to the wonderful superiority of the Greeks in the art of colonization, the worthy bishop adds, —

"If the art of founding such colonies as theirs be indeed one of the *artes perditæ*, it is well to be sensible of the difference and the cause of it, that we may at least not deceive ourselves by calculating on producing similar effects by dissimilar and inadequate means.

SECTION VII.—QUACK SALVE FOR BAD SORES; OR, THE TREE OF ENGLISH SOCIETY TO BE TRANSPLANTED TO THE COLONIES!

And what is the *panacea* which this worthy bishop, *who has evidently had no colonial experience,* proposes for the remedy or cure of these serious national evils? We must allow him to state it in his own words :—

"The main cause of this difference may be stated in few words. We send out colonies of the limbs, without the belly and the head ;—of needy persons, many of them mere paupers, or even criminals ; colonies made up of *a single class* of persons in the community, and that the most helpless, and the most unfit to perpetuate our national character, and to become the fathers of a race whose habits of thinking and feeling shall correspond to those which, in the meantime, we are cherishing at home. The ancients, on the contrary, sent out *a representation of the parent state—colonists from all ranks.* We stock the farm with creeping and climbing plants, without any trees of firmer growth for them to entwine round. A hop-ground left without poles, the plant matted confusedly together, and scrambling on the ground in tangled heaps, with here and there some clinging to rank thistles and hemlocks, would be an apt emblem of a modern colony. They began by nominating to the honourable office of captain or leader of the colony, one of the chief men, if not the chief man of the state, — like the queen-bee leading the workers. Monarchies provided a prince of the blood-royal; an aristocracy its choicest nobleman; a democracy its most influential citizen. These naturally carried along with them some of their own station in life,—their companions and friends; some of their immediate dependents also—of those between themselves and the lowest class; and were encouraged in various ways to do so. The lowest class again followed with alacrity, because they found themselves moving *with*, and not *away from* the state of society in which they had been living. It was the same social and political union under which they had been born and bred; and to prevent any contrary impression being made, the utmost solemnity was observed in transferring the rites of pagan superstition. They carried with them their gods—their festivals—their games; all, in short, that held together, and kept entire the fabric of society as it existed in the parent state. Nothing was left behind that could be moved,—of all that the heart or eye of an exile misses. The new colony was made to appear as if time or chance had reduced the whole community to smaller dimensions, leaving it still essentially the same home and country to its surviving members. It consisted of a general contribution of members from all classes, and so became, on its first settlement, a mature state, with all the compo-

nent parts of that which sent it forth.   It was a transfer of
population, therefore, which gave rise to no sense of
degradation, as if the colonists were thrust out from a
higher to a lower description of community."

Again, speaking of the emigration of the humbler
classes—"the uneducated clown, the drudging mechanic"
—the Bishop proceeds :—

" He has been accustomed, perhaps, to see the squire's
house and park; and he misses this object, not only when
his wants, which found relief there, recur; but simply
because he, from a child, has been accustomed to see
gentry in the land."

And how is this desideratum to be supplied, that a
veritable colonial aristocracy may exist, so that the
" uneducated clown, or drudging mechanic," may enjoy
the interesting and enlivening prospect of a "squire's
house and park, and of gentry in the land" of his adoption?   Why, the Bishop shall again answer the question
himself :—

"Offer an English gentleman of influence, and competent fortune (though such, perhaps, may fall short of
his wishes) a sum of money, however large, to quit his
home permanently and take a share in the foundation of a
colony; and the more he possesses of those generous traits
of character which qualify him for the part he would have
to act, the less likely is he to accept the bribe.   But offer
him a patent of nobility for himself and his heirs,—offer
him an hereditary station in the government of the future
community; and there will be some chance of his acceding
to the proposal.   And he would not go alone.   He would
be followed by some few of those who are moving in the
same society with him—near relations, intimates.   He
would be followed by some, too, of an intermediate grade
between him and the mass of needy persons that form the
majority of the colony—his intermediate dependents—

persons connected with them, or with the members of his household. And if not *one*, but some half-dozen gentlemen of influence were thus tempted out, the sacrifice would be less felt by each, and the numbers of respectable emigrants which their united influence would draw after them so much greater. A colony so formed would fairly represent English society, and every new comer would have his own class to fall into; and to whatever class he belonged he would find its relation to the others, and the support derived from the others, much the same as in the parent country. There would then be little more in Van Dieman's Land, or in Canada, revolting to the habits and feelings of an emigrant than if he had merely shifted his residence from Sussex to Cumberland or Devonshire,—little more than a change of natural scenery."

And again the worthy bishop adds :—

"The desirable consummation of the plan would be, that a specimen or sample, as it were, of all that goes to make up society in the parent country should *at once* be transferred to its colony. Instead of sending out seedlings, and watching their uncertain growth, *let us try whether a perfect tree will not bear transplanting* : if it succeeds, we shall be saved so much expense and trouble in the rearing; as soon as it strikes its roots into the new soil it will shift for itself,"

To the same effect, the late Charles Buller, Esq., M.P., in his famous speech on Systematic Colonization, delivered in the House of Commons on the 6th April, 1843, insists upon the same specific of a complete transference of the whole fabric of English society to the colonies.*

"If you wish colonies to be rendered generally useful to all classes in the mother-country—if you wish them to be prosperous, to reflect back the civilization, and habits, and feelings of their parent stock, and to be and long to remain integral parts of your empire—*care should be taken*

* Inserted as an Appendix to Mr. Wakefield's work.

that society should be carried out in something of the form in
which it is seen at home—that it should contain something, at
least, of all the elements that go to make it up here, and that it
should continue under those influences that are found effectual
for keeping us together in harmony.   On such principles alone
have the foundations of successful colonies been laid.
Neither Phœnician, nor Greek, nor Roman, nor Spaniard—
no, nor our own great forefathers—when they laid the
foundation of an European society, on the continent, and
in the islands of the Western World, ever dreamed of
colonizing with one class of society by itself, and that the
most helpless for shifting for itself. The foremost men of
the ancient republics led forth their colonies; each expedition was in itself an epitome of the society which it
left; the solemn rites of religion blessed its departure from
its home; and it bore with it the images of its country's
gods, to link it for ever by a common worship to its ancient
home. The government of Spain sent its dignified clergy
out with some of its first colonists. The noblest families
in Spain sent their youngest sons to settle in Hispaniola,
and Mexico, and Peru. Raleigh quitted a brilliant court
and the highest spheres of political ambition, in order to
lay the foundation of the colony of Virginia; Lord Baltimore and the best Catholic families founded Maryland;
Penn was a courtier before he became a colonist; a set of
noble proprietors established Carolina, and intrusted the
framing of its constitution to John Locke; the highest
hereditary rank in this country below the peerage was
established in connection with the settlement of Nova Scotia,
and such gentlemen as Sir Harry Vane, Hampden, and
Cromwell did not disdain the prospect of a colonial career.
In all these cases the emigration was of every class. The
mass, as does the mass everywhere, contributed its labour
alone; but they were encouraged by the presence, guided
by the counsels, and supported by the means of the wealthy
and educated, whom they had been used to follow and

honour in their own country. In the United States the constant and large migration from the old to the new states is a migration of every class; the middle classes go in quite as large proportion as the labouring; the most promising of the educated youth are the first to seek the new career. And hence it is that society sets itself down complete in all its parts in the back settlements in the United States; that every political, and social, and religious institution of the old society is found in the new at the outset; that every liberal profession is abundantly supplied; and that, as Captain Marryatt remarks, you find in a town of three or four years' standing, in the back part of New York or Ohio, almost every luxury of the old cities."

In short, Mr. Buller's *panacea* is precisely the same as the Bishop's—the tree of English society must be carefully taken up, with a good ball of earth round the roots, and transplanted whole and entire to Canada or Australia. I suspect, however, that both the Bishop and Mr. Buller got this tree originally from the Wakefield Nursery; for it was generally understood that, in the year 1840, when the article of which the following is an extract was published in the *Colonial Gazette*, on the 21st of May, of that year, Mr. Edward Gibbon Wakefield was the mainspring and chief supporter of that journal:—

" It has been mooted of late years, whether colonization be not one of the lost arts. The question was suggested by a comparison between the signal advancement of the colonies of Ancient Greece, which commonly equalled, and sometimes surpassed, their Parent States in less than a century, and the slow progress of modern civilization towards wealth and greatness. But the question was solved as soon as asked: if the art of colonization were lost it has been recovered, by the inquiry which has made known the cause of rapid advancement in the one case, and of stagnation in the other.

" In ancient colonization the powers of society were

transplanted complete. The colony was matured before its departure, by the most careful preparation.; it comprised all ranks and classes—the most eminent citizens in war and learning; a martial army for land or sea; and abundance of slaves, as the means of ample production. It carried with it, too, renowned teachers for intended schools; and the sacred fire, which was religiously preserved, for temples to be built. Its removal was like the transplanting of a full-grown tree, with sufficient precautions for its growth in a new situation; so that the only change was the change of place.

"Modern colonization, on the other hand, has, for the most part, been a loose scramble, and, at best, very defective in some important particulars. A good half, it has been reckoned, of the settlements which have emanated from modern Europe, actually perished from want of foresight and preparation; and the most prosperous of them have exhibited a long struggle of a moral or economical kind, which might have been averted by the adoption of the Greek principle of forecast and completeness."

This idea, which passed for a profoundly original one at the time, *took* remarkably well in the United Kingdom. It made the complete round of the British periodical press, and served, like the celebrated Paganini's single fiddle-string, as the cord on which every "able editor" in the land, whether metropolitan or provincial, played off his "articles," or "series of articles," on "Systematic Colonization," forsooth! explaining, till the thing became perfectly nauseous, that what *he* meant by "colonization" was not "emigration," or a mere "shovelling out of paupers;" but the transplantation to the colonies of the whole tree of English society and civilization, roots and all. It may be taken for granted, therefore, that, in the flourishing settlement of *No-man's-Land*, which was doubtless formed about that period, on the newly-discovered principle of colonization, this tree will be found growing with remarkable luxuriance; so that the famous Arabian "bird called the Roc" will build its nest every year in its topmost branches, while that ancient mariner, "Sinbad the Sailor," will be seen reposing under its shade.

The fact is, this idea of the transplantation to a colony of the whole tree of English society, is the merest fallacy imaginable. It has no foundation whatever either in reason or in experience; and the circumstance of its having *taken* so remarkably at the time it was put forth, only shows how exceedingly gullible both the press and the people of England uniformly are on all subjects relating to the colonies. The truth is, they see and feel universally that they are all wrong somehow, and "out of order" in their colonial system; and they catch at any Morrison's or Holloway's Pills that may be offered them to "put them to rights." And when such national "pills" are duly "gilded," and advertised, by men of mark in the world, like the late Mr. Buller, Bishop Hinds, and Mr. Wakefield, who is there who would not provide himself with a *four and sixpenny box ?*

The simple truth is, the tree of English society is incapable of transplantation to any colony under the sun. It would never stand the salt water. It would be sure to lose its vegetative power in crossing the Line. And if it lived at all to reach Australia or New Zealand, it would soon wither and die in the midst of the far stronger and healthier indigenous vegetation.

The idea of the transplantation of the tree of English society to the colonies proceeds on the notable assumption that, if such a transplantation took place, the different parts of society—the trunk, the roots, the branches, and the leaves—would preserve the same relative proportions to each other, and maintain the same relative distances as in the parent soil. Now any person who has had the slightest Colonial experience knows that the very reverse of this is the fact. Suppose, for instance, that the population of a whole English county could be transplanted—each individual with the precise amount of property and qualifications he possesses at home—to some favourable locality, comprising perhaps a million of acres of land of average quality in Australia, the goodly tree of English society would be nowhere recognizable in a single twelvemonth ; the relative proportions of its different parts would be hopelessly destroyed, and the relative distances perhaps in no instance preserved. The man who had carried out plenty of money with him, without the requisite ability to lay it out advantageously, would be sure to lose it, if not in extravagant living, at least in unnecessarily expensive improvements, and in unprofitable and ruinous speculations; while "the uneducated clown," Joe Tomkins, perhaps, who commenced as a day labourer, and had reared a comfortable cottage for his family with his own hands on the bit of ground he had purchased with his first savings, would very soon work himself up into the possession of a well-cultivated and well-stocked colonial farm ; and as he looked around him on his rapidly increasing property, and his fat white-haired urchins of colonial children playing happily around him, instead of being oppressed with the absence of "the squire's house and park," about which the worthy Bishop fancies he must be perpetually dreaming, he will have learned to sing, what was once the old English, but is now the colonial song—

> "When Adam delved and Eve span,
> Where was then the gentleman ?"

"Ha! but I am much mistaken if that is not the old squire himself, riding up leisurely among the trees yonder, on his old racer. He has been spending a great deal of money to no good purpose in draining a swamp, and has, unfortunately, got rather behind. He is coming, I dare say, to ask some assistance from Tomkins, who was formerly a commmon labourer in his parish in England; and often very badly off. He used then to call him Joe; but times are a little changed now. I will just make a note of their conversation.

Joe Tomkins.—Good morrow, Squire.

Squire.—Good morning, Mr. Tomkins! Pray, would you oblige me with the loan of one of your teams for a day or two, to help me in with my stuff; for these fellows are leaving me in dozens for the diggings, and we are sadly behind with everything?

Joe Tomkins.—With all my heart, squire; I'll send you two of my lads, with a couple of teams; for we have got all *in* here, and can help a neighbour at a pinch.

Squire.—Thank you! Thank you! Mr. Tomkins."

The idea, therefore, that colonization, properly so called, bears any resemblance in its nature and results to the transplantation of a full-grown tree from its native soil in England to some favourable field beyond seas, is utterly untenable; being based on an assumption which is contrary alike to reason and to uniform experience. What then, it may be asked, does colonization resemble? Why, suppose a chemist should take a handful of chemical salts, all of different component parts and qualities, and throw them all together into some common solvent, say boiling water, —they will all dissolve, and nothing but the pure element will appear for a time to the naked eye. But as the water cools and evaporates, a number of specks, or centre-points of crystallization, will appear throughout the liquid; and these will gradually attract the floating particles of congenial character, till the whole mass arranges itself into new forms of crystallization, as perfect and beautiful as the first, but in all likelihood totally different in their component parts and qualities. In like manner, take people in any number from all classes of society in the mother-country,—from the prince to the peasant,—and set them down

N

together upon the shore of some colony or new-found-land, the original qualities and proportions of the different component parts of the mass will soon disappear; society, so to speak, will assume a new form of crystallization, exhibiting totally different phases and qualities from the first; and nature's own aristocracy will rise to the surface in the process, and assume, by universal consent, the place to which it is entitled. For it is pre-eminently absurd, and contrary to all experience, to suppose that society can possibly exist in any country without exhibiting *heads* as well as *tails*. With the permission, therefore, of Mr. Wakefield, Bishop Hinds, and the executors of the late Mr. Buller, I will hew down this beautiful tree of theirs, and *burn it off*, as we colonists do with the real tree, as it stands very much in the way of efficient colonization.

Before doing so, however, I must have one word more with the Bishop about the notable expedient of creating nobilities for the colonies, which he suggests as a *sine qua non* towards efficient colonization. This is the more necessary, as the idea has since been started in New South Wales; where it was actually proposed, by Mr. W. C. Wentworth and others, when called to frame a Constitution for that colony, which was ratified in the Imperial Act of 1855, that an order of Colonial Nobility should be created by her Majesty, to be attached to the possession of a certain amount of property, and to be transmissible by hereditary descent: and that out of these rich and rare materials an Upper House of Legislation should be constructed, on the good old hereditary principle; it being a well-ascertained fact that the ability to make wise and good laws for any people is transmissible by natural descent from any person who owns a certain amount of landed property! But as the idea was scouted by the common sense of the colonial public, it is quite unnecessary to say anything further on the subject.

SECTION VIII.—THE TRUE CAUSE OF THE INSIGNIFICANT AMOUNT OF BRITISH, AS COMPARED WITH GRECIAN COLONIZATION—BAD GOVERNMENT AND THE LUST OF EMPIRE ON THE PART OF THE MOTHER COUNTRY.

Spain and Portugal, which, at the era of the doubling of the Cape of Good Hope and the discovery of America, by the Spaniards and Portuguese, respectively, were the first Maritime Powers of Europe, had preceded England in the heroic work of Colonization by a whole century at least ; but England—without ever attempting beforehand to bring the whole question of Colonization to the light of reason and the test of historical experience, as she ought to have done, or to ascertain the law of nature and the ordinance of God in regard to it, and without caring in the least as to whether her own procedure in the matter was, or was not, in accordance with the sacred and inalienable rights of men—merely adopted the false principles which these powers had established in the management of their colonies, and blindly followed the superlatively bad example they had set her.

" The leading principle of colonization in the Maritime States of Europe" (Great Britain among the rest), observes a well known writer of last century, " was commercial monopoly. The word *monopoly* in this case admitted a very extensive interpretation. It comprehended the monopoly of supply, the monopoly of colonial produce, and the monopoly‚ of colonial manufacture. By the first, the colonists were prohibited from resorting to foreign markets for the supply of their wants ; by the second, they were compelled to bring their chief staple commodities to the mother-country alone; and by the third, to bring them to her in a raw or unmanufactured state, that her own manufacturers might secure to themselves all the advantages arising from their further improvement. This latter

principle was carried so far in the Colonial system of Great
Britain as to induce the late Earl of Chatham to declare, in
Parliament, that the British Colonists in America had no
right to manufacture even a nail for a horse-shoe."*

"The maintenance of this monopoly," says Dr. Adam
Smith, " has hitherto been the principal, or, more properly,
perhaps, the sole end and purpose of the dominion which
Great Britain assumes over her colonies. * * * The
monopoly is the principal badge of their dependency, *and
it is the sole fruit which has hitherto been gathered from that
dependency.*"†

It would be difficult to determine which of the Maritime States of Europe, Great Britain included, was the
most arbitrary and exacting, the most irrational and
suicidal, in the management of this monopoly. Spain was
doubtless the first in the order of time, but Great Britain
was not a whit behind her in folly and injustice. "The
commercial policy of the Spanish government," says Mr.
Merivale, "towards its continental colonies has been often
described, and exhibits the most perfect monument of
systematic tyranny, of which any age has furnished an
example." "As late as 1803, when Humboldt was at
Mexico, an order was despatched from Madrid for the
rooting up of all the vines in the northern dependencies of
that province."‡

Again—"Power was exclusively in the hands of Spaniards, and most colonial offices were sold in Madrid."
"Of 170 viceroys," say the Revolutionists of Buenos
Ayres in their first manifesto, "who have governed the
provinces of America, four only have been Americans; of
610 captains general and governors, only fourteen."

---

* Bryan Edward's *History of the West Indies*, vol. ii. p. 565.
† *Wealth of Nations*, book ɪv. chap. vii.
‡ Merivale's *Lectures on Colonization*, vol. i. p. 7 & 9.

"Even the very clerks of the government offices were almost exclusively European."*

Their very revenues were abstracted for purposes and objects in which the colonists had no concern whatever. "Mexico, in Humboldt's time, furnished annually 6,000,000 dollars, over and above all expenses of government and defence."†

But Great Britain proved a very apt pupil under the teaching of her chosen instructresses, Spain and Portugal. For if the British Government did nothing, comparatively, to *promote* colonization in America before the War of Independence, it did enough, in every possible way, and with singular success, to harass and oppress the actual colonists, and thereby virtually to put a stop to colonization altogether. For this is the whole secret of the paltry and insignificant results of British colonization up to that memorable period, as compared with the magnificent results of the colonization of the ancient Greeks. This antagonistic action of the British Government, in regard to American colonization, previous to the revolutionary war, was unfortunately not peculiar to any one Royal house or government—it was alike the characteristic of all; the difference to the American colonists being only in the degree of badness: for even the Revolution of 1688 could scarcely be called a revolution for them. Even the "Glorious and Immortal Memory" is associated with acts of the grossest injustice and tyranny in America; and the affair of Glenco is not the only blot on the fair escutcheon of William the Third. I shall subjoin a few illustrations of the truth of this statement from the multitude of a similar kind that might easily be adduced.

In the year 1661, when the people of Massachusetts apprehended some attack upon their chartered rights on

* Merivale's *Lectures*, vol. i. p. 10.
† Merivale's *Lectures*, vol. i. p. 20.

the part of Charles the Second, "The General Court," as
we are informed by the historian Grahame, "appointed a
committee of eight of the most eminent persons in the
colony to prepare a report, ascertaining the extent of their
rights, and the limits of their obedience; and, shortly
after, the court, in conformity with the report of the committee, framed and published a series of declaratory
resolutions, expressive of their solemn and deliberate
opinion on these important subjects. It was declared
that the patent (under God) is the original compact
and main foundation of the provincial commonwealth, and
of its institutions and policy; that the governor and
company are, by the patent, a body politic, empowered
to confer the rights of freemen; and that the freemen so constituted have authority to elect annually their
governor, assistants, representatives, and all other officers ;
that the magistracy, thus composed, hath all requisite
power, both legislative and executive, for the government
of all the people, whether inhabitants or strangers, without
appeal, except against laws repugnant to those of England;
that the provincial government is entitled by every means,
even by force of arms, to defend itself both by land and sea
against all who should attempt injury to the province or its
inhabitants ; and that any imposition injurious to the provincial community, and contrary to its just laws would be
an infringement of the fundamental rights of the people of
New England."*

These declaratory resolutions were accordingly transmitted
to the king by deputies, who were appointed, and sent home
expressly for the purpose, by the provincial legislature ;
but all the efforts and influence of these deputies could not
prevent the instituting of legal proceedings against the
colony in the infamous law courts of the period, to deprive
it of its charter, and to reduce it under the arbitrary

* Grahame's *History of the United States,* i. 310.

government of the Crown. From circumstances, however, which it is unnecessary to detail, the forfeiture of the charter of Massachusetts was not formally declared till after the accession of James the Second. As soon as that monarch had ascended the throne, other deputies were sent home to England, to plead the cause of the colonists with the king; who, agreeably to his usual custom, received them roughly, and demanded an unconditional surrender of the charter, on the part of the colonists, which the deputies of course refused. A writ of *Quo Warranto* was therefore issued against the colony in the year 1683, and the charter was at length adjudged to be forfeited, on the most frivolous pretences, on the 2nd of July, 1685. The chartered right of the colony to elect its own governor being thus taken away, Sir Edward Andros, an unprincipled tool of James the Second, was appointed Governor of New England during the reign of that monarch, and continued in power till the Revolution of 1688.

"But why," the reader will doubtless ask, "why rake up the unjust and oppressive acts of that infamous and dismal period, as if its acts of injustice and oppression had ever been either recognised or approved of by any subsequent government of England? The charter of the metropolitan City of London was declared to be forfeited in precisely the same way, and at precisely the same period as the colonial charter of Massachusetts; but was it not speedily restored again by our great deliverer, William of Orange, whose 'glorious and immortal memory' all true Englishmen must ever revere?" There was no doubt a good and sufficient reason for this very politic procedure of William; for he knew well, that if he had refused to restore the charter of the City of London, the people of England would very soon have sent him back again to Holland. But unfortunately it was far otherwise with the charter of Massachusetts, which King William *refused to restore*, although deputies had actually been sent over

from America to solicit its restoration; thereby meanly
taking advantage of the knavery of his predecessor.
The people of Massachusetts accordingly never recovered
the rights and privileges which had been solemnly guaranteed to them, on the faith of the Crown, under the
Royal Charter of Charles I.,* till the revolution of
1776—the only revolution that was ever of any service to
America. But the people of England—those sworn friends
of freedom and of the rights of men—where were *they*, and
what did *they* do all the while? Why, they just cared as
little for a mere colony *then* as they do *now;* they sided
with their Government, and left it to do as it pleased with
the colonies, as they have always done, and as Sir George
Lewis very honestly informs us they will do yet in any
similar case.

" In any struggle for power between their own country
and the dependency, the people of the dominant country
are likely to share all the prejudices of their government,
and to be equally misled by a love of domination and by
delusive notions of national dignity."*

"It was with great reluctance," adds the historian of
America, "that King William surrendered to the American colonies *any* of the acquisitions which regal authority
had derived from the tyrannical usurpations of his predecessors; and his reign was signalized by various attempts

---

* By the Charter of Incorporation granted to the colony of
Massachusetts Bay, in the year 1628, by Charles the First, the first
governor of the company and his council were named by the king:
the right of electing their successors was vested in the freemen of the
corporation. The executive power was committed to the governor and
a council of assistants; the legislation to the body of freemen, who
were empowered to enact statutes and ordinances for the good of the
community, not inconsistent with the laws of England.—Grahame's
History of the United States, i. 206.

* Lewis, *on the government of Dependencies*, p. 254.

to invade the popular rights which at first he had been compelled to respect or to restore."†

Witness the following clause of an Act of Parliament of the 7 and 8 William III., establishing an arbitrary authority over the colonies :—

"Be it further enacted and declared by the authority aforesaid, that all laws, bye-laws, usages, or customs at this time, or which HEREAFTER shall be in practice, or endeavoured, or pretended to be in force or practice, in any of the said plantations, which are in any wise repugnant to the before-mentioned laws, or any of them, so far as they do relate to the said plantations, or any of them, or which are anywise repugnant to this present Act, *or to any other law hereafter to be made in this kingdom,* so far as such law shall relate to and mention the said plantations, *are illegal, null and void, to all intents and purposes whatsoever.*"*

When Sir Edmund Andros, James the Second's Governor of New England, demanded a surrender of the charter of Connecticut, the precious document was brought forth by the officer in charge of it, and laid upon the table of the General Court ; of which the members were doubtless looking at it mournfully, as they conceived, for the last time, when the lights were suddenly extinguished, and the charter was carried off in the dark by some person unknown, and concealed in the hollow of a tree till after the Revolution of 1688. By that charter the command of the militia of the province was assigned to the Governor of Connecticut, who was appointed to his office by popular election. Notwithstanding this chartered right, however, King William, in the year 1693, commissioned Fletcher, *his* Governor of New York, to command the troops of Connecticut. Fletcher accordingly proceeded to Connecticut, and in the presence of the assembled troops began to read his

† Grahame's *History of the United States*, ii. 232.
* 7 and 8 William III. cap. 7., sec, 9.

commission from the king. The colonial officer, however, in command of the troops under the Governor of Connecticut, ventured to remonstrate against this unconstitutional proceeding; but Governor Fletcher, disregarding his remonstrance, and continuing to read his royal commission, the officer commanded the drums to beat, to drown his voice, which they did accordingly. Fletcher was furious at this interruption, and stormed and raged accordingly; but the Connecticut officer very coolly ordered the drums to beat the louder, and the excitement becoming general, the "Glorious and Immortal Memory's" Governor of New York was literally *drummed* out of the province of Connecticut, which was thenceforth left to be governed according to law! It would scarcely be credited, if it were not the fact, that within five years of the glorious and happy Revolution of 1688, the very creature of that Revolution, William the Third, should have attempted, through his functionaries in America, to do the very same thing that had so shortly before cost one of the Stuarts his head, and another his crown—viz., to substitute the royal will for the laws of the land. But the good people of England had no intention, it seems, in making a Revolution for themselves, to make one also for America. They left the Americans to perform that necessary service for themselves, and they did so accordingly.

"The preservation of the original charter of Connecticut had always been a subject of regret to the Revolution government of England; and various attempts were successively made to withdraw or abridge the popular franchises which it conferred. We have remarked the encroachment attempted by King William in the year 1693 on the chartered rights of the province, and the determined opposition by which his policy was defeated. In the year 1701 a more formidable attempt was made to undermine those rights altogether, by a bill which was introduced into the English House of Lords for rescinding all the existing

American charters, and subjecting the relative provinces to the immediate dominion of the Crown."*

Of the great and good deeds of Queen Anne for the promotion of colonization in America, I shall only mention one, which is sufficiently characteristic.

" On the removal of Nicholson from the government of Virginia in 1704, this dignity was conferred as a sinecure office on George, Earl of Orkney, who enjoyed it for *thirty-six years*, and received in all £42,000 of salary from a people who never once beheld him among them."†

The accession of the House of Hanover seems to have mended the matter very little in regard to the treatment of the American colonies by the Whig government of the period.   For

" In the very first year of the king's reign (George I., anno 1715) a bill was introduced in the British Parliament for *abolishing all the charters of the various provinces of New England*."‡

How a bill of such beneficent intentions towards the American colonists could have broken down, under the paternal government of the Whigs, it is difficult to conceive; for the ministry of the period were not destitute of the power to do good when they pleased, and were by no means scrupulous about the means of doing it, in so far as money could effect their object.   Nay, the same historian informs us, that about this period, and until the Revolution of 1776, " the whole strain of British legislation with regard to America disclosed the purpose of raising up a nation of customers for the merchants and manufacturers of the parent state, and acknowledged the idea that *the American communities existed solely for the advantage of Britain*."§

* Grahame's *History of America*, iii. 32.   † *Ibid*, iii. 67.
       ‡ *Ibid*, iii. 72.   § *Ibid*, iii. 137.

There can be no doubt of the truth of this assertion; for even the famous Earl of Chatham, patriot though he was, declared in Parliament, in explanation and illustration of the British constitution in regard to colonies, as I have stated above, that "the American colonists had no right to manufacture even a horse-shoe nail," without the express permission of the Sovereign Power. But the British government of the period had evidently been taking their lessons in colonization from a very experienced master in the art, the king of Spain; for, according to Professor Heeren, "the original character of the Spanish colonies, namely that of mining settlements, led naturally to commercial restrictions. A free admittance to foreigners, under such circumstances, would have been absurd. The advantages of general trade, if at all considered, held a very inferior rank; the main object was to import into Spain, and to Spain alone, the immediate treasure of America. Even to the Spaniards it might have been evident that the prosperity of the colonies was not likely to be advanced by these means—but *the prosperity of their colonies, as usually understood, was no design of theirs.*"*

That no opportunity of harassing and oppressing the American colonies might be neglected, and that no British monarch should be precluded from a share in this good work, an abortive attempt was made to tax the Americans, in the reign of George the Second; and on its abandonment, another vigorous effort was made in Parliament to abolish the colonial charters.

"Another measure," observes the historian, "which succeeded the relinquished design of taxing the American colonies, was the repetition of an attempt, of which we have already witnessed several instances, to invade their chartered systems of liberty. A bill was introduced into the British Parliament in the year 1748, by which all the

* *Heeren, ubi supra,* 58

American charters were abolished, and the king's instructions to the provincial governors were rendered equivalent to legal enactments."*

The tyrannical aggressions of the ministry of George the Third upon the liberties of America, which led at length to the Revolution of 1776, and the freedom and independence of the American colonies, are sufficiently known to render it quite unnecessary to show what that venerated British monarch did for the promotion of colonization in America. It is deeply to be lamented, indeed, by every lover of his country, that the iniquitous conduct of a band of heartless and unprincipled men, in that gloomy period of our national history, should have given birth to a spirit of bitter hostility towards the British name on the part of a large portion of the citizens of the United States—a spirit which will doubtless subsist for generations to come. There was no such feeling towards their mother country, on the part of the Greek colonies of antiquity; and we shall show in the sequel the reason why.

It must be evident from these brief sketches, which might easily be multiplied to any number, so as to exhibit innumerable acts of the most unprincipled and tyrannical character, on the part of British governors of the colonies during the period in question, that the only object which the British government ever pursued, in connection with colonization, throughout the whole course of the colonial history of Great Britain, previous to the war of American Independence, was *empire*—and that the only passion with which 'that government was ever actuated towards the colonies was the *lust of empire*.†

It must be equally evident that, in the pursuit of this

---

* Grahame, iii. 308.

† I have heard it said by a person in one of the first departments of the state, that the present contest (with the American colonies) is for DOMINION on the side of the colonies, as well as on ours: and so it is indeed; but with this essential difference: *we* are struggling for

worthless *shadow*—in the gratification of this unhallowed
lust—all the proper and legitimate objects of colonization
were sacrificed and lost. For while every petty Grecian
state had its own colony, or series of colonies, each of which
became a mother-country in its turn, and was often, as in
the cases of Syracuse and Miletus, probably four times the
extent of the parent state, both in wealth and in population,
the whole population of the British colonies, after a period
of a hundred and seventy years, did not exceed two millions
and a half, at the commencement of the War of Independence. Such at least is the estimate of Mr. M'Gregor, a
highly competent authority. But of that amount upwards
of half a million were Africans; and of the remaining two
millions, at least one-fourth were the descendants of
foreigners! Considering the extent, population, and resources of the United Kingdom, this result of British
colonization, for so long a period, is not only insignificant
but humiliating; whether we regard colonization merely
as a noble and *heroic work*, with Lord Bacon, or view it in
the far higher and Christian light of its being the peculiar
mission of Britain in the modern world. It is abundantly
evident, at all events, that so insignificant an amount of
colonization as this result gives, when contrasted with the
colonizing power of Great Britain, could never have secured
to the mother-country the attainment of any one of the
proper and legitimate objects of colonization in any sensible
degree.

There can be no doubt, therefore, that it was simply and
solely the impolitic and suicidal attempt to combine with
colonization the pursuit of *empire*, and the exercise of an
unrighteous domination over subject states and people,
beyond seas, who had a natural, inherent, and indefeasible

dominion over OTHERS; *they* are struggling for SELF-dominion—the
noblest of all blessings.—*Observations on Civil Liberty, and the Justice
and Policy of the War with America.* By Dr. Price. 1766. p. 74.

right to their freedom and independence, that made *us*, as the great colonizing nation of modern times, to differ so widely in this most important respect from the ancient Greeks; who had precisely the same national mission as ours in the ancient world. For who, except under the pressure of the direst necessity, would have chosen to forego the rights and the enjoyments of freemen in their fatherland, to share the hard fortunes of those self-expatriated men who were doomed to pass their dreary existence in countries so wretchedly and so disgracefully governed as the British colonies must have been, so far as Great Britain could have her finger in the colonial pie, previous to the War of American Independence?

It was under these circumstances of persecution at home, and tyranny and oppression abroad, that the Thirteen original colonies of America, like Israel in Egypt, grew and prospered; and became at length, from the smallest beginnings, through the indomitable energies of a British people, under the ennobling influences of their thorough Protestantism, a great nation.*

---

* I have much pleasure in presenting the candid reader with the following very remarkable Roman Catholic testimony to the influence of the thorough Protestantism of the founders of the earlier British Colonies of America, in moulding the institutions and in bringing about the national independence of that country.

"If we open history to examine the origin and the successive development of the United States of America, we shall meet a handful of poor and serious Protestants, exiled from their country for their religious opinions, and who came to establish themselves in the immense and fertile solitudes of the New World, to seek their own bread by the copious sweat of their brow; the population which they formed was then agricultural and commercial, was enterprising and active, was laborious and persevering, because its founders could not live without these qualities. Separated and delivered over to their own individual exertions, it was necessary that they should assist each other energetically; and among themselves a spirit of fraternity was developed, which multiplied without confounding individual strength.

The amount of British colonization out of which this nation arose, was insignificant in the extreme ; and the character and history of that colonization form one of the blackest pages in the annals of our country. But perhaps Great Britain never learned the art of colonization until after the American War. Let us see then if it be so from the result of her efforts since.

SECTION IX.—THE LUST OF EMPIRE, AND BAD GOVERNMENT, THE CHARACTERISTICS OF BRITISH COLONIZATION FROM THE WAR OF AMERICAN INDEPENDENCE TILL THE ADVENT OF RESPONSIBLE GOVERNMENT FOR AUSTRALIA, IN THE YEAR 1856.

One might have supposed that the Declaration of American Independence, and the calamitous results of her own folly and madness in attempting to counteract that great national revolution by a mere impotent display of physical force, would have taught Great Britain a salutary lesson, and led her to effect an immediate and thorough reform in her whole system of colonization ; but Great Britain was unfortunately too old and too proud to learn anything, even in this excellent " free school for

Separated from the bosom of the Catholic Church by their Protestant doctrines, they grew up, imbued with the contempt of her authority, and professed the dogma of the superiority of private reasoning ; *hence their sentiment of exalted and haughty independence.* Separated, lastly, by many leagues from their metropolis, they were accustomed to depend upon themselves without the necessity of any extraneous aid. Then a day arrived on which they considered their emancipation necessary, and without any change or transition, the sentiment of their laboriousness made them great, their position made them independent, and their customs and religion made them Republican. With them, as a French writer says, the name came after the substance, and the republic was constituted before it was proclaimed."—*El Universal,* (*a Mexican Paper*), Mexico, 1 Jan., 1853. Translated by the New York Correspondent of the *Times,* 26th March, 1853.

adults;" and the consequence has been, that her coloniza-
tion system has been incomparably worse since the War of
American Independence than it ever was before. Let the
following sketch of the actual state of things, in the
British colonies of Australia, up to the very recent period
I have indicated, bear witness to the fact:—

Imprimis, unlike the colonists of Virginia under Charles
I., no conceivable number of British subjects, congregated
together in *any* part of Australia were recognized as
having a right either to frame a constitution for their own
government, or to be consulted to give their concurrence
beforehand to one to be formed for them in England.
They might petition for one, and they might have to
repeat that petition for years together, as the people of
Port Phillip had to do for ten long years —suffering the
utmost inconvenience, hardship, and injustice, all the
while—before they got one at all; and when they did get
one at last, it might not have the slightest resemblance
to the one they would have chosen forthemselves. But the
humiliating fact was, they had no choice in the matter;—
like common beggars, British colonists had to take what
was offered them *by their betters*, or go without.

Item, the franchise was fixed *by authority*, and so fixed as
to exclude from all political rights and privileges a large
proportion of the intelligence and moral worth of the
colony; and the natural and necessary consequence was,
that a large proportion of the community became either
perfectly indifferent about their government, or animated
with the fiercest hatred towards the institutions of their
adopted country.

Item, instead of being allowed to choose their own
legislators, they were uniformly nominated by the Crown,
or in other words, by the Secretary of State for the Colonies,
or his principal Colonial functionary, the Governor; and
in all likelihood, they were so nominated that, for any real
service they were of to the community—otherwise than by

o

voting on all possible occasions against its proper interests—
a majority of these nominees might have been represented
by as many empty beer-barrels, with moveable heads on,
to second motions! A partial reform of this most iniquitous
system of government was effected at the instance of Lord
Stanley, afterwards Earl Derby, in the year 1842, when a
Legislative Council, to consist of two-thirds elective
members and the remaining third of Crown nominees, was
conceded to the Australian Colonies. But even after that
measure of reform was conceded, the Treasury Bench of
the first Legislative Council of New South Wales, constituted under Lord Stanley's Act, was a perfect *Refuge for
the Destitute;* and it was quite humiliating to see the sorry
figure its occupants made. Yet these were the men who
were holding the highest offices, as Heads of Departments,
and receiving the largest salaries in the country!

Item, nearly a third of the Ordinary Revenue of the
colony, besides the whole of the Land Revenue, was taken
out of the control of this mockery of a Legislature by Act
of Parliament, and appropriated for the payment of salaries
greatly above either the necessities of the case, or the
means of the people—as for instance, giving a salary
(£5,000 a year) to the Governor of less than two hundred
and fifty thousand colonists,—our number before the
Separation of Victoria,—equal to what is allotted to
the President of the United States, the first magistrate or
head of a sovereign and independent nation, numbering
upwards of thirty millions of souls! Nay, this salary was
afterwards increased—at the instance of a servile
worshipper of the rising sun—Sir William Denison,
forsooth!—to £7,000 a year!

Item, the little knot of officials, Crown nominees, and
servile colonists, into whose hands so preposterous a system
virtually threw the whole legislation of the colony,
arranged the Electoral Districts by an Act of the Local
Legislature, as they were permitted and authorised to do

by Act of the Imperial Parliament, so that fifteen thousand of the citizens of Sydney should have no more political weight or influence in the country, than fifteen hundred of the inhabitants of a frontier district seven hundred miles distant from the seat of government; the reason for this *artful dodge* being, that the inhabitants of Sydney were anxious for political improvement and general reform, while the inhabitants of the frontier district were almost exclusively tenants of the Crown and their servants, who could of course be very easily managed, especially at so great a distance.

Item, under this artful system, and in order to extend the influence and increase the number of the retainers of the Local Executive, the large revenue which was raised in the colony, as compared with its actual population, was expended in great measure in the maintenance of unnecessary offices, or in the payment of salaries greatly disproportioned to the services rendered to the community; insomuch that the construction of many public works of urgent necessity for the welfare and advancement of the colony, such as roads, bridges, tanks, reservoirs, breakwaters, &c., &c., was either not undertaken at all, or retarded and stopped for want of funds, while the appropriations even for the education of the colonial youth were paltry in the extreme.

Item, instead of having a fixed and liberal system for the disposal of waste land, as in the United States of America, the system in the Australian colonies, previous to the advent of responsible government, was changed, like the wages of Jacob, ten times, to the unspeakable annoyance and loss of the colonists; while the system in operation for many years thereafter was often so illiberally and oppressively administered, and the delays interposed by interested parties were so extremely vexatious, as to prove in numerous instances absolutely ruinous to the *bona fide* settler.*

---

* It is quite amusing to hear Lord Stanley, afterwards Earl Derby —

To form some idea of the arbitrary and irrational character of the system of government that prevailed under British domination in the Australian colonies, till the establishment of responsible government in 1856, it is only necessary to glance at the leading principles of the colonial administration of Earl Grey, who may be regarded as the last British Colonial Minister under the old *régime*. If his lordship, therefore, had been studying how he could best alienate the affections of the Australian colonies from the

after giving the colony of New South Wales the regular sham of a Constitution, of which I have just sketched out the leading features—in the year 1842, expressing his hope, in a despatch to the Governor, of date 5th September of that year, that the colonists would be duly grateful for the " small mercies they were going to receive."

" In conclusion, I have only to express my anxious, but confident hope, that the Act which I now transmit to you, conferring upon the inhabitants of New South Wales, powers so extensive for the administration of their own local affairs, will be received by them with feelings corresponding with those which have induced Her Majesty, by my advice, to divest herself of so large a portion of her authority over the internal management of the colony, and, with the aid of Parliament, to grant so large a measure of self-government ;—that the powers thus vested in the Local Legislature will be wisely and temperately exercised ;—and that her Majesty may have the high satisfaction of witnessing, as the result of her gracious boon to the colony, its continued advance in religion and morality; its steady progress in wealth and social improvement ; and the permanent happiness and contentment of her people.—I have the honor to be, sir, your most obedient, humble servant,

" STANLEY."

The following Notes, appended to a Return to an Address of the Legislative Council of New South Wales, in the year 1846, exhibiting the amount derived from the sales of waste land throughout the territory, during the ten years from 1836 to 1845 inclusive, will show the way in which this most important department of the public service was managed in the colonies under Downing Street domination.

" In the year 1831, Lord Ripon's regulations for the abolition of free grants, and the sale by auction of all Crown lands, were first promulgated in the colony.

mother-country, so as to ensure the speedy dismemberment
of the empire—which he now so strongly deprecates—
he could scarcely have adopted a fitter course of procedure
for the attainment of his object than the one he pursued
with remarkable steadiness and perseverance, during the
six years of his administration. Lord North, the real
author of the American Revolution, was evidently his
"Great Apollo;" and the spirit of that defunct statesman,

"1839.—In this year the minimum price was raised from 5s. to 12s.
per acre.

"1841.—In this year the system of sale at a fixed price of 1l. per
acre was introduced into the district of Port Phillip.

"1842.—In this year the system of sale by auction was resumed
throughout the colony, at a minimum upset price of 12s. per acre for
country lands, with liberty to select portions not bid for at the upset
price.

"1843.—In this year the minimum price was raised to £1 per acre,
by the Act of the Imperial Parliament 5th and 6th Victoria, cap. 36."

Here were six different systems, all established by authority, in
successive operation, for the disposal of land in New South Wales,
within the short period of twelve years! But what else could be
expected under a system of government which was so constantly
changing its head or main-spring as the Colonial Office? The
testimony of the late G. R. Porter, Esq., Secretary to the Board of
Trade, is most important on this subject. It is as follows :—

"With the exception of the analogous office of President of the
Board of Controul, the ministry of the Colonies has, during the
present century, been changed more frequently than any other of the
great offices of State. There were, during forty-eight years, eighteen
Secretaries of State for this department, one of whom, Earl Bathurst,
held the seals for fifteen years; so that the average tenure of the
remaining seventeen was under eighteen months. On the occurrence
of each of these changes the whole system of our colonial policy has
been liable to alteration; although, if there be one department of
Government which more than any other requires to be conducted upon
fixed principles, assuredly it must be that to which are confided the
variety of interests involved in the Colonial dependencies of the
kingdom, the inhabitants of which have no voice in the national
councils."—*The Progress of the Nation.*" By G. R. Porter, Esq.,
F.R.S. London, 1851. Page 725.

whose name will ever be associated with the disasters and dishonour of his country, was in reality the evil genius of the Colonial Office from the period of Earl Grey's accession to power, in the year 1846.

The grand object of Earl Grey's administration was to force upon the Australian colonies a continuance of the transportation system, in direct opposition, it is alleged, to his own express pledges on the subject, and certainly to the almost unanimous protest and remonstrances of the colonists. A great deal of casuistry was employed by the Colonial Office and its men of business, of that peculiar description which characterized the special pleading of the department in the case of the West India dispatches, to prove that Earl Grey never pledged himself not to continue transportation to Van Dieman's Land. But I confess I regard it as a matter of very little moment indeed whether he pledged himself or not; for I have yet to learn that the opinion of any Secretary of State, on any subject whatever affecting the interests of colonists, is to be weighed for one moment against the deliberate opinion of a whole series of British colonies. Every insult was heaped upon the colonies, and especially upon the unfortunate colony of Van Dieman's Land, in connection with this matter; every discreditable manœuvre was resorted to to steal a march upon them, and to worm out of them something that might be interpreted as an expression of acquiescence in the meditated infliction; everything was sacrificed to promote the convict policy of Earl Grey.

I had the honour, as one of the two Representatives of the city of Sydney in the Legislative Council of New South Wales, during the year 1850, to present the most numerously signed petition that had ever been presented to the Colonial Legislature, against the renewal of transportation to that colony. It had 36,589 names attached to it—names of persons of all ranks in society, and from all parts of the colony.* But although I had cordially participated from the first in the anti-transportation movement, and had protested, in the strongest manner, against the continuance of transportation to any of the actual colonies of Eastern Australia, or to any part of the eastern coast of that continent, I took occasion, in my speech on the subject in Council—as I had also done before a Select Committee of the House of Commons in the year 1837—to express my decided approval of transportation in the abstract, as a species of punishment for crime. I could not therefore be regarded as a prejudiced witness in the case, or as being actuated by mere party spirit, in opposing a measure of importance in the eyes of the Colonial Office. On the contrary, I considered the continuance of transportation as one of the political necessities of the British Empire; and I regarded the punishment itself, if properly carried out, as both humane and reformatory in a very high degree. But as there was no political necessity for the continuance of transportation to Van Dieman's Land, or for its extension to any part of the eastern coast of Australia, it was folly in the extreme on the part of Earl Grey—it was something akin to political insanity, like Lord North's—to force upon the colonies a measure so exceedingly distasteful, and thereby to imperil their connection with the British Empire. The Australian Anti-Transportation League, which his Lordship's impolitic measures virtually called into existence, was one of the characteristic features of the times It gave the colonists the important idea of a Union of the Colonies. It taught them, moreover, that union was strength; and it furnished them with an instrument which they may use on some other occasion, and with still greater effect.

Earl Grey's Australian Colonies Bill of 1850 was supposed, by ill-informed people at home, both in Parliament

* The number of signatures to the petition in favour of the resumption of transportation—on the same occasion—was only 525.

and out of it, to have been a great improvement on the previous system. It was not so by any means. It lowered the franchise, indeed, from twenty to ten pounds—a concession, be it remarked, for which the colonists were indebted, not to the House of Commons, but to the House of Lords—but in leaving the appointment of the Electoral Districts to the actual Legislature, it virtually provided for the establishment of a worse system of government than the one previously in existence. Earl Grey was not left in ignorance as to the probable issue of so unwarrantable an experiment. Sir William Molesworth had stated distinctly, in his speech on the Australian Colonies Bill, that the interests of the colonists could not be safe in the hands of the actual Legislature; and that it was therefore the bounden duty of the Colonial Office to have sent out instructions to the Local Executive, to ensure the carrying out of the Imperial Act on the principles of common sense and common honesty. But as no such instructions were sent out with the Act, and as the Act itself was actually carried out by the Government-packed Legislature to which the colony was subjected at the time, Earl Grey was justly chargeable with the entire result, agreeably to the maxim *Quod facit per alium, facit per se.* The colonists were thus deprived of their political rights, as I have shown in the case of the city of Sydney, under the mockery of an Act of Parliament, which official influence was permitted to mutilate on its passage, so as to deprive the colonists of the benefits it designed. It was generally believed, indeed, in New South Wales, that all this was clearly foreseen in Downing Street, and was artfully contrived in order to elicit from the mock Legislature, which would thus be created, an expression of opinion in favour of a resumption of transportation to that colony.

This peculiar species of political dishonesty—in vitiating the electoral system of the colonies, so as to repress, or prevent the expression of public opinion, and to ensure, pliant majorities in the Colonial Legislatures, for the carrying out of the principles of arbitrary government—was one of the regular devices of Lord North and his associates, and one of the fruitful causes of the American Revolution.

"In North Carolina, at this juncture," observes the historian, "a general ferment was excited by the efforts of Dobbs, the Royal Governor, so to alter (partly by creating new boroughs and counties, and partly by other measures,) the system of popular representation, as to ensure to the Crown an entire ascendant over the deliberations of the provincial assembly. From these measures, after he had pursued them so far as to kindle a high degree of public spirit in the province, he was at last compelled to depart, by the resolute opposition of the assembly, accompanied by such expressions of popular indignation as strongly betokened a revolt against his authority."*

Again, "On a question from New Jersey in 1773, with respect to the number of representatives from certain counties. or places, the attorney-general Raymond advised the King that he might regulate the number to be sent from each place, or *might restrain them from sending any at his pleasure.* In 1747, on a similar question from New Hampshire, the Crown lawyers, Ryder and Murray, informed his Majesty that the right of sending representatives to the assembly was founded, originally, on the commissions and instructions given by the Crown to the governors of New Hampshire." "These questions, Pitkin (an American writer) very justly observes, could be settled only by a Revolution."†

A third particular in which Earl Grey, as the Autocrat for the time being of all the colonies of Britain, identified himself with the real authors of the American Revolution, and in which he even surpassed King James the Second, King William the Third, and Lord North himself, was the

* Grahame's *History of the United States*, iv. 75. (Anno 1760.)
† *Ibid.* vol. iii. p. 58.

appointment of a Governor-General for the Australian
colonies, under the sole authority of the Colonial Office,
and without an Act of Parliament whatsoever. The idea
of combining the whole of the American colonies under one
general government, and subjecting them to a Governor-
General, to be under the sole authority of the Crown,
originated with a British monarch, whose opinions and
practice, in what his worthy grandfather used to call
"kingcraft," doubtless deserve all honour and imitation,—
I mean King James the Second!!! The fact itself, with
the views and objects of its worthy projector, is thus
detailed by the historian of America :—

"The project of a general government, embracing all the
colonies, *which had been devised by James the Second*, but
rendered abortive by the Revolution, was now (1692)
revived by this enterprising politician (Nicholson, governor
of Virginia), who beheld in it at once the most effectual
means of securing the absolute authority of the Parent
State, and the fairest promise of his own ascent to the
pinnacle of provincial greatness. By his merit in promoting
an object so agreeable to the English Court, added to his
boasted influence and experience in America, he hoped to
entitle himself to the appointment of Governor-General;
and this ambitious vision seems to have mainly influenced
his language and actions during his second presidency in
Virginia."*

Again, "He [Governor Nicholson] cooperated (anno
1698) with his friend, Colonel Quarry, another functionary
of the Crown in North America, in the composition of the
memorials which were presented in Quarry's name to the
Commissioners of Trade and Plantations in England.
These memorials represented the colonists of America, and
the Virginians in particular, as deeply imbued with
republican principles; strongly recommended immediate

* Grahame's *History of the United States*, vol. iii. p. 12.

recourse to the most rigorous measures for preserving the ascendancy of the Royal prerogative; and especially suggested, "that all the English colonies of North America be reduced under one government and one viceroy, and that a standing army be there kept on foot to subdue the enemies of the Royal authority."*

But the American colonists, of the Anti-Revolution period, were too watchful over their own rights and liberties, ever to permit such an appointment as that of a Governor-General to be made in their midst; and the project had therefore to be abandoned, with every inclination in the proper quarters to carry it out. But mark the progress of the true principles of government in *our period!* Without consulting either House of Parliament, and certainly without consulting the Australian colonies, Earl Grey merely nods† to his subordinates; and forthwith the parchment, with the sign manual attached, is duly issued, and a Governor-General is created for Australia! This Downing Street demonstration, however, proved a signal failure. So sheer an insult was the appointment considered to the colonies generally, that some of them, as for instance South Australia, got up an expression of indignation on the occasion; but so utterly useless, as well as uncalled for, was the appointment, that the rest scarcely thought it worth while to be angry.‡

The man whom Earl Grey *delighted to honour* with the appointment of Governor-General of Australia was Sir

---

* Grahame's *History of the United States*, vol. iii. p. 15.

† *Nutu* quatit Olympum, (scil. Jupiter)—VIRGIL.

‡ It is very questionable policy, as well as an evidence of very bad taste, to introduce upon the stage a functionary of this kind, who is really not wanted, and for whom there is nothing earthly to do. The maxim of Horace is as good in politics as it is in poetry:

" Nec Deus intersit, nisi dignus vindice nodus
    Inciderit."—HORAT. *Ars Poetica.*

There was certainly no such *nodus* in the case in question.

Charles Augustus Fitzroy, of the ducal House of Grafton, who was then Governor of New South Wales, and had previously been Governor of the island of Antigua, in the West Indies.

In the general opinion of the colonists, which, I cannot but think, was perfectly correct, Sir Charles Fitzroy was a man with neither head nor heart—

> " *Sans* eyes, *sans* ears, *sans* taste, *sans* everything."

From the distinguished position which his Excellency and his two sons—one of whom was his private secretary—held in the colony, they were necessarily the observed of all observers; and their influence on the community was correspondingly great. I am sorry to say that that influence was unspeakably evil; and if the reader should wish to ascertain its nature and character more particularly, he will only require to turn up the famous letter of Junius, No. 87, addressed to the Duke of Grafton a century ago, and look at the photograph of a noble lord of the period therein exhibited. In one word, there was no place in New South Wales that could furnish so large a contribution to the Scandalous Chronicle as Government House, Sydney, during the administration of Sir Charles Augustus Fitzroy— there was no *back slum* in London or Westminster that stood more urgently in need of a thorough clean out.

But why repeat such grievances, it may be asked? Why, simply to shew what the colonies have often had to suffer during the past, and to prevent the recurrence of such flagitiousness in the future.

" Of all constitutions," observes one of the ablest writers of the present day, and one who is certainly no bigot— " Of all constitutions, forms of government, and political methods among men, the question to be asked is even this, What kind of man do you set over us? All questions are answered in the answer to this.*"

* T. Carlyle's *Latter Day Pamphlets.*

To the same effect observes Mr. Merivale :—" It never should be forgotten, that the selection and encouragement of fit men is, if possible, even of more consequence than the adoption of fit measures."*

The great Socrates, also, was precisely of the same opinion, as to the necessity of having fit and proper persons at the head of a State. "In order to be well governed," he observes, " the head of our Republic must be a man of undoubted virtue, of cultivated taste, and of strict integrity."†

"No nation, or people," I quote from the able writer on America whom I have repeatedly cited, " can ever be safely indifferent to the moral character of its political chiefs and leaders "‡ and therefore if that character happens to be notoriously bad in any particular instance, it ought, for the benefit of society, to be publicly and fearlessly exposed. No doubt, it may be somewhat hazardous to make the attempt; but, as Sir Walter Scott observes in his Diary, "If we do not run some hazard in our attempts to do good, where is the merit of them ?"§ It was an ancient practice with the Colonial Office to send out men for the highest appointments in the colonies who

* Merivale, vol. ii. p. 161.

† Notre Republique sera donc bien gouvernee, si elle a pour Chef un homme qui joigne la connaissance du bien a celle du beau et de justice. Plato's *Republic*, Book ii. French Translation. Paris, 1794.

‡ The Americans were generally imbued with the persuasion (which some notable events in their subsequent experience tended to illustrate and confirm), that *a nation can never be safely indifferent to the moral characters of its political chiefs and leaders;* and that private virtue and prudence afford the surest test of the purity and stability of patriotic purpose and resolution.—*Grahame*, vol. iv. p. 316.

" The moral principle," says Dr. Channing, "is the life of communities." And again :—" Liberty has no foundation but in private and public virtue.—Dr. Channing's *Essay on war.*

§ Sir Walter Scott's Life, by Lockhart. Diary, vol. vi. p. 138.

were bankrupt alike in character and in purse;* and if this
practice was continued to a very late period in New South
Wales, it was doubtless because the people had previously
had so little to say in the management of their own affairs.
"I confess," says Oldmixon, an American annalist of the
earlier part of last century, "it gives me a great deal of
pain, in writing this history, to see what sort of governors
I meet with in the Plantations."† And, in reference to a
much later period, another writer on America observes :—

"It unfortunately happened for our American provinces,
at the time we now treat of, that a government in any of
our colonies in those parts was scarcely looked upon in any
other light than that of an hospital where the favourites of
the ministry might lie till they had recovered their broken
fortunes; and oftentimes they served as asylums from their
creditors."‡

If Her Majesty could have commissioned the Prince of
Darkness to represent her in the colony during the period
that terminated with the government of Sir Charles Fitz
Roy, I doubt not but his sable Excellency would have
received a Farewell Address of respect and regret at the
close of his felicitous administration. Of course, there
were such addresses presented to Sir Charles Fitz Roy on
his leaving the colony, not only by the Legislature, but by
certain of the clergy of more than one denomination.
Feeling deeply interested, as I did, in the character and
reputation of my adopted country, I submitted the following amendment on the Farewell Address to His Excellency
by the Legislative Council of the period, on the 1st
December, 1854 :—

---

*   Who having lost his credit, pawned his rent,
             Is therefore fit to have a government.— POPE.
The practice is very different now under responsible government.
† Oldmixon, quoted by Grahame, vol ii. p. 302.
‡ Wynne (an American writer), also quoted by Grahame, vol. iii.
p. 236.

" That this Council, on the eve of its prorogation, and of the departure for England of his Excellency Sir Charles Augustus Fitz Roy, desires to record its deliberate opinion—

" 1. That his Excellency's Administration has, throughout, been a uniform conspiracy against the rights of the people of this land.

" 2. That, from the lamentable inefficiency of his Excellency's Government, as well as from its utter inability to meet the wants of an unprecedentedly important crisis, this colony, which was evidently designed by nature to take the lead in the Australian group, has fallen from the high position which it might otherwise have easily maintained, and become, in the estimation of her Majesty's Government, of the British public, and of the civilized world, only the second in the list.

" 3. That in order to maintain and perpetuate the antipopular system which has uniformly characterised his Excellency's Government, the funds of the colony have been lavishly expended in the maintenance of unnecessary offices and the payment of extravagant salaries, while public works of urgent necessity to the community, in all parts of the territory, have been postponed and neglected.

" 4. That no such efforts, as were indispensably necessary under the extraordinary circumstances of the times, have been made during His Excellency's term of office, to supply the colony with an industrious population of the working classes from the mother country, and that the efforts of private individuals to supply this great desideratum have uniformly been frowned upon and systematically discouraged.

" 5. That notwithstanding the extraordinary interest which is now taken in Australia by the European public, no efforts at all worthy of the name, have been made during His Excellency's Government, in the way of geographical

discovery, either by land or sea, with a view to the opening
up of this vast *terra incognita,* for the progressive settlement
of a European population, although the able and energetic
Governor of a neighbouring colony has been gaining im-
perishable laurels by demonstrating the practicability of
navigating the great river which forms the southern
boundary of New South Wales for nearly 2000 miles; and
that while Great Britain and the United States of America
have been vieing with each other in their search for Sir
John Franklin and his companions in the icy regions of
the North, the lamented Leichhardt, a name not less
illustrious in the annals of geographical discovery, has been
left to perish miserably in the central desert of Australia,
and no effort, at all worthy of the colony, has been made to
search either for himself or his remains.

" 6. That instead of relaxing in any way the oppressive
character of the land system, in accordance with the obvious
intent and spirit of the Orders in Council, His Excellency
has voluntarily exceeded the powers entrusted to him for
the time being by the Imperial authorities, in rendering
that system still more oppressive, and thereby curtailing
unnecessarily the rights and privileges of a mis-governed
and down-trodden people.

" 7. That the moral influence which has emanated from
Government House during His Excellency's term of office
has been deleterious and baneful in the highest degree to
the best interests of this community; and that the evil
example which has thus been set in the highest places of
the land has tended, more than anything else that has
occurred in this colony these thirty years past, to bring
Her Majesty's Government into contempt, and to alienate
from Her Majesty the affections and respect of the
Australian people."

I did not expect that this amendment would be carried;
but the names of the gentlemen who voted with me in a
minority of six against twenty-eight, will doubtless satisfy

the reader as to the propriety of the step I had thus taken, and the worthless character of the administration that had come to its close. The six members who formed the minority were Mr. Cowper, the present Premier; Mr. Parkes, late Colonial Secretary; Mr. Campbell and Mr. Flood, both afterwards Ministers of the Crown; Mr. Bligh, a magistrate of the territory, and myself.

Another instance of the complete identification of Earl Grey with his

"Most noble, reverend, and approved good masters"

of the Lord North school, was the idea which his lordship repeatedly put forth, that the governors of all the British colonies should have their salaries paid by the mother country, or, in other words, that they should be *a sort of out-door paupers, supported by the parishes in England!* Whether any of the Australian colonies would be abject enough to consent to such a proposal, the real object of which was to make the governors the complete tools of their Downing Street Paymasters, I shall not say; for under a government-packed Legislature, with perhaps a million a-year to appropriate in salaries for offices of all kinds, whether necessary or not, there will always be plenty of people abject enough for anything—plenty of "four-footed beasts and *creeping things*:* but it is positively refreshing, while it tends to raise one's opinion of human nature, to contemplate the manner in which so insidious a proposal was received by the patriots of the olden time in America. The following passage from the American historian relates to events that took place during the administration of Governor Hutchinson, the *last* Royal Governor of the Colony of Massachusetts:—

"Hutchinson had enjoyed his commission as governor

* They actually grasped at the idea in the Legislature of New South Wales—just as a beggar would at a sixpence!!!

P

but a very short time, when he acquainted the provincial assembly that he no longer required a salary from them, as the king had made provision for his support. By this measure, the British Court expected gradually to introduce into practical operation the principle for which it had already contended, of rendering the emoluments, as well as the communication and endurance of executive functions in America, wholly dependent on the pleasure of the Crown; and doubtless it was supposed that the Americans would give little heed to the principle of an innovation of which the first practical effect was to relieve themselves from a considerable burden. But the Americans valued liberty more than money, and justly accounted it the political basis on which reposed the stability of every temporal advantage. Hutchinson's communication was maturely considered; and, about a month afterwards, the assembly, by a message, declared to him that the royal provision for his support, and his own acceptance of it, was an infraction of the rights of the inhabitants recognized by the provincial charter, an insult to the assembly, and an invasion of the important trust which from the foundation of their commonwealth they had ever continued to exercise."*

Again, on his subsequent "avowal, that he could no longer authorise a provincial provision for the judges, as the king had undertaken to provide for *their* remuneration also, the assembly instantly passed a resolution declaring that this measure tended to the subversion of justice and equity; and that while tenure of judicial office continued to depend on the pleasure of the king, 'any of the judges who shall accept of and depend upon the pleasure of the Crown for his support, independent of the grants of the assembly, will discover that he is an enemy of the con-

* Grahame's *History of the United States of America*, vol. iv. p. 323.

stitution, and has it in his heart to promote the establishment of arbitrary power in the province.'"*

But the crowning Act of Earl Grey's administration—the Act most directly illustrative of the thoroughly arbitrary principles of British domination in the colonies—was, what is called the Squatting Act of 1846. This Act, which at once established in the Australian colonies a system precisely similar to that which so long characterized and so often convulsed the ancient Roman republic, and led to the numerous agrarian agitations of Roman history, was passed almost immediately after his Lordship's accession to office, at the instance of a comparatively small portion of the colonists, the occupants of the Waste Lands. It authorised long leases of vast tracts of these lands at a merely nominal rental, and established a right of preemption, at the minimum price, on behalf of the occupants; thereby virtually confiscating the public lands of the colony, locking them up from the industrious and virtuous emigrant, and subjecting numerous families and individuals of that class to the greatest hardship, loss and ruin.

I happened to arrive in England, on one of my voyages from New South Wales, a few weeks after this Act was passed; and having still retained, at the express desire of my constituents, the character of a representative of the people of that colony, and Mr. Under-Secretary Hawes having told me, on my calling at the office in Downing-street, that as there was a series of regulations to be appended to the Act, under the designation of Orders in Council, which were to have the full force of the Act, Earl Grey would be glad if I would offer any suggestions I might deem of importance, before these Orders in Council should be finally adopted, I did so accordingly—stating that although Australia was remarkably destitute of navigable waters,

* Grahame's *History of the United States of America, Ibid.*

it was not so absolutely, as there were various rivers
along the coast available for navigation, for greater or
lesser distances from the Pacific; and recommending that
it should be an Order in Council that four miles should be
reserved from the operation of the Squatting Act, along all
navigable water for the settlement of an agricultural
population—the land on the banks of these rivers being
generally of very superior quality. I had mentioned the
Richmond River, in particular, as one that had not less
than three hundred miles of navigable water in the main
river and its tributaries. But the Land and Emigration
Commissioners, to whom the preparation of the Orders in
Council was referred, instead of adopting the simple and
intelligible principle I had indicated—the mere adoption of
which would have proved a boon of incalculable value to
the industrious classes of the colony, and ensured the
settlement of hundreds or perhaps thousands of families of
that class along all our rivers—chose to refine upon my
principle, and made it an Order in Council that two miles
on either bank of the Richmond River should be reserved
from the operation of the Squatting Act for the settlement of
an agricultural population—*for twenty miles from its mouth.*
But the Richmond River, like certain rivers in England,
struggling as it were for an exit through the sand banks
thrown up by the surges of the Pacific, is only five miles
from the ocean at the distance of twenty miles from its
mouth; and the whole of the land for that distance on both
banks of the river is a mere mangrove swamp, utterly
useless either for man or beast. The present Chancellor of the
Exchequer, the Right Honourable Robert Lowe (who was
then serving his apprenticeship in legislation as a member
of our Colonial Legislature), when the Order in Council
was published in the colony, could scarcely find words to
express his astonishment at the folly and madness of the
authors of this particular Order in Council, of which he
could not possibly divine the origin. He will understand

the matter now, and will doubtless do me justice in the case, as he has done on other occasions in New South Wales. Indeed, I account it one of the *memorabilia* of my life that when that very eminent man resigned his seat as a nominee member of our Legislative Council, in 1844, previous to his being chosen, as he was on the first vacancy, as an elective member, he did me the honour to ask me, as a member of our Select Committee on National Education, to move his very able Report in the Legislature, which I did accordingly in a speech of three hours, during the whole of which Mr. Lowe was present in the House.

During the year 1848, I had the honour of being examined before a Select Committee of the House of Lords on Emigration, of which the late Lord Monteagle was Chairman. His Lordship, who had been making enquiries on the subject beforehand, made me relate the incident about the Richmond River to their Lordships' Committee : and when I had done so, he observed,—"You mean to say that the Commissioners reserved all the bad land for the settlement of an agricultural population, and gave all the good land away to the squatters?" to which I replied, —"That is precisely my meaning, my Lord." Lord Wharncliffe, who was one of the Committee, laughed at the absurdity of the thing ; but it was no laughing matter to the colonists. The banks of the Richmond River and its tributaries were then inhabited by a numerous body of cedar-cutters, who could make excellent wages at that rough occupation, and many of whom were married and had numerous families. One of these persons, a married man with a large family, had accumulated in this way the sum of £800, which he was earnestly desirous to invest in the purchase of a homestead or small farm for his family on the river banks. But there being no land for sale at the time on the river, and the poor man being ordered off the squatter's run on which he had been living on suffer-ance, he went to the nearest public house in a fit of despair, and persevered in a course of the wildest dissipation till he had spent the whole of his money. And this was only one of many similar cases of the kind.

As to the operation of the Act in regard to the squatters, two gentlemen of that class who had taken up large runs on another river in the same part of the colony—the Clarence River—exercised their pre-emptive right, as the holders of these runs, to purchase at the minimum price of one pound an acre, one square mile each or 640 acres of the land on the river banks, which, if my recommendation had been adopted, would have been reserved for the settlement of an agricultural population; and they immediately raised the price of the land to persons of that class to thirty pounds an acre!

Such, then, was the miserable and suicidal policy which Great Britain has been pursuing until yesterday, as it were, in the government of her Australian colonies, ever since the War of American Independence. Like some old withered beldame, she has been gratifying to the full her *lust* of empire, and sacrificing everything that was really valuable and desirable for the gratification of this un-hallowed passion—the hopes and prospects, nay, the very existence, of myriads of her people at home, and the welfare and advancement of myriads of her people abroad. It is recorded as one of the golden sayings of the good King Henry of Castile, "that he feared the curses of his people more than the weapons of his enemies." Would God we had had rulers in Britain in times past that really feared the curses of their people, either at home or abroad! Deep and hollow, like a voice from the sepulchre, they rose to the listening ear of heaven from the cheerless haunts of wretchedness in every city of the land; and they were wafted across the ocean with every breeze from her remotest colony!

In short, as the Roman historian says of his own country and people, so may we of ours, in reference at least to the heroic work of colonization. *Primo pecuniae, dein imperii cupido crevit; ea quasi materies omnium malorum fuere.* "First the love of gain, and then the lust of empire—these have been the principles of British colonization, and the source of innumerable evils."*

To revert for one moment to Earl Grey—my impression of the calamitous character of his Lordship's administration, as Principal Secretary of State for the Colonies, was so strong at the time, that I addressed a letter to his lordship, before leaving England on my return to Australia, in November, 1849, which gave great offence at the Colonial Office, and led to a series of unsuccessful efforts in the Colony, where the influence of Downing-street was almost irresistible, to put me down. The last paragraph of that letter was as follows:—

"As far as regards the Australian Colonies, your Lordship has for three years past been knocking at the gate of futurity for the President of the "United Provinces of Australia" : be assured, my Lord, he is getting ready, and will shortly be out; and he will astonish the world with the manliness of his port and the dignity of his demeanour. As in duty bound, he will make a profound obeisance to your Lordship, in the first instance, in grateful acknowledgment of the concern which your Lordship has had in his paternity: he will then take his place in the great family of nations, with a proud consciousness of the brilliant career upon which his country has entered, when delivered at length from the baleful domination of Downing-street. He will require no soldiers to enable him to keep his seat, like Louis Napoleon. He will have no foul blot of slavery to defile his national escutcheon, like Zachary Taylor."†

---

* Sallust. Catalin. c. x.

† Zachary Taylor was then President of the United States, as Louis Napoleon was of the National Assembly of France. My letter

SECTION X.—THE GRECIAN SPECIFIC FOR SUCCESSFUL COLONIZATION.
—FREEDOM AND INDEPENDENCE FOR THE COLONIES.

To return to the ancient Greeks—I have stated in a
former section of this chapter, that the mother-country of
that wonderful people, Greece Proper, was actually smaller
than Scotland ; and there is reason to believe that its
population, even at the period of its greatest glory, was
not greater than that of Scotland at the present day.*

What, then, was the secret of the wonderful success of
the Greek colonies of the ancient world ?   Why, the answer
is plain and obvious to every person who will honestly
admit the fact—THEY WERE FREE AND INDEPENDENT FROM
THE FIRST.   This, conjoined with the spirit and energy of
the people themselves, was the cause, and the sole cause,
of their rapid advancement and extraordinary prosperity.

"Different commonwealths," says a great European
authority on the Law of Nations, "may be formed out of
one by common consent by sending out colonies in the
manner usual in old Greece.   For the Romans afterward
(who are followed now by the nations of Europe), when
they sent a colony abroad, continued it under the jurisdiction of the mother-commonwealth or Greater country.
But the colonies planted by the Greeks, and after their
method constituted particular commonwealths, were obliged

to Earl Grey was reprinted entire by an enthusiastic colonist of Port
Phillip, and circulated all over the district.

* Even if we add all the islands, the square contents of Greece are
a third less than those of Portugal.

Ancient Greece :—From the German of A. H. L. Heeren, Professor
of History at Göttingen.   By George Bancroft.   London. 1845.
Page 16.

The area of Portugal is 38,700 square miles : that of Greece is therefore 25,800, while that of Scotland is 29,600.

only to pay a kind of deference and dutiful submission to their mother-commonwealth."*

"The migrations of the Greek colonists," says Bishop Thirlwall, " were commonly undertaken with the approbation and encouragement of the States from which they issued ; and it frequently happened that the motive of the expedition was one in which the interest of the mother-country was mainly concerned, as when the object was to relieve it of superfluous hands, or of discontented and turbulent spirits. But it was seldom that the Parent State looked forward to any more remote advantage from the colony, or that the colony expected or desired any from the Parent State. There was in most cases nothing to suggest the feeling of dependence on the one side, or a claim of authority on the other. The sons, when they left their home to shift for themselves on a foreign shore, carried with them only the blessing of their fathers, and felt themselves completely emancipated from their control. Often the colony became more powerful than the parent, and the distance between them was generally so great as to preclude all attempts to enforce submission. But though they were not connected by the bands of mutual interest, or by a yoke laid by the powerful on the weak, the place of such relations was supplied by the gentler and nobler ties of filial affection and religious reverence, and by usages which, springing out of these feelings, stood in their room, and tended to suggest them where they were wanting. Except in the few cases where the emigrants were forced, as outcasts from their native land, they cherished the remembrance of it as a duty prescribed not merely by nature, but by religion. The colony regarded its prosperity as mainly depending on the favour of the tutelary gods of the State to which it owed its birth. They were invited to share the newly-conquered

* Puffendorf's *Law of Nature and Nations*, Book VIII., chap. xii., sec. 5.

land, and temples were commonly dedicated to them in the new citadel, resembling as nearly as possible, in form and position, those with which they were honoured in the mother-country; their images here renewed the old model; and it is not improbable that the priests who ministered to them were sometimes brought from the ancient seats. The sacred fire, which was kept constantly burning on the public hearth of the colony, was taken from the altar of Vesta in the Council-hall of the elder State. The founder of a colony, who might be considered as representing its parent city, was honoured after his death with sacred rites, and as a being of a high order; and when the colony in its turn became a parent, it usually sought a leader from the original mother-country, to direct the planting of the new settlement. The same reverential feeling manifested itself more regularly in embassies and offerings sent by the colony to honour the festivals of the parent city, and in the marks of respect shown to its citizens who represented it on similar occasions in the colony. But the most valuable fruit of this feeling was a disposition to mutual good offices in seasons of danger and distress."[*]

"The Greek colonies," says Baron Niebuhr, "were planted at a distance from the Parent State, usually by persons who emigrated to escape from commotions and civil feuds, and not under the direction of the government at home; or if a colony went forth in peace, and with the blessing of the Parent State, and the latter retained honorary privileges, still *the colony from the beginning was free and independent, even when founded to serve as a safe mart for commerce.*"[†]

---

[*] *History of Greece.* By the Rev. Connop (now Bishop) Thirlwall, Fellow of Trinity College, Cambridge, vol. ii. p. 98.

[†] Niebuhr's *History of Rome*, vol. ii. p. 43. In a posthumous work, Niebuhr repeats the same idea in the following language :

"The very fact that *the mother-city made no claims to rule over her colonies, as modern States do in regard to theirs*, and that the colonies, in

To the same effect, the laborious and accurate M'Culloch, in his Dictionary of Commerce, under the Article *Colonies*, observes:

"The Greek colonies of antiquity seem to have been chiefly founded by citizens whom the violence and fury of contending factions forced to leave their native land; but they were sometimes formed for the purpose of relieving the mother-country of a redundant population, and sometimes also for the purpose of extending the sphere of commercial transactions, or of providing for their security. The relations between the mother-country and the colony depended, in a great measure, on the motives which led to the establishment of the latter. When a colony was founded by fugitives, forcibly expelled from their ancient homes, or when it was founded, as was frequently the case, by bodies of voluntary emigrants, who received no assistance from, and were in no respect controlled by, the Parent State, it was from the first independent; and even in those cases in which the emigration was conducted under the superintendence of the parent city, and where the colony was protected by her power and influence, the dependence was, mostly, far from being absolute and complete. *The great bulk of the Greek colonies were really independent States;* and though they commonly regarded the land of their forefathers with filial respect, though they yielded to its citizens the place of distinction at public games and religious solemnities, and were expected to assist them in time of war, they did so as allies only, on fair and equal terms, and never as subjects. Owing to the freedom of their institutions, and their superiority in the arts of civilized life to the native inhabitants of the countries among whom they were generally

cases of emergency, assisted the parent city, produced in antiquity a cordial relation between the mother city and her colonies; of which we find but few exceptions, as, e. g., between Corcyra and Corinth."— Niebuhr's *Lectures on Ancient History.* Translated by Dr. Schmitz, of the High School, Edinburgh, 2 vols. London, 1852.

placed, these colonies rose, in a comparatively short period,
to a high pitch of opulence and refinement; and many
among them, as Miletus and Ephesus in Asia Minor,
Syracuse and Agrigentum in Sicily, and Tarentum and
Locri in Italy, not only *equalled, but greatly surpassed, their
mother cities in wealth and power.*"

"The connexion existing between the colonies and the
mother-cities," observes Professor Heeren, "was generally
determined by the same causes that led to their formation.
In these cases when a city had been founded by malcontent
or banished emigrants, all dependence on the mother-
country was naturally out of the question; and even in the
colonies established for the purposes of trade, that dependence was but feeble and brief; the mother-cities failing in
power and not in will, to enforce it. *The very independence
of so many colonies,* made (almost without exception) in
countries pre-eminently favoured by nature in productions
and climate, and so situated as to oblige the inhabitants to
navigation and commerce, *must have given a great impulse to
the civilization of the Hellenic race, and may be regarded as the
main cause of its rapid progress and wide extension; wider
indeed than that of any other nation in the ancient world.
What a variety of political ideas must have been formed among
a people, whose settlements, more than a hundred in number, had
each its own peculiar form of government !*"*

Nay, so ennobling was the spirit of freedom and independence in the Colonies of Greece, that whereas the idea
of a colonial author under the British system of colonial
domination, (which seemed effectually to repress all the
nobler faculties of men), was apt to raise the smile of in-

---

* *A Manual of Ancient History, particularly with regard to the
Constitutions, the Commerce, and the Colonies, of the States of Antiquity.*
By A. H. L. Heeren, Knight of the North Star of the Guelphic Order;
Aulic Councillor and Professor of History in the University of
Göttingen, &c. London, 1847. Page 127.

credulity or contempt on the face of the learned vulgar at home, not a few of the immortal writers of Greece were mere colonists, and the splendour of their genius reflects an unfading lustre on their father-land to the present day. Homer, the first of the Grecian poets, was an Ionian Greek, colonist, of Asia Minor; and so also was Herodotus, the first of her historians.*

Even Mitford, whose history appears to have been written for the express purpose of bringing all popular government into discredit, and of inducing men to submit without murmuring to arbitrary rule, admits this remarkable fact in the following language :—

"Few of the Grecian colonies were founded with any view to extend the dominion of the mother-country. When a State by a public act sent out a colony, the purpose was generally no more than to deliver itself from numbers too great for its territory, or from factious men, whose means of power at home were unequal to their ambition. Corinth, however, early, and in later times Athens, had sometimes further views. Possessing naval force, they could give protection, and exact obedience; of which the Grecian commonwealths in general could do neither. For the most part, therefore, in the colonies, as in Greece itself, *every considerable town claimed to be an independent State; and* unless oppressed by a powerful neighbourhood, *maintained itself by its own strength and its alliances.*"†

---

* Of the Greek colonies, the most ancient, and in many respects the most important, were those along the western coast of Asia Minor, extending from the Hellespont to the boundary of Cilicia. * * * Here, in the native country of Homer, the father of Grecian civiliza-tion, of Alcaeus, and of Sappho, poesy, both epic and lyric, expanded her first and fairest blossoms; *and hence, too, the mother-country herself received the first impulse of moral and cultivated taste.*—Heeren, ubi supra, page 127.

† *History of Greece.* By William Mitford, Esq., vol. i. p. 385.

The maritime state of Corinth,* as this historian informs
us, was the first Grecian State that attempted to lord
it over her colonies, and to hold them in subjection.
Thucydides informs us of the first attempt of this kind
which she seems to have made, and of the spirited manner
in which it was repelled. The Locrians, a Corinthian
colony on the north coast of the Gulf of Corinth, having, in
the usual way of the times, exhibited their determination
to think and act for themselves, the haughty Corinthians,
who seem to have been a regular Tory community of the
old school, designated them as " refractory subjects," and
proceeded to treat them accordingly. But the Locrians
firmly asserted their freedom and independence; protesting,
in a remonstrance which they addressed to the Corinthian
government, and of which the historian has given us the
substance, "that they had emigrated, not to become the
slaves or subjects, but the equals of the Corinthians, and
that this had been the original understanding and condition of their emigration."† It is humiliating to be obliged
to acknowledge that, with all our boasted civilization, and
our professed Christianity, we have all along as a great
colonizing people been so far behind these ancient Pagan
Greeks, who so fully understood, and so nobly and successfully vindicated, the principles of manly freedom, two
thousand five hundred years ago!‡ In the noble art of

---

* The territory of this powerful Maritime State, the mother country
of so many famous colonies, was only four miles square.

† 'Ου γαρ ἐπι το δουλοι, αλλ' ἐπι το ὁμοιοι ειναι, ἐκπεμπονται·
Non enim ut servi sint, sed ut pari jure sint, dimittuntur,—Thucyd.
lib. i. c. 37.

‡ "In the circuit we have traversed," observes an able writer by
no means favourably disposed to the claims of colonists in modern
times, "no vestiges have appeared of any disposition, in the several
parent states, to impose taxes on the colonies, or even to retain

colonization, they were unquestionably our masters; and
we shall never practise that art successfully till we follow
their illustrious example. They planted colonies on every
shore, and everywhere they prospered—simply because the
colonists were everywhere their own masters, and had no
Colonial Office to thwart their efforts, and to blast their
prosperity!

The brightest and palmiest period of Grecian colonization appears to have been the seventh and sixth centuries
before the Christian era; of which Bishop Thirlwall speaks
in the following language of well-merited admiration :

"How far political changes were connected with the
prime spring of that wonderful activity which was displayed
by the Asiatic Greeks, more especially the Ionians, in the
seventh and sixth centuries before our era, can only be
conjectured. It seems probable that the fall of the ancient
aristocracies which succeeded the heroic monarchy, and the
emulation between a growing commonalty, and an oligarchy
which grounded its political claims solely on superior
wealth, were conditions, without which the Ionian genius
would not have found room to expand itself so freely. On
the other hand, the inferior degree in which the Dorians
and Æolians were animated with the spirit of commercial
adventure, may have been owing to their political institutions, not less than to a difference in their national
character. It is however certain that in the two centuries
just mentioned the progress of mercantile industry and
maritime discovery was coupled with the cultivation of the
nobler arts, and the opening of new intellectual fields, in a
degree to which history affords no parallel before the

sovereignty over them."—*History of the colonization of the Free States
of Antiquity*, p. 47. London, 1777.

And again :—

"The only connection known, for many ages, between the Mother-
country and the (Greek) colony was that of affection and alliance."—
Ibid, p. 32.

beginning of the latest period of European civilization."[*]

"Among the (*Ionian*) towns," says Professor Heeren, "the most remarkable were Miletus, Ephesus and Phocaea. Miletus was the principal seat of trade. In the days of her prosperity, she was, next to Tyre and Carthage, the first emporium of the world. Her sea trade was chiefly carried on in the Euxine and the Palus Mæotis, whose shores, on all sides, were occupied by her colonies, amounting, according to some authorities, to more than a hundred. By means of these settlements she monopolized the whole of the northern trade in pulse, dry fish, slaves and furs. Her land trade was carried on by the great *military* road, constructed by the Persians, far into the interior of Asia. Four harbours admitted her vessels; and her naval power was so great, that she had been known, more than once, to fit out, unaided, fleets of from eighty to a hundred sail. The people of Miletus and their colonies were not only sovereigns of the Black Sea, but likewise extended their trade over the whole of Southern Russia, and eastward to the regions beyond the Caspian Sea; that is, to Great Bukharia."[†]

The enemies of public freedom, and especially of republican institutions, are fond of representing the government of the petty republics of ancient Greece as "a constituted anarchy;" but the magnificent remains which they have left us of their inimitable architecture—the undoubted evidence of their civilization and refinement—sufficiently demonstrate that the government under which such buildings could have been erected must have been both strong and stable, and that both government and people must have been pre-eminently the patrons of the liberal arts. Although the Greeks were unfortunately unacquainted with the representative principle, which, I agree

---

[*] Thirlwall's *History of Greece*, vol, ii. p. 105.
[†] Heeren, *ubi supra*, p. 130

with Chateaubriand in thinking, is rather to be traced to the
polity of the primitive Christian Church, than to the forests
of Germany, the colonies of each of the three great races
that occupied the west coast of Asia Minor, formed distinct
federations of sovereign and independent republics; which
had regular places of meeting, and which were doubtless
serviceable in maintaining a good understanding among
their component parts.

" The meetings of the Ionians," says Bishop Thirlwall,
" were held in a spot at the northern foot of Mount Mycale,
called from its destination—that of receiving the whole
Ionian body—Panionium, and consecrated to the national
god, Poseidon. In them too the religious or festive object
was almost exclusively predominant. Yet it would appear
that in early times there was among the Ionians a tendency
of disposition and of circumstances toward a closer union
than subsisted among either their northern or their
southern neighbours."[*]

These federations, however, were sufficiently loose, and
from circumstances with which we are unacquainted, were
soon dissolved.

"The Ionian cities," adds Bishop Thirlwall, "were
soon completely isolated. No provision was made either
for defence against foreign enemies, or for the maintenance
of internal tranquility : there was no common treasury, nor
tribunal, nor magistrate, nor laws. Yet it may have been
very early, though the time is uncertain, that the Lycians
set an example of the manner in which the advantages of a
close federal union might be reconciled with mutual independence. They distributed their twenty-three cities into three
classes: the cities of the first rank possessed each three votes,
those of the second two, those of the least one, and each contributed to a common fund in proportion to its weight in the

* Thirlwall's *History of Greece*, vol. ii. p. 102.

Q

common council. This was held, not in any fixed place, so as to raise one city to the rank of a capital, but in one appointed for the time by common consent. A supreme magistrate and other officers were here elected; and a court was instituted for the decision of all disputes that might arise between members of the confederacy; the cities contributing in proportion to their rank to fill the places in the national judicature and magistracy: in the same assemblies were discussed all questions relating to peace and war, and the general interests of the united states. Had the Greeks on the western coast of Asia adopted similar institutions, their history, and even that of the mother-country, might have been very different from what it became.

"But whatever ill effects may be attributed to their want of union, it does not seem immediately to have checked the growth, or to have diminished the prosperity of the several cities. They may perhaps have shot up the more vigorously and luxuriantly from the absence of all restraint. This advantage undoubtedly also resulted from the abolition of the monarchical form of government, which probably took place everywhere within a few generations after the first settlement, though the good was balanced by great evils."*

But even taking it for granted that the Grecian republics were merely " constituted anarchies," there is much truth, as well as meaning, in the observation of the learned historian of the *Middle Ages*, which applies equally to the ancient Grecian republics, and to those of modern Italy: " The wildest excesses of faction are less dishonouring than the stillness and moral degradation of servitude."† The ancient Greeks doubtless felt with our great writer and poet, Sir Walter Scott, when he observed, " The feast of

* Thirlwall's *History of Greece*, vol. ii p. 103.
† Hallam, vol. i. p. 483.

fancy will be over with the feeling of independence."[*]
And they would certainly have sympathised with the poet,
when he says, in the very spirit of their own immortal
bards,

> " Sound, sound the clarion, fill the fife ;
> So all the sensual world proclaim,
> One crowded hour of glorious life
> Is worth an age without a name."[†]

Agreeably to the maxim of the eminent French philosopher
—" L'usage que nous devons faire de notre liberté, c'est
de nous en servir autant que nous le pouvons;"[‡]   " The
use we ought to make of our liberty, is to avail ourselves
of it as much as we can "—agreeably to this maxim, when
the Greeks were precluded from the full enjoyment of their
national freedom in one city or state, they emigrated, and
straightway recovered it in the founding of another.

It cannot be denied, indeed that, in the course of the
great Persian war, and chiefly as one of the natural results
of that event, an important change took place in the
political condition of a considerable number of the Grecian
colonies, and that, from being independent before, not a
few of these communities became thenceforth mere
tributary states.   In such a crisis as that war presented for
the whole Greek nation, the idea of a common treasury, to
which each state should contribute in proportion to its
means, for the general expenses of the war, as well as of a
common head to direct both offensive and defensive operations, was perfectly natural : and who so fit to undertake
the highly responsible and delicate duty of managing this
national treasury, of fixing the due proportions for each of

* Diary, in Life by Lockhart, vol. vi. p. 163.
† Sir Walter Scott.
‡ Malebranche, *De Inquirenda Veritate,* lib. i. cap. 2.—French
Translation.

the allies, and of undertaking the general management of
the war, as the metropolitan City and State of Athens?
The two great Powers of Greece at that period were Athens
and Lacedæmon or Sparta; the former a naval Power, like
Great Britain, and the latter a military Power, like France:
but as a large portion of Greece consists of islands and
lands accessible chiefly by sea, it was natural that the
maritime power should acquire the predominance over the
inferior States. Annual contributions, however, for any
common object are always dangerous to the liberties of
such States; for when once acquiesced in by the weaker
party, and a precedent established, a ready pretext for
their continuance will always be found by ambitious and
unscrupulous statesmen: insomuch that a political connection originating in the friendly alliance of sovereign and
independent states, is sure to ripen into the supremacy and
domination of one, and the compulsory subjection of all
the others. Hence the real result of the Persian war was
not so much the liberation of Greece as the elevation of
Athens to the rank of a metropolitan Power or dominant
country at the head of a great federation of tributary and
subject states. "The Athenians," says an able but
anonymous writer in the interest of Great Britain in the
course of the American troubles, " the Athenians, suddenly
acquired the sovereignty of almost all the islands of the
Archipelago, and of the whole of the eastern coast of that
sea. The Ionian colonies became their zealous friends, and
the Æolians their subjects. Both followed their standard
in war, and advanced contributions for the public expense."*

When the relation of a dominant country and a series of
dependencies had thus been established between Athens on
the one hand, and the free colonies of Ionia and Æolia on

* *History of the Colonization of the Free States of Antiquity*, p.
58. London, 1777.

the other, the Athenians appear to have reckoned on the permanence of this relation, and to have carried matters with a very high hand towards these subject states; for in the course of the famous Peloponnesian war, or the long and desperate struggle between Athens and Lacedæmon for the supremacy of Greece, the Lesbians, who had never been a colony of Athens at all, took the first opportunity to revolt, and joined the Lacedæmonians.

"The Lesbians, *an Æolian colony,*" observes the same writer, "revolted from the Athenians in the fifth year of the war, and joined the Lacedæmonians. The Athenians were provoked beyond measure by *this unnatural and ungrateful rebellion.* In the first transports of their resentment, they passed the most cruel and bloody vote, that all the males of Lesbos, arrived at the age of puberty, should be put to death, and the women and children sold for slaves; and they sent the same day a ship with commissioners to see the decree put into execution.

" When their passions subsided, they began to reflect on what they had done. A meeting of the citizens was therefore convened next day. The former sentence was reviewed, and after much contention, it was carried, by a small majority, to prevent the execution of the former order. The deputies of Lesbos, who had come to plead their cause at Athens, returned on board this last vessel. They procured changes of rowers, that one party might sleep while the other was employed. They offered them the most palatable provisions, and promised the highest rewards, to procure their most vigorous exertions. The former ship had departed full twenty-four hours before them, and they could not overtake her in her course. They arrived, however, before the Athenian commander had finished the reading of the first order. The Lesbians were immediately assembled, and informed both of their danger and their safety."*

* *History of the Colonization of the Free States of Antiquity,* page 58. London, 1777.

When the Lacedæmonians acquired the supremacy of Greece, as the result of the Peloponnesian war, they seem to have outdone the Athenians in the tyranny they exercised over the subject or tributary states; proving, if the thing required any proof, that the liberties of any one people can never be safe in the hands of another. But these successive instances of successful usurpation over the inferior states of that country, on the part of the two great naval and military powers of ancient Greece, are no evidence whatever against the views I have given above of the principle on which colonization uniformly proceeded among the ancient Greeks, viz., that of entire freedom end national independence.

"If the Corinthians tell you," observe the deputies of the city of Corcyra, a Corinthian colony, in their address to the people of Athens, when soliciting an alliance with the latter,—"if the Corinthians tell you that it is not right for you to form an alliance with us, because we are their colony, they ought to learn that a colony is obliged to respect its mother-country, only when well used by it. If, on the contrary, it is ill-used by it, it becomes its enemy. It is not to be its slave that it is sent forth as a colony by the mother-country, but to enjoy entire freedom, and to have the same rights and the same prerogatives as its mother-country."*

Indeed the Athenians themselves never pretended to base the authority they exercised, in the period of their power and glory, over the subject states of Greece, on the right of a mother-country to rule over its colonies ; for it was notorious that certain of these states, as for instance the Lesbians, were not Athenian colonies at all. When certain of the minor states called in question the right of Athens to exercise such authority shortly before the Peloponnesian war, the Athenian commissioners put the matter

* Thucydides, lib., i. 34, 38.

on its right footing, by replying very coolly, as the historian informs us, "In all past times the strongest have been masters : we are not the authors of that law ; it is founded in nature."[*] In short, the Athenians pretended to no higher right in the authority they exercised over other states, whether colonies or not, than that of the famous Rob Roy Macgregor—

> " That they should take who have the power,
> And they should keep who can."

In regard to the mutual good feeling that continued to subsist for ages between the mother-country and the many Grecian colonies that were successively planted in Europe, Asia, and Africa, on this principle of entire freedom and independence, I will only give two instances in proof of the fact : the first in the case of a Corinthian, and the second in that of an Athenian colony. "The Syracusans," observes the writer I have just quoted, "oppressed by the tyranny of Dionysius the younger, and harassed and plundered by the Carthaginians, applied to Corinth for aid (in the 108th Olympiad). They received first the famous Timoleon for their general, and ten gallies loaded with supplies; to which afterwards were added ten more, furnished in the same manner. Timoleon banished Dionysius, and expelled the Carthaginians. He made free all the Greek cities in Sicily, and established democracy in Syracuse. The constant wars, however, with which, for a long time, Sicily had been wasted, had almost depopulated the country. Timoleon, therefore, supplicated Greece for a recruit of inhabitants. He caused it to be proclaimed through all the states of Peloponnesus, that the senate and people of Syracuse offered habitations and land to all persons who

---

[*] C'est de tout tems que les plus forts sont les maitres ; nous ne sommes les autcurs de cette loi ; elle est fondee dans la nature.— Thucydides, lib. i. 84. French Translation.

should repair thither to possess them. The reputation of Sicily for opulence and fertility was so great, that no fewer than 50,000 people emigrated to take possession of the vacant territories; and before this event, 5000 persons had arrived from Corinth."*

The other instance is remarkably in point, and is only the more interesting, as the manifestation of kindly feeling which, it shows, subsisted between the mother-country and her colonies, led to a series of the most memorable events recorded in the history of nations, and eventually gave the Greeks the empire of the world.

When Cyrus, king of Persia, was preparing to subjugate the Grecian cities of Asia Minor, Aristagoras, the political chief of the Ionian city of Miletus, who had been stirring up his fellow-countrymen to resist "the barbarians," was deputed by the Ionian Confederation to proceed to Greece, to solicit assistance in their approaching struggles in the *Old Country*. He accordingly proceeded in the first instance to Lacedæmon, which was then the head of the most powerful and warlike of the states of Greece. But he was unsuccessful in that quarter, the Lacedæmonians, who were of the Dorian race, being rather a phlegmatic and unimpressible people; and he therefore proceeded to Athens, the recognised head of the Ionian family, and of which his own native city, Miletus, had been an ancient colony. Aristagoras accordingly addressed the sovereign people of that illustrious City and State in their national assembly; reminding them that Miletus was an ancient colony of their own, and soliciting assistance, on behalf of the Ionian Confederation of Asia Minor, against "the barbarians," the common enemy of the Grecian name. This appeal proved irresistible; the generous Athenians immediately voted the assistance required, and twenty ships of war were

* *History of the Colonization of the Free States of Antiquity,* page 46. London, 1777.

accordingly dispatched, in aid of their oppressed and struggling fellow-countrymen, and soon rendezvoused in the harbour of Miletus. No doubt, as Herodotus informs us, "these ships were the beginning of evils both to Greeks and barbarians;"* for this generous and fraternal procedure on the part of the Athenians undoubtedly led to the invasion of Greece by the Persians, and to the subsequent subversion of the Persian Empire by Alexander the Great. But it is impossible not to admire the generous spirit that animated the Athenians on the occasion, in so readily affording the assistance required in their necessity by the people of Miletus, although nearly four hundred years had elapsed since the original settlement of that city by an Athenian colony. And is Christianity, in the middle of the nineteenth century, less likely to maintain a generous and kindly feeling between a mother-country and her free and independent colonies, than the worship of Jupiter and Apollo five centuries before the Christian era? Shame on the men who for one moment could seriously entertain a sentiment so unwarrantable in itself, and so supremely dishonouring to the Christian name!

SECTION XI.—AMERICAN COLONIZATION—ITS PRINCIPLES AND RESULTS.

In a work which I published in the year 1840, on my return to London from a tour of observation in the United States, entitled, *Religion and Education in America,*† I showed that those states and territories of the American Union, which have been either acquired or settled since the War of Independence, including the great valley of

* *History of Greece.* By William Mitford, Esq., vol. iii. p. 61.
History of Greece. By John Gillies, Esq., L.L.D., vol. i. p. 369.
† *Religion and Education in America.* Ward, Paternoster Row. London, 1840.

the Mississippi, bear precisely the same relation to the original Thirteen States, as the numerous colonies of Britain do to the United Kingdom. They are to all intents and purposes the colonies of the United States; for as far as the relation of a mother-country and a colony is concerned, it is of no importance whatever, whether the latter is planted on the same continent or island as the mother-country, or is separated from it by vast tracts of intervening ocean. This idea, I perceive, has since been put forth by John Arthur Roebuck, Esq., M.P., in his work, entitled, *The Colonies of England*, with a view to contrast the progress and extent of colonization in the United States with its progress and extent in the British Empire, since the peace of 1783.

And with what a contrast does this view of the two countries present us! The United States commenced their national existence with a population of less than three millions, and that population is already increased considerably more than ten-fold; the increase being chiefly in the colonies, in which a population of upwards of fifteen millions have been called into existence, making all due allowance for the natural increase of the population of the original Thirteen States. But Great Britain, with a much larger population to start with,—a population five times greater than that of the United States in the year 1783,—had only a colonial population, properly so called, previous to the era of the gold discoveries, of about a million and-a-half! In short, while Great Britain was enjoying, as abundantly as America, the Divine benediction implied in the first commandment given to mankind, *Be fruitful and multiply*, she had utterly neglected her proper duty, so clearly enjoined in the second part of that commandment, *Replenish the earth and subdue it*,—she had not been filling the world with her cities, like America; she had not been making the wilderness and the solitary place rejoice with the happy abodes of a numerous, virtuous, and Christian population.

In order, however, to set this matter in its proper light, it will be advisable to limit the field of vision to a particular instance of American, as compared with British, colonization; and the instance I shall take is that of New England, or the group of Northern Free States, consisting of Massachusetts, Connecticut, Rhode Island, New Hampshire, Vermont, and Maine. New England, I have already had occasion to observe, was colonized, almost exclusively, by the twenty thousand Puritan emigrants who settled in that country between the years 1620 and 1640; the subsequent additions of population from the mother-country being quite insignificant. In the year 1790, when the first census of the United States was taken, the population of New England amounted to 1,009,522; having doubled itself every twenty-seven years or thereby, from the year 1640. During the next fifty years, however, it little more than doubled itself, its amount in 1840 being only 2,229,859; but this arose entirely from the enormous emigration of the intervening period, which we are now to compare with that of Great Britain,—the great colonizing power, forsooth, of modern times. The population of Great Britain, therefore, or rather of the United Kingdom, in the year 1790, was 14,000,000, and it had not even doubled itself during the next fifty years; the amount in 1841 being only 27,041,031. In so far therefore as the internal increase is concerned, there is no great disparity, although the balance is considerably in favour of New England. In regard, however, to their respective colonizing powers, the two countries were remarkably different from each other; their population being respectively as follows, viz:—

Old England—Population in 1790 = 14,000,000.
New England—Population in 1790 = 1,009,522.*

* The population of Great Britain doubles itself every 48 years, and that of the United States every 30 years; but the numbers I have given are sufficiently near the truth for all practical purposes.

I will not introduce any disturbing element into the question, by reminding the reader that Great Britain had the advantage of all the American Loyalists to start with, in Nova Scotia and elsewhere; for it is quite evident that these Loyalists must have been the merest handful of people,—and the circumstance constitutes, without exception, the most condemnatory sentence that has ever been pronounced upon the colonial policy of the British Empire to the present day. That after an imperial rule of upwards of a hundred and fifty years,—with all the numberless means of acquiring and consolidating power, extending influence, and practising corruption, which that rule had given the mother-country throughout this long period, —there was nobody to take her part in the great struggle with her colonies but the miserable handful of American Loyalists;

> " 'Twas strange, 'twas passing strange !
> 'Twas pitiful, 'twas wondrous pitiful !"

> " For dust was thrown upon her sacred head,
> And no man cried, *God bless her !* "

but this insignificant handful of American Loyalists, who certainly never dreamt that the Americans would gain the day !

Behold, then, these two brave countries,—Old England and New England,—starting fair in this race of colonization, in the year of grace 1790; the former with her fourteen millions of people and her boundless resources in ships, colonies, and commerce; the latter with only one million of people, almost all as poor as Lazarus, as they had but just escaped *with the skin of their teeth* from an unnatural and calamitous war !

It is an interesting and very remarkable fact in the history of the internal emigration and colonization of the United States, that it has uniformly proceeded upon a parallel of latitude from the point of departure; the Northern, Middle, and Southern States throwing off their respective swarms of emigrants every year to the regions due west of them respectively; deflecting very little, if at all, from that parallel either north or south. Since the annexation of Texas and California, indeed, this order of things has been somewhat deranged; but from the peace of 1783, till the year 1840, it had been, with only few, and these unimportant, exceptions, the general rule in the United States; each state, or group of states, colonizing the unoccupied territories due west of itself. New England, as being the most densely peopled, as well as the most limited in extent, and the least fertile, portion of the original Union, was first in the field as a colonizing country; for emigration had thus become a matter of necessity for the inhabitants of that region, and the highly favourable accounts that were received from time to time from the first emigrants to the westward, soon rendered it a perfect passion; insomuch that the emigration from New England alone, which had commenced soon after the peace of 1783, reached in one year at the commencement of the present century when the whole European emigration to America was perfectly insignificant, the almost incredible amount of 300,000 souls!*

The country that was first colonized in this way from New England was the western portion of the State of New York, and the State of Ohio; both of which countries are literally New England colonies. A large portion of the waste lands in these extensive regions had been allotted by the National Congress, as the only recompense which the country had to give them for their services, to the soldiers

---

* Dr. Seybert, an eminent American statistical writer, estimates the number of foreign emigrants who arrived in the United States from the year 1790 to the year 1810, at 120,000 altogether, or 6,000 per annum; and Mr. McGregor estimates the number from 1810 to 1820 at 114,000. These were evidently but inconsiderable additions, when compared with the natural increase from the American stock.

of the Revolution; many of whom sold their tickets of location for the merest trifle to the leaders of the successive colonies from New England. One of these tickets happened to be given by his client, an old Revolutionary soldier, to a country lawyer in the state of New York, as the only fee he could offer him for conducting and gaining a law-suit for him. The lawyer placed it in his desk, as an article that might one day have some assignable value, but had none then. A good many years thereafter, when the flood-tide of New England emigration had been flowing for years in the direction of the region to which this location ticket referred, the lawyer wrote to a friend in the western country, inquiring what the value of his property thereabout might be—and the answer he received was "Seventy-five thousand dollars, and rapidly rising!" It was the possession of this property that enabled that lawyer, who proved to be a men of superior ability, to devote himself to the service of his country, first in the legislature of his native State, and afterwards as a member of Congress, at Washington, where I had the honour of being introduced to him, in the year 1840, as President of the United States. The distinguished individual I allude to was Mr. Martin Van Buren.

When the emigrants from New England had spread themselves over the western portion of the State of New York and the whole State of Ohio, they afterwards over-ran and occupied successively the subsequently formed States of Indiana, Illinois, and Michigan. It is perfectly fair, therefore, to consider the whole of these countries as the colonies of New England; for although a considerable number of emigrants from the Middle States, and also from Europe, settled in all of them from time to time, a much larger number of New Englanders had in the mean time been scattered over the whole of the other States of the Union, and particularly over the State of Kentucky, in the various capacities of professional men, merchants, traders, and artisans of all kinds, as well as planters and farmers. The population of these New England colonies, in the year 1840, was as follows, viz ;—

Western half of the State of New York . . .	1,214,460
Ohio	1,519,467
Indiana	683,315
Illinois	474,403
Michigan	211,705

Total Colonial population of New England in the year 1840 . . . . = 4,103,349

Such then were the magnificent results of the colonizing efforts of New England during a period of fifty years ; commencing, although it did, with a colonizing power of only one million of souls, and the scantiest resources otherwise. But the entire colonial population (properly so called) of Great Britain, originating, although it did, in a colonizing power of fourteen millions of people, with boundless resources of every kind, amounted, in or about the year 1840, to not more than 1,161,009 souls ; even throwing the whole convict emigration of the Empire, with all its increase, for fifty years, like the sword and belt of Brennus, as a make-weight, into the scale !

It is worthy of special observation that the State of Ohio, which contained a population of a million and-a-half in the year 1840, was settled in the very same year (the year 1788) as New South Wales, of which the whole population in the year 1841 was only 130,856, considerably less than a tenth part of the population of the American State.[*]

Surely then if the art of colonization has been lost, as it

---

[*] The first settlement in Ohio was formed in 1788 ; but its growth was impeded, for several years, by sudden wars, and by the exaggerated notions which prevailed of the unhealthiness and other perils of the wilderness. In 1840, however, it contained 1,519,000 inhabitants and was then the third state in the Union. Merivale, vol. ii. p. 47.

seems to have been, in Old England, it has been found again in New England; for I question whether even the ancient Greeks ever surpassed the New Englanders in that noble art, that *heroic work*.

What then is the reason—for there surely must be some adequate reason—for the prodigious difference in the two results? Why, the answer is plain and obvious to the meanest capacity;—America, like the ancient Greeks, gives her colonies freedom and independence from the first; whereas Great Britain, until a very recent period, uniformly withheld everything like manly freedom from her colonies, treated them with the coldest neglect and the grossest injustice, and harassed and oppressed them in every possible way with the incubus and the curse of her Colonial Office. Yes! instead of insulting her colonies by offering them, what certain *soi-disant* colonial reformers in England think it would be a great deal indeed for Great Britain to offer hers, viz., municipal independence—which signifies allowing them to manage for themselves in all little matters, and leaving all important ones to be managed for them at home, or, in other words, the Colonial Office—instead of insulting her colonies by offering them municipal independence, America gives them at once complete independence; that is, the entire control of all matters affecting their interests, as men and as citizens, in every possible way. In short, America realizes the *beau ideal* which, the ancient Locrians indignantly reminded the Corinthians, was the implied condition of their own emigration—she makes her colonies in every respect like herself; she treats her colonists not as her slaves or subjects, but as her equals.

In particular, whenever a number of American colonists, equal to about one-fourth of the number of the inhabitants of the British colony of New South Wales, in the year 1840 —that is, 60,000 altogether—are congregated in any American colony, they have a right, under the American colonization system, to meet together and form a Constitu-

tion for themselves. They may have a Legislature, either
of one or of two Houses, as they please; they may fix the
franchise either high or low, as they choose; they may elect
whatever public officers they may think necessary for the
management of their affairs, and pay these officers whatever salaries they think proper! they may make the best
possible arrangements that suggest themselves to their own
minds for the construction of roads and bridges, the maintenance of schools and colleges, the dispensation of justice,
and the punishment of crime; and they may choose
whomsoever they consider the fittest and properest persons
to represent them in the National Legislature, to deliberate
upon all those great questions of foreign relations, peace
and war, customs' duties, public lands, and the general
post office—in which they have a common interest with the
rest of the nation. In one word, America gives her
colonies all that the ancient Greeks ever gave theirs—entire
freedom and independence; admitting them upon perfectly
equal terms with herself into the great National Confederation.

And the result is precisely what might have been
anticipated—colonization directs itself towards the Waste
Lands of the United States, while those of the British
Colonies, with a much better climate, are passed by and
disregarded. Witness the emigration from the United
Kingdom during the years 1852 and 1853: it amounted

In 1852, to 368,764.
In 1853, to 318,680.

And whither did these emigrants direct their steps? Why,
not fewer than 224,000 in 1852 and 225,258 in 1853
emigrated from Great Britain and Ireland to the United
States, while the emigration to British America, during the
same years, respectively, was, in 1852, only 33,563; and
in 1853, only 30,563; and to Australia, in 1852, 87,000;
and in 1853, 59,931. Notwithstanding, therefore, the

R

powerful impulse that was given to emigration throughout
the United Kingdom, by the discovery of gold in Australia,
the full tide of emigration from Great Britain was still
directed towards the United States, and the claims of the
British colonies, with all their superior advantages, were
treated with derision.   In one word, this humiliating state
of things was entirely the result of bad government and
the lust of empire on the part of Great Britain.

It may not be out of place to glance at the results of
this lust of empire and bad government of the colonies, on
the part of Great Britain, in the interesting and important
light of her duty and obligations as the head of European
Protestantism.

At an early period after the great Protestant Reformation, Great Britain was elevated to the high and honourable
position of the first Protestant nation in Christendom ; and
there was given her a colonial empire such as no other
Protestant nation has ever possessed.   Her peculiar mission
among the nations—her high and holy mission—was therefore to colonize the waste places of the earth with her
Protestant people ; and we have only to look at the
magnificent results of the colonization of New England,
that noblest colony ever planted by man, to have
some idea of what Britain might have done for
the cause of God and of protestantism, had she only done
her duty, had she only fulfilled her mission.   In two
centuries exactly, the twenty thousand Puritans of New
England had become a great people of two millions and-a-
quarter ! and during the last half century before the close
of that period, they had called into existence a colonial
and thoroughly Protestant population besides, of upwards
of four millions of souls !

" We often hear it said," observes the eloquent historian
of England, " that the world is constantly becoming more
and more enlightened, and that this enlightening must

be favourable to Protestantism, and unfavourable to Catholicism. We wish that we could think so. But we see great reason to doubt whether this be a well founded expectation. We see that during the last two hundred and fifty years the human mind has been in the highest degree active; that it has made great advances in every branch of natural philosophy; that it has produced innumerable inventions tending to promote the convenience of life; that medicine, surgery, chemistry, engineering have been very greatly improved; that government, police, and law have been improved, though not to so great an extent as the physical sciences. Yet we see that during these two hundred and fifty years Protestantism has made no conquest worth speaking of. Nay, we believe that as far as there has been a change, that change has, on the whole, been in favour of the Church of Rome."*

"In fifty years from the day on which Luther publicly renounced communion with the Papacy, and burnt the bull of Leo before the gates of Wittenberg, Protestantism attained its highest ascendancy, an ascendancy which it soon lost, and which it has never regained. Hundreds, who could well remember Brother Martin a devout Catholic, lived to see the revolution, of which he was the chief author, victorious in half the States of Europe. In England, Scotland, Denmark, Sweden, Livonia, Prussia, Saxony, Hesse, Wirtemberg, the Palatinate, in several cantons of Switzerland, in the Northern Netherlands, the Reformation had completely triumphed; and in all the other countries on this side of the Alps and Pyrenees, it seemed on the point of triumphing."†

Admitting, therefore, the indisputable fact, that the progress of the Reformation was suddenly checked throughout European Christendom within fifty years after the burning of the Pope's bull at Wittenberg, it is a fact

---

* Macaulay's *Essays*, vol. iii. p. 208.　　† *Ibid.* p. 221.

equally indisputable, that just about the period when Protestantism received its great check in Europe, Great Britain, as the first of the Protestant nations of Europe, had a vast colonial empire given her beyond seas, which she has been constantly increasing from time to time to the present day; and within that vast empire, the field for the maintenance and extension of her national Protestantism, by means of British colonization, has been open and unlimited these two hundred and fifty years. And what has Great Britain done for the extension of our common Protestantism over that vast field these two centuries and a half? Literally nothing that deserves to be mentioned! All her efforts in this way throughout this long period sink into insignificance compared with those even of her own colony of New England in half a century; for it is another indisputable fact, although Lord Macaulay has not mentioned it, as he ought to have done, that the United States of America is the only country in Christendom in which Protestantism has really been extending its area—*lengthening its cords and strengthening its stakes*—these two hundred and fifty years; and this extension has taken place principally, if not exclusively, since the era of Freedom and Independence.

If Great Britain, therefore, is to be considered the *bulwark of the Reformation*, it can only be in the sense of keeping it back, and confining it within the ancient territorial limits which it had already attained only a few years after the death of Luther. Her gross neglect or misuse of the power which Divine Providence had given her of extending it far and wide over continent and isle, by means of· British colonization, "stereotyped the Reformation at that early period, and it has ever since been printed from the same plates." And this result, as I have shown sufficiently, has in no respect been due to any want of enterprise or energy on the part of her people, but simply and solely to her own unhallowed lust of empire—to her uniform and systematic refusal of that self-government, that freedom and independence, to which her colonists had an inherent and indefeasible right by the law of nature and the ordinance of God.

Instead, therefore, of pluming herself for the services she has rendered to the Protestant Reformation, let Great Britain hang her diminished head, and listen in silence to the sentence that awaits her, for having virtually ruined its interests and betrayed its cause. For it is entirely owing to her neglect of duty, her breach of trust, in regard to this vital interest of Protestantism, that the Reformation cannot now number up millions and millions more of a people of British origin and Protestant religion, in countries that are still tenanted only by the grizly bear and the timid kangaroo. Whether the lamentable shortcomings of Great Britain, in the non-fulfilment of her high and holy mission, as the first of the Protestant nations of Europe, are not sufficient to involve a forfeiture of her colonial empire in the high court of heaven, it is not for me to determine; but methinks I see the handwriting against her upon the wall—methinks I hear this forfeiture declared by a voice from the Eternal!

The loss annually sustained by the British nation, through this gross mismanagement of the British colonies, has been incalculable, while the gain to the United States has been correspondingly great; for much, if not all, that we lost through our *bad* system, they gained through their *good* one. In particular, no foreigners emigrate voluntarily to the British colonies, with the exception of those attracted of recent years by the fame of the Gold Diggings; but the influx of foreigners—many of them people of substance as well as of respectable standing in society—into the colonies of the United States is very great; and the Union receives annually a large accession both of wealth and strength from this source. In the year 1853 not fewer than 119,474 Germans landed in the United States at the Port of New York alone, besides the many thousands who had landed at the more southern ports of Philadelphia, Baltimore, Charleston, Savannah and New Orleans. And many of these German immigrants are people of considerable wealth. By dint of great exertion in certain quarters, there has been a considerable German emigration to South Australia and Victoria; but the voluntary and self-originated emigration from Germany is all to the United States; and the fact can only be regarded as a strong condemnation by foreigners of our colonization system, as compared with that of the United States.

But the number even of British subjects, of the middle and more respectable classes of society, who annually emigrate to the United States, is, as I have already demonstrated, beyond all comparison greater than that of those who emigrate voluntarily to the British colonies. I have myself known many instances of persons of this class who greatly preferred our Australian climate to that of the United States, and who would gladly have cast in their lot with a British rather than with an American community; but who had made up their minds at last to emigrate to America from their thorough detestation of our colonial system. Now, when it is considered that every inhabitant of the United States consumes only about seven shillings and sixpence worth of British produce and manufactures annually, whereas every inhabitant of the Australian colonies consumes from seven to tenpounds' worth—[Population of New South Wales in 1869=485,358. Imports, £3,544,285, or £7 7s. per head]—the loss which Great Britain sustains in this way must be immense.

But the strangest and most humiliating fact of all, in illustration and in condemnation of our colonization system, as compared with that of the United States, is the wholesale emigration to America from Ireland for a long series of years past, and the abject character and condition of a large proportion of the emigrants. These emigrants, it is well known, are "the hewers of wood and the drawers of water" in the United States; they are employed in all manner of servile work, as diggers of canals, as labourers upon the earth-works of railways—in doing every thing, in short, that the humblest American workman disdains to do. Now, what a humiliating and degrading condition is this for any Country in Christendom, and especially for any portion of the United Kingdom, to be reduced to—to be a mere breeding state, like Virginia before the late war, for the rearing of "white niggers," as they are technically called over the water, for the haughty republicans of America! The very idea is sufficient to make one's blood boil with virtuous indignation. "Look at Ireland," said the Duke of Sotomayor to Lord Palmerston, when his lordship was tendering his advice, somewhat unseasonably, as to the internal government of Spain under the late Bourbon dynasty in that country. "Look at Ireland!" For my own part, as a Christian man, I cannot help thinking that it would have been far less dishonourable to Great Britain to have been defeated either at Trafalgar or Waterloo, than to have allowed a foreigner, and that foreigner a Spaniard too, to speak these three words to a British Minister. It is no disgrace to a great nation to be defeated in a just cause, taking it for granted that the cause in both these cases was a just one, which is somewhat doubtful; but it is a deep disgrace to any nation to allow whole masses of its people to sink into such a condition of social degradation as to warrant the whole volume of charges implied in the speech of the Duke of Sotomayor, "Look at Ireland!" We may naturally feel indignant at Cicero's telling us, as we shall find he does, that there was nothing to be got in Britain in his time but slaves, and even these of so inferior a class, that one could not pick out either a schoolmaster or a fiddler from a whole ship-load of them! But there is a much worthier object for our indignation here; for what is the wholesale emigration from Ireland to the United States but a species of "white slavery," with which we condescend to furnish America, simply because her colonization system is incomparably better than ours, and because that better system alone enables her to employ our surplus poor, whom we are glad to get rid of, after having first degraded them to the level of slaves? For I have no hesitation in expressing my decided opinion that, if the extraordinary facilities which the British empire affords for colonization were only turned to account, every over-burdened class of society in the United Kingdom would be relieved; competition in every branch of business would be diminished; poverty and destitution would in great measure disappear from the face of society, and crime would be wonderfully lessened in amount. It is her colonies that serve as the safety-valve for America; and I am confident the time is not too late even yet for her present colonies to prove the safety-valve for Great Britain also. The extent of destitution and suffering that result from a redundancy of population is much greater, and the amount of emigration that is necessary to have a salutary effect upon a country suffering from such a redundancy, is much smaller than is generally supposed. It is the last ounce that breaks the back of the camel—it is the last drop that makes the pitcher overflow.

SECTION XII.—ROMAN COLONIZATION, AND THE ROMAN COLONY OF BRITAIN.

Baron Niebuhr, in his celebrated History of Rome, gives the following definition of a Roman colony :—

"A colony is a company of people, led at the same time and in one body to a certain place furnished with dwellings, in order to live there under certain legal conditions : they may be citizens or dependents sent out to form a commonwealth, according to a decree of their state, or of that to

which they are subject; but not such as have seceded
during a time of civil dissension."[*]

There was therefore this essential difference between a
Grecian and a Roman colony, that whereas the former,
although occasionally the result of an act of the state, was
not necessarily so, and was often indeed an association of
families and individuals opposed to the party in power, the
latter was always the result of a decree of the Senate.
The Grecian colonists almost uniformly defrayed the
expenses of their own emigration and settlement; while
the Roman, like the earlier settlers in New South Wales,
had grants of land and a free passage *out*, with rations and
other indulgences, including an ample supply of slave
labour, from the State. The Grecian colonies, moreover,
were founded, either to relieve the Mother-country of the
pressure of a redundant population, or to provide places of
refuge and settlement for those, whether unquiet spirits or
not, for whom the Mother-country had become a great deal
too hot; but the Roman colonies were formed expressly to
extend the limits of the empire, or to hold, by military
occupation, territories which had been acquired by force of
arms. The Grecian colonies were therefore free cities,
supporting themselves by agriculture and commerce, and
defending themselves from the surrounding barbarians, till
they could subjugate and civilize them, by their own warlike prowess : the Roman colonies were mere garrison
towns on the frontiers of the empire, and the lands were
held by the leading colonists on a tenure somewhat similar
to that of the feudal system, each large estate being a
knight's fee.[†]

---

[*] Niebuhr's *Rome*, vol. ii. p. 43.

[†] McCulloch, in his *Dictionary of Commerce*, under the Article
Colonies, gives the following account of the Roman colonies. "The
Roman colonies were, for the most part, founded by and under the
authority of Government; being intended to serve both as outlets for

It was under this peculiar system of colonization that the island of Britain was conquered and colonized by the Romans under Julius Cæsar, about fifty years before the Christian era; and the following incidental notice, which is given us in the letters of Cicero, of the state of the island at that early period, and of the Roman estimate of its inhabitants and capabilities, is certainly by no means flattering to our national vanity.

" We are all on tiptoe to hear of the issue of the war in

poor and discontented citizens, and as military stations, or garrisons, to secure the subjection of the conquered provinces over which they were scattered. The most intimate political union was always maintained between them and the Mother-city. Their internal government was modelled on that of Rome; and, while their superior officers were mostly sent from the capital, they were made to contribute their full quota of troops and taxes, to assist in carrying on the contests in which the Republic was almost constantly engaged."

The last of the Roman colonies, was that of Dacia, a province which had been conquered by the Emperor Trajan at the commencement of the second century. It comprised the extensive country on the left bank of the Danube, including part of Hungary, Transsylvania, and the principalities of Moldavia and Wallachia, which was recently the seat of war between the Russians and the Turks. The Dacian colony consisted of 30,000 soldier-colonists; and it is somewhat remarkable that the descendants of these colonists, who are a comparatively poor people, employed in pastoral pursuits and agriculture along the flanks of the Carpathian mountains, still speak a barbarous dialect of the Latin language to the present day. (See *Overland Journey from Constantinople to London*. By Rev. — Walsh, Chaplain to the British Embassy at Constantinople. London, 1823.)

This conquest of Dacia by the Emperor Trajan is thus alluded to by the contemporary poet Statius, in the first Book of his *Thebais*, as translated by Pope:—

> Nor yet attempt to stretch thy bolder wing,
> And mighty Cæsar's conquering eagles sing;
> How twice he tamed proud Ister's rapid flood,
> While Dacian mountains streamed with barbarous blood;
> Twice taught the Rhine beneath his laws to roll,
> And stretched his Empire to the frozen Pole.

Britain: for it appears that the approaches of the island are defended with works of prodigious strength. As for money, it has already been ascertained that there is not one silver sixpence to be got in the island, and there is not the slightest hope of booty, except from slaves; and I presume you will scarcely expect any schoolmasters or fiddlers from such a quarter."*

Cicero's correspondent, Atticus, had probably requested him to purchase for him some well-educated slave, probably as a private tutor for his nephews, Caius and Marcus, and especially to teach them instrumental music; but no British-born slave of that period possessed such high qualifications! The reader will probably suppose that it would be out of the question to talk of slaves from the British islands in any part of the world now. If so, let him only look at Ireland emigrating wholesale to the United States.

There was a good deal of hard fighting, as usual, in the Roman conquest of Britain,† of which the reader who desires it will find a full and particular account in the proper place; but Britain, or rather the southern portion of the island, was fairly conquered at last, and proclaimed a Roman colony with the customary formalities; liberal grants of the waste lands in the island being held forth to intending emigrants of the requisite qualifications, with

---

* " Britannici belli exitus expectatur. Constat enim aditus insulæ esse munitos mirificis molibus. Etiam illud jam cognitum est, neque argenti scrupulum esse ullum in illa insula, neque ullam spem prædæ, *nisi ex mancipiis:* ex quibus nullos puto te literis aut musicis eruditos expectare." Cicero. *Epist. ad. Atticum*, lib. iv. 16.

† The Roman conquest of Britain appears to have been a work of great difficulty, and a whole series of bloody battles was required to effect it—first with the different tribes of Britons, and afterwards with the Picts and Scots or Caledonians—from the landing of Julius Cæsar in the year 50 before Christ, till the conquest of Agricola at the close of the first century of the Christian era.

the other indulgences enumerated above. From the first *Eclogue* of Virgil, which may be regarded as a sort of *Anti-Emigration Circular* of the day, we learn that Britain was one of the regular *Emigration Fields* of the empire for carrying off the redundant population and the unquiet spirits of Italy, during the reign of the Emperor Augustus; although it does not appear to have stood very high in public estimation at Rome, being regarded by intending emigrants in much the same light as the *Falkland Islands* in our own time. This is pretty evident from Virgil's mentioning it last of all, with anything but a note of recommendation; for he hints that where there might be a possibility of getting home again from other colonies, there was no hope of returning if you went *there*.

> " At nos hinc alii sitientes ibimus Afros,
>   Pars Scythiam, et rapidum Cretæ veniemus Oaxem,
>   Et penitus toto divisos orbe Britannos.."

> " But we, alas, must leave our native land,
>   To pitch our tents on Afric's burning sand,
>   Or range the Scythian wilds with weary feet,
>   Or build our wigwams on the streams of Crete ;
>   Or, sadder still ! on Britain's distant shore,
>   Ne'er to be seen or known of mankind more !"

In short, Britain was virtually as far from Italy in Virgil's time, as New Zealand is from England in ours ; while the dangers of the voyage were incomparably greater, considering the comparative facilities of ancient and modern navigation.

And yet the island did get colonized notwithstanding, and became in time a first-rate Roman colony ; the garrison towns all over the country being transformed successively, as they became wealthy and populous, into Roman municipal cities, enjoying, within certain well-defined limits, the privilege of self-government, and exhibiting in no inconsiderable degree the civilization and refinement of Rome.

The numerous English cities and towns of the present day, of which the names end in *chester, cester, caster*, and even *castle*, mark the sites of these ancient Roman municipalities, which were originally only *Castra* or *Castella, Camps* or *Forts*; and they exhibit, in the most unmistakable manner, the extent and progress of Roman colonization in our island. It extended at one time as far north as the Friths of Clyde and Forth, where the Emperor Antoninus threw a wall across the island, the remains of which are now called "Graham's Dike," to protect the colonists from the incursions of the Scots and Picts of the north. These barbarians, like the Caffres of the present day, came down occasionally upon the colonists in great force, carrying off much valuable booty to their hills; and it was even alleged, as is stated by the historian Gibbon, that they were somewhat addicted to cannibalism, "preferring the shepherd to his flock."* These incursions became so frequent and disastrous that the Emperor Severus at length contracted the limits of the colony by throwing a second wall across the island from the Solway Frith to the German Ocean; and within these limits it continued to increase and prosper till the beginning of the fifth century, when it numbered not fewer than ninety-two considerable towns, including thirty-three municipal cities, having all the

* This is related of a Caledonian tribe of the period, whose headquarters were somewhere near the site of the present city of Glasgow, and who were called the *Attacotti*. But Gibbon was probably not aware that savages are in the habit of accusing other tribes of their own countrymen, with whom they are at variance, of cannibalism, to prejudice the civilized race against them, and thereby to serve their own purposes. There is nothing more common among the aborigines of New South Wales. I am somewhat concerned in this matter personally, being a native of the town of Greenock, near Glasgow. If the ancient savages of that neighbourhood ever did eat any Roman colonists, it is evident, to use the language of the Rev. Sidney Smith, that they must have "disagreed" with them, as their posterity have an utter aversion to everything Roman now.

privileges and appendages of such cities throughout the
Roman empire.* As an interesting particular in the

* There were actually three walls erected by the Romans across the
island of Britain, while that island, or rather the southern portion of
it, was a Roman colony; and the circumstance affords us no mean idea
of the formidable character of the ancient Caledonians, or Scots and
Picts, whom these walls were intended to keep out of the colony. The
first wall was erected under the Emperor Adrian, in the year 120, by
his prefect, or Governor of Britain, Julius Severus. It was a rampart
of earth, covered with turf, extending from the mouth of the Tyne to
the Solway Frith, about eighty Roman miles. About twenty years
later, in the reign of Antoninus Pius, A.D. 140, the Caledonians having
in the meantime broken down this rampart in various places, and
ravaged the colony, the Emperor directed his Prefect, or Governor
of Britain, Lollius Urbicus, to proceed against them, which he did
accordingly, constructing at the same time a second wall or rampart,
thirty-seven miles long, from the Frith of Forth to the Frith of
Clyde. It was formed of turf, on a foundation of stone, and was
four yards in thickness, with a moat or fosse in front. But the
Caledonians had as little respect for this second wall as they had
had for that of Adrian; and in the year 208, the Emperor
Septimius Severus marched against them in person at the head of his
numerous army in Britain; but having experienced great losses in the
inhospitable country, he deemed it better to abandon the northern
portion of the colony to the barbarians altogether, and accordingly
constructed a third wall across the island nearly in the same line with
that of Adrian, from Newcastle-on-Tyne to the Solway Frith. This
wall was built of freestone and was eight feet thick and twelve in
height. It was upwards of sixty-eight English miles in length, and
had a tower or castle of sixty feet square every three quarters of a
mile throughout its whole extent. And between every two of these
castles there were four turrets of twelve feet square, 300 yards apart
from each other. This wall was called by the Britons "Mursever,"
or Valsever," evidently a corruption of *Murus*, or *Vallum Severi*. The
poet, Spenser, knew it by the latter name, and calls it Gualsever.

Next there came Tyne, along whose stony bank
That Roman monarch built a brazen wall,
Which mote the feebled Britons strongly flank
Against the Picts, that swarmed over all,
Which yet thereof Gualsever they do call.

Spenser's Faery Queen.

history of the times, as exhibiting the state of Roman civilization in the colony of Britain, we learn from the poet Juvenal, who flourished in the reign of the Emperor Nero in the first, and of Trajan in the second century, that it was customary, in his time, for young gentlemen of Britain, who were studying for the bar, with a view to the practice of their profession in the Roman courts of the municipal cities of the island, to cross over to France for their education.*

Such, then, was the state of Britain at the commencement of the fifth century. It was a Roman colony of four hundred and fifty years standing; wealthy and populous, with all the appendages and advantages of Roman civilization, and having a degree of freedom, moreover, under the municipal institutions of Rome, such as no British colony of the present day in Australia was permitted to enjoy until the advent of responsible government in the year 1856. And yet there was one thing wanting—that one thing which the Greek colonies uniformly had from the first—that is, their entire freedom and national independence; and the first opportunity that presented itself of achieving these great benefits and blessings for their adopted country was accordingly seized with avidity by the Roman colonists of Britain, who thenceforth became free and independent.†
This important event, so deeply interesting to every Briton, but especially to every British colonist, is related in the

*   "Gallia causidicos docuit facunda Britannos:
       De conducendo loquitur jam rhetore Thule."—*Juvenal.*

† This most interesting event is described in the following manner by the descendants of the ancient Britons themselves. "Having oppressed the island for four hundred years, and exacted an annual tribute of three thousand pounds of silver, they (that is the Romans) departed for the land of Rome, to repel the invasion of the black horde, leaving behind them only women and children of tender age, who all became Cambrians."—*Welsh Chronicle, quoted in History of the Conquest of England by the Normans.* By A. Thierry, vol. i. p. 7.

following language by the eloquent historian of the *Decline and Fall of the Roman Empire :*—

"Whilst Italy was ravaged by the Goths, and a succession of feeble tyrants oppressed the provinces beyond the Alps, *the British island separated itself from the body of the Roman empire.* The regular forces which guarded that remote province, had been gradually withdrawn; and Britain was abandoned, without defence, to the Saxon pirates and the savages of Ireland and Caledonia. *The Britons, reduced to this extremity, no longer relied on the tardy and doubtful aid of a declining monarchy. They assembled in arms, repelled the invaders, and rejoiced in the important discovery of their own strength.* Afflicted by similar calamities, and actuated by the same spirit, the Armorican provinces (a name which comprehended the maritime countries of Gaul, between the Seine and the Loire) resolved to imitate the example of the neighbouring Island. They expelled the Roman magistrates, who acted under the authority of the usurper Constantine; and a free government was established among a people who had so long been subject to the arbitrary will of a master. *The independence of Britain and Armorica was soon confirmed by Honorius himself, the lawful Emperor of the West, and the letters, by which he committed to the new States the care of their own safety, might be interpreted as an absolute and perpetual abdication of the exercise and rights of sovereignty.* This interpretation was, in some measure, justified by the event. After the usurpers of Gaul had successively fallen, the maritime provinces were restored to the empire. Yet their obedience was imperfect and precarious; the vain, inconstant, rebellious disposition of the people, was incompatible either with freedom or servitude; and Armorica, though it could not long maintain the form of a republic, was agitated by frequent and destructive revolts. *Britain was irrecoverably lost* (anno 409). *But as the Emperor wisely acquiesced in the independence of a remote province, the separation was not embittered by the reproach of tyranny or rebellion; and the claims of allegiance and protection were succeeded by the mutual and voluntary offices of national freedom.*

"This revolution dissolved the artificial fabric of civil and military government, and the independent country, during a period of forty years, till the descent of the Saxons, was ruled by the authority of the clergy, the nobles, and the municipal towns. Zosimus, who alone has preserved the memory of this singular transaction, very accurately observes, that the letters of Honorius were addressed to the *cities* of Britain. Under the protection of the Romans, ninety-two considerable towns had arisen in the several parts of that great province; and, among these, thirty-three cities were distinguished above the rest, by their superior privileges and importance. Each of these cities, as in all the other provinces of the empire, formed a legal corporation, for the purpose of regulating their domestic policy; and the powers of municipal government were distributed among annual magistrates, a select senate, and the assembly of the people, according to the original model of the Roman constitution. The management of a common revenue, the exercise of civil and criminal jurisdiction, and the habits of public counsel and command, were inherent to these petty republics; and when they asserted their independence, the youth of the city, and the adjacent districts, would naturally range themselves under the standard of the magistrate.*

From this very interesting narrative, we learn —

1. That the colonists of Britain, although enjoying a considerable degree of freedom under the admirable municipal institutions of Rome, nevertheless embraced the first opportunity that offered, of achieving their entire freedom

* Gibbon's *Decline and Fall of the Roman Empire*, vol. iv. p. 169. London, 1825.

8

and national independence; which were afterwards formally guaranteed to them by the Emperor Honorius : and,

2. That for forty years, previous to the Saxon irruption, the government of the island was administered by a Confederation of Sovereign and Independent Republics, on the model of the ancient Republic of Rome.

It was no disparagement to the Roman colonists of Britain, that their country was so speedily overrun, and their whole national system subverted and destroyed by the northern barbarians. In that gloomy and disastrous period, this was the common fate of every Roman province in succession, till Rome itself fell, and was sacked by the Goths. A people long habituated to the arts of peace were but ill fitted to withstand the furious onset of the half-savage hordes of the north, especially at a time when fire-arms were unknown; but the circumstance that every vestige of Roman civilization, as well as of the Roman language, was swept away, and no trace of either left in the Anglo-Saxon institutions, or the Anglo-Saxon tongue of the country, sufficiently declares how hard a struggle the Anglo-Saxons must have had ere they conquered the island, and how every successive city, as it fell, must have been put to the sword by the ruthless conquerors.

There is only one reflection that suggests itself on the review of this transaction,—and it is this : if the Roman colonists of Britain were entitled to their freedom and independence, under the reign of the Emperor Honorius, when they seized upon that freedom and independence themselves, why should we, the British colonists of Australia, be refused our freedom and independence also under the reign of Queen Victoria ?* Is it because we are

* There is a remarkable coincidence in the case of the ancient Roman colonists of Britain with our own, which is well worthy of special notice. In the year 409, when they put forth their Declaration of Independence, they had thirty-three Municipal cities or

nearer. Great Britain, than the ancient Roman colonists of
Britain were to Rome ?   This will surely not be pretended.
What then will stand in the way of the attainment of
our natural and inherent rights as British Colonists,
able and willing to manage our own affairs in every
thing ?   Nothing, I answer, but that unhallowed lust

Borough towns in the island, and fifty-eight inferior towns and
villages. Now as the rank of a Roman municipality would scarcely
be conferred on any city or town in Britain till it had attained a
population of 4,000 souls, and as population in these times of war and
inroad, was much more concentrated in walled towns and strongly
defended villages than at present, there is reason to believe that
nearly one-half of the entire population of the Roman colony would
be resident in towns, and that the entire population would amount to
at least half a million of souls. Now if half a million of Roman
colonists in Britain did a praiseworthy and noble action, as every
honest right-hearted man will allow they did, in asserting their freedom and independence in the fifth century, why should a million
and-a-half of British colonists in Australia be precluded from following
their noble example in the nineteenth century ? Are we less intelligent
or less able to defend ourselves than the Roman colonists of Britain at
the period in question ?

The following was probably something like the amount and distri-
bution of the population of the Roman colony of Britain at the era of
its independence in the year 409.

Thirty-three Municipal Cities or Boroughs, viz. :—

London, the Capital of the Colony 10,000
Four other Cities at 7000 each . . . . = 28,000
Ten   Ditto   at 5000 each . . . . = 50,000
Eighteen Ditto   at 4000 each . . . . = 72,000

Smaller Towns and Villages.

Twenty at 2000 each . . . . = 40,000
Twenty at 1500 each . . . . = 30,000
Eighteen at 1000 each . . . . = 18,000
_____

Total Town population 248,000
Rural population 252,000
_____

Total population of the Roman Colony of Britain
A. D. 409 . . . . = 500,000

of empire that has been the fruitful source of "woes un-numbered" to Great Britain already—nothing but that vain pursuit, on the part of a deluded people, of an empty shadow, for which the invaluable substance is sacrificed and lost.   Let Her Majesty be only advised to follow the good example of the Emperor Honorius, and no part of the present Colonial Empire will ever be half so valuable in its actual condition, even to Great Britain, as free and independent Australia.

SECTION XIII.—THE RESULT OF THE COMPARISON STATED.

If the comparison I have thus instituted between ancient and modern, Grecian and British colonization is both fair and just—and I challenge all and sundry to prove that it is not—it follows that much, if not the whole, of what we are in the daily habit of hearing from all quarters, as to the benefits and blessings of "belonging to the British Empire," in the sense of being mere dependencies of that empire, and of being governed as such, is either the sheerest cant or the grossest delusion.   Nay, it is a mere artifice of the devil, to extend and perpetuate human misery, by setting men's minds and hearts against the adoption of those beautiful and perfect arrangements, which the All-wise and beneficent Creator has established, for the welfare and advancement of society in this lower world.

So far, indeed, from the British government of the colonies, properly so called, having ever been either a benefit or a blessing to these colonies, it has uniformly, and without one solitary exception, been the bane and the curse of the colonies, from the time when the first of them was planted, under that Solomon of his age, King James the First, till the advent of popular institutions for the Australian colonies in the year 1856.   And if it has been "destructive" to the best interests of the colonies, as

Heeren testifies it has, it has been infinitely worse for the mother-country herself. With a virgin soil and a propitious sky, with a luxurious climate and a country of boundless resources, we colonists can struggle on, even under the worst government, and prosper notwithstanding. But—to take a single instance of the genuine *domestic* effects of this lust of empire on the part of Great Britain, this grasping at the shadow and losing the substance, this virtual stoppage of the healthful perennial stream of emigration that would otherwise have flowed from an overcrowded country for two centuries and-a-half—what can you do, in your present circumstances, ye poor needle-women of England? Instead of pining in the hopeless wretchedness of your cheerless lot, ye might, every one of you, had Great Britain only discharged her proper duty to herself, and to you, in the matter of colonization, have been the happy mothers of hopeful children in the colonies; and your sons and your daughters would have been extending our noble language, our equitable laws, our free institutions, and our Protestant religion over every continent and every isle.

Mr. Wakefield doubtless speaks of "a peculiarity of *colonies*, as distinguished from *dependencies* in general, which furnishes a reason," as he conceives, "for wishing that they should belong to the empire. I mean," he continues, "the attachment of colonies to their mother-country. Without having lived in a colony—or, at any rate, without having a really intimate acquaintance with colonies, which only a very few people in the mother-country have, or can have—it is difficult to conceive the intensity of colonial loyalty to the empire. In the colonies of England, at any rate, the feeling of love towards England and of pride in belonging to her empire, is more than a sentiment; it is a sort of passion which all the colonists feel, except Milesian Irish emigrants. I have often been unable to help smiling at the exhibition of it. In what it originates I cannot say:

perhaps in a sympathy of blood or race, for the present
Anglo-Americans feel in their heart's core the same kind of
love and respect for England that we Englishmen at home
feel for the memory of Alfred or Elizabeth : but, whatever
may be its cause I have no doubt that love of England is
the ruling sentiment of English Colonies."*

Now, with all his acuteness, Mr. Wakefield has here
confounded two things that are essentially distinct from
each other, viz., "the love of England," and "the love of
her empire," or government, in the sense of a strong desire
to be, or to continue, under it.   The love of England—
meaning the love of the country, of its people, of its institutions, and of its prosperity—is a generous and manly
feeling, which, I am most happy to admit with Mr.
Wakefield, is the characteristic of *all British colonies* : and
so far from there being anything either strange or unaccountable in it, as Mr. W. seems to imagine, it is the
most natural thing in the world.   For, according to the
Scotch proverb, "Blood is thicker than water ;" or in other
words, "we shall always be more kindly-affectioned
towards our *own* kindred, our *own* country, our *own* race,
than towards mere strangers or foreigners," *provided always
that no disturbing element shall have intervened*, as in the case
of the war of Independence in America ; which I am sorry
to say has generated very extensively somewhat different
feelings in that country from those which Mr. Wakefield considers universal.   But Mr. Wakefield is decidedly in the
wrong in taking it for granted, as he does, that this love of
England, which is both natural and universal in British
colonies, necessarily implies a desire to live under her
government, as mere dependencies of her empire.   I deny
that it does.   I deny that the two things have the slightest
connection with each other: and it is throwing dust in the
eyes of the people of England, and rendering them stone-

* *Art of Colonization, &c.*, p. 101.

blind both to their interest and their duty, to persuade them that they have; or that the equally generous and manly desire of freedom and independence, on the part of British colonists in certain circumstances, implies anything like a hatred of England, or of her people, of her institutions, or of her prosperity. Away with such folly—such madness!

In a passage I have quoted above, the great Hugo Grotius, one of the ablest and best interpreters of the law of nature and nations that has ever lived, lays it down as a universal and unquestionable maxim, that in such circumstances as those of the British colonies of North America and Australia, respectively, *novus populus sui juris nascitur*, "a new and independent nation is born." And Heeren, no mean authority in politics either, confirms this maxim, by stating, in a passage I have already quoted above, that "the desire of independence is natural to agricultural colonies, because *a new nation gradually becomes formed within them.*" And this natural, and therefore divinely implanted desire, with the new and multiform attachments from which it flows, constitutes one of the strongest principles—one of the strongest passions—of human nature. In short, the love of England, and the desire of national independence, on the part of British colonists in the circumstances I have indicated, are in perfect harmony with each other, like all the other works of God; which both of these generous and manly feelings undoubtedly are. It is highly presumptuous, therefore, to say the least of it, for mortal man to imagine that *his puny* arrangements for the welfare and advancement of society in this lower world, should be preferable to those of the Supreme Creator, and Lord of all—that *his* notorious device of Downing-street, for instance, as a centre of emanation for all power and authority in the uttermost parts of the earth, should be a better device for the government of such countries as British America and Australia, than the one indicated in the law of Nature and the ordinance of God ; which proclaims with a voice from heaven, that these countries should be free and independent.

There has doubtless been a disturbing element at work in the case of British America, which has deranged in some degree the natural tendencies of things in that country—I mean the two American wars, and the feelings of bitter hostility they unhappily engendered on both sides of the boundary line ; for such feelings are the regular stock-in-trade of your "British empire men," and your "zealots for British connection," as opposed to the advocates of national independence. Then there are the antipathies of race, *within* the boundary line. But we are happily free from all such disturbing elements in Australia. There are no hostile races *here*, as in Canada; there are no unreasonable antipathies towards America, to make us profess what we do not feel; and least of all, is there any temptation in the Australian colonies to the folly of *annexation*, in the Canadian sense of the phrase. We love England as warmly as Mr. Wakefield can wish us to do, and from our inmost hearts we will ever *pray for her prosperity* ; but we cherish at the same time that generous and manly desire of national independence, which God and nature have implanted in our breasts.

Mr. Wakefield has also fallen into a serious mistake in considering " the attachment of colonies to their Mother-country a peculiarity of colonies, as distinguished from dependencies in general, which furnishes a reason for wishing that they should belong to the Empire." On the contrary, it furnishes no such reason whatever, but the very reverse. The British subject who goes to any of the other dependencies Mr. Wakefield speaks of—to the East or West Indies, for example ; to Ceylon; to the Mauritius ; to Hongkong, Singapore or Labuan; to Aden, St. Helena, the Bermudas, Gibraltar, Malta, or Heligoland—uniformly carries his *patria*, or country, along with him, *in imagination*, and returns to it *in reality*, as soon as he can; never for one moment seeking for another *patria* or country in any of these dependencies. But the British colonist, properly so called, leaves his *patria*, or native country, for ever, and seeks for another *patria*, or adopted country, in the land of his emigration.* It must be obvious, therefore, that Mr. Wakefield's wish that those colonies, in which hundreds of thousands of his fellow-countrymen have actually found the *patria*, or country, they were in search of, when they left their native land, "should belong to the empire," rather than the other dependencies in which there can be no such *patria* either sought for or found, is, to say the least of it, somewhat unreasonable.

* This is the remarkably appropriate language in which emigration and colonization are uniformly described by the ancients: "*Nos* PATRIAM *fugimus*—PATRIAM *quærentes.*—Virg. "*Causa* RELINQUENDI QUÆRENDIQUE PATRIAM."— Seneca, as quoted above.

CHAPTER III.

THE FUTURE AUSTRALIAN EMPIRE.

SECTION I.—THE PRESENT CRISIS, AND THE CONSUMMATION TO WHICH IT POINTS.

"I anticipate with others," observed Lord John Russell, on the second reading of the Australian Constitution Bill of 1850, "that some of our colonies may so grow in wealth and population that they may feel themselves strong enough to maintain their own independence in amity and alliance with Great Britain. I do not think that that time is yet approaching. But let us make them, as fast as possible, fit to govern themselves. Let us give them, as far as we can, the capacity of ruling their own affairs. Let them increase in wealth and population; and, whatever may happen, we of this great empire will have the consolation of saying that we have increased the happiness of the world."

Through the unexpected discovery of gold in Australia, a change, which no mortal could anticipate at the time, has passed upon the Australian Colonies since these memorable words were spoken by Lord John Russell twenty years ago; and the consummation to which they point, and which was then regarded merely as a remote contingency, is now almost universally admitted as an impending reality. By that wonderful event, which took the whole civilized world by surprise, the Australian Colonies were virtually wrenched out of the hands of the Imperial Government, just as a boat is wrenched out of the hands of a rower in the rapids of an impetuous river; and they are now swept along by the current towards freedom and independence, with a velocity of motion which the Imperial Government may doubtless direct for the accomplishment of the highest national objects, but which it is utterly powerless either to stem or to check. During the interval that has elapsed since Lord John Russell addressed to the House of Commons the words I have quoted, the Australian Colonies have virtually lived half a century; and the way in which they have successively carried out a whole series of important measures of reform in their respective political systems, since the inauguration of responsible government for the colonies in 1856, proves to demonstration their entire fitness for that COMING EVENT, which Lord John Russell anticipated with such kindly feelings twenty years since.

That his lordship was not mistaken as to the opinions, on this subject, *of others*, of the highest standing in society, as men and as statesmen, will appear from the following quotations :—

"If a dominant country understood the true nature and advantages arising from the relation of supremacy and dependence to the related communities, it would voluntarily recognise the legal independence of such of its own dependencies as were fit for independence; it would, by its political arrangements, study to prepare for independence those which were still unable to stand alone; and it would seek to promote colonization for the purpose of extending its trade rather than its empire, and without attempting to maintain the dependence of its colonies beyond the time when they need its protection."*

"The colonies, which we are founding in America, Australasia, and Africa, will, probably, at some future day, be powerful nations, who will also be unwilling to remain

* *Essay on the Government of Dependencies.* By George Cornewall Lewis, Esq., 334. London, 1841.

in subjection to any rule but their own. But this withdrawal from our metropolitan rule ought not to offend or wound us as a nation; we should feel in this case as a parent feels when a child has reached unto manhood—becomes his own master, forms his own separate household, and becomes, in his turn, the master of a family. The ties of affection remain—the separation is not the cause or the effect of hostility. Thus should it be with a mother-country and her colonies. Having founded them, and brought them to a sturdy maturity, she should be proud to see them honestly glorying in their strength, and wishing for independence. Having looked forward to this time as sure to come, she should prepare for it. She should make such arrangements in her system as to put all things in order for this coming change in the colony's condition, so that independence may be acquired and friendship retained. The colony would, in such a case, continue to feel towards the mother-country with kindness and respect; a close union would exist between them, and all their mutual relations would be so ordered as to conduce to the welfare of both."*

" Under the present system of management Great Britain derives nothing but loss from the dominion she assumes over her colonies."†

"It is the trade of the colonies that renders them beneficial to the mother-country; *our trade, as it is now, and always has been conducted, centres in Great Britain.*"‡

"Let the trade to North America be what it may, of little importance or otherwise, it is a mere begging the question, and a most disingenuous artifice to insinuate that

---

* *The Colonies of England.* By John Arthur Roebuck, Esq., M.P., p. 170.

† *Wealth of Nations*, c. vii.

‡ *Instructions to the Representatives of the City of Boston, in the Legislature of Massachusetts*, May, 1764.

this trade will be lost, if a separation from the colonies should ensue. On the contrary, it is more probable that, when all parties shall be left at full liberty to do as they please, our North American trade will rather be increased, than diminished by such a measure. Because *it is freedom, and not confinement, or monopoly which increases trade.*"[*]

But these enlightened and patriotic sentiments and views were far in advance of the age in England a hundred years since—the era of the American troubles.

"Only one Englishman at this crisis," (anno 1771) observes the historian of America, "had the sagacity to perceive that the views and pretensions of Britain and America were quite incompatible, and that, in the warmth of the controversy, these conflicting views had been so far disclosed and matured, that a cordial reconciliation was no longer possible. This was Dr. Josiah Tucker, Dean of Gloucester, one of the most learned and ingenious writers on commerce and political economy that England has ever produced. With a boldness equal to the comprehension of his views, he openly recommended, in several tracts which he published about this time, an entire separation of the two countries, and a formal recognition of the independence of the American States. The doctrine which he inculcated was, that *when colonies have reached such a degree of wealth and population as to be able to support themselves, the authority of the parent State whence they emanated, must necessarily be trivial and precarious; and that, consequently, in all cases of this kind, it is the dictate of prudence and sound policy that the parties, instead of waiting to be separated by emergent quarrel and strife, should dissolve their connection by mutual consent.* Such, he contended, was now the situation of the British colonies in America; and in urging upon Britain the consequent policy of releasing them from further controul, he

* Dean Tucker's *Humble Address, Recommending Separation from America,* p. 61. Gloucester, 1775..

maintained with much force and good sense that this measure would be attended with a great alleviation of the national expense, without any real diminution of the national gain. For this unpalatable counsel the doctor was regarded as a wild visionary, both by those of his countrymen who supported, and by those who opposed the measures of their government. But time illustrated his views and honoured his wisdom."*

The celebrated Edmund Burke, and the well-known ethical writer, Soame Jenyns, both threw all the influence of their names and their fame at this period into the scale of war with America—the former characterising the truly politic and patriotic scheme of Dean Tucker as puerile and childish; and the latter showing up the Americans in a poem, after expatiating for a while over the wide fields of freedom, *voluntarily throwing themselves back once more into the arms of Britain!* It is scarcely necessary to remind the reader that this poetical fancy was but indifferently realized. These distinguished men proved "blind leaders of the blind," and the nation, under their guidance, "fell into the ditch." Dean Tucker's was the true wisdom, because it was in accordance with the law of nature and the ordinance of God. The American historian whom I have just quoted adds in a note, "Watkins, in his life of the Duke of York, relates, that after the independence of America had been irrevocably conceded by the Treaty of Paris, George the Third, meeting Tucker at Gloucester, observed to him, 'Mr. Dean, you were in the right, and we were all in the wrong.'"†

It is interesting and instructive, in such a crisis as the present in the history of our nation, thus to contrast the

* *History of the United States of North America, from the Plantation of the British Colonies till their Revolt and Declaration of Independence.* By James Grahame, Esq., 1836, vol. iv. p. 307.

† Grahame, vol. iv. p. 308.

very different circumstances and prospects of British colonists, a century ago, when the first great Act of Separation was in progress, as compared with those of our own happier times. I am not singular, therefore, in holding the opinions I advocate in these pages, as to the inherent and indefeasible right of any community, such as a British colony, able and willing to sustain and protect itself, to declare its entire freedom and independence, irrespectively altogether of the opinions of parties in the mother-country, whether in office or not. The Rev. Dr. Witherspoon, President of the College of Princeton, New Jersey, in America, had only been six or eight years out of Scotland, where he had previously been one of the most eminent parochial ministers in that country, when he was elected a member of the first National Congress of the United States, and signed the famous declaration of independence at Philadelphia, in the year 1776.* The sentiments of Dr.

* I was told by persons of the highest intelligence in America, when in that country in the year 1840, that, next to Washington, there was no man to whom the Americans considered themselves more deeply indebted for the achievement of their national freedom and independence, than Dr. Witherspoon. His high character and eminent talents had given effectual support to the cause of freedom, which he had embraced at an early period in their great national struggle ; and during the subsequent progress of that struggle, when things were at the gloomiest, and not a few even of his coadjutors were ready to give up the contest as utterly hopeless, Dr. Witherspoon repeatedly reanimated their drooping spirits, and encouraged them to those renewed efforts which were ultimately crowned with success. But no sooner were the liberties of his country effectually secured, than, without looking for either office or emolument for himself, he returned, like an old Roman, to his quiet college, and even volunteered a pilgrimage to Scotland, where his name and character had always stood very high, to engage ministers, and candidates for the ministry, for those parts of his adopted country which had been left desolate by the war, and to collect funds for their settlement.

It is somewhat remarkable that one of my own earliest recollections should have been connected with the memory of this great and good

Witherspoon, and also of the celebrated John Wesley, on the relations of mother-countries and their full-grown colonies, will appear from the following extract from the able and excellent historian of America :—

" It was the opinion of Dr. Witherspoon and many other persons of sincere and profound piety in America, that when collisions arise between different authorities in the same empire, every man possesses the right of choosing which side he shall support, bounded by the duty of consulting the interests of religion and liberty, and of respecting the opinions and wishes of the majority of the community. The scriptural precepts referred to by the Quakers and other advocates of submission, they thought were intended (in so far as their application might be supposed universal), to inculcate the duty without defining

man, and especially with that event of his life to which I have just alluded. My mother, who was born in the year 1770, used to tell me, when a little boy, that the first Charity Sermon she had ever heard was one preached in the open air at Beith, in Ayrshire, Scotland, where she was then on a visit to a relative, by the Rev. Dr. Witherspoon, *from America*. She was fourteen years of age at the time, which must consequently have been in the year 1784, the year after the Peace. Dr. Witherspoon had been the parish minister of Beith many years before; and the concourse of people from the surrounding country was so great on the occasion, that the parish church could not hold them, and the service had to be held in an adjoining field, where Dr. W. preached from a moveable pulpit, or as it is technically called, in the west of Scotland, *a tent*. My mother used to describe to me his venerable appearance and snow-white locks, and the peculiarly impressive character of his oratory, the whole scene having evidently made a deep and indelible impression upon her mind. I was afterwards at school for a short time in Beith; and the schoolmaster, in whose house I resided, had the same feeling of veneration for the memory of Dr. Witherspoon. These apparently trivial circumstances naturally led me at an after period to enquire into the public career of Dr. Witherspoon, especially when visiting the College over which he had presided in New Jersey, and may perhaps have had some influence in shaping out my own.

the limits of obedience to civil authority, and to recommend a peaceable, moderate, and contented disposition, and averseness to wanton and unnecessary change. John Wesley was at first opposed, upon religious principles, to American resistance, and in letters to the Methodists in America, endeavoured, without effect, to dissuade them from embracing the cause of their country. But *he very soon changed his opinion, and even encouraged the Americans to revolt, by expressions of his good wishes and approbation.*"*

We have much reason, therefore, to be thankful to the God of Heaven, the Supreme Ruler among the nations, that our lot has been cast in much happier times than those of British colonists in America in the days of Dr. Wither-spoon and the Rev. John Wesley. We have reason to bless God that our Rulers in England are "men of under-standing, who know the times," and what it is incumbent upon them to do for this great people both at home and abroad.

SECTION II.—HOW THAT CONSUMMATION IS TO BE REALIZED.

Taking it for granted that the intercolonial negotiations and conferences now in progress† will issue very shortly in the establishment of a Customs League, a Uniform Tariff and a political federation of all the actual colonies of Eastern Australia, viz.: New South Wales, Victoria, Tasmania, South Australia and Queensland, I am decidedly of opinion that that great measure, for which we are now morally certain Her Majesty's Government and the Imperial Parliament are fully prepared, should, for

* Grahame's *Hist. of the United States*, vol. iv. p. 315. Also, Southey's *Life of Wesley*.

† While these pages are passing through the press, a Conference of delegates from four of the five actual Australian Colonies is sitting in Melbourne, on the subject of a Uniform Tariff for *all* these Colonies.

T

various reasons to be stated in the sequel, be consummated as speedily as possible. Assuming, therefore, that a political federation or union of the five actual colonies has been effected, with provision for the future admission into the Union of the two embryo colonies of Capricornia and Carpentaria, all that would be requisite—the consent and concurrence of the respective Colonial Legislatures having been previously obtained—would be an Act of the Imperial Parliament conceding entire freedom and independence to the Australian Union, and recognizing it thenceforth as a Sovereign Power in the world.

Such an Act—an Act of the Imperial Parliament, voluntarily conceding and establishing the Independent Sovereignty of the Australian Union—would, in my humble opinion, be a right honourable and highly Christian Act on the part of the Imperial Government and Legislature. To call into existence, at the uttermost ends of the earth, as if by the wand of a magician, a Government exhibiting all the peculiar features and possessing all the best characteristics of her own—to give birth, as it were, to so mighty a nation as the Australian nation will eventually, and at no distant period, become, a nation moreover

This is the first step in the necessary process; and a second has actually been taken at the same time, in the appointment of a Select Committee of the Victorian Assembly to take into consideration the subject of a federation of the Colonies. The motion was made by C. Gavan Duffy, Esq., on the 2nd June, 1870, and was to the following effect:—" That a Select Committee be appointed to consider and report upon the steps necessary to be taken in order to obtain a conference of delegates from the Parliaments of the Australian Colonies on the subject of a future federation of the colonies; such committee to have power to send for persons and papers, and to sit during the adjournments of the House, and to consist of the following members, viz. :—Mr. (now Sir James) M'Culloch, Captain M'Mahon, Mr. Michie, Mr. Fellows, Mr. Higinbotham, Mr. Aspinall, Mr. Casey, Mr. Kerford, Mr. Rolfe, Mr. Berry, Dr. Macartney, and the mover; three to form a quorum."

evidently destined to exert a powerful influence for good over a vast extent of the earth's surface, as well as over a very large proportion of the whole family of man—what are all the triumphs of Cressy and Agincourt, of Trafalgar and Waterloo, compared with the honour and glory that would redound to the British Government and nation from such an Act as this!

It were neither expedient nor desirable, however, that, in conceding entire freedom and independence to any of her colonies, Great Britain should allow them to form a number of petty independent States, like the ancient Republics of Greece, or those of Italy in the Middle Ages. It will be far preferable for the Australian colonies, as well as for the general interests of humanity, that they should form one large State, through a confederation of separate and independent provinces, like the United States of America.* As separate and independent communities, the present Australian colonies would be comparatively insignificant, and would have no weight or influence in the family of nations; but seven such provinces combined, with the whole eastern coast-line towards the Pacific as the measure of their empire, would at once form the first Power in the Southern Hemisphere, and prove a formidable rival (and the only rival that great country is ever likely to have out of Europe) even to the United States.

Now Great Britain will have it completely in her power to accomplish this great object of the future, simply by ignoring the separate provinces, and treating only with the future Federal Union.

It may doubtless be alleged that the future condition of the Australian Colonies, after they shall have become free and independent, is a matter with which Great Britain can

* The undoubted tendency of the last three centuries has been to consolidate what were once separate States or Kingdoms into one great nation. Dr. Arnold; but I have lost the particular reference.

have nothing to do, and in which she can have no influence on the one hand, and no interest on the other. But this would be a great mistake. The history of the past informs us that the characteristic of all the people or nations of Teutonic origin, as it was unquestionably that of the ancient Greeks, is a strong love of freedom, and an equally strong repugnance to centralized government of any kind, "A government formed after one standard," observes Professor Gervinus, one of the great lights of modern Germany —"A government formed after one standard—power concentrated in one hand—has neither suited the Teutonic people nor the genius of the Protestant religion. The type of their government has rather been, from the beginning of history to this day, a confederation of people and States, such as those of Germany and Switzerland, the Hanseatic League, the Netherlands and America; where, although their centralized government might perhaps be somewhat disjointed, no maturer political experience or theory could draw it closer together."*

And again:—"The federal union which united the Dutch provinces was neither firmer nor politically better planned than in Switzerland or Germany; and the same characteristic may be remarked in every confederation of Teutonic origin, even in America, that they only combined in times of danger, and that, notwithstanding the constitution, the tie is loosened on a return of security."†

There was extreme difficulty in forming a General Government, even for the little Republics of Switzerland; and even after such a government had been formed, certain of the Cantons reserved to themselves the right of separate action as Sovereign and Independent States!

"The original Cantons of Switzerland," observes the distinguished ecclesiastical historian, Dr. Merle d'Aubigné, "had renounced the right of forming fresh alliances,

---

* *Introd. to Hist. of 19th Cent.*   † Idem, *ibidem.*

without the general consent of the confederates ; *but Zurich and Berne had reserved to themselves this power.*"*

It was the instinct of self-preservation that originally united the Seven United Provinces of the Netherlands against the overwhelming power of Spain; and it was the same instinct that united the original Thirteen Colonies of America against the tyranny of England. In both cases there was the utmost difficulty in preventing the entire separation of the different provinces when the pressure from without was withdrawn. Hence the urgent necessity for the Imperial Government's exercising such a power, as might easily be exerted at present over a series of subject colonies, in binding up into one magnificent volume the future Seven United Provinces of Eastern Australia. Only permit these provinces to become free and independent without any previous provision of this kind, and their future condition in reference to each other would be one of the most difficult problems imaginable. I repeat it, therefore, if it is desirable for Great Britain herself, as well as for Australia and the whole civilized world, as it unquestionably is, that the colonies of Eastern Australia, in the event of their becoming free and independent, should form one Great Nation, instead of a series of small ones, she must provide for that issue beforehand, in the way I have suggested; for otherwise, there is but little likelihood of its being realized at all. Under the present colonial system, there are always petty jealousies subsisting between the different colonies, even of the same group; which, if they were all Sovereign and independent, might prove a source of repulsion rather than of attraction.

I repeat it, it is not for the interest either of Great

* Les Cantons primitifs de la Suisse avoient renoncé au droit de former de nouvelles alliances, sans le consentement de tous; *mais Zurich et Berne s'en etaient reservé le pouvoir. Histoire de la Reformation*, Tom, iv. p. 525.

Britain, or of the world at large, to permit the formation
of a number of petty sovereignties in this hemisphere;
and so long as it is in the power of the Mother-country to
bind together the whole of the eastern provinces into one
great nation—one mighty power of the future in the
Pacific, that will condescend to play " no second fiddle " to
Brother Jonathan, but will claim perfect equality with him
from the first—her proper course in the matter is plain and
obvious, and cannot be mistaken.

There is an obvious reason for designating the several component parts of the future Australian Union the SEVEN UNITED
PROVINCES, rather than the Seven United States, of Australia. With the latter of these designations, we should
be constantly in danger of being mistaken by ignorant
people for component portions of the great American
Union. Besides, as the Seven United Provinces of *Old
Holland* have long since been merged into a kingdom,
there can be no possible objection to our appropriating the
long famous designation of *The Seven United Provinces* in
New Holland.

It must also be borne in mind, as an additional reason
for a somewhat different designation for our Union, from
that of our friends on both sides of the American Continent, that the SEVEN UNITED PROVINCES OF AUSTRALIA
will comprise a vastly greater extent of territory than any
equal number of the United States. The territory comprised in the Australian Union will be nearly equal in
extent to that of twenty of the United States of America.

SECTION III.—THE FORM AND CHARACTER OF THE FUTURE FEDERAL
OR NATIONAL GOVERNMENT OF AUSTRALIA.

The Federal or National Government of the Seven
United Provinces would in all likelihood, be a reflex of the
actual Colonial Legislatures. Corresponding to the Legis-

lative Council and Legislative Assembly of each of the present colonies, there would be a Senate and a House of Representatives, with a President and Vice-President, to have cognizance and exclusive control over all Foreign Relations, over Trade and Customs, and over the Post Office. The House of Representatives should represent the population of the Union; each province returning a number of members equal to the multiple it should contain of a certain minimum amount of population—say twenty thousand: the Senate should represent the different provinces on a footing of perfect equality; each province returning the same number of Senators—say three. The Senators of the National Legislature, I would propose, should be elected by the Legislative Council and Legislative Assembly of each province, meeting together for that express purpose in the same hall, as is customary on certain prescribed occasions in the Norwegian Storthing.*

But where, it may be asked, have we men to fill such high offices as those I have indicated—a President, for instance, and a Vice-President, of the Union, with all the other offices which such an organization would imply? Why, I have no hesitation in expressing my belief and conviction that both on the Treasury benches and in the ranks of Opposition in our actual Legislatures, we have men perfectly able to discharge all the functions required under a National Government, with credit to themselves and with satisfaction and benefit to the public.

I have taken it for granted that, in the event of Australia becoming free and independent, she would adopt, as a matter of course, a Republican form of government. I look upon this as a settled point, in the present circumstances and condition of the civilized world—not, however, as being the result of reasoning from abstract principles, but simply *ex necessitate rei*, from the necessity of the case.

* *Vide* Laing's Travels in Norway.

"Whether opposed or not," says the eminent French writer, Victor Hugo, "whether acknowledged or rejected, republicanism, all illusions apart, is the future, either proximate or remote, the inevitable future of nations : "*— and if so, much more so of those essentially plebeian communities, such as our own colonies, that are gradually passing into the condition of nations.

And again :—" Republicanism is the manifest and irresistible portion of the civilized world."†

To the same effect, Mr. Merivale, the able writer on Colonies and Colonization, observes :—" The state of society in provinces thus circumstanced, is and must be essentially republican, whatever may be the character of their institutions."‡

"Universal Democracy," observes Mr. Carlyle, in accordance with these sentiments, " whatever we may think of it, has declared itself as an inevitable fact of the days in which we live; and he who has any chance to instruct, or lead, in his days must begin by admitting that."

"And again :—" Democracy is hot enough here, fierce enough; it is perennial, universal, clearly invincible, among us henceforth."§

" The preparation for the future is widely diffused, and if the results are of a kind for the moment to discourage the eager and impatient, the promises of the age are so great and so confident, that even the most faint-hearted rouse themselves to a belief that a time has arrived in which it is a privilege to live."¶

And these are not merely the sentiments and opinions of philosophers, politicians and statesmen—they are those of the most eminent divines, both of our own country and of foreign nations. To give only one instance of each—

* Victor Hugo. *Napoleon the Little.*   † Idem. *Ibid.*
‡ Merivale, vol. 1. p. 112.   § *Latter Day Pamphlets.*
¶ Gervinus—*Introd. to Hist. of 19th Cent.*

"I am convinced," says the celebrated Robert Hall, "there is no crime in being a republican, and that while he obeys the laws, every man has a right to entertain what sentiments he pleases on our form of government, and to discuss this with the same freedom as any other topic."

"His character," observes the distinguished author of the *History of the Reformation*, when describing the great Swiss Reformer, Zwingle,—"His character, his habitual intercourse with men, contributed, as much as his sermons, to gain their hearts. He was at once a true Christian and a true republican. The equality of all men was not merely a hackneyed phrase with him: written in his heart, it pervaded his whole life."*

"I reprobate no form of government upon abstract principles," says the celebrated Edmund Burke, that ardent admirer of the limited monarchy of the British Constitution. "There may be situations in which the purest democratic form will become necessary. There may be some (very few and very particular circumstances,) where it would be clearly desirable."†

There are therefore cases in which one particular form of government would be suitable, and no other. There are other cases in which that particular form would not

---

* Son caractere, sa maniere d'être avec tous les hommes, contribuoient, autant que ses discours, a gagner les cœurs. Il etait a la fois un vrai chretien et un vrai republicain. L'egalité de tous les hommes n'etait pas pour lui une phrase banale; ecrite dans son cœur, elle se retrouvait dans sa vie—Caractere de Zwingle. D'Aubigné, ii. 451.

† *Reflections on the Revolution in France.* To the same effect Lamartine observes, as follows:—"If a people is at one of those epochs when it is necessary to act with all the intensity of its strength, in order to operate within and without one of those organic transformations which are as necessary to people as is a current to waves or explosion to compressed powers—a republic is the obligatory and fated form of a nation at such a moment.—*History of the Girondists*, vol. i. p. 25. Now the Australian people are unquestionably at such an epoch at the present moment.

suit at all. No sane person, for example, would propose any other form of government than that of a limited monarchy for Great Britain and Ireland; imbedded as that form is in the whole structure of society, as well as in the habits and feelings, and in all the cherished traditions and associations of the people. But what foundation is there at this moment, or has there ever been, for such a form of government in Australia? Where is the long descent of a monarch from the ages of darkness and feebleness in that country? Where are the hereditary aristocracy—the ornament and support of thrones—and the feudal system, its ancient appendage in Australia? Where are the associations *there* that embalm that form of government in the hearts of the British people? Again, democracy, such as that of the ancient States of Greece, might have been practicable where the state consisted only of a single city and its surrounding territory, and where the whole of the free-men could easily be assembled, on all important occasions, in the great square of the capital; but it would be utterly impracticable either in Great Britain or in Australia. The only form of government indeed that is at all practicable in the latter country is that of a representative and federa-tive republic, or a confederation of smaller republics headed up into one great one for all matters of common interest exclusively. In short, I am a Republican, as far as the future government of Australia is concerned, not from any pre-conceived idea of the exclusive excellence of that form of government, or of its fitness for all cases and circum-stances, and still less from an ignorant contempt for other forms of government, and in particular for the limited monarchy of the British Constitution; but simply from a candid and dispassionate view of all the circumstances of our particular case, and from the settled conviction to which I have thus been led, that it is the only form of govern-ment at all practicable for free and independent Australia.

The people of England are doubtless rather sensitive on

this point. They are strongly and conscientiously attached
to their own limited monarchy, and believe that it is by far
the best form of government for their country—for the
preservation of all that is valuable in its institutions, and
tor the maintenance of the liberties of its people. But they
are no political propagandists. They believe that other
people may live as well as they do under very different
forms of government, and they admit that there are cases
in which their particular form would be utterly impracticable.*

* Forms of government possess a diversity as legitimate as the
diversity of character, of geographical situation, and of intellectual,
moral and material development amongst the nations. Like individuals, they have their different ages: the principles which govern
them have successive phases. Monarchical, Aristocratic, Constitutional
and Republican Governments, are the expression of these different
degrees of maturity in the genius of the people. They demand more
liberty in proportion as they feel themselves more capable of supporting
it; they require more equality and democracy in proportion as they
are more inspired with justice and love of the people.—*Lamartine's
Circular to the Diplomatic Agents of the French Republic*, 1848.

There are two maxims on this subject that are commonly retailed in
society, and that pass current for much more than they are worth.
The first is that of Pope, in his *Essay on Man* :—

> For *forms* of government let fools contest ;
> Whate'er is best administered is best.

Pope's real meaning in this carelessly-expressed sentiment, as he
afterwards explained himself in one of his letters to Dr. Atterbury, the
Nonjuring Bishop of Rochester, was simply that the right administration of any form of government was of far more importance to the
subject than its mere theoretical perfection. The other maxim,
delivered in the form of a compliment to one of the Roman Emperors,
by the courtly poet Claudian, is—

> Nunquam libertas gratior extat,
> Quam sub rege pio.

Liberty is never sweeter than under a virtuous prince; meaning a despotic
emperor, like those of Rome. But how much more dignified, how
much more accordant with the principles of eternal justice, as well as
with the moral nature and essential dignity of man, than either of

Besides, the republican form of government has now
been tried for a century in the United States, by a
people of precisely the same origin as the colonists of Australia ; and, its bitterest enemies even being judges, it has
succeeded in that case beyond all expectation ;* and there

these slavish maxims, the sentiments of the distinguished American
moralist, Dr. Channing :—

" I know," says that writer, " that tyranny " (or a despotic form of
government) " does evil by invading men's outward interests, by
making property and life insecure, by robbing the labourer to pamper
the noble and king. But its worst influence is *within*. Its chief
curse is, that it breaks and tames the spirit, sinks man in his own
eyes, takes away vigour of thought and action, substitutes for
conscience an outward rule, makes him abject, cowardly, a parasite,
and a cringing slave. This is the curse of tyranny. It wars
with the soul, and thus it wars with God." " It has often
been said, that a good code of laws, and not the form of government,
is what determines a people's happiness. But good laws, if not springing from the community, if imposed by a master, would lose much of
their value. The best code is that which has its origin in the will of
the people who obey it ; which, whilst it speaks with authority, still
recognises self-government as the primary right and duty of a rational
being, and which thus cherishes in the individual, be his condition
what it may, a just self-respect." " Free institutions contribute in no
small degree to freedom and force of mind, by teaching the essential
equality of men, and their right and duty to govern themselves."

But even Pope, in his wiser mood, expresses himself like a man :—

Who first taught souls enslaved, and realms undone,
Th' enormous faith of many made for one ?
That proud exception in all Nature's laws,
T' invert the world and counterwork its cause ?

Essay on Man.

* The democratic constitution of America," observes Professor
Gervinus, " is the choice of the people. This state grew unobserved
in the far West, and came forth from obscurity just as Russia reached
her full maturity in the East ; they attained to historical importance
at the same time ; Napoleon raised Russia to the acme of her greatness,
and America purchased from him the power of displaying her strength
on a wider field, and opposing her popular influence to the dynastic
despotic influence of Russia. The aspect of this rapidly unfolding,

is surely no conceivable reason why it should not succeed equally well in Australia.

It may doubtless be alleged that the Republican form of government has been twice tried in France, and has entirely failed in both cases. But the reason of that failure is obvious, and peculiar to France—I mean the existence of a vast standing army within the French

free, happy state, without a king, aristocracy, or state church, has a wonderful attraction to the people of all nations, and exercises a direct influence over them, which, though at first little noted, is now too powerful to be stopped in its onward course. Its fortunes attract the attention of the people of Europe, who are wearied with their worn-out institutions ; and by the facility of constant intercourse, tidings of the most prosperous among the emigrants is rapidly spread among the lower classes of society. To this propagandism, which has never been sufficiently appreciated, may be added the active exertions of literature, which has become proportionally democratic throughout Europe. Numbers from the educated classes, who earn their daily bread by this literature, extend a hand in sympathy to those below them, and assist at the work of democracy." "Monarchical policy has nothing but an uninfluential dependent part of the press to maintain its moral power on the field, against this united and equal force, capable of the most marvellous political co-operation ; the provincial assemblies, from which alone a practical political education could have been derived, have been suppressed and undermined, and even where they have the semblance of existence, have lost the confidence of the people and become useless, because they have only a semblance. The field is therefore left open to democratic principles. They progress in every path ; in the violent one of revolution, where in the agrarian law of the doctrines of socialism they have received their most terrific watchword ; still more effectually along the quiet pathway of ideas and habits which undermine power. More and more they influence the thoughts of men. Revived usages, the political opinions and practice of individuals and of Governments, even of those which are opposed to democracy, are all governed by it. The changes in property, the equal right of inheritance, educational institutions open to all, facility of intercourse, everything tends to the approximation of classes." "This is the great feature of the time."—Gervinus' *Introd. to Hist. of 19th Cent.*

territory.* This grand source of the repeated failure of a
republican form of government in that country was foreseen
and predicted by an eminent statesman of our own country
to whom I have repeatedly referred—the Right Hon.
Edmund Burke—from the very commencement of the First
French Revolution.

"Armies," observes Mr. Burke, "have hitherto yielded
a very precarious and uncertain obedience to any senate,
or popular authority; and they will least of all yield to an
assembly which is only to have a continuance of two years.
The officers must totally lose the characteristic disposition
of military men, if they see with perfect submission and
due admiration, the dominion of pleaders; especially when
they find that they have a new court to pay to an endless
succession of those pleaders, whose military policy, and the
genius of whose command (if they should have any), must
be as uncertain as their duration is transient. In the
weakness of one kind of authority, and in the fluctuation
of all, the officers of an army will remain for some time
mutinous and full of faction, until some popular general,
who understands the art of conciliating the soldiery, and
who possesses the true spirit of command, shall draw the
eyes of all men upon himself. Armies will only obey him
on his personal account. There is no other way of
securing military obedience in this state of things. But
the moment in which that event shall happen, the person
who really commands the army is your master—the master
of your whole republic."†

In this oracular language was predicted the rise of the
first Napoleon, when he was only a subaltern in one of the

---

* To reconcile the existence of an army of a hundred and fifty
thousand men, [now six hundred thousand] of a navy of a hundred
ships of the line, and of a frontier guarded by a hundred fortresses,
with the existence of a free government, is a tremendous problem.
Sir James Mackintosh, *Vindiciae Gallicae.*

* Ubi supra.

Royal Regiments of Artillery; and the Empire arose on the ruins of the Republic in accordance with this very remarkable prediction. The re-establishment of the Empire, therefore, under circumstances precisely similar, was not to be wondered at. On the contrary, it was an event to be expected every hour, so long as the French Republic continued to maintain a standing army of upwards of half a million of men.*

It may doubtless be alleged that the Americans, although Republicans, have a standing army, which has been considerably increased since the acquisition of California and the territories adjacent; but that army is very small, and it exists chiefly for the occupation of certain forts or garrisons on their frontiers, for their occasional wars with the Indians, as in Florida, and for the protection and defence of certain points within their vast territory, which are supposed to require the presence of an armed force. But the theory of the American Constitution is to have no regular standing army; and the well grounded jealousy of republicans on this point is remarkably evinced in the uniform and steady refusal of their Congress—until very lately, when the great civil war, so happily terminated, necessitated a change in their naval and military system,—to create any higher rank than that of Major-General in their army, or of Post Captain or Commodore in their navy. Even as it is, however, the extraordinary and apparently increasing deference that has been paid to military fame in the United States is one of the worst features in their political system, and indicates great danger ahead.† Free and independent

* The other two rocks, on which the barque of the second French Republic unfortunately split, were an army of public functionaries under the influence and controul of a centralized government, and the connection of Church and State.

† There have already been not fewer than six Military Presidents of the United States, viz:—General Washington, General Jackson, General Harrison, General Taylor, General Pierce, and now General

Australia, however, would be much less exposed to any
such danger than the United States. The process of
annexation, in the event of our obtaining our National Independence, would go on naturally and spontaneously with
us, as will be evident in the sequel, and without involving
the country in collisions with any power in the civilized
world. At the same time, it would be very desirable that
Australia, when free and independent, should, as early as
possible, be possessed of a small fleet or navy—for surveying purposes, for the protection of trade and the suppression
of piracy and kidnapping in Polynesia and the Eastern
Islands of the Indian Archipelago, as well as for the
extension of civilization and the influence and benefits of
the Union among the Islands of the Western Pacific. A
respectable navy, to consist chiefly of armed steam-vessels,—
of which the Victorian war-steamer Cerberus would probably be the commencement—would require to be formed
for these purposes at a very early period in the history of
the nation; but Australia is happily too far removed from
the rest of the civilized world, to be engaged, if left to
herself, in any war, either of aggression or of defence, for a
century to come.

As it is still rather fashionable, in certain quarters at

Grant. It is a bad sign; and the lust of conquest, with which we seem
to have inoculated them, from India and elsewhere, is evidently in
keeping with it. Montesquieu has shewn that success or victory in war
is as fatal to the existence of a Republic as defeat. It was the great
naval victory of Salamis that ruined the commonwealth of Athens; it
was its triumph over the Athenians that ruined the Republic of
Syracuse—transforming it into a military despotism. "It is not the
country," says Lamartine, "which runs the greatest danger in war; it
is liberty. War is almost always a dictatorship; soldiers forget insti-
utions for men;—thrones tempt the ambitious;—glory dazzles
patriotism. The *prestige* of a glorious name veils the design on
national sovereignty; the republic doubtless desires glory, but she
desires it for herself and not for Cæsars, or Napoleons." Lamartine's
Circular to the Diplomatic Agents of the French Republic, 1848.

least, to decry everything like popular government, or
democracy, that is, government by and for the people, I
shall append in a note the character given us of the ancient
Grecian democracy, by the distinguished statesman and
historian, Mr. Grote, as also by the Edinburgh Reviewer;
together with an extract of a speech on the same subject,
by the illustrious Pericles, the political chief of the
Athenian democracy.*

* Democracy in Grecian antiquity possessed the privilege, not only
of kindling an earnest and unanimous attachment to the constitution
in the bosoms of the citizens, but also of creating an energy of public
and private action, such as could never be obtained under an oligarchy,
where the utmost that could be hoped for was a passive acquiescence
and obedience. The theory of democracy was pre-eminently seductive;
creating in the mass of the citizens an intense positive attachment, and
disposing them to voluntary action and suffering on its behalf, such as
no coercion on the part of other governments could entail. Among
the Athenian citizens it produced a strength and unanimity of positive
political sentiment, such as has rarely been seen in the history of
mankind, which excites our surprise and admiration the more when
we compare it with the apathy which had preceded. Because democracy happens to be unpalatable to most modern readers, they have
been accustomed to look upon the sentiment here described only in its
least honourable manifestations—in the caricatures of Aristophanes,
or in the empty common places of rhetorical declaimers. But it is not
in this way that the force, the earnestness, or the binding value or
democratical sentiment at Athens is to be measured. We must listen
to it as it comes from the lips of Pericles, while he is strictly enforcing
upon the people those active duties for which it both implanted the
stimulus and supplied the courage; or from the oligarchical Nicias in
the harbour of Syracuse, when he is endeavouring to revive the
courage of his despairing troops, for one last death struggle, and when
he appeals to their democratical patriotism as to the only flame yet
alive and burning even in that moment of agony.—Grote, vol. iv.
p. 237—9.

The intellectual and moral pre-eminence which made Athens the
centre of good to Greece, and of the good to after generations, of which
Greece has been the medium, was wholly the fruit of Athenian institutions. It was the consequence, first, of democracy, and secondly, of

U

SECTION IV.—THE CERTAIN RESULT OF FREEDOM AND INDEPENDENCE
FOR AUSTRALIA—PEACE WITH ALL THE WORLD.

The first and certain result of the establishment of a
Sovereign and Independent Power in Australia would be
*Peace with all the world for all these colonies, whatever wars
might be waged in Europe;* and surely this is a consideration
of no trifling importance. Our harbours would doubtless
be open and welcome to all European belligerents, if they
chose to come so far from home to decide their quarrels;
but there would be no fighting allowed within three leagues
of our coast. This is now recognized as the law of nature
and nations, and we may rest assured that it would not be
violated in our case by any of the civilised nations of
Christendom. It was the profound peace enjoyed by the
United States in the infancy and non-age of their national
existence, during the long series of wars that ravaged and

the wise and well-considered organization by which the Athenian
democracy was distinguished among the democratic institutions of
antiquity. The Athenian constitution was a democracy, that is
government by a multitude, composed in majority of poor persons—
small landed proprietors and artisans. It had the additional democratic
characteristic, far more practically important than even the political
franchise; it was a government of boundless publicity and freedom of
speech.—Edin, Rev., Oct. 1853.

We live under a constitution such as in no way to envy the laws of our
neighbours—ourselves an example to others rather than imitators. It
is called a democracy, since its aim tends towards the Many, and not
towards the Few; in regard to private matters and disputes, the laws
deal equally with every one; while in respect to public dignity and
importance, the position of each is determined, not by class influence,
but by worth, according as his reputation stands in his particular
department; nor does poverty or obscure station keep him back, if he
has any capacity of benefitting the State. And our social march is
free, not merely in regard to public affairs, but also in regard to
tolerance of each other's diversity of tastes and pursuits.—*Pericles to
the Athenians, in Thucydides,* quoted by Grote. vol. vi. p. 193.

desolated Europe after the first French Revolution, that gave America her first and fair start in the world. Her people were then at peace with all the world, and they simply improved the precious opportunity which this gave them, when almost the whole world besides was at war.

I shall be told indeed that the present is a time of peace, and that there is no likelihood of any general war in Europe that could affect us in any way. That such a war is possible, however—nay, that it is not improbable in certain well-understood contingencies—no person of any political discernment can deny. In the estimation of men of real discernment in such matters, Europe—with her multitudes of unoccupied and uneasy classes, and the revolutionary principles that characterize them—is at present reposing on a volcano, ready to burst forth at any moment, and to involve the European world in a general conflagration. I have no doubt whatever that Her Majesty's present ministers sincerely desire, in all their political arrangements, to comply with the apostolic injunction, *If it be possible, as much as lieth in you, live peaceably with all men.** But it is sometimes not possible, either for individuals or for nations, to live peaceably with others; and in such cases it may be necessary, in accordance with the political morality of the times, even for the most peacefully disposed nation to

"Cry havoc! and let slip the dogs of war."

In short, we have no security whatever that Great Britain shall not at some future time, and possibly very soon, be engaged in war with one or other of the Great Powers of Christendom—with France, with Russia, or with America. And what would be the result to us, as mere colonies of Britain in such an event? Why, these Golden Lands

---

* Rom. xii. 18.

would in all likelihood be the very first point of attack, from the fame of their wealth and the hope of plunder in our cities—not indeed from any hostile feeling towards us, as colonists, on the part of the belligerents, but simply to cripple and annoy our mother-country.

I have already alluded to the hostile attitude of Russia towards these colonies, as dependencies of Britain, when her fleet wintered in the harbour of New York, within the last few years, to pounce, as it was alleged, upon Sydney and Melbourne, in the event of any interference on the part of England, such as was then anticipated, in the affairs of Poland.

There is at present, indeed, an *entente cordiale* between England and France; and it is the obvious interest of both countries to maintain a good understanding with each other. But how long such a state of things may last, no man can tell. "There are cases," as the Abbé Millot well observes, "in which the destiny of entire nations depends upon a single head."* And is it not pre-eminently so in France at present? Besides, the disastrous day of Waterloo is not yet effaced from the memory of France; and although a large majority of the people of both countries are now earnestly desirous of the continuance of peace, it is not always the majority that determine the movements of great nations. Nay, we know as a positive fact that, under every form of government in France during the last forty-five years, there have been numerous and highly influential Frenchmen of all ranks in society, from the highest downwards, whose waking thought by day and whose dream by night it has constantly been to wipe out the national disgrace of Waterloo in some great measure of hostile aggression upon England. The *mania* in France for a war with England, during the administration of M. Thiers, 'in the reign of

---

* Il est des circonstances où la destinée des peuples depend d'une seule tête.—*Millot.*

Louis Philippe—when the Prince de Joinville published his famous pamphlet on the subject of an invasion of England—is well known. The idea was also entertained under the Republic, even at the time when French Commissioners were attending the Great Exhibition in London on the part of their National Government. "On the 31st of October, 1849," says the *Edinburgh Reviewer* for July, 1853, "the Legislative Assembly of the French Republic passed a law ordering that an investigation should be instituted into the whole state of the navy by a Commission of fifteen members of the Assembly, to be elected by ballot from the whole number. The Commission thus appointed had accordingly been in existence two years when the famous Coup d'Etat annihilated both it and the Government under which it had its origin. But a copy or two of the unpublished Reports of the Commission, which the Imperial Government forthwith suppressed, happened to reach England; and these Reports sufficiently disclosed the workings of the French mind on the subject of the national relations with Great Britain, and the intense desire that prevailed extensively in influential quarters in France to humble the pride, to annihilate the commerce and to destroy the resources of England by a whole series of acts of aggression on a large scale on the first favourable opportunity.

"We must first establish," said M. Collas, the Secretary of the Commission, "the number of ships of the line that France can and ought to put to sea the day that war is declared. On this head we have a certain basis. *Our adversary is known. It can only be England*," M. Collas proposed a scheme, expressly adapted in time of peace, "to prepare for the moment when *all the possessions of England might be attacked at once*, and especially her trade at the outset of the war."

The Report also proposed that they should keep afloat a sufficient number of cruisers (in the words of M. Collas)—

"to display the French flag at all times in all the seas of the globe; * * and, on a declaration of war with England, *to strike her possessions everywhere at once,* as soon as the declaration of hostilities was made known." Particular reference was made to the purpose which such cruisers might be made to serve in the Pacific and Indian Oceans; for "if war broke out," says the worthy Secretary, "these ships, perfectly armed and equipped, would be apprised of it by *the steam communications through Suez and Panama; and before France and England could send a fleet to sea, they would commence the destruction of the commerce of the enemy all over the globe."*

It is all very well to tell us, as Earl Russell has recently been doing in a collection of his speeches and dispatches that has just been published, that "so long as her colonies desire to continue their allegiance, England is pledged to defend them from aggression to the last shilling and the last man." But His Lordship has surely forgotten that, while France has scarcely a colony worth either taking or defending, we have about fifty altogether, and in all parts of the habitable globe. The French admirals who gave evidence before the Committee of the National Assembly of 1849, gave it as their deliberate opinion that the French Navy of that period was quite equal to that of England; and it is matter of notoriety that it has ever since been increasing in strength as greatly and as rapidly as our own. To talk of England, therefore, defending each and all of her fifty colonies in the event of a war with France is simply a piece of empty bravado. As I have already stated in a former section of this work, the Earl of Ellenborough gave it as his opinion in the House of Lords, sixteen years since, that the idea of England being able to defend Canada against the United States in the event of a

* *Edinburgh Review,* for July, 1853. Article, *The French Navy,* passim.

war with America, was out of the question; and he therefore recommended that the Mother-country should at once
take the initiative in the case by taking the requisite steps
for the peaceful and entire separation of the North American Colonies from the United Kingdom—a recommendation
in which Lord Brougham heartily concurred.

As little could Great Britain be able to defend us from
all hostile aggression, in the event of a war with France.
It is surely no disparagement either to the disposition or to
the ability of Great Britain to make such an acknowledgment. For supposing that her whole Flying Squadron
were engaged in defending either the Cape or New
Zealand, what would become of us in the mean time? Or
if we, the Australian Colonies, should be the main point
of attack, as in all likelihood we should be in such an
emergency, where would there be anything like adequate
defence for so many other helpless colonies? Great Britain
would have enough to do to defend her own shores in such
a crisis.

Earl Russell, it appears, is still full of the notable
scheme of a Congress of Colonial representatives to be
held from time to time in London, and to contribute, on
the part of their respective constituents, the associated
colonies, three or four millions a year to the National and
Military Estimates of the Mother-country, for the defence
they are to enjoy under her continued protection. Such a
Congress, I maintain, would be of no practical utility,—and
even if it did assemble, I am quite sure it would never vote
the three or four millions Earl Russell requires for the
defence of the Empire. Why?—why, because the thing is
quite unnecessary; the only desideratum for the maintenance
of peace in the Colonies being Freedom and Independence.

In the event of Great Britain being involved in war with
any of the great powers of Christendom, Mr. Higinbotham,
an eminent member of the Legislature of Victoria, virtually
proposes that we should not only take part as principals

in the quarrel, whatever it might be, and proclaim war against that particular enemy of Britain, but that we should undertake the entire responsibility of arming and defending ourselves against the enemy in question at our own cost and charge. This, I conceive, to be the only meaning of the following Resolution, as one of a series recently submitted by Mr. Higinbotham to the Legislature of Victoria :—

"The people of Victoria, possessing by law the right of self-government, desire that this Colony should remain an integral portion of the British Empire ; *and this House acknowledges, on behalf of its constituents, the obligation to provide for the defence of the shores of Victoria against foreign invasion, by means furnished at the sole cost, and retained within the exclusive control, of the people of Victoria.*"

Now I object entirely to this doctrine of Mr. Higinbotham's. I maintain that, as British colonists, we have nothing to do with the quarrels of Britain with other powers ; and if she is either unable or unwilling to defend us from the consequences in which these quarrels may involve us without any fault of our own, the sooner the connection ceases the better will it be for both parties. In an article in the *Morning Advertiser, Auckland, New Zealand, of the 15th February,* 1870, the Editor quotes from the *London Times,* a passage to the following effect :—" We would suggest to the colonists to consider how far they are protected, by the mere fact of acknowledging the sovereignty of this country, from foreign ambition or from mutual struggle * * * We are quite content that they should devote all their attention to their own interest, and for that purpose we cheerfully, and with some pride, afford them the security which the name of the British Empire confers." On this passage, the New Zealand Editor makes the following just and spirited remarks :—

" New Zealand is dismissed with the paternal blessing

of the *Times*, and a promise of the shadow of Britannia's shield. It has evidently not occurred to the *Times* that the colonists may consider the security conferred by the name of the British Empire as of more than doubtful value. A connection of the sort described by the *Times* is so eminently one-sided as to be altogether valueless. We can see plainly enough how the wrath of Britain's enemies might be visited on us through such a connection, but we fail to see how it is to be averted. A war between Britain and France, or Britain and Russia, might lead at any moment to the sudden inroad of a French or Russian squadron, against which we should have to fall back upon "the security"—so cheerfully granted—which the name of the British Empire confers. Is it to be wondered at that colonists should begin to examine a little more closely into the value of this security? Is it not likely that they may begin to think that such a connection is hardly worth retaining?"

In one word, the only way in which the British colonists of Australia can ever be ensured from all hostile aggression, so as to enjoy the inestimable blessings of peace, whatever wars might be waged in Europe, would be their erection into a Sovereign Power and the concession by the mother-country of their entire freedom and independence.

SECTION V.—BENEFICIAL RESULTS TO BE ANTICIPATED FROM THE ESTABLISHMENT OF A SOVEREIGN AND INDEPENDENT POWER IN AUSTRALIA FOR THE REGIONS BEYOND.

There is an urgent necessity at this moment for the creation of a Sovereign and Independent Power in Australia, in order to afford the requisite moral support and material protection to the friends of civilization and good government now inhabiting the islands of the Western Pacific Ocean. One of the numerous groups of islands in that vast ocean—I allude to the Fiji Islands—is at present in a very critical condition.* The extraordinary fertility of these islands, and the suitableness of their soil and climate for the growth of intertropical productions, have, within the last ten or twelve years, induced a comparatively large number of Europeans, with not a few Americans, to settle in the Fiji Islands; regular mercantile companies having been formed for the purpose in Sydney and Melbourne, while numerous adventurers, who have acquired colonial experience in New South Wales and Victoria, are proceeding thither from time to time on their own account, and are now purchasing large tracts of land from the natives, often I fear in a very questionable way, and obtaining as labourers on their respective plantations, and sometimes, I suspect, by very questionable means, the natives of other groups of islands in the same expanse of ocean. There are already as many as two thousand white men on these islands; and as the native chiefs are all independent of each other, and no sovereign authority recognised in the group, there is an urgent necessity for the immediate establishment of a regular government in the islands; deeds of violence being done, and the grossest outrages perpetrated with impunity.

With a view to this very desirable consummation, the principal chiefs petitioned Her Majesty, through the then resident British Consul, Mr. Pritchard, to take possession of the islands as a British colony, on the 14th December,

* The Fijian Archipelago consists of about eighty islands situated in the Western Pacific, between the 15th and 19th degrees of south latitude. The principal island of the group is about a hundred miles in length and fifty in breadth; and the second is ninety miles long by twenty-five broad; the rest, with a few exceptions, being much smaller. The entire population of the group is about 200,000. The Wesleyan missionaries, who have occupied the Fiji Islands with great zeal and devotedness for many years past, have succeeded to a very considerable extent in the civilization and christianization of the natives.

1859; a previous cession of the sovereignty having been made by Thakombau, the principal chief, on the 12th October, 1858. Colonel Smith, an experienced officer in the service, was accordingly deputed by Her Majesty's Government to proceed to the Fiji Islands, to ascertain their state and prospects generally, and to report on the subject of the Petition. Colonel Smith was accompanied by Dr. Seemann, a scientific German gentleman and litterateur, who was appointed to investigate and to report upon the natural history of the Islands. Dr. Seemann arrived in Sydney, on his return to England from the Fijis, towards the close of the year 1860; and I had the pleasure of being a fellow-passenger with him, by the P. and O. Company's steamers from Sydney by the Red Sea to Alexandria in Egypt, or rather to the Isthmus of Suez, in the year 1861. Colonel Smith's report, it seems, was unfavourable for the petitioners; and the islands have consequently remained in their original state of anarchy and barbarism, without any settled government, to the present day. Public meetings have repeatedly been held in the islands, with a view to the formation of a regular government, but there being no paramount authority available in the case, without effect.

In this emergency, various expedients have been successively proposed and rejected. It has been strongly recommended, for instance, to annex the Islands to the United States. It is also understood that the French Authorities in New Caledonia are quite prepared to accept the Sovereignty of the Fijis for His Imperial Majesty, Louis Napoleon;* and it has even been suggested to cede

* The Fijians," says an officer of the Royal Navy who has visited the Islands, " have a great dread of falling into the hands of the Americans or the French. They dislike the former on account of the demands made upon them by the United States, mentioned above "— (alluding to a seemingly unwarrantable claim made upon them by an American Consul, and enforced in a somewhat arbitrary manner by

the Islands to the North German Confederation. But the large majority of the white inhabitants being British subjects, another attempt is now making, with the concurrence of the more influential native chiefs, to induce Her Majesty's Government to reconsider their former decision, and to erect the islands into a British Colony. There is reason to believe, however, that, with the present views of the Imperial Government, this second effort will be equally unsuccessful with the first ; as the bitter experience which Her Majesty's Ministers have had in New Zealand is not likely to induce them to embark in any other doubtful scheme of colonization in the Western Pacific—especially with an aboriginal race in the Fijis, equally numerous and not unlike the Maories in their warlike propensities.

It would be the easiest thing imaginable, however, if a Sovereign and Independent Power were organized and established in Australia, for that Power either to annex, or to establish a protectorate in and on, the Fijian Islands ; and thereby to ensure to their inhabitants, both native and European, all the benefits and blessings they could ever derive from being a colony of Britain.

But the Fijis are not the only group in the Western Pacific that would be likely to experience inestimable benefits and blessings from annexation to the future Australian Empire. The group of the New Hebrides, still nearer the Australian coast than the Fiji Islands, and next to that group in extent, as well as in beauty and fertility,

the Captain of a U. S. man-of-war), " and the French are to be feared and hated throughout the South Seas in consequence of their proceedings at Tahiti. This feeling is kept up in the minds of the natives of Polynesia from the threats constantly held out by the French Missionaries of their islands being taken possession of by France. But the chiefs of Fiji would gladly see the English Flag hoisted in their land, and under that influence it would not be difficult to induce them to submit to the authority of one supreme chief as King of Fiji. *Sketches in Polynesia,—the Fijis. Blackwood's Magazine, for July, 1869.*

could also be annexed, and subjected to an Australian protectorate, for purposes which I shall state more particulary in the sequel, with the greatest facility.

And so also could the Solomon Islands, the group in which the late enterprising but unfortunate Benjamin Boyd proposed to establish his Papuan Republic, when he was murdered by the savages on one of these islands, the island of Guadalcanar, about twenty years since.

And last of all, though not least, the future Australian Empire would, in all likelihood, as one of its first acts, annex, with a view to the establishment of an Australian protectorate in and over it, the great island of New Guinea, and so extend our limits to the Equator.

Nay, I am strongly of opinion that if a Sovereign and Independent Power were called into existence in Australia, in whose harbour French ships would always be as safe if not as welcome as British, Louis Napoleon would not be unwilling to make over to us, for a reasonable consideration, his colonies of New Caledonia and Tahiti, as his uncle the first Napoleon did Louisiana and Florida to the United States. There can be no doubt whatever that the island of New Caledonia, in particular, was taken possession of by the far-seeing French Emperor, to serve as a Naval and Military station for his troops and ships, in the event, at one time by no means improbable, of a war with England. But if Australia were free and independent, and her harbours always available, whatever wars might rage in Europe, there would be no further necessity for the retention of that costly toy.

Besides, the French have neither the tact nor the spirit for the heroic work of colonization ;* and if such a colony as New Caledonia now is would be a mere drag upon the

* A respectable French upholsterer from Paris, with whom I had become acquainted in Sydney, went down to New Caledonia shortly after the formation of that colony ; but he soon returned to Sydney, and

Treasury in England, if it were a British colony—how
much more so must it not be as a colony of France? In
one word, I am strongly of opinion that Australia,
Sovereign and Independent, is destined in the good providence of God, and for the greatest and noblest purposes,
to exercise a beneficent protectorate at no distant period
over all the isles of the Western Pacific down to the
Equator.

SECTION VI.—ESTIMATE OF THE PROBABLE INFLUENCE OF AUSTRALIA,
AS A SERIES OF SEPARATE COLONIES, IN PROMOTING EMIGRATION
FROM THE UNITED KINGDOM.

The grand question of the day in England is that of
Emigration : and considering that the population of the
United Kingdom is increasing at the rate of a quarter of a
million per annum, while the difficulty of obtaining employment and comfortable subsistence for the industrious
classes is also constantly increasing, it is no matter of
wonder that that question should be one of intense interest
to every lover of his country. How, then, it will be asked,
will Australia respond to the desires and necessities of the
mother-country, whether as a series of separate colonies as
at present, or as a Sovereign and Independent State ?
These two questions, I shall endeavour to answer con-
secutively.

So early as the year 1835, when the colony of New South
Wales extended from Cape Capricorn to Bass's Straits, and
the fund arising from the sale of its waste lands on the
Wakefield principle—that is, appropriating the proceeds

when I asked him how he had done so, he told me his countrymen
did not understand colonization, like the English, and there was therefore no field for him. On asking him what the population of the
country might be, he replied, characteristically enough, *Trente colons,
et cinq cents soldats !* Thirty colonists and five hundred soldiers

for the promotion of emigration—was becoming considerable, I published a series of papers in Sydney, pointing out the paramount importance of that fund for ensuring the welfare and advancement of the colony, through the progressive introduction into its territory of numerous industrious and virtuous families and individuals from the mother country. In these papers I laid down and advocated the two following principles, viz. :—1st. That the Waste Lands of Australia were not the property of the actual colonists, but of all the inhabitants of the British Empire ; and 2nd. That the best mode of expending the funds accruing from the sale of these lands was in the promotion of the emigration of industrious and virtuous families and individuals from the mother-country to Australia, in numbers proportioned to the population of each of the three kingdoms respectively. These principles were cordially received and approved by the colonists ; and it will doubtless not be uninteresting to the reader to be informed of the manner and degree in which they have been adhered to or carried out during the long period of thirty-five years that have since elapsed. This information I shall give accordingly in the few following sketches.

As soon as the fund accruing from the sale of the waste lands had become considerable, the Imperial Government created a distinct department—that of the Land and Emigration Commissioners—for the due expenditure of the fund in the promotion of emigration to Australia, by giving to suitable families and individuals a free passage out. With this view, the Commissioners engaged for the most part experienced Surgeons in the Royal Navy, to select suitable emigrants in all parts of the United Kingdom, and to proceed with them, in ships chartered by the Commissioners, to New South Wales ; which then included the districts of Port Phillip and Moreton Bay, now the great colonies of Victoria and Queensland. In this way, numerous farm-labourers were despatched from the agri-

cultural districts of England, particularly from the County
of Kent; pastoral emigrants from the Highlands of Scotland; mechanics of various handicrafts from Dundee and
the Clyde in Scotland, and from Londonderry in Ireland;
and farm-labourers from the South and West of Ireland.

Simultaneously with the appointment of the Government
Commissioners, the Local Government issued Orders upon
the Land Revenue to the amount of £15 for each Statute
adult immigrant landed in the colony, to any respectable
colonists who desired to import from the mother-country
any number of hired servants, labourers, or shepherds, on
their own account. But as not one in a hundred of the
colonists of the period had the means of selecting and
engaging such emigrants in the United Kingdom themselves, the business of directing the emigration that was
then taking place to New South Wales, fell, with very few
exceptions, into the hands of the Government. I happened
to be identified with one or two of these exceptions myself,
one of which had rather a singular result.

Having deemed it necessary, in the year 1836, to proceed
to England, to engage and bring out certain ministers of
religion, schoolmasters, and missionaries to the aborigines,
my brother, Mr. Andrew Lang, of Dunmore, Hunter's
River, late Member of the Legislative Council of New
South Wales, and the late George Rankin, Esq., J.P., of
Bathurst, obtained orders of this kind from the local
Government for the importation of a hundred families each
of the classes of persons required at the time in the Colony.
These orders were assigned to me by the gentlemen I have
mentioned, for the double purpose of enabling me to select
a large number of reputable and industrious families for
the Colony, and of facilitating my arrangements for the
passage out of the persons I wished to bring out with me
on my return. Two pretty large vessels were accordingly
engaged for this purpose, and were filled with suitable
emigrants of my selection; the orders on the land revenue

in both cases being simply transferred to the shipowners as their security for payment on the safe arrival of their vessels at their port of destination. In one of these vessels there was a body of clerical and lay German missionaries, numbering thirty adult persons in all, whom I had been permitted by the Home Government to convey out at the cost of the land revenue, for the formation of a German mission to the aborigines at Moreton Bay; the history and the beneficial influence of which in the neighbourhood, for a long series of years thereafter, are well-known in that part of the territory, although the mission itself, like all the other missions to the aborigines of that period, proved a failure.

My brother's order had included fifty families of vine-dressers from France or Germany, whom I had agreed to select and bring out on condition of their having a minister and schoolmaster of their own nation and communion, as Mr. Lang intended at the time to form an extensive vine-yard on his property on the Hunter; the late Dr. Leichhardt, the unfortunate explorer, having given it as his opinion that that part of our territory was admirably adapted for the cultivation of the vine. As such emigrants, however, were not then procurable in France—French *vignerons* having no desire to leave their native country—and as there were great difficulties in the way of German emigrants of the humbler classes passing down the Rhine through Holland,* I succeeded at length, through a French Protestant clergyman of the place, in engaging about fifty families of German vine-dressers at Havre de Grace in France, who had emigrated from their native country, with the intention of proceeding to America by way of Havre;

---

* The British Consul at Rotterdam, whom I saw there on the subject, informed me that the Dutch Government would not allow the German vine-dressers to enter Holland without a bond or guarantee from the British Government that they should not return to it as paupers.

v

but having expended all their means were there stopped short. About 250 of these emigrants, both male and female, embarked at Havre on board the French ship, "La Justine," the captain of which was a Protestant, whom I had met with in a mercantile house connected with the Colony, in London. The captain touched at Rio de Janeiro, in the Brazils, for fresh provisions. There is a large German population in that city, as I ascertained when I was there myself in the year 1823; and the arrival in their harbour of a whole ship-load of vignerons from the fatherland was quite an event among the Germans, and every inducement was held forth to the captain simply to land his passengers on the wharf; the Brazilian Government, which had taken a great interest in the matter, having offered him a large amount if he should do so— more than sufficient to remunerate him for all the expenses of his voyage. But the captain was an honourable man; and being under engagement to my brother and myself,* he refused to do so, and proceeded again to sea. But the Germans in Rio having made their countrymen on board believe that they were going to a penal settlement, and would all be made slaves of on their arrival; and having secretly supplied them with arms, they rose upon the captain at sea, and compelled him to take them back to Rio. My brother and myself, however, were honorably relieved of all the obligations we had undertaken in the case; and I have since ascertained that the vignerons of the "La Justine" formed a settlement for the growth of the vine in the mountainous country a few miles from Rio, near the Emperor Don Pedro's summer palace; that they had there built a town called Petropolis in honor of the

---

* I had drawn for £1,000 upon my brother, who duly endorsed the draft, to enable the French captain to fit out and provision his vessel; and I had engaged, on my brother's behalf, that he should be paid £3 for each adult emigrant landed in the Colony, in addition to the amount guaranteed in the Government order.

Emperor, who took a great interest in the settlement, and often visited it, and that all the places about have regular German names. It was no doubt a great and irreparable loss to Australia at the time.

In short, the Emigration System of the period, under the management of the Emigration and Land Commissioners, had been introducing into the Colony for a series of years, up to the year 1839 inclusive, a very large and constantly increasing number of a superior class of emigrants from all parts of the United Kingdom; and the progressive advancement of the Colony in its moral and religious character, as well as in its material interests, was evident and gratifying in a very high degree.

A change, however, of an unexpected and disastrous character came over the spirit of our colonial dream of onward and steady progress as a thoroughly British community. In the year 1839, the Land Fund, which had been constantly increasing, especially from extensive purchases of land and town allotments in the district of Port Phillip, and which had actually reached the very large amount of £100,000 a year, very naturally excited the cupidity of the merchants of Sydney, who conceived that if they could only get the management of the fund into their own hands, they could make handsome fortunes out of it, as some of them actually did. With this view a hue and cry was got up against the Government system of emigration; the gullible portion of the colonial public being led to believe, from certain calculations that were artfully placed before them on the part of the merchants, that the Department of Emigration would be managed much more economically and much better for the community, if it were virtually taken out of the hands of the Government Emigration and Land Commissioners, and placed directly in those of the people themselves.

Unfortunately, the local Government of the day—that of the late Sir George Gipps and his nominee Council—were blind enough not to oppose or resist this suicidal agitation; and the consequence was that the expenditure of the large and constantly increasing Land Fund available for the promotion of immigration, was in great measure if not entirely taken out of the hands of the Government Commissioners, and handed over to a few mercantile speculators in the city of Sydney. Orders on the Land Fund were doubtless issued by the local Government to colonial proprietors, intending or rather professing to import immigrants as hired servants or labourers on their own account, at so much per head for each statute adult; but as not one in twenty of these colonists had any means of selecting and engaging such persons in the United Kingdom, these orders were simply transferred to some mercantile house in Sydney engaged extensively in the immigration business, and having partners, agents, and correspondents in London. These London agents were generally shipbrokers, who in some cases merely paid the Sydney merchant so much per head for all the orders for emigrants he could obtain in the Colony. In other cases there was a regular partnership between the London shipbroker and the Sydney merchant; at all events there was no check or supervision exercised in either case over the shipbroker, as to how or where he was to obtain his emigrants: he had merely to send out so many statute adults to enable him to obtain the regular bounty, and like all mercantile men he endeavoured to find them in the cheapest market.

That market was the south and west of Ireland; where the London shipbrokers had their whippers-in engaging emigrants for New South Wales at so much per head, and forwarding them, with but little or no enquiry either about their character or qualifications, to the Australian emigrant ships—to the general rendezvous of the period in Plymouth Sound—by the Dublin or Cork steamboats trading to London. For as vessels could always be chartered to sail from London at a cheaper rate than from any of the outports of the kingdom, while cargo to fill up with and cabin passengers were more likely to be found there than in any outport, the Australian emigrant ships chartered by the London shipbrokers sailed from London, to touch at Plymouth—after getting safely over the worst part of the voyage, the passage down channel—to receive their complement of Irish bounty emigrants in that port.

I happened, towards the close of the year 1840, in returning to the Colony from England, to see this whole process, which had then been but recently inaugurated, and of which I had no previous conception, carried out in all its details. Having accidentally missed my passage out by a vessel from Liverpool, instead of returning to London from that port, I engaged my passage by a bounty emigrant ship which was then about to sail from London, to touch at Plymouth Sound—proceeding as I did first to Dublin and then to Plymouth. On reaching Dublin, I was surprised beyond measure to find the steamer from thence to Plymouth crammed quite full with steerage and deck passengers, who had just been collected by the charterer's agent in the south and west of Ireland, and were proceeding to the bounty emigrant ship by which I had engaged my own passage in Plymouth Sound. That vessel I afterwards found had embarked all her cabin passengers but myself, with all her provisions and water, and all the cargo for which she could find stowage, in the London Docks, and had merely to touch at the Sound for her bounty emigrants from Ireland; who were simply transferred from the deck of the Dublin steamer to that of the Australian emigrants ship, without ever touching the English soil, although in the *correct* statistics of the day they were all rated as emigrants from England.

The vessel by which I had thus made my passage to New South Wales on the occasion referred to was the sixth which the charterers had sent out in this way to

Sydney and Melbourne during the year 1840. But there were various other firms in the trade, who followed precisely the same course; collecting their emigrants by means of agents, who were paid at so much per head, in the South and West of Ireland, and forwarding them by the Cork and Dublin steamboats to meet the Australian emigrant ships in Plymouth Sound. The proportion of Protestants to Roman Catholics by not a few of these vessels, was only one in eighteen! A large proportion moreover of this accession to the intellectual, moral, and religious character of the Colony, were from the county of Tipperary, the most famous in all Ireland for deeds of violence and blood.

In short, while it was notorious that nine-tenths of all the funds arising from the sale of waste land in New South Wales had been contributed by Protestant purchasers chiefly from England and Scotland, it was nevertheless the fact that, under the system introduced, at the instance of certain unprincipled mercantile speculators in Sydney, of conducting emigration to Australia in private bounty emigrant ships from London, to touch for the most part at Plymouth, at least two-thirds of the whole amount of that revenue was expended in bringing out to the Colony Roman Catholics from Ireland!

Such a state of things undoubtedly implied either the grossest neglect or the grossest mismanagement in some quarter or other; and it is impossible to acquit the local Government of the period of the great culpability that attached to it, either for permitting its existence in the first instance, or for its continuance for a single hour after its real character had become known. The fact was that, in the year 1838, Sir George Gipps and his two Councils had found New South Wales a thoroughly Protestant Colony; but in the short space of three years thereafter, they had done more, through their gross neglect of the proper duties of their office, to transform it into a mere province of the Popedom, than had been done by all the injudicious acts of all their predecessors for fifty years before! It was no excuse for men occupying so exceedingly responsible a situation as that which these gentlemen held at the time to plead that they did not foresee the consequences of the measures they had sanctioned in regard to immigration. They ought to have foreseen them; and the confession of their inability to have foreseen them was simply a confession of incapacity. They ought never to have entrusted to unprincipled speculators (for common sense might have taught them that the Bounty Immigration business was sure to fall into such hands under the system they had created) such enormous powers for good or for evil as were thus so flagrantly abused.

I was the first to sound the alarm on the occasion; which I did in a letter addressed to the Protestant landowners of New South Wales, entitled "The Question of Questions! or, is this Colony to be transformed into a province of the Popedom?" which was published as a pamphlet in Sydney, in the year 1841. During the following year the subject was taken up also in the nominee Legislative Council of the period, by the late Bishop Broughton, who showed, from a reference to the immigration statistics of the day, that during the eighteen months that had elapsed from the 1st January, 1841, to the 30th June, 1842, there had been imported into the Colony, at the public expense, 25,330 (twenty-five thousand three hundred and thirty) immigrants, of whom not fewer than 16,892 (sixteen thousand eight hundred and ninety-two), or two-thirds of the whole number were from Ireland, chiefly Roman Catholics from the south and west, and only 8,438 (eight thousand four hundred and thirty-eight) from England and Scotland together; Ireland having thus had four times her proper share of the benefit afforded to the United Kingdom, through immigration to Australia, in proportion to her population as compared with that of Great Britain.

Besides, a very large number of these immigrants from

the south and west of Ireland were altogether unsuited to
the circumstances and wants of the Colony; as witness the
following extract of the evidence of the late Dr. Thomson
of Geelong, given before a Select Committee of the Legislative Council (of which he was himself a Member) on
Immigration, in the year 1843; Sir Charles Nicholson,
Bart., Chairman :—

" 25. By the Colonial Secretary : Generally speaking,
do you find men who come from towns willing to engage as
labourers or shepherds in the country? There is a disin-
clination on the part of such persons to go into the interior.
We have had a great many immigrants brought to Port
Phillip who are utterly useless; in point of intellect they
are inferior to our own aborigines.

" 26. What do they represent themselves as being?
Labourers.

" 27. By Dr. Lang : Where do they come from? The
south of Ireland."

Lest I should myself be suspected of cherishing an anti-
Irish, and especially an anti-Catholic, feeling, so as to lead
me either to countenance or to practise injustice towards
that class of our fellow-subjects, I can challenge all and
sundry to point to a single instance of anything of the kind
in my public procedure for the last forty years ; during the
whole of which period I have ever acted on the principle of
a *fair field for all, and no favour for any*. At the same time
I have all along been strongly of opinion that it was alike
the interest and the bounden duty of all who had the best
interests of Australia at heart, to do all that in them lay to
make the Australian Colonies British and not Irish
Colonies—to maintain a somewhat similar proportion
between the different nationalities in Australia to that
which obtains in the United Kingdom,—and especially to
prevent our fair country from becoming like Ireland, a
mere province of the Popedom. And therefore I regard
those unprincipled men, who for their own personal ag-

grandisement established the Bounty System of Immigration for New South Wales, as well as the Government that enabled them to carry out their nefarious schemes, as having been guilty of a species of high treason to Australia.

Providentially, perhaps, for the Colony, a period of deep and general depression ensued in the years 1842-1845, during which the Land Fund having fallen to nothing, bounty immigration ceased for a time; but in 1846, when the Colony was again reviving from this state of general depression, and the resumption of immigration in some form or other was generally expected, I resolved to proceed to England, as I did accordingly, at my own cost and charges, to give an impulse throughout the United Kingdom to Protestant emigration to Australia. I did so, I confess, as it seemed, in my estimation, a matter of life and death to the Colony; for I had ascertained that a great effort was making at the time to give the future immigration a thoroughly Romish character. Before doing so, however, I made a pretty extensive tour in the districts of Port Phillip and Moreton Bay, now the great Colonies of Victoria and Queensland, to make myself acquainted with the general capabilities of the country and the wants and wishes of its inhabitants.

I was absent from the colony on that occasion nearly four years—from 1st July, 1846, till March 11th, 1850—during which I traversed the United Kingdom in various directions, from the Bristol Channel to the Orkney and Shetland Islands; publishing and circulating books and pamphlets on the subject of my mission, which I had got up for the purpose, partly in the Colony and partly on my voyage home; lecturing and delivering addresses on Australia as an eligible field for emigration, and especially for the cultivation of cotton and the sugar-cane by European free labour, and publishing a series of letters with the same view in various influential and widely circulated journals.

In particular, I delivered such lectures or addresses in various parts of England, generally to very large and enthusiastic audiences,—as, for instance, in Exeter Hall, London, and in two other localities at the West End; in Manchester, on two different occasions; in Liverpool; in Leeds; in Newcastle; in Birmingham; in the cities of Bristol, Gloucester, and Bedford; at Hitchin, in Hertfordshire; and in Newport, Monmouthshire. The meeting in Exeter Hall was presided over by the Honorable D. Kinnaird, who took a great interest in emigration to these Colonies, and particularly in Protestant emigration. In Manchester, the meetings were presided over by Thomas Bazley, Esq., M.P., President of the Chamber of Commerce in that city, who had taken a deep interest in the cultivation of cotton at Moreton Bay. The meeting at Leeds was presided over by the ex-Mayor (also ex-M.P.) for the Borough, and those at Newcastle and Bristol by the Mayors of these cities. The meeting at Bedford was held in pursuance of a requisition requesting me to visit that city, and signed by the Mayor, by ministers of all denominations, including those of the Established Church, and by a large number of the most respectable inhabitants. The room engaged for the meeting was the Shire Hall, the largest in the city. It was filled to suffocation on my arrival; but as there were far more outside than within, the meeting was adjourned to a large square adjoining, where a waggon was fixed in the place usually occupied in a similar way at elections, from which I addressed a most attentive audience of more than two thousand persons, for nearly two hours, in the stillness of a summer eve. Something of a similar kind had taken place in Bristol, where I twice addressed large assemblages of people, there being not fewer than fifteen hundred present on the second occasion. Of these meetings detailed reports were published in the local journals; in which the subject of emigration to Australia, and the advantages it

held forth to the swarming myriads of England, were successively brought under the notice of thousands who had
never heard a syllable on the subject before.

In Scotland I delivered a series of four lectures in the
City of Glasgow, towards the close of the year 1847, and
other two to large audiences in the Trades' Hall of that
city, early in 1849. These lectures or addresses were
repeated in Edinburgh, and in the towns of Ayr, Kirkin-
tilloch, Kirkcaldy and Cupar; in Aberdeen; in the towns of
Elgin, Inverness, and Oban; at Wick in Caithness; at
Kirkwall and Stromness in the Orkney Isles, and at Lerwick
in the Shetland Islands. Lady Franklin, with whom I had
had the honour of becoming acquainted when her unfortunate
husband was Governor of Van Dieman's Land, happening
to be a fellow-passenger with me in the steamer to the
Orkney and Shetland Islands (whither she had gone to
make ineffectual inquiries about Sir John and the Polar
Expedition) took a deep interest in my object, both from
her intimate acquaintance with the Australian Colonies
and their resources, and also from the remarkable redundancy of female population in these islands arising from
the maritime character of their male population, and the
frequent and fatal accidents on their dangerous coasts; and
I learned afterwards that Her Ladyship had quite a daily
levee at the inn, after I left the islands, from the number
of respectable young Shetland and Orkney Island females
who waited upon her to express their desire to come out to
Australia, and to ascertain by what means they could get
out passage free. But the benevolent efforts of Lady
Franklin, as well as my own endeavours, in favour
of these reputable Scotch Protestant females, were unfortunately neutralized by Earl Grey and his subordinates
in the Colonial Office, who, at the instance of well-known
and deeply interested parties, had allowed the disposable
funds of the Colony at the period in question to be absorbed
in sending us out not fewer than 2,219 Irish females under

the denomination of orphans, and almost exclusively Roman Catholics, during the eighteen months ending on the 30th June, 1849. This was done in direct contravention of a principle embodied, at my suggestion, in the Report of the Select Committee of the Legislative Council on Immigration, for the year 1845, to the following effect :— "Whatever number of emigrants may henceforth be introduced" (that is, by Government, at the public expense) "ought to be derived in equal proportions from the three kingdoms." But Downing Street in those days was unhappily amenable neither to law nor to reason.

In Ireland (which I visited twice during my stay in the mother country) my efforts in favour of Australian emigration were confined to the province of Ulster, where I delivered addresses on the subject to large and deeply interested audiences, in Belfast, Coleraine, Londonderry, Armagh, and Banbridge. In Coleraine, the meeting, which was large and enthusiastic, was presided over by the late John Boyd, Esq., M.P. for the Borough; in Londonderry, Sir Robert Bateson, Bart., presided; and in the City of Armagh, W. Paton, Esq., Agent for the Primate of Ireland. By these means not only was the subject of Australian emigration and its advantages brought under the notice of multitudes of persons of all classes of society and in all parts of the three kingdoms, but the minds of men generally were thereby undergoing the requisite preparation for taking advantage, with intelligence and success, of the great impending crisis, when the discovery of gold in Australia astonished the whole civilized world, and attracted tens of thousands to its shores.

I have already observed that the grand turning point in the history of the Australian Colonies was the advent of responsible government, and the establishment of popular institutions, in the year 1856. A Draft Constitution had been drawn up by the Legislative Council of New South

Wales, in the year 1853,* which was approved of and enacted by the Imperial Parliament in 1855 : the Colony granting Her Majesty a Civil List, and Her Majesty conceding in lieu of it to the Colonial Legislature all the *Droits* of the Crown, and in particular all the Waste Lands of the Territory in absolute and perpetual possession. Now I have no hesitation in stating—as one of the representatives of the people in the Legislature of New South Wales, for upwards of a quarter of a century—that, if the rights and interest of Great Britain, as a great colonizing Power, had been taken into consideration on that most important occasion, by the Secretary of State for the Colonies, a very different arrangement, and one of transcendant importance to the Mother-country, might have been effected with perfect facility. The importance of immigration, both to the Mother-country and to the Australian Colonies had then been so long and so extensively acknowledged, that if the Secretary of State, whose bounden duty it was to have duly considered the rights and interests of both parties in the case, had merely insisted on attaching to the Imperial Act a proviso to the effect that one half of the funds accruing from the sales of all Waste Lands in Australia should be appropriated, for a certain period at least, to the promotion of emigration from the United Kingdom, the arrangement would have been cordially acceded to by the Australian public. The extreme importance of the case, and the course which it was incumbent upon Her Majesty's Government to have pursued in the matter, had been indicated by myself in the following pages of a work, which was published in London in the year 1852, three years before the Constitution Act was passed.

" As one of the main objects of colonization is to provide an eligible outlet for the redundant population of the

* I happened to be absent in England at the time and had consequently no share in its authorship.

Mother-country, I would take it for granted that Great Britain would never concede independence to any colony, or group of colonies, at all adapted for such a condition, without providing for the carrying out of this great object as fully as if the colony, or group of colonies, had continued a dependency or group of dependencies."

"The particular reasons why it would not be expedient for Great Britain to surrender the absolute controul of the waste lands to the provincial governments, are,. *First*, that if these lands were to be surrendered unconditionally to the provincial governments, these governments might determine that no part of the proceeds arising from their sale should be appropriated for the promotion of immigration : and *Second*, that even although the provincial governments might appropriate a portion of the land revenue for immigration, the probability is that there would be no restriction imposed as to where the immigrants should come from ; so that Great Britain would reap no *special* advantage from the arrangement, and might possibly be excluded from *any* advantage from it through the competition of foreigners. Ideas of this kind have of late, and especially since the discovery of gold, been put forth again and again in New South Wales; and I have oftener than once incurred some degree of obloquy myself, in the Legislative Council of that colony, for insisting, as I have uniformly done, that the waste lands are *not* the property of the actual colonists, as certain influential members of Council are in the habit of regarding them, but of the British empire,—to be administered, however, for the mutual advantage of the mother-country and the colony. At the general election in New South Wales, in 1851, several of the candidates put forth the idea that, as the discovery of gold would send out plenty of emigrants to the colony, no part of the land fund ought in future to be appropriated for immigration purposes, but that the whole of it should be applied for the construction of roads and bridges, &c. But Great Britain has a deep interest in preventing any such measure from being carried,—she has a deep interest, on behalf of her industrious and virtuous poor, in insisting upon the continuance of the present arrangement for the appropriation of at least one-half of the land fund for the promotion of emigration from the United Kingdom."

" I am therefore decidedly of opinion that Great Britain should on no account surrender the absolute controul of the waste lands to any mere provincial legislature, and that she should make it a *sine qua non*, in a Treaty of Independence with the General or National Government, that one-half of the proceeds of the sales of all waste lands throughout the Union, should be appropriated as at present for the promotion of emigration from Great Britain and Ireland."

" This arrangement would effectually ensure a thoroughly British population for the Australian provinces ; which, I confess,—with the best possible feelings towards foreigners of all nations,—I regard as a matter of essential importance for their welfare and advancement. Under such an arrangement also, the National Government of the Australian Union would virtually be a mere *agency*, and as far as the mother-country is concerned, an *unpaid agency*, for carrying out the first grand object of colonization for Great Britain, viz., the providing of an eligible outlet for her redundant population. The Australian provinces would therefore, although formally free and independent, be in reality a series of *Tributary States* to Great Britain ; paying her a large amount of *tribute* for the promotion of emigration from her shores every year: for although the benefit would be mutual and equal, the arrangement would necessarily take the form of a large annual contribution to the British treasury from Australia—

probably not less in amount than £150,000 (a hundred and fifty thousand) a-year."*

"I can imagine no difficulty whatever in the way of the carrying out of such an arrangement as I propose, or of the creation of the requisite guarantees to ensure the fulfilment of the proposed condition. Great Britain would have this completely in her own power, and could easily enforce the fulfilment of such a condition, if there were the slightest disposition exhibited on the part of the Australian Government to set aside the treaty. But this is scarcely conceivable; for the arrangement would be so beneficial to both parties that there could be no disposition to withdraw from the terms of the engagement. I would limit the arrangement, however, to the period of FIFTY YEARS. If at the close of that period, a future generation of Australians should deem it expedient to renew the treaty, on the same conditions, they would have it in their power to do so; but if not, they would be free to do as they pleased. And in the mean time, I can think of nothing that would be likely to interrupt the friendly intercourse that would be sure to subsist between the two countries, on a basis of such reciprocal advantage."†

---

* The revenue which may be derived from the sale of wild land is the fund out of which the cost of introducing emigrants is best defrayed. This is the suggestion which, in reality, forms the great discovery of Mr. Wakefield, and does the greatest credit to those who have supported and enforced his views. About the speculative parts of his scheme many doubts may be entertained; respecting this there can scarcely be two opinions. Merivale, vol. ii. p. 51.

† The work quoted above was entitled, *Freedom and Independence for the Golden Lands of Australia; the right of the Colonies, and the interest of Britain and of the world.* By the Author of this work, London, 1852. It was doubtless a premature attempt to carry the point aimed at in this volume. The world had not got so far ahead as to receive such a proposition eighteen years ago. I am happy to find, however, that it has *now* got up to my stand point *then.* My own opinions on the subject are of an old date.

I had therefore given the Colonial Office the best advice for the interests of Britain in the year 1852. But as the famous Dean Swift says—"No wonder men will not take advice, when they will not even take warning." Such warning had undoubtedly been given to the Colonial Office, five years before the passing of the Constitution Act of 1855, as will be seen from the following extract of a letter from Earl Grey to the Governor of New South Wales, of date, Downing Street, 27th May, 1851. "I have received your Dispatch, No. 239, of the 31st December last, forwarding an Address from the Legislative Council of New South Wales to the Queen, setting forth the amount expended upon Immigration from the Land Fund since the year 1836, and the debt incurred upon it for the same object, setting forth the advantages derived from that outlay to the mother-country, and urging that it is no part of the duty of the colonists to pay for the importation of emigrants."*

There was therefore the more urgent necessity, on the part of the Principal Secretary of State for the Colonies, to watch over and to protect the interests of Great Britain in so momentous a crisis as that of the concession of absolute power over the waste lands of the Colonies to the local legislatures ; as it was evident from this Dispatch that there was actually a party in the Colonies at that period opposed to the appropriation of any part of the Land Fund for the purposes of Immigration. It is, therefore, with extreme regret that I have to inform the reader that the nobleman to whom, as Secretary of State for the Colonies at the time, we are mainly indebted for this unaccountable dereliction of public duty to the mother-country, was one whom I have always regarded with the highest respect and esteem—Lord John, now Earl Russell.

* Council Paper.

By Clause II. of the Imperial Act, 18 and 19 Vict., Cap. 54, passed 16th July, 1855, it is enacted that—"The entire management and control of the Waste Lands belonging to the Crown in the said Colony, and also the appropriation of the gross proceeds of the sales of any such Lands, and of all other Proceeds and Revenues of the same, from whatever source arising within the said Colony, including all Royalties, Mines, and Minerals, shall be vested in the Legislature of the said Colony."

And it is also enacted by Clause L. of the same Act, as follows :—" The said several sums mentioned in Schedules A. B. and C. shall be accepted and taken by Her Majesty, her Heirs and Successors, by way of Civil List, instead of all Territorial, casual, and other Revenues of the Crown (including all Royalties) from whatever source arising within the said Colony, and to the disposal of which the Crown may be entitled either absolutely or conditionally, or otherwise howsoever."

The three Schedules above referred to are as follows :—

Schedule A.

Salaries of Public Offices £20,550

Schedule B.

Pensions chargeable. £13,950

Schedule C. (now in process of extinction).

Public Worship £28,000

This famous Act was passed on the 16th July, 1855— Lord John Russell being then Secretary of State for the Colonies. The following paper, for which I am indebted to the courtesy of George F. Wise, Esq., Agent for Immigration in New South Wales, being an abstract of his yearly Reports for three different periods—will show the reader how immensely valuable to Great Britain, as a field for Emigration, was the magnificent estate which was thus virtually thrown away.

INFORMATION RESPECTING IMMIGRATION FROM THE UNITED KINGDOM
TO NEW SOUTH WALES,

From 1838 to 31st December, 1851—19 Years.

Assisted Immigrants Introduced.	Cost of Convey- ance, Superintendence, &c., &c.			Paid by Immigrants, or out of Imperial Fund.			Paid by Resi- dents in this Colony under Remittances Regulations.			Total charged on the Colonial Fund for Introduction of Immigrants.			Unassisted Immigrants Arrived.
No.	£	s.	d.	£	s.	d.	£	s.	d.	£	s.	d.	No.
58,261	918,141	12	3	17,812	9	9	*nil.*			900,329	2	6	14,038

INFORMATION RESPECTING IMMIGRATION FROM THE UNITED KINGDOM
TO NEW SOUTH WALES,

From 1st January, 1852, to 31st December, 1859—8 Years.

Assisted Immigrants Introduced.	Cost of Convey- ance, Superintendence, &c., &c.			Paid by Immigrants, or out of Imperial Fund.			Paid by Resi- dents in this Colony under Remittances Regulations.			Total charged on the Colonial Fund for Introduction of Immigrants.			Unassisted Immigrants Arrived.
No.	£	s.	d.	£	s.	d.	£	s.	d.	£	s.	d.	No.
66,714	1,005,674	11	5	*nil.*			38,948	0	5	966,726	11	5	17,388

INFORMATION RESPECTING IMMIGRATION FROM THE UNITED KINGDOM
TO NEW SOUTH WALES,

From 1st January, 1860, to 31st December, 1869—10 Years.

Assisted Immigrants Introduced.	Cost of Convey- ance, Superintendence, &c., &c.			Paid by Immigrants, or out of Imperial Fund.			Paid by Resi- dents in this Colony under Remittances Regulations.			Total charged on the Colonial Fund for Introduction of Immigrants.			Unassisted Immigrants Arrived.
No.	£	s.	d.	£	s.	d.	£	s.	d.	£	s.	d.	No.
21,295	297,445	5	3	*nil.*			97,333	4	2	200,112	1	1	8,532

From the first part of this Abstract, the reader will perceive that during the nineteen years ending 31st December, 1851, when Victoria had just become a separate Colony, New South Wales had contributed from her Land Fund the sum of £900,329 2s. 6d. for the promotion of emigration from the United Kingdom to Australia. During the second period, of eight years, till the separation of Queensland, the said colony had contributed for the same purpose £966,726 11s. 5d.; and during the third period of ten years, from the separation of Queensland, the contribution by New South Wales towards the same object had been £200,112 1s. 1d. And as Victoria has been contributing in the same way from her own land-fund for the last eighteen years, and Queensland from hers for the last ten, the reader will be able to form some idea of the value of that splendid estate which the British people have now virtually lost through the act and deed of their own Government.

For it will be observed that while the sum contributed by New South Wales for emigration to that Colony during the second period, of eight years, was £966,726 11s. 5d., or at the rate of £120,840 3s. 11d. per annum; the contribution for the last decennial period was only £200,112 1s. 1d., or at the rate of £20,011 4s. 1d. yearly. The cause of this remarkable diminution of the fund available for *immigration*, as it is called in the colonies, was that both of the two ministers for lands, under the two different governments that have held office during the past ten years in New South Wales, were strongly opposed to any appropriation of public money for that purpose altogether; the one alleging that all that was requisite to induce a flow of immigration from the mother-country, was to reduce the minimum price of land which is now a pound, to ten shillings, or rather to five shillings an acre; while the other held and advocated the notable principle, that if either land or the worth of it should be given to or for immigrants from Europe, it ought *a fortiori* to be given to actual colonists—thousands, or rather tens of thousands, of whom had in their own persons or in those of their parents received their portion already in a free passage to the colony at the expense of its land fund !

In this state of things a sort of compromise was effected, under which the contribution for immigration from the land fund of New South Wales during the last decennial period was expended under the system of what is called "Assisted Immigration," or that of allowing actual colonists to contribute so much per head for the passage out of their friends or relations, the Government paying the larger portion of the cost from the Land Fund. But this system, although equitable and just in theory is very much the reverse in practice; for it is taken advantage of almost exclusively by Irish Roman Catholics, upon whom it may be said by way of explanation, that the usual influences are brought to bear, to enable them to increase the number of "the faithful" in the land, by getting out their relatives from home. At all events the result of the Assisted Immigration system, which has been virtually a sort of semi-pauper system, during the last decennial period, was an immigration of 16,623 souls, of whom not fewer than 10,296 were Irish Roman Catholics, while the whole number of Protestants of all denominations from the three kingdoms was only 6,327.

During my stay in England in the years 1847-49, I was successful, after great personal sacrifices as well as much personal labour, in sending out about six hundred Protestant nonconformists in three different ships to Moreton Bay, now Queensland; chiefly to cultivate the cotton plant and the sugar-cane by means of European free labour in that settlement; having unexpectedly observed, on my first visit to that part of our territory in November, 1845, the peculiar adaptation of the soil and climate for these Tropical products, and the practicability of their

cultivation in Australia by means of European free labour.*
On that occasion I had laboured long but unsuccessfully
both in the Mother-country and in the Colony to establish
the principle that, instead of coming out as semi-paupers
in the Government Emigration ships, to which I found
reputable persons in all parts of the mother-country greatly
averse, the emigrant who paid his own passage should be
entitled on his arrival, to a *bonus* in land, to defray or assist
in defraying the cost of his passage. All my efforts, however, were unsuccessful ; but no sooner was the separation
of Queensland effected, and a new Colony proclaimed and
established, in December, 1859, than the Government of
that Colony got an Act passed, in its first Parliament, in
1860, establishing the principle in question, and publicly
recognizing it as mine—thereby guaranteeing to every
adult immigrant, whether male or female, thirty acres of
land, a *bonus* which has since been increased to forty acres.
And with what result? Why, during the first eight or
nine years from the passing of that Act the population of
Queensland had been more than quadrupled, and so many
persons and families of a superior class had arrived in the
Colony, that for years together the capital at the colonial
banks was increased by immigration at the rate of £20,000
sterling a month or nearly a quarter of a million a year !

Precisely the same result was realized in New Zealand,
where a *bonus* of forty acres of land was held forth for
every adult immigrant paying his own passage out, and

---

* This idea, which, when I first announced it in London, Manchester, and Glasgow, in the years 1847-1849, was almost universally
regarded and stigmatized as absolutely chimerical and absurd, is now
regarded somewhat differently. The idea is now—no longer a matter
of mere speculation : it is an unquestionable reality, an accomplished
fact, for in the year 1868, the export of cleaned cotton, almost the
entire produce of British free labour, from Queensland, was not less
than 6000 bales ; and there were also at the same time upwards of two
thousand acres of land under the sugar-cane in that Colony.

where the population more than quadrupled itself in ten years. But in New South Wales, where there was no such *bonus* offered to the intending emigrant, the population remained stationary during the whole decennial period, with the exception of the natural increase from births; the increase from Assisted Immigration being balanced by the simultaneous emigration which had taken place to Queensland, to California, and to New Zealand. That emigration—so utterly discreditable to a country with so splendid a climate as that of New South Wales, with a territory equal in extent to that of the United Kingdom and all France put together, and with millions of acres and millions more of the finest land lying utterly waste—was occasioned, I verily believe, by the stagnation and depression arising from the complete stoppage of immigration, and of the influx of capital, industry, energy, and enterprise that would certainly have accompanied it, had such a system as that of Queensland been established in New South Wales, and had Lord John Russell only done his duty to the mother-country in 1855.

"The colonies," says an able writer, "contain virgin soil sufficient to employ and feed five times as many people as are now crowded into Great Britain and Ireland. Nothing is needed but arms to cultivate it, while here, among ourselves, are millions of ablebodied men unwillingly idle, clamouring for work, with their families starving on their hands. What more simple than to bring the people and the land together! * * * The land, we are told impatiently, is no longer ours. A few years ago it *was* ours, but to save the Colonial Office trouble we made it over to the local government, and now we have no more right over it than we have over the prairies of Texas. If it were so, *the more shame to the politicians who let drop so precious an inheritance.**

* Article entitled *England and Her Colonies.* By James Anthony Froude, M.A.—*Frazer's Magazine*, January, 1870.

Had the principle which I recommended so strongly in 1852—that of appropriating one-half of the funds arising from the sales of waste land for the promotion of emigration from the United Kingdom to Australia—been established by the Imperial Parliament in 1855, as it might have been with perfect facility, it would have served as a fly-wheel for the regulation of the social machinery of the colonies in the department of immigration, as well as a safety valve for carrying off one of the dangerous elements of society, both at home and abroad. There would have been no necessity under such a system for the introduction of more labour where it was not wanted in any of the colonies; and there would have been the means of holding out a *bonus* to emigration to the employer of labour, as was done so successfully during the last decennial period in Queensland and New Zealand. For it is quite as reasonable that the middle classes of society, the employers of labour of every grade, should have a *bonus* on emigration in the shape of a certain extent of land, as that the mere labourer should have such a *bonus* in the shape of a free passage out. The waste lands of the colonies belonged to both alike, till Lord John Russell allowed the Imperial Parliament to give them away. I am equally opposed with Mr. Wakefield and Bishop Hinds to a mere emigration of paupers; and I hold it to be one of the urgent necessities of the times that a *bonus* in land should be held forth to all who can pay their own passage to Australia. I will just show from a single instance how such a system would work, even on a very limited scale. A respectable tradesman, a rope-spinner, from my native town of Greenock, in the West of Scotland, having emigrated to Australia, thought he could do better for himself in his business by crossing over to New Zealand, where he soon managed to establish himself in a rope-walk near the town of Auckland, in the Northern Island, for the manufacture of the *phormium tenax* or New Zealand flax into cordage. Requiring additional labour for his business, he sent home for two workmen of the same craft, whom he had known in Greenock, offering them a free passage out, which he obtained for them by paying into the Treasury of the province £18 for each, and which they willingly accepted. On their arrival he received from the provincial Government forty acres of land for each of them; but he told them at the same time that if they preferred having the land themselves and would pay him by instalments from their wages what he had paid for their passage out, they should have it by all means. Preferring the land, they were soon able to pay for it, and they are now respectable land-holders in New Zealand. From the wretched government of our colonies in times past, Emigration has got a bad name at home, and is scarcely considered respectable. It was never in such bad odour when the heroic work of colonization was in the hands of the glorious Greeks.

Having, at the last General Election in 1869, declined re-election for the Parliament of New South Wales, in which I had been one of the representatives of the city of Sydney for many years past,* I recently embodied the views to which I have just given expression, in a pamphlet entitled "Immigration; the grand desideratum for New South Wales: and how to promote it effectually," as the subject will in all likelihood be dealt with in the ensuing session of that Parliament. But it will doubtless be seen from what I have stated above that the question, as to what amount of assistance our Colonial Legislatures may be disposed to render to the Mother-country in the promotion of immigration from the United Kingdom, or whether they will give any assistance at all, will depend entirely on the collective wisdom of each; and the experience of the last decennial period is by no means encouraging. There is a regular

* I had the honour of receiving a Requisition on the occasion, from more than two thousand of the electors of West Sydney.

Anti-Immigration League in existence in Victoria, **and** there is a considerable number of persons of the same opinion in New South Wales. But I am happy to state that there is a large majority of the people of the latter colony strongly in favour of an extensive immigration from the mother-country, and strongly disposed to make the requisite sacrifice, in the way of a *bonus* in land, for the accomplishment of so important an object.

SECTION VII.—POINTS OF IDENTITY, AND POINTS OF DIFFERENCE BETWEEN THE FUTURE NATIONAL GOVERNMENT OF THE SEVEN UNITED PROVINCES OF AUSTRALIA, AND THAT OF THE UNITED STATES.

In accordance with the principles and practice of popular government, the National Government of the future Australian Union would, doubtless, be identical in its form and structure with that of the United States. There would be a House of Representatives, to represent the Australian people numerically, according to population, and to be elected for a certain period. There would also be a Senate, to represent the Provinces, in equal numbers for each and on equal terms. And there would be a President, to be elected for a certain term of service, either directly or indirectly, by the nation, and to be eligible, as in America, for one additional term only.

Such a Constitution would of itself form a complete answer to the objection that has been urged in certain quarters, viz., that in the event of a federation of the Colonies, there would be no security or protection for the smaller and weaker provinces against injustice or aggression from the larger and stronger; for the smallest and weakest province would have precisely the same number of representatives in the Senate or highest political court of the nation as the largest and strongest.

Besides, there would be a Supreme Court for the Federal

Union, consisting of the most experienced judges in the land, who would be armed with sufficient power by the Constitution to administer justice between any two of the provinces, and especially to protect the weak against the powerful. The Supreme Court of the United States has discharged all such duties for nearly a century past with consummate ability and with entire success.

There is an urgent necessity at this moment for the creation of such a high Court of Appeal in Australia, on the ground of the requisite dispatch desired as well as on that of expense; the long delays and the great expense incurred in appeals to the Privy Council under our present system, being a very serious grievance in all the colonies. Doubtless we could scarcely expect to find men for such an office of such eminence in their profession as the great Law Lords at home; but there would be no difficulty in finding a sufficient number of fit and proper persons to form a Supreme Court, or Court of Appeal, under the National Government that would at once command the confidence, and ensure the respect of all the United Provinces.

With these points of coincidence, there will also be others of great difference between our future National Government and that of the United States. The much greater extent of each of the Seven United Provinces, as compared with the average extent of the different States of the American Union, will of itself constitute a great difference between the two cases. The island, or colony of Tasmania, the smallest of the Seven Provinces, has an area of 27,000 square miles*—an extent of territory considerably greater than that of all the following five of the smaller States of the American Union put together—viz., Massachusetts, New Jersey, Connecticut, Delaware, and Rhode Island. Victoria, with her extended boundary, would be

* I had stated it at 24,000 in a former section of this work, It was an error.

considerably larger than the five following of the larger States, viz., New Hampshire, Vermont, Maryland, South Carolina, and Michigan, while the Australian provinces along the Pacific—from Cape Howe to Cape York—would each be as extensive as four of the largest States in the American Union. This peculiarity of our position would render the Provincial Governments of Australia much more important in their National System, as integral portions of the Federal Union, than the State Governments of America. It might also detract somewhat from the honour and glory of the Federal Government, as one of the great Powers of the world. But I cannot see that any practical inconvenience would result from this peculiarity of our Constitutional system.

Another great point of difference between the future National Government of Australia and that of the United States is that, whereas the possession and management of the waste lands of the country are vested by the Constitution of the United States in the Federal Government, the waste lands of Australia would in all likelihood remain in the possession and under the exclusive management of the Provincial Parliaments respectively. I cannot see that such a system as that of the United States, in regard to the waste lands of the country, could be adopted with propriety, or even with safety, in Australia. The Provincial Governments would be quite competent to manage the waste lands within their respective boundaries; and I am confident they would never allow the funds accruing either from the management or the sales of these lands to be placed in a common Treasury, like that of the United States, to be divided rateably among the Provinces, according to the population of each, or applied to the general purposes of the National Government. Besides, there would be no necessity for uniformity of system, either in the management of the waste lands throughout the Union, or in the appropriation of the funds arising from their management or sale. Each Provincial Parliament could manage all such internal matters best for itself. The revenue arising from the Custom House, or from direct taxation of any kind, would be something altogether different from the Land Revenue of the different provinces, and could be dealt with safely as a National Fund from the first.

Again, the question of Immigration is one that can have no place in the American system, in the way of appropriating any portion of the funds arising from the sale of the waste lands for its direct promotion. But that question is all-important for Australia, and will continue to be so for a long time to come. As it is evident, however, that there will be great differences of opinion in regard to it, it will unquestionably be best for each Provincial Parliament to deal with the whole subject for itself.

I do not suppose that there would be any necessity for a standing army in Australia, in the event of our obtaining entire Freedom and Independence.* It was long after the Americans had become a nation before they found anything of the kind at all necessary, either for defence or for aggression. On visiting the city of Charleston, South Carolina, in the year 1840·–that is more than twenty years before the late war, in which that city bore so conspicuous a part—I found that the barracks for the Royal troops during the colonial regime had been transformed into a College after the peace of Paris in 1783. It was a good idea; and as the last of Her Majesty's troops are now ordered home, I

---

* I had likewise, in those days, a mortal antipathy to standing armies in time of peace; because I always took standing armies to be only *servants, hired by the master of the family for keeping his own children in slavery;* and because I conceived that a prince who could not think himself secure without mercenary troops, must needs have a separate interest from that of his subjects; although 1 am not ignorant of those artificial necessities which a corrupted ministry can create for keeping up forces to support a faction against the public interest.—Dean Swift, *Letters to Pope,* 1720.

presume the Colonial Parliaments will have to decide very shortly to what purpose the Military Barracks in the different colonies shall henceforth be appropriated. I have already hinted that a few armed steam-vessels will be necessary for surveying purposes, for the protection of commerce, for the prevention of piracy and kidnapping, and for the general advancement of civilization both among the islands of the Western Pacific and those of the eastern portion of the Indian Archipelago. With regard to the latter of these very promising fields for commercial enterprise and speculation, as it will be the evident interest of the Australian Government and nation to take the earliest opportunity of establishing relations with the Eastern Islands of the Archipelago, of which the natural productions are the richest of those of any country on the face of the earth,* there is reason to believe that one of

---

* The Indian Islands present to us an immense country more easy of access to the merchant and navigator than any other portion of the globe, owing to the tranquillity of the seas which surround them, that, like so many canals, or great navigable rivers, throw the communication open, and render it easy from one extremity to another. This great advantage peculiarly distinguishes them from the continuous territory of the Continent of Africa, from a great part of that of Asia, and from some of that of America. * * * In a commercial point of view, the immediate neighbourhood of the Indian Islands to the greatest nations of Asia is one of their most prominent characteristics. With respect to fertility of soil they are eminent. Their mineral and animal productions are various, rich, and extensive. They afford in luxuriance the vegetable productions common to other tropical climates, and some which are peculiarly their own, and which refuse to grow in cheapness and perfection anywhere else. It is at the same time to be remembered of these last, that they have been and still are in more universal request among men in any rank of social improvement, than the productions of any other portion of the globe.

The Indian Islanders, blessed with an abundance of fertile soil, which cannot be exhausted for ages, will be for an indefinite time in a condition to supply the more civilized world with its cheap and various produce, and necessarily in a condition to pay for the manufactured

the first of the national undertakings of the Federal Union will be to form a railway from the Murray River, where it reaches its northernmost limits in latitude 34°, to the Gulf of Carpentaria. It is a remarkable fact that Fort Bourke on that line is equidistant from all the three capitals of the three southern continental colonies—from Sydney, from Melbourne, and from Adelaide. From the northernmost point which the Murray River reaches in its long course from the Snowy Mountains to its embouchure in Encounter Bay, in the province of South Australia, a little to the eastward of the boundary of that province, the distance to the Head of the Gulf of Carpentaria is about a thousand geographical miles. The intervening country is remarkably level and well-fitted for the construction of a railway; and about half way between the two extremities of the line, as well as at the head of the Gulf, there is an extensive tract of country of a superior character, either for agriculture or grazing. Now there can be no doubt that in a few years hence a railway will be constructed from the point I have indicated on the Murray to the Gulf of Carpentaria. That point is nearly equidistant from Melbourne and Adelaide, the course being *up* the river to the former of these capitals, and *down* towards the latter; while Fort Bourke, nearly four degrees farther north on the probable line of route, would be equidistant from Sydney and Brisbane overland, as well as from Melbourne and Adelaide by the Murray. Such a line of railway as I

necessaries or luxuries of the latter. The value and extent of the intercourse between them will increase, it is almost superfluous to insist, in the proportion in which freedom and good government will enable them to exchange their respective productions, at the smallest cost, and in the greatest abundance—a maxim too trite and obvious to be here dwelt upon, had it not, in all periods of our intercourse with these countries, been either notoriously neglected, or rather had it not been acted in direct opposition to. *Crawford's History of the Indian Archipelago*, vol. III., pages 275, 277.

have indicated would thus bring all the four capitals
within a few days journey of one of the most important
geographical points in the whole world. A splendid prospect for commerce would thus be opened to all these
colonies !

As to the cost of a Federal or National Government for
Australia, I do not suppose that there would be any difficulty in providing the requisite funds. We should never
think of giving the governors of the different provinces
anything like the same salaries under such a system as we
give them now ; and there are various other salaries in all
the present Colonies that would admit of similar curtail-
ment. The President of the United States has a salary of
not more than £5000 a-year; why should ours have more ?
The highest salary given to the Governor of any particular
State of the American Union is that of the Governor of
Louisiana, which is not more than £1500 a-year. Why
should any Governor selected from among ourselves have
more ? It would neither be asked for nor expected by any
colonist; and the saving to be effected in that particular
item of expenditure alone would go a long way towards
the support of a Federal Government for the Seven United
Provinces of Australia.

SECTION VIII.—ESTIMATE OF THE PROBABLE INFLUENCE OF AUS-
     TRALIA, AS A SOVEREIGN AND INDEPENDENT STATE, IN PROMOTING
     EMIGRATION FROM THE UNITED KINGDOM.

Having shewn in a former section of this chapter, how
Great Britain had herself bartered away for a thing of
naught the moral and political power she once possessed
for the promotion of Emigration to Australia, and the consequent uncertainty of the future action of the respective
Provincial Parliaments in this most important matter, I am
now to show what Australia, as a Sovereign and In-

dependent State, might not only be expected to do, but could easily accomplish, in the way of promoting an extensive emigration from the United Kingdom, for a long series of future years.

I am therefore decidedly of opinion that, in the event of the Seven United Provinces of Australia being recognized by the Mother-country, and admitted into the great family of nations, as a Sovereign and Independent State, it should immediately take possession of the Fiji Islands, of the New Hebrides group of Islands, and of the Solomon Islands —all in the Western Pacific Ocean and in the Southern hemisphere—not, however, with a view to the permanent annexation of these three groups of islands, as part and parcel of the Australian Empire; but simply with a view to the setting up of regular government in the respective groups, through the formation of a series of Australian Protectorates, for the civilization of the Aborigines on the one hand, and the creation of a vast Emigration Field for the progressive settlement of perhaps half a million of the redundant population of the United Kingdom on the other.

With a view to demonstrate the entire practicability of this great enterprise of the future, I shall first give a slight sketch of the three groups of Islands I have enumerated ; I shall then shew the peculiar fitness of these groups of Islands as Emigration Fields, for the progressive settlement or colonization of a European population, and shall afterwards indicate the manner in which such colonization might be effected to a very great extent, so as eventually to repay perhaps the whole cost to be incurred in the first instance.

To begin with the FIJI ISLAND group—

" The Fiji group includes the islands lying between the latitudes of 15 deg. 30 min. and 20 deg. 30 min. S., and the longitudes of 177 deg. E., and 178 deg. W., comprising among others, what were named by Tasman, " Prince William's Islands," extending over about 40,000 square miles of the South Pacific, and forming a connecting link between the abodes of the Malayan and Papuan races which inhabit the widely spread Polynesia."[*]

"The two principal islands of the group, all of which are lofty, picturesque, and fruitful, are Viti Levu (Great Fiji), which is eighty-five miles long by forty broad, and Vanua Levu (Great Land), ninety-five miles by twenty-five or thirty; and there are besides, nearly one hundred inhabited islands of all sizes, containing a population which has been variously estimated at from 75,000 to 300,000 souls, the mean of these numbers being probably not far from the truth."[†]

The two islands thus indicated by Captain (now Admiral) Erskine are more particularly described as follows, by the Rev. Mr. Williams:—

Vanua Levu (Great Land) is more than one hundred miles long, having an average breadth of twenty-five miles. Its western extremity is notable as being the only part of Fiji in which sandal wood can be produced. The opposite portion of the island is deeply indented by the Natawa Bay, which is forty miles long, and named by the natives, "the Dead Sea." The population of Vanua Levu is estimated at 21,000. Its scenery much resembles that of

Na Viti Levu (the Great Fiji), which measures ninety miles from east to west, and fifty from north to south. A great variety of landscape is found in navigating the shores of Great Fiji. To the S. E. there is tolerably level ground for thirty miles inland, edged, in places, by cliffs of sandstone five hundred feet high—the luxuriant and cheerful beauty of the lowland that gives place to the gloomy grandeur and unbroken solitude of the mountains. To the

---

* *Fiji and the Fijians*, by Thomas Williams, Missionary in Fiji. London, 1858.

† *Journal of a Cruise among the Islands of the Western Pacific.* By John Elphinstone Erskine, Capt. R.N. London. 1853.

S. W. are low shores with patches of brown barren land; then succeed narrow vales, beyond which rise hills, whose wooded tops are in fine contrast with the bold bare front at their base. Behind these are the highest mountains in the group, bleak and sterile, with an altitude of 4,000 or 5,000 feet. Westward, and to the coast, high land is close to the shore, with only narrow strips of level ground separating it from the sea. Proceeding northward some of the finest scenery in Fiji is opened out.*

"*Taviuni*," says Mr. Williams, "commonly called Somosomo, from its town of that name being the residence of the ruling chiefs—is too fine an island to be overlooked. It is twenty-five miles long, with a coast of sixty miles, and consists of one vast mountain, gradually rising to a central ridge of 2,100 feet elevation. Fleecy clouds generally hide its summit, where stretches a considerable lake, pouring through an outlet in the west a stream which, after tumbling and dashing along its narrow bed, glides quietly through the chief town, furnishing it with a supply of fresh water. A smaller outlet to the east discharges enough water to form a small but beautiful cascade. This lake is supposed to have as its bed the crater of an extinct volcano, an idea supported by the quantity of volcanic matter found on the island. However wild and terrible the appearance of the island once, it is now covered with luxuriance and beauty beyond the conception of the most glowing imagination. Perhaps every characteristic of Fijian scenery is found on Somosomo, while all the tropical vegetables are produced here in perfection. It has only a land-reef, which is often very narrow, and in many places entirely wanting, breaking towards Tasman's Straits, into detached patches."†

* *Fiji and the Fijians.* By Thomas Williams, late Missionary in Fiji. London, 1858.
† Williams—*Ibid.*

"Almost all the islands," adds Captain Erskine, "we saw had lofty picturesque peaks, and the soil, of decomposed volcanic rocks, both on the hills and in the plains, appeared to be of exuberant fertility; that of Vanua Levu—the second island in point of size—being perhaps the least so."

The following statements by the missionaries of the progress of European vegetables will show to what extent and with what ease they may be produced:—

"Of turnip, radish, and mustard seed, after being sown twenty-four hours, the cotyledon leaves appear above the surface. Melons, cucumbers, and pumpkins spring up in three days; beans and peas make their appearance in four. In four weeks from the time of planting radishes and lettuce are fit for use; and in five weeks marrowfat peas."

"Immense quantities of yams are produced, and taro is cultivated by means of irrigation, the ditches being used for the purpose both at Lakemba and Levuka."*

Then as to the climate and temperature of the islands:—

"The temperature is nearly uniform; the greatest extremes of heat and cold being experienced inland. My meteorological journal kept at Lakemba in 1841, and ten years later at Vanua Levu, shows 62 deg. as the lowest, and 121 deg. as the highest temperature noted. The low temperature here recorded, is ascribed in part, to a river running close by my house. The mean temperature of the group throughout may be stated at 80 deg. Very hot days are sometimes preceded by very cold nights."*

The Fiji Islands have been occupied for upwards of twenty years past by Protestant Missionaries of the Wesleyan Communion, through whose zealous and self-

---

* *Journal of a Cruise among the Islands of the Western Pacific.* By John Elphinstone Erskine, Capt. R.N. London, 1853.

* *Fiji and the Fijians.* By Thomas Williams, late Missionary in Fiji. London, 1838.

denying labours very many of the natives have embraced, and now profess, Christianity.

The second of the groups to which I have referred above is that of the NEW HEBRIDES Islands, which are situated as nearly as possible within the same range of latitude, although considerably farther to the westward, and therefore so much nearer Australia. They are described in the following language by the Rev. A. W. Murray :—

" The New Hebrides are situated between latitude 14 deg. 20 min. N. and 20 deg. 4 min. S. ; and longitude 166 deg. 41 min. and 170 deg. 21 min E. They extend about 400 miles, N.N.W. and S.S.E. The northern island was discovered by Quiros in 1606. He regarded it as a part of the southern continent which at that time was supposed to exist. The group was visited by Bougainville in 1768. Besides ascertaining that the land was not connected, but composed of islands, he did but little ; and it was reserved for our own great navigator, Cook, to complete the discovery. He visited it in 1774, discovered all the southern islands, and more or less fully explored the whole of it. He gave it the designation it now bears. It is remarkable that a group so extensive, and possessing resources so great, should have continued so long comparatively unknown. This has been owing, doubtless, chiefly to the savage character of the inhabitants ; and, when these are brought into a state which shall render it safe for foreign visitors to approach their shores, the islands will, in all probability, speedily be laid open to the world, and their resources made available to the purposes for which they are adapted. With the exception of the Fijis and New Zealand, there is no group in the South Pacific that will bear comparison with the New Hebrides. In extent, population, and resources, they have no other rival. There are no fewer than *thirty* inhabited islands, two of which are about two hundred miles in circumference. Besides these, there are a number of inhabited islands, in the immediate vicinity of the larger ones, of which no notice is taken in geographical works, and which have no place on any chart. The names of the principal islands of the group, proceeding from the north in a south-easterly direction, are *Espiritu Santo*, the largest island of the group; *Mallicolo*, the next in size; *Bartholomew's*; *Leper's Island*; *Aurora*; *Pentecost*; *Ambrym*, or *Chinambrym*, as the natives call it; *Apee*; *Paum Islands*, two in number; the *Pyramid*; the *Monument*, so named because of its shape; *Two Hills*; *Shepherd's Isles*, five in number; *Three Hills*; *Montague*; *Hinchinbrook*; *Vaté*, or *Sandwich Island*; *Erromanga*; *Nina*; *Tanna*; *Fotuna*, and *Aneiteum*. All these islands are inhabited, some of them thickly so for heathen lands. Of course we can only guess at the population. It is very probable that it may not be less than one hundred and fifty thousand. The islands of the New Hebrides are, so far as our knowledge goes, all of volcanic origin. They resemble in their general appearance the islands of Eastern Polynesia. In beauty and fruitfulness they are not a whit behind the finest of these. Some of them, Ambrym for example, are perfect gems. The writer has seen many beautiful islands both in Eastern and Western Polynesia, but one more lovely than the island just named he never beheld."[*]

As the Fiji Islands have been occupied successfully, for a long series of years past, by missionaries of the Wesleyan Communion, the New Hebrides Islands have been occupied for a similar period, and with equally gratifying results, by ordained missionaries from the Presbyterian Churches in Scotland and Nova Scotia.

The first of the Islands of this group that was occupied for missionary purposes by the Presbyterian missionaries,

[*] *Missions in Western Polynesia*, from their commencement in 1839 to the present time. By A. W. Murray, twenty-five years a Missionary in Polynesia in connexion with the London Missionary Society. London, 1863.

and of which, I am happy to say, the population is now entirely Christian, was *Aneiteum*, of which the following notices are given by the Rev. Mr. Murray :—

"It was discovered by Captain Cook, in 1774, and by him named Anatum, a name by which, except in missionary circles, it is still generally known. It is the most southerly island of the New Hebrides. It lies in south lat. 20º, and east long. 170º. It is forty miles in circumference, and has a population of 3,600.* It is lofty, some of its mountains rising to the height of 3,000 feet. Its general character is mountainous; but it has a considerable amount of good agricultural land. It is well wooded and watered. Large quantities of kaurie pine are found of excellent quality, and a great variety of other wood, which might be turned to valuable account. But the chief distinction of Aneiteum, among the islands of the southern division of the New Hebrides group, consists in its harbour. This is of a very superior character. It is spacious, and sheltered from all points except the west, to which it opens. It is easy of ingress and egress, the entrance being wide and free from obstruction. Anchorage for vessels of any size is found at a convenient depth of water and with good bottom, and the circumstances must be very extraordinary that would endanger any vessel properly secured. A considerable number of vessels have of late years resorted to the island.

"The island of Aneiteum is seen from a great distance; some say sixty miles. It is a beautiful island. Hill and valley, mountains of every shape and size, intersected by deep ravines, cultivated spots, and barren tracts, covered with scrub, or entirely without vegetation, diversify the scene and give it a lively and picturesque appearance."

The next of the Islands of this group that have been

---

* It has been greatly diminished since by a fatal epidemic that overspread the island a few years ago.

occupied—in the first instance most unfortunately for all concerned, but subsequently under better auspices—by the Presbyterian missionaries, is *Tanna*:—

" It is a lovely island, by far the richest and most beautiful of all the islands of the southern division of the New Hebrides. It was discovered by Captain Cook, on the 5th of August, 1774, and was estimated by him to be about thirty miles in length, and from nine to twelve miles in breadth. It is therefore about eighty miles in circumference. The population is probably about ten thousand ; the estimate of some is much higher, and they may be correct. The island presents a very interesting appearance. It is mountainous, but the mountains being generally rather low, and round, or table-topped, and covered with dense forests to their summits, it appears soft and beautiful, rather than grand and imposing. 'The purple peak, the pointed spire,' the frowning battlement, and hoary cliff, which look so grand and picturesque on many of the islands of Polynesia, are not found on Tanna. Tanna, however, has its own beauties and objects of interest, many and great. The most striking natural object on the island is a volcano, which has been in a state of constant activity from the days of Cook, and no one knows how long before, to the present time.

"Any one approaching the island now finds Cook's description just as apt as it was when he penned it. 'The light seen in the night,' he says, ' we now find to have been a volcano. A rumbling noise was heard, and it threw up great quantities of smoke and fire.' Again he remarks : ' On Thursday, the 11th, during the night, the volcano was very troublesome, and threw out great quantities of fire and smoke, with a most tremendous noise, and sometimes we saw great stones thrown into the air.' Nothing strikes one as more remarkable than the prodigious stones it emits. Immense blocks are scattered around the neighbourhood of the crater, which at different times have been thrown out. At the distance of miles the ground is hot and cracked; and smoke is seen issuing from fissures in several places. Hot springs abound in the neighbourhood; and vast quantities of sulphur are found. Sulphur is now becoming an article of export. There are several craters, some of which are extinct. Two or three are generally in a state of activity; and occasionally the noise is, as Cook describes it, tremendous, being heard at a distance of forty miles. The mountain is not high, and over an area of perhaps three or four miles it is covered with ashes and scoria.

"The island is amazingly fertile. All the usual productions of Eastern Polynesia are found, and others also, such as figs, The yams of Tanna are perhaps the largest of any to be found in Polynesia, or anywhere else. Cook says, 'One of our people weighed a yam which exceeded fifty-five pounds.

"Port Resolution, in which Cook anchored, is a tolerable harbour; it is formed by a bay, or creek, about three-quarters of a mile deep, and about half that broad, the head of which is only about four miles from the volcano. It is situated on the north side of the most easterly point of the island, and is about thirty miles distant from Aneiteum."

The island of *Erromanga* so famous, or rather so infamous, for the brutal murders, first of the Rev. John Williams 'and his coadjutor the Rev. Mr. Harris, in the year 1839, and afterwards of the Rev. Mr. Gordon and his wife, from Nova Scotia, has since been reoccupied, after a period of temporary abandonment, by a brother of the late Mr. Gordon, also from Nova Scotia, who with a Christian heroism and devotedness worthy of the very best ages of the Christian church, has voluntarily come forth from his native land, to occupy the very scene of his brother's murder.

"The island is of a triangular shape. According to Cook,

it is seventy-five miles in circumference. It is not, as a whole, equal to Tanna in fertility and beauty; still, it is a fine island, and in many parts it is not devoid of beauty. It is mountainous, and some of the mountains are so high that they can be seen at a distance of forty miles. A large part of the south-east, or windward side of the island, looks rugged and barren.

"The island which next claims our notice," says the Rev. Mr. Murray, "is the finest of any that has yet gained our attention. The native name of the island is *Vaté*, or *Faté*; but Cook, its discoverer, gave it the name of Sandwich Island, in honour of the Earl of Sandwich, who was, at the time of the discovery, first lord of the Admiralty. Cook did not examine the island minutely. He appears, however, like subsequent visitors, to have been delighted with its appearance." He remarks, "The surface whereof appeared very delightful, being agreeably diversified with woods and lawns." The island has indeed a charming appearance. Captain Erskine, who visited it in H.M.'s ship Havannah, in 1849, writes as follows:—"The weather being somewhat cleared before sunset, we were enabled to see a little more of the features of the island. The usual belt of vegetation extended on all sides for a few hundred feet above the level of the sea, a white sandy beach running along the shores. Above the first range, especially on the mainland which forms the south side, of the harbour, the surrounding hills are of varied and most picturesque forms, being in general bare of trees, but covered with apparently rich pasture, in some places brown, as if burnt for purposes of cultivation. The rainbow tints caused by the setting sun gave a peculiar beauty to the landscape, and many of the officers considered that none of the islands we had yet visited offered so beautiful a scene as that which lay before us." This is high praise, considering that the gentlemen whose opinion Captain Erskine records had visited the finest Islands of Eastern Polynesia, the beauty

of some of which has been generally considered to be un-
rivalled in any part of the world.

" *Vaté*, according to Cook, is fifty-four miles to the north
of Erromanga, and seventy-five miles in circumference.
We have seen but one side of the island. On that there
is a large track of low land, extending in most part many
miles towards the interior, which is occupied by lofty
mountain ranges, and hills of various shapes and sizes.
The principal mountains are of considerable height, though
not, we think, equal to those of Erromanga.

"Another feature which gives the island a great superiority over all the islands of the New Hebrides to the
south, are its magnificent bays and harbours. In the other
islands, if we except the harbour of Aneiteum, there is
nothing to compare with them, and we doubt if there is a
single island throughout the whole of Eastern Polynesia so
well furnished with harbours as is the island of Vaté.
The finest harbour on the island, so far as our knowledge
goes, is that which is known as "Havannah Harbour."
This name was given to it by Captain Erskine when he
visited it in the voyage already referred to. The harbour
is formed by the mainland of Vaté on the south and east
sides, and on the west and north by two islands."

The Rev. Mr. Gordon, of Erromanga, has recently paid
a lengthened visit of four months to the island of *Espiritu
Santo*, the northernmost and by far the largest in the New
Hebrides group. This was the particular island of that
group that was first discovered, in the year 1606, by the
Spanish navigator, Fernando de Quiros, who, supposing it
a part of a great southern continent, spent the remainder
of his life in memorializing the Court of Madrid for troops
to enable him to conquer it for the King of Spain. But
the Spanish monarch of the period was fortunately too
wise in his generation for such folly, and De Quiros seems
to have died of a broken heart.

Mr. Gordon having met with two natives of Espiritu Santo

at Erromanga, learned the language of the country from them, and carried them back with him to their native isle. He met with a cordial reception from the inhabitants, and had no difficulty in maintaining friendly relations with them. His report as to the climate was particularly favorable for a country in so low a latitude; and he seems to have anticipated no danger to European health or life from a residence in the island.

" The soil of the New Hebrides," says Captain Erskine, " among which are several active volcanoes, is generally of exuberant quality."*

The third of the three groups of islands in the Western Pacific, of which I proposed to give a slight sketch, is that of the SOLOMON ISLANDS, discovered by the Spanish navigator, Alvaro de Mendana, in the year 1597, and lying in latitude 10° S., and longitude 160° E. They are eighteen in number, and some of them—particularly the islands of Santa Ysabel, Guadalcanar, San Christoval, Buonavista, Florida, Sesargo, and Santa Ana—are of large size.

"*Santa Ysabel,*" says Mendana, "was inhabited by people who had the complexion of mulattoes, with curly hair and little covering to their bodies; who worshipped serpents, toads, and such like creatures; whose food was cocoa nuts and roots, and who, it was believed, ate human flesh; for " the chief sent the general a present of a quarter of a boy, with the hand and arm. *Buonavista* is twelve leagues in extent, very fertile, and well peopled, the natives living in regular villages or towns. On *Florida,* twenty-five leagues in circuit, the natives dyed their hair red, collected together at the sound of the conch-shells, and ate human flesh. *Sesargo* was well inhabited, produced plenty of yams and bread-fruit, and here the Spaniards saw hogs. *Santa Ana,* was well peopled and fertile. The Spaniards observed here hogs and fowls."

* Captain Erskine, R.N.—*ubi supra.*

"The island of *San Christoval*," says Mr. John Webster, who accompanied his friend the late Benjamin Boyd, Esq., in the last cruise of the Wanderer, and who spent some time in that island, is about seventy miles long, and quite a *Terra Incognita* to the civilized world. For beauty of scenery and natural resources it cannot be surpassed. Its magnificent harbours, its pleasant climate and rich soil, combine to render it a spot, which, at no distant time, will be inhabited and cultivated by the Anglo-Saxon race. I consider it a splendid country for growing sugar, coffee, cotton, indigo, spices, and other productions of the Asiatic Islands. The country is but thinly populated. The natives cultivate little patches of yams, canes, and sweet potatoes, just sufficient for their own use. I observed none of them with more than one wife. The females attended to household duties and cooking. They appear to be well treated by the men, whose time is occupied in fishing and in cultivation. There seems to be little authority possessed by any one. Isitado (the principal chief), alone, appeared to have some influence. Each family claims certain lands and trees, and they seem to live in harmony with each other. But, from the fact of their always going armed, I have no doubt they are on bad terms with the neighbouring tribes, and the trophies of war exhibited on their houses, shew that frequent and bloody encounters take place."*

The Solomon Islands are a much more extensive group than either the New Hebrides or the Fiji Islands. The late Benjamin Boyd, Esq., was so charmed with their appearance, from what he saw of them during his short stay at San Christoval, in the year 1851, that he had formed the design of establishing in these islands what he called a Papuan Republic; not knowing perhaps that such

* *The last cruise of the Wanderer* : By John Webster, Sydney, no date.

a proceeding on the part of a British subject would have been contrary to law. From San Chistoval he proceeded with his splendid yacht, the "Wanderer," to the neighbouring island of Guadalcanar, where, going ashore one morning with a single attendant, he was suddenly surprised and murdered by the natives; just as the Rev. John Williams and his fellow-labourer, Mr. Harris, had been, about twelve years before, in the island of Erromanga, from a similar and most melancholy act of indiscretion.

As to whether these three groups of islands could be colonized successfully, and with safety as to health and life, by a European race, I would remind the reader that God "formed the earth to be inhabited," and therefore never intended that such transcendantly beautiful parts of it, as these islands, should lie waste. That Europeans can stand an intertropical climate, and retain their bodily powers and their mental faculties unimpaired, is evident from what is actually taking place both in Queensland, far to the north-ward, between the Tropics, and in the voluntary emigration to Fiji, where the climate is spoken of in the most favourable terms.

"The example of the vigorous race of genuine European blood," observes the able historian of the Indian Archi-pelago, "bred in the hot plains of South America, under the very line, would seem satisfactorily to prove that the long entertained notion that the European race undergoes, from the mere effect of climate, a physical degeneracy when transported to the native countries of the black or copper-coloured races, is no better than a prejudice. The different races of men appear to preserve their distinctions wholly independent of climate. In hot countries, the first settlers feel, indeed, the inconveniences of heat, but the constitu-tion of their descendants immediately adapts itself to the climate which they were born to inhabit."[*]

* _Crawford's Indian Archipelago_, iii. 273.

"In climates very warm," says Humboldt, "*and at the same time very dry*, the human species enjoys a longevity perhaps greater than what we observe in the temperate zones. This is especially the case whenever the temperature and climate are necessarily variable. The Europeans who transported themselves at an age somewhat advanced, into the equinoctial part of the Spanish colonies, attain there for the most part, to a great and happy old age."[*]

In another of his works, Baron Humboldt tells us that "there are in the hot plains of America, near the equator, men of the genuine European race, who are as athletic as the peasantry of Spain, and perform all sorts of field labour in the sun without inconvenience."[†]

Here, then, are three noble Emigration Fields in the Western Pacific Ocean, in which, I have no hesitation in expressing my belief and conviction, that as many as half a million of all grades and classes of the redundant population of the mother-country might be settled progressively, in a comparatively short period, and with perfect facility, under a Protectorate to be established in each of the three groups of islands by the future Federal Government of the Seven United Provinces of Australia. Such a Government would have extraordinary facilities of various kinds for the accomplishment of so noble an object—such indeed as no other Government upon earth could possibly have. Nay, I believe the whole enterprise would pay itself, if not entirely, at least in great measure, while the impulse it would give to every form of industry, both at home and abroad, and to commerce generally, would prove of incalculable importance to the mother-country, as well as to the Australian Union. The principle I would rely on for the carrying out of the great object I have indicated, is the one discovered and advocated by the late Edward Gibbon

---

[*] *Humboldt's Political Essay on New Spain*, i.
[†] *Crawford ubi supra.*

Wakefield, viz., the appropriation of the funds accruing from the sales of the waste lands in the colonies for the promotion of emigration.*

Supposing then that such a Sovereign Power as I have indicated should be called into existence by the mother-country, and a Protectorate established under its authority for each of the three great groups of the Western Pacific — what are the steps that would require to be taken or the course to be pursued, for carrying out the great object in view, and how are the funds to be raised to meet the necessary expenditure?

Before answering these questions, I would observe,

1. That the aboriginal population of all the three groups of the Western Pacific, is not nearly one-tenth, if even one-twentieth, part of what these islands could easily sustain, if occupied by an industrious European population.

---

* Besides the three groups I have mentioned, there is still another in the Western Pacific, extending 400 miles in length by 160 in breadth, which a respectable Scotch shipmaster, a fellow-townsman of my own, who has just returned to Sydney from a successful voyage in search of pearl shells along the north-west coast of Australia, considers of a superior character, both in beauty and fertility, to either the New Hebrides or the Solomon Islands, with both of which he is well acquainted, having been long in the way of visiting them. The group I refer to is the Louisiade Archipelago, lying between lat. 10 deg. and 13 deg. south, about two or three hundred miles south-eastward from the south-east Cape of New Guinea. These islands are exceedingly fertile, and are inhabited by a tall, able-bodied, athletic people of the Papuan race, with whom my informant has had no difficulty in maintaining friendly relations. If I recollect aright the Louisiade Archipelago was either discovered or visited by Admiral D'Entrecasteaux, in his voyage in search of La Perouse. But to think of myriads of people in all the three kingdoms on the very point of starvation, while hundreds of islands, like those I have been describing, are lying comparatively waste—the thing is monstrous; it is surely discreditable, in the highest degree, to a commercial and professedly Christian nation, with such extraordinary facilities for colonization as we undoubtedly possess.

There are exceptional cases, but this may safely be taken as the general rule.

2. That the natives of these islands are almost universally desirous that white men should settle among them—if, from no higher motive, at least from a natural desire to obtain, in some way or other, a portion of the valuable property—to them invaluable—which the white man is sure to introduce among them.

3. That although naturally treacherous—at least in particular instances, for it is by no means universally the case—and apt to overpower and massacre any solitary white man, or small party of white men, who might venture among them, and thereby place themselves at their mercy, as is evident from the two melancholy cases I have mentioned above, there would be no danger to be apprehended for Europeans settling down among them, in any particular locality, in sufficient numbers to defend themselves, as the old Greek colonists had to do universally in Asia Minor and elsewhere. And when once European superiority is established among them, or rather when they are satisfied that there are no hostile designs entertained towards them, they soon become tractable, friendly, and submissive enough. And

4. That the natives of all these islands are quite willing to alienate large portions of their lands to Europeans for what they would themselves consider a fair equivalent; but which would generally be a very small amount to Europeans.

Now if such lands or portions of land were purchased exclusively by and for the Government to be established in the different groups respectively, so as, in the phraseology of the United States, "to extinguish the Indian titles" by fair and honourable means; and if all purchasing from the natives by private individuals were to be disallowed in every case, and the lands so acquired to be sold at

Y

something like their intrinsic value to European immigrants, a large and constantly increasing fund would very soon be realized by such Government, after the establishment of the settlement, for the promotion of European Emigration.

And if that fund were to be anticipated to a certain extent, as it easily might be, with perfect safety, by European capitalists, and expended, first, in making the preliminary surveys, and the other preparatory arrangements indispensably necessary for the formation of permanent settlements in each of the three groups; and secondly, in giving a free passage out to numerous families and individuals of the humbler and industrious classes, to form such settlements, under the leadership and direction of fit and proper persons, who could easily be found for the purpose in all the actual Australian colonies, the great undertaking might be inaugurated simultaneously and successfully in all the three groups.

Supposing, then, that an emigration of this kind were effected to the requisite extent, there would speedily ensue a considerable and rapidly increasing emigration of families and individuals of a superior class, who would willingly pay their own passage out, to turn the great resources of the islands to a proper account, by availing themselves of the wonderful facilities they afford for the purpose, as well as of the native and European labour that would, in such circumstances, be easily procurable.

With a view to stimulate such emigration, I would propose that substantial encouragement should be held forth for all such emigrants, by ensuring them of a *bonus* in land or town allotments, sufficient to form, at the customary price of the settlement, a fair equivalent for the cost of their passage out; and I would also propose that this *bonus* should be extended to foreign immigrants, especially to Germans, Swiss, and Scandinavians, that is, natives of Denmark, Sweden, and Norway who, *next to ourselves*, generally make the best colonists.

I would propose, finally, that the European capitalist, or capitalists, advancing the funds requisite for the carrying out of this great undertaking, should have security for the due repayment of such funds, together with interest at a stipulated rate, over all the Public Lands of the particular Protectorate, for the benefit of which the funds advanced should be expended, under the guarantee of the Australian Union.

For the complete success of this great undertaking, which I am confident would be fraught with benefits and blessings incalculable to the United Kingdom, and would in all likelihood lead to the progressive emigration of perhaps half a million of all classes of the redundant population of the mother country, and their speedy and successful settlement in the beautiful Isles of the Western Pacific Ocean, I am satisfied that the establishment of a Sovereign and Independent Power in or on the Pacific would be indispensably necessary. This, in my humble estimation, is a *sine qua non* in the case. I would not propose, however, to subject the Australian Union to a single farthing of expense in carrying out the undertaking. This must all be borne in the first instance by the capitalists advancing the necessary funds, which, as a matter of course, they would not do unless they were satisfied with the security offered. But in these days of Turkish bonds, Greek bonds, Spanish bonds, and South American bonds, I can have no doubt whatever that Australian bonds, on the security of all the waste lands of the three great groups of the Western Pacific Ocean, provided that a great emigration to these groups of islands were taking place simultaneously, would be willingly taken by the great capitalists of the world.

Supposing, then, that the London capitalists were satisfied with the proposed security, and the necessary funds forthcoming, the well-known preliminary steps for the formation of a settlement in a new country would fall to be taken for each of the groups of islands in Australia; where the Colonial experience of all who might be employed in any capacity in commencing the undertaking would doubtless prove an important and valuable element for ensuring its success. An armed steam-vessel would accordingly be sent forth with a strong surveying staff for each of the groups in the first instance; while the requisite means would be taken to conciliate the natives and to obtain a footing in the country, through the purchase of suitable blocks of land for the occupation and settlement of a European population.

Simultaneously with these operations on this side, the requisite ways and means would be taken in the mother country for the selection of numerous families and individuals of suitable character and qualifications from amongst the humbler and industrious classes of society; who would be forwarded passage-free to their destination in vessels chartered for the purpose by the Land and Emigration Commissioners and entirely under their management and surveillance. These emigrants would all be the future purchasers of land and town allotments in their places of settlement, and would thus eventually reimburse the capitalists for the cost of their passage out.

Without deeming it necessary to enter any further into details for the carrying out of the enterprise, there are one or two important questions to which it may be advisable to advert before concluding this part of the general subject. It will be asked, therefore, how the government to be set up in any of these groups of islands is to be supported—whether through the establishment of a Custom-house, as in all the actual colonies of Australia, or by some system of direct taxation. In reply to this question I would observe that the communities to be formed in all the three groups of islands will in all likelihood be agricultural and not pastoral communities like those of Australia; the land being much more fertile as a general rule, and therefore likely to be held in much smaller portions, while there is reason to believe that it would not be at all suitable for sheep-farming. In such circumstances it may be safely inferred that when the insular communities are fully established, the consumption of dutiable commodities in the islands would be as large as that of the Australian colonies; which in New South Wales amounts at present to between seven and eight pounds for every man, woman, and child of the entire population. There would be no difficulty in supporting an efficient government with such a revenue as this.

But there are great, and in my opinion valid, objections to the establishment of a Custom-house system for such communities. It would be much too costly on the one hand, from the number of petty offices which it would tend to create,* while it would be inefficient and demoralizing on the other. For all such communities as those proposed for the South Sea Islands, I would unhesitatingly adopt the sentiment of the poet, although I have forgotten his name—

> " Free as the winds, and changeless as the sea,
> Should trade and commerce unrestricted be.
> Wherever land is found, or oceans roll,
> Or man exists from Indus to the Pole,
> Open to all, with no false ties to bind,
> The world should be the market of mankind."

It can be no reason why there should be a Custom-house in any of the Isles of the Pacific, for the levying of duties on foreign trade, that there is one in England, another in France, a third in the United States, and a fourth in Australia. The circumstances of the countries contrasted, in all these cases, are totally different from each other. Besides, the universality, whether of a custom, or of a Custom-house, is no better argument for its propriety, than its great

---

* La multiplicité effrénée des offices est la marque assurée de la decadence prochaine d'un etat.—*Sully.* The unrestrained multiplication of offices is the sure sign of the approaching fall of a State.

antiquity; and it is well observed by an able French writer, "Ancient customs are sometimes great abuses, which are only the more dangerous the more respectable they are considered."*

Custom-houses, also, are a great obstacle in the way of trade, and frequently a perfect *incubus* upon it. It is universally acknowledged that the public lose far more in the additional price they have to pay for their taxed commodities, than the State derives from the taxes in the shape of duties: and all this loss has to be sustained by the community.†

---

* "Les anciennes coutumes ne sont quelquefois que de grands abus, d'autant plus dangereux qu'on les croit plus respectables."—*L' Abbé Millot.* To the same effect, the celebrated Christian Father, Cyprian, in his Epistle to Stephen, Bishop of Rome, when testifying against Roman traditions, observes, "Consuetudo sine veritate, vetustas erroris est."—*Custom, without truth for its basis, is merely the antiquity of error.* The same excellent observation will apply equally to Custom-houses.

It is somewhat singular that in one of the most ancient treaties of peace and commerce in existence—viz., between the Carthaginians and Romans,—free-trade and no Customs' duties forms one of the stipulations. Polybius (Book 3. chap. 22.) has preserved a copy of a treaty of peace and commerce between the Romans and Carthaginians, concluded so early as in the year after the expulsion of the kings of Rome, under the consulship of Junius Brutus and Marcus Horatius ; that is, 28 years before the expedition of Xerxes into Greece, and 246 from the building of Rome. It is remarkable for the entire freedom of trade which it establishes between the rival republics, while it jealously guards against expeditions of war and invasion. The Free-trade proviso, translated into Latin by Isaac Casaubon, is as follows:—

"Qui ad mercaturam venerint, ii vectigal nullum pendunto, extra quam ad præconis aut scribæ mercedem." *Let those* [Romans] *who come* [to Carthage] *for purposes of trade, pay no Customs' duties, with the exception of the fees of the auctioneer and the clerk of the market.*

† "The last remedy which I would propose is one which I feel persuaded would not only be attended with beneficial results to New Zealand, but also to all the Australian colonies :—it is the doing away with the Customs, and declaring the ports of New Zealand free. The

In one word, taxes levied through the Custom-house are unequal in their pressure, and consequently unjust in their operation : as they are paid chiefly by the humbler classes, who are least able to bear them. The industrious mechanic, for example, consumes perhaps as much sugar and tea as the squire himself, especially if his wife happens to be a tidy body, and at all fastidious in her taste ; but he virtually contributes greatly more to the State.

I trust, therefore, that there will be no custom-house system ever established in the Isles of the Western Pacific. Indeed, without an army to support, without a Custom-house establishment, and without an Established Church, there will be no difficulty in supporting the Government establishments necessary for these insular commuuities by some form of direct taxation.

The other question, to which I would advert, is, in view of the fatal consequences to which a false step in the matter might possibly lead, one of national interest and importance —I mean the Land Question in the Fiji Islands. I have already shewn that the lawlessness now prevalent in these islands, from the want of any settled government in the group, urgently calls for the interposition of a Sovereign authority of some kind from without ; and as Her Majesty's

impetus that such a measure as this would give to trade in this and the neighbouring colonies is incalculable. The loss in revenue could easily and equitably be made up by means of a property and income tax, which I doubt not the people would cheerfully pay. The present taxes on imported goods are made to press heavily on the honest trader alone; the facilities for smuggling being so great in a country possessing such fine harbours, and such an extensive coast line as New Zealand, as to require a more efficient Coast Guard than that of England or Ireland for its prevention. To such an extent is smuggling carried on in the article of tobacco alone, that a short time ago it could in this country be bought at 10*d.* per pound, duty paid, or said to be paid, while the duty itself was a shilling."—*New Zealand in 1842, or the Effects of a bad Government on a Good Country.* By S. M. D. Martin, M.D., Auckland, New Zealand, 1842.

Government has already refused to establish such authority
in Her Majesty's name, or to make the Imperial Government responsible in any way for the maintenance of peace
and the administration of justice in the group, there is the
more urgent necessity for the " COMING EVENT," to which
this volume points, being realized as speedily as possible ;.
as in the present state of things in the Western Pacific
Islands generally, it would be far from desirable that the
Sovereignty of the Fijis should fall into the hands of any
other Power than that of Britain, or of one emanating
directly from Great Britain.   But the present state of the
land question in these islands only renders the necessity
for the establishment of a regular government in the group.
still more urgent.

Towards the close of the year 1835, I had occasion to
visit Van Dieman's Land, now Tasmania, in the discharge
of clerical duty in connection with the Presbyterian Church
of that colony.   The people on both sides of the island.
were in a state of extraordinary excitement at the time.   A
few months before, certain adventurers from Van Dieman's.
Land had crossed over Bass's Straits, which separates that
island from the main land, and had discovered very extensive tracts of the finest land, whether for agriculture or for
grazing, around Port Phillip on the opposite shore.   Taking
it for granted that this country was a *terra incognita,*
belonging to nobody and open alike for all comers—being,.
as it was, five or six hundred miles from Sydney, and quite
unknown to the people of New South Wales—the colonists
of Tasmania were all at once seized with a regular mania
for acquiring landed property on the largest scale in Port
Phillip.   Companies were accordingly formed, among
whom the land was divided into portions like German
Principalities; certain black natives, who were easily found
for the emergency, were recognized for the time being as
lords of the manor, and instructed to append their marks.
to documents drawn up with the strictest regard to English.

Constitutional law—I need not say also with the sharpest practice – thereby ratifying their own voluntary and entire alienation of their splendid domain for so many blankets, tomohawks, knives, &c.; and the same being signed, sealed, and delivered before competent witnesses, certain lawyers of the highest standing in the insular colony, who, it was well known, were themselves deeply concerned in the speculation, pronounced the deeds valid documents and the whole transaction one in perfect accordance with the laws of the land. But the late Sir Richard Bourke, who was then Governor of New South Wales, and who, I believe, had reported the whole case to the Imperial Government and been duly authorized to pursue the course which he actually took in the matter, publicly declared the whole transaction unwarrantable and illegal, and the pretended deeds from the natives null and void.

Early in the year 1839, I happened to touch at New Zealand on my way to Europe by Cape Horn; for our vessel having sprung a leak, when we were only a few days out from Sydney, we were obliged to make for the Bay of Islands, towards the northern extremity of New Zealand, for the requisite repairs. During my stay of ten days or a fortnight in that port, I saw and heard of much that was then going on in New Zealand, and especially of the wholesale manner in which unprincipled Europeans, who had been living for years in the island, had been virtually robbing the natives of their lands. The hands even of the agents of the Church Missionary Society, both clerical and laic, were anything but clean in the matter; and certain, especially, of the lay missionaries were carving out for themselves regular principalities at the expense of the natives. Mr. S. for example, a lay missionary from New South Wales, had bought a large tract of eligible land from the natives, having a frontage of from four to five miles on one of the navigable rivers in the Bay of Islands, for a check shirt and an iron pot. The same functionary had another estate which he had procured in a similar way, towards the North Cape. Mr. F., a journeyman coach-maker, and by no means of apostolic character, in the town of Parramatta, in New South Wales, when he was engaged as a lay missionary for New Zealand on the civilizing system, which was then in operation on the Society's Mission Station in that group of islands, had purchased from the natives a tract of land to the north-ward of the River Thames, having a frontage of from thirty-five to forty miles on the east coast of the island towards the Pacific Ocean. I could not learn how far back from the sea Mr. F's land extended, or what the valuable *consideration* had been for this princely estate. Messrs. C. and D., who had been originally sent out as missionary agriculturists, also on the civilizing system, had selected their domains on a somewhat similar scale with those of the S. and F. estates, on the Hokianga River, on the west coast, while those of Messrs. K. and K. were situated towards the North Cape. In short, the Society's Mission had, *in deference to the views of men of the highest intelligence in all other matters*, been conducted for a time in great measure on the civilizing system—to civilize the New Zealanders, for-sooth, and then to christianize them—and this was the result. The Rev. Mr. B. the Superintendent of the Mission for a time and a J.P. for the island, with whom I was a fellow-passenger to England in the year 1824, told me himself that, with the assistance of his son, Samuel, who was afterwards drowned in the island, he had ploughed and sown with wheat eleven acres of ground during the year 1823, after having grubbed up the whole of the land, which had been overgrown with tall ferns, with his own hands. The Wesleyan Mission of the period had been conducted on a different principle, the missionaries of that communion being expressly forbidden by the funda-mental rules of their Society from acquiring property in land or from trading in any way. -But one of their number having been dismissed for immorality, had become a general merchant or trader, and was one of the largest proprietors of land, acquired of course in the way I have indicated, at the period of my visit, in the island.

When such things were done in quarters from which something better was to have been expected, what could be looked for in others? Indeed, short as my stay was in the island, I had a whole list of cases given me on perfectly reliable authority, of the most heartless villainy on the part of the Europeans in their dealings with the natives, and of the degradation, misery, and ruin entailed upon the New Zealanders by their means.

Resolved, as I was, to expose this state of things to the Government and the public on my return to England, I learned—1st, That a Company, of which the late Earl Durham was Governor, had been formed in London for the Colonization of New Zealand; 2nd., That a Bill for this purpose had been submitted to Parliament in the year 1838, but had been thrown out, chiefly at the instance of the Church of England and Wesleyan Missionary Societies, under the philanthropic but mistaken idea that the establishment of a British Colony in the Island would be detrimental to the welfare and advancement of the aboriginal race; 3rd., That Lord John Russell, then Principal Secretary of State for the Colonies had, doubtless in consequence of that Bill having been rejected, set his face strongly against the colonization of New Zealand; and 4th., That the Company, despairing of an Act of Parliament in their favour, had been buying up the Deeds, (beautifully engrossed on parchment, in the New Zealand and English languages, with the requisite signatures and seals in the legal form) of the great landholders of New Zealand; being determined to carry out their object as they best could, and expecting to sell the large estates of which they had thus got possession, at a pound an acre, to intending emigrants from the United Kingdom, to whom they were to offer the bonus of a free passage out.

In these circumstances I published a pamphlet, entitled. "*New Zealand in* 1839; or Four Letters, to the Right Hon. Earl Durham, Governor of the New Zealand Land Company, &c., &c., on the Colonization of that Island, and on the present condition and prospects of its Native Inhabitants." London: Smith, Elder, and Co., 1839. In this pamphlet, from which I shall make a few illustrative extracts, I pointed out the actual condition and prospects of New Zealand, of which I have already given a few sketches, and the grand mistake that had been made in the rejection of the Bill for the Colonization of the Island. I then strongly and earnestly recommended that Her Majesty should at once assume the Sovereignty of the Island and declare it a British Colony—in the interests of humanity, civilization, and christianity; and especially for the preservation from ruin and extinction of a noble race of aborigines—recommending in particular that Her Majesty should assume the right of preemption over all the lands of the future colony, and erect a court of competent jurisdiction to examine into and decide upon all alleged purchases from the natives, in accordance with the grand principles of equity and justice. I next shewed—and this was the strangest point in the case to all concerned at the time—how all this could be done at once without an Act of Parliament at all. For as Norfolk Island and New Zealand were within the original commission of the first Governor of New South Wales, and as acts of sovereignty had been performed in the latter Island by former governors of that colony, in the appointment of justices of the peace to exercise their functions within its territory, it could be occupied and colonized at once, without any additional authority, as a dependency of New South Wales. And after shewing the Company in my pamphlet how utterly worthless were the titles they held to their estates in New Zealand, and.

the discreditable way in which these estates had been procured, I strongly recommended them to surrender all their Deeds to the Crown, and to look for justice and to go about the accomplishment of their object in a more legitimate way.

The following are a few extracts from the pamphlet in question, which, it will be seen, are not inapplicable to the case of the Fiji Islands at this moment :—

"So far from being able to establish and to support a regular government on European principles, the New Zealanders are actually unable to protect their own patrimonial territories from the grasp of European rapacity, even when practised by unaccredited individuals, acting without the sanction of any Government whatever. It is the obvious interest however of such individuals to speak with great deference of the New Zealand chiefs,—of their being the heads of an independent nation, and of their ability to form a government on European principles for their own territory : for so long as such ideas are entertained in England, they will be enabled to rob the natives of their land unquestioned and unobserved, under the pretext of having bought and paid for it ; and to produce regular deeds of sale and purchase, on some future convenient opportunity, for lordships as extensive as those of the Percies and the Howards.

"In short, the New Zealanders can only be regarded as mere children, incapable of managing their own property, except through the agency of some liberal, enlightened, and Christian Government, acting as their trustee ; and I beg to assure your Lordship, that unless some such Government interfere speedily on their behalf, by the establishment of a system of general guardianship for the protection of the natives on the one hand, and the enactment of equal laws, both for natives and Europeans on the other, there is no prospect for the New Zealand nation but that of gradual demoralization and speedy extinction. From the causes

that are now in operation, chiefly through their intercourse
with Europeans, the number of the natives, for a large
extent of country around the Bay of Islands, as well as for
a considerable distance to the northward and southward of
that Bay, has been diminished at least one-half, during the
last fifteen years; and it is the opinion of the most
respectable Europeans on the spot, that if the present
system is allowed to continue much longer, the period of
their final extinction, in the northern division of the
northern island, cannot be far distant.

"This consummation, so strongly to be deprecated by
every genuine philanthropist, is likely, my Lord, to be indefinitely accelerated by the prevalence of a system which
has recently come into operation in New Zealand, and
which is at present acted upon in that island to an extent
of which your Lordship and the British public can have no
conception;—a system, moreover, which it is alike the
interest and the bounden duty of the British Government,
as the great colonizing power of modern Europe, and the
natural protector of the aborigines of every land to which
the all-pervading commerce of Great Britain extends, to
put a stop to immediately.

"Tracts of eligible land, of sufficient extent to constitute
whole earldoms in England, have already been acquired in
New Zealand, by the merest adventurers,—by men who
had arrived in that island without a shilling in their
pockets, but who had had influence enough to obtain credit
for a few English muskets, a few barrels of gunpowder, a
few bundles of slops, or a few kegs of rum or tobacco in
Sydney or Hobart Town. And thus, my Lord, after being
despoiled of their pigs and potatoes, and their other articles
of native produce, in pretended barter for the veriest trifles,
the poor natives, who, your Lordship and the British public
have been told again and again, are capable of establishing
a regular Government of their own, are, at length wheedled
out of their land,—their only remaining possession,—and

reduced at once to a state of hopeless poverty and moral degradation.

"It is absolutely distressing, my Lord, to observe the effects which this system of unprincipled rapacity is already producing upon the truly unfortunate natives of New Zealand, in conjunction with the other sources of demoralization to which I have already alluded. The more intelligent of the natives perceive and acknowledge their unfortunate condition in these respects themselves; but they are spellbound, as it were, and cannot resist the temptation to which the offer of articles of European produce and manufacture infallibly exposes them. Like mere children, they will give all they are worth to-day for the trinket or gewgaw, which they will sell for the veriest trifle to-morrow. Pomare, an intelligent native chief, who speaks tolerably good English, but who has already alienated the greater part of his valuable land in the neighbourhood of the Bay of Islands, observed to one of my fellow-voyagers, 'Englishmen give us blankets, powder, and iron-pots, for our land; but we soon blow away the powder, the iron-pots get broken, and the blankets wear out; but the land never blows away, or wears out.' The master of the vessel, in which I have just returned to England, had resided for a considerable time at the Bay of Islands, about eight or ten years ago, as the master of an English whaler, and was consequently well known to the natives in that part of the island. On going ashore at the village of Kororadika, the day after we had cast anchor, he called at the house of a native chief, of the name of Riva, with whom he had formerly been well acquainted, and asked him, how he had not come on board his ship, to welcome him, as he used to do, when he heard of his arrival in the Bay. 'I was ashamed to go,' replied the noble-minded, but unfortunate chief, 'because I had no present to offer you. Formerly, when I went to see my friends, I always carried them a present of pigs or potatoes; but I am a poor man now. I have

sold all my land, and I have nothing to give my friends.'
Riva is as fine a looking man as I have ever seen; tall,
muscular, and athletic; with an expression of kindliness
on his open countenance, which it is impossible to mistake,
notwithstanding the tattooing with which it is disfigured.
But his poverty, my Lord, is not the worst feature in his
present circumstances. Having no land to reside on, as he
formerly had, at some distance from the Bay, he is compelled to take up his permanent residence in the village of
Kororadika, among the lawless crews of the English,
French, and American whalers that frequent the port; his
daughter, one of the handsomest native women I have
seen, being actually living, at the time I visited the island,
in open concubinage with a civilized brute, who commands
an English whaler out of London, and who, I was credibly
informed, has a wife and children in this city.

" If I am not greatly in error, the opposition exhibited
to the New Zealand Colonization Bill, during the last session
of Parliament, originated chiefly among the friends and
supporters of Christian Missions, and especially among the
friends and supporters of the Church of England Society's
Mission to the Aborigines of that Island. I confess, my
Lord, there was something generous, philanthropic, and
Christian in the very aspect of this opposition; and no
wonder therefore that it should have been completely successful in preventing the passing of the Bill. It professed
to treat with profound respect the rights and interests of
one of the noblest races of Aborigines on the face of the
globe. It professed to sympathise with the feeble efforts
of that race to rise to a higher level in the scale of humanity,
and to occupy a prominent place in the catalogue of civilized
nations. And more than all this, it professed to deprecate
the serious obstacles which a community of European colonists might in all likelihood throw in the way of the general
reception of the Christian religion by the natives of New
Zealand. I am sorry, however, to be called on, from a

sacred regard to the interests of truth, as well as to the cause of humanity and the Christian religion; I am sorry, my Lord, to be obliged to state, that the anticipations of unmingled benefit to the Aborigines of that island, which were thus founded on the prospect of their being left entirely, for the future, to the charities of the Church Mission in New Zealand, were alike unwarranted by the past history, and by the present condition, of that mission.

"The Church of England's Mission to New Zealand was formed at the instance of the late Rev. Samuel Marsden, Principal Episcopal Chaplain of New South Wales, in the year 1812, but was not properly in operation till the year 1814. It was originally established, and for a long time systematically conducted, on the principle of *first civilizing and then christianizing*, the natives; and for this purpose, a large number of artizans, of various handicrafts, were engaged, some in England, and some in New South Wales, as lay-missionaries, to teach the natives the various processes of civilized life. Reversing the apostolic plan, the missionary carpenter, the missionary boat-builder, the missionary blacksmith, the missionary plowman, the missionary rope-spinner, &c. were all set to work at their various occupations, and the natives were expected forthwith to follow their example. In fact, the mission settlement in New Zealand was for a long time a complete lumber-yard, or factory, in which all sorts of labour were going on but the proper labour of a missionary—the very clergyman, for there was only one on the island, being in no respect different from a common agricultural labourer, except that he mounted a pulpit and read prayers in a surplice every Sunday.*

---

* My attention had been directed at a very early period to the character and results of what is known as the civilizing system, in the conduct of missions to the Heathen—so highly extolled as that system is in all the higher walks of literature in which the subject happens to be alluded to—and I embodied my views and experience in regard to it, in the following verses, which were written in very peculiar circumstances.

z

VERSES

WRITTEN WITHIN SIGHT OF THE NORTH-EAST CAPE OF
NEW ZEALAND, AUGUST 1830.

"ANTARCTIC isle! thy mountains rise
All dimly o'er the western main;
But gladly I regale my eyes
With the blest sight of land again!
O, 'tis a welcome sight to me
Amid this wild and billowy sea!

"Thy shores, methinks, sequester'd isle,
Might form a fitting dwelling-place
For men devoid of earthly guile,
For mortals of a heavenly race;
For underneath thy cloudless skies
Fancy might form a Paradise.

"Far different is the race that swarms
Along thy rivers, lakes, and bays:
All horribly disguised their forms,
All treacherous their savage ways;
Barbarian war their chief employ,
And deadliest cruelty their joy.

"The vile assassin's hideous yell,
The murderer's terrific roar,
The music and the speech of hell
Are heard along thy shelving shore;

During a voyage to England by Cape Horn in 1830, our vessel, after
doubling the North Cape of New Zealand, encountered a violent
gale of eight or nine days, from the south-east; and it was
during that gale, with the New Zealand mountains in sight from the
ship's deck, that the verses were written; for much of my literary
work, including no small part of this volume, has been done at sea. I
may add that the Church of England Mission in New Zealand has
long abandoned the civilizing system, although I think it was well that
the experiment was made somewhere, to show how different God's
thoughts and ways are from those of the very wisest of men.

While men, like lions in their den,
Feast on the quivering limbs of men!

" See yon tall chief of high command,
   With face tattoo'd and bearing proud;
The feast of blood already plann'd,
   He eyes his victim in the crowd.
His horrid mien and matted hair
Might well befit a tiger's lair.

" Beneath his shaggy flaxen mat,
   The dreadful marree* hangs conceal'd;
Nor is his dark and deadly thought
   By look, or word, or act, reveal'd;—
The fated wretch fears no surprise
Till suddenly he shrieks, and dies!

" How shall we tame thee, man of blood?
   How shall thy wild Antarctic isle,
Won by philanthropy to God,
   With British arts and science smile?
How shall New Zealand's sons embrace
The habits of a happier race?

" Let agriculture tame the soil,"
   The philosophic sage exclaims;
Let peasants ply their useful toil
   Along the wide Antarctic Thames;
So shall New Zealand's sons embrace
The habits of a happier race."

" Wisdom, thy name is folly here!
   The savage laughs thy plans to scorn.
Each lake supplies him dainty cheer;
   He sates his hunger with the fern,
And contemplates with proud disdain
Thy furrow'd fields and yellow grain.

---

* The marree is a short hatchet, resembling a butcher's cleaving-knife, and is sometimes made of fish-bone, though generally of serpentine stone finely polished. The handle is perforated, and it is usually attached by a piece of cord to the internal part of the mat or plaid worn by the New Zealanders.

" ' Let European arts be plied,'
    Again the learned sage commands,
' And be the great sledge-hammer tried
    To civilize the savage lands :
The axe, the chisel, and the saw
Lead to religion, peace, and law.'

" Deluded sage, th' attempt were vain :
    The savage scorns thy science too,
And asks with pitiful disdain,
    ' What ship outsails my war-canoe ?'
Of all thy gifts there is but one
He prizes—'tis thy murdering gun.

" ' Go, preach the Gospel,' Christ commands ;
    And when he spake the sov'reign word
New Zealand's dark and savage lands
    Lay all outstretch'd before their Lord :
He saw them far across the sea,
Even from the hills of Galilee.

" In all their ignorance they lay
    Before the Saviour's piercing eye ;
And He who makes the darkness day,
    Thus pitied all their misery :
' Proclaim to yonder savage race
The tidings of redeeming grace.

" ' Let the wild savage know the God
    Whose Providence his life sustains,
And Him who shed His precious blood
    To save him from eternal pains ;
So shall his brutal warfare cease,
So shall he learn the arts of peace !' "

" Yes ! " Preach the Gospel," Christ commands,
    ' To every soul, the world around :
In barbarous, as in learned lands,
    Still let the Gospel trumpet sound,
Till every dark and savage isle
In Eden's primal beauty smile.' '

" Yes ! though despised in every age,
   Thy word of power, Almighty Lord !
Can put to shame the wisest sage,
   And civilize the rudest horde ;
Can cheer the deepest, darkest gloom,
And make the dreariest desert bloom.

" Great Source of light ! O, be it given
   To every minister of thine,
To wield this instrument of Heaven
   With zeal and energy divine,
Till every isle of this vast sea
Be won to virtue and to Thee !''

" If such occupations had been indispensably necessary
for the support of the mission, it would not only have been
allowable but praiseworthy to have pursued them. But
they were alike unnecessary and unwarranted ; and the
result, as might have been expected, was, that they had
just as little influence in civilizing, as it may be supposed
they had in christianizing, the natives. The native *waré*
or house, and the native canoe, both of which occasionally
display considerable taste and ingenuity, were quite sufficient for all the purposes of the New Zealander in his un-
christianized state ; he was sufficiently acquainted with
agriculture to enable him to procure in abundance all the
necessaries of life ; and of all the missionary artizans who
were sent out by the Church Missionary Society to effect
his civilization, the missionary blacksmith, who could mend
his broken musket, and thereby enable him to commit
murder upon his fellow-man, was in reality the only one
whose talents commanded his unfeigned respect. Indeed,
as a general maxim, I would say that it is by no means
particularly desirable that the New Zealanders should
acquire a knowledge of European arts till they have embraced the religion of Europeans, when they will acquire
them as a matter of course. Pomare, the chief I have

already mentioned, offered, in the month of February last, to dispose of all his right and title to Barrier Island, at the mouth of the River Thames,* for a small English schooner of the value of £200. But what was the object of the savage in desiring to get possession of the schooner? Why, it was simply that he might be able to carry all his fighting-men, in one body, to some part of the coast where the natives are still unacquainted with the use of fire-arms, and where he could consequently plunder and murder them at discretion, after the example of the old buccaneers of America.

Not to interrupt the regular course of the argument of this volume, or to tire out the reader with didactics rather than facts, I shall insert, in an Appendix at the close of this work, the remaining quotations I had marked from my Pamphlet entitled, *New Zealand in* 1839.

I have already stated that Lord John Russell was strongly opposed, in the first instance, to the colonization of New Zealand; and the rejection of the New Zealand Colonization Bill in 1838 only served to strengthen his opposition to the measure, as it seemed to preclude all hope of obtaining the requisite Parliamentary sanction. But the publication of my pamphlet threw quite a new light upon the whole subject, in shewing to demonstration that New Zealand could be colonized at once as a Dependency of New South Wales, without any further Parliamentary sanction My recommendation to that effect was accordingly received and adopted forthwith by the Colonial Office —I need scarcely add without acknowledgment †—fresh influence having been brought to bear upon the

* An island of forty miles in length, with more than one fine harbour.

† Oh no! they never mentioned it! But this was only another instance of a very ancient practice not unknown three thousand years ago, as witness the following case:—" There was a little

Office by the New Zealand Company, who volunteered at once, in accordance with my suggestion, to surrender all their Deeds to the Crown, and to abide the award of a regularly constituted government. Still, however, to show with what extreme reluctance and dislike the measure was regarded by the Colonial Office,— as if they had been either afraid or ashamed of it—the whole thing was managed in the shabbiest possible manner; Captain Hobson, R.N., the first Governor of New Zealand, being sent out almost clandestinely, in the first instance, merely as a British Consul, or rather Detective, to obtain a cession of the Sovereignty of the Island (what a bright idea!) to Her Majesty the Queen, from all such New Zealand chiefs as might be willing to concede it, and only in the last instance, in case of any unexpected and great emergency, to assume the Sovereignty of the Island for Her Majesty the Queen.

Such a case of extreme emergency very soon arose, and Captain Hobson was not unequal to the occasion; for within nine days of the time when he hoisted the British flag in the Middle Island of the New Zealand group, and proclaimed the whole group a British Possession, a French ship, with all the necessary equipment for the purpose, arrived in that island to proclaim it a French Colony under Louis Philippe, then King of the French.

A Dispatch, announcing the determination of her Majesty's Government to colonize New Zealand as a dependency of New South Wales, was in due time addressed by Lord Normanby, who had in the mean time succeeded Lord John in the Office, to Sir George Gipps, then Governor of New

city and few men within it, and there came a great king against it, and besieged it, and built great bulwarks against it. Now there was found in it a poor wise man, and he by his wisdom delivered the city; yet no man remembered that same poor man."—*Ecclesiastes* ix. 14-15.

South Wales; and no sooner was the official proclamation published in the *Government Gazette* of that colony, than a perfect *furore* for estate and principality purchasing in New Zealand—precisely similar to that of 1835 in Tasmania, when the discovery of the El Dorado of Port Phillip was announced in the insular colony—arose in Sydney and elsewhere in New South Wales. One of the remarkable incidents of that period—as remarkable of its kind as any in history—and peculiarly applicable to what is now passing in the Fiji Islands, is recorded in the following extract from Volume First of my Historical and Statistical Account of New South Wales, Third Edition, London, 1852.

The earlier portion of the administration of Sir George Gipps, the ninth Governor of New South Wales, was rendered memorable from the settlement of New Zealand as a dependency of New South Wales. On my way to England, in the year 1839, I spent a short time in that island; and after carefully observing the state of affairs in it, I published a pamphlet on my arrival in London, entitled *New Zealand in* 1839; in which I strongly recommended to Her Majesty's Government the propriety of taking immediate possession of that whole group of islands as a dependency of Great Britain—showing that they had been considered as included in the original charter of New South Wales, by the earlier Governors of that colony, some of whom had even commissioned magistrates to act in New Zealand. The settlement of the island as a dependency of New South Wales was authorised in the first instance; and Captain Hobson, R. N., the first Governor, was sent out originally as a sort of British Consul, with instructions to acquire lands for the Crown on the best terms he could from the natives, but with authority to act upon the recommendation I had given, if he should deem such a course expedient and necessary. Captain Hobson adopted that course accordingly, by taking possession of the whole group for Her

Majesty the Queen: and it was fortunate for his country, and for the best interests of humanity, that he did; for if he had delayed doing so a single week longer, the middle, or largest, island of the group would have been a colony, and in all probability a convict colony of France. Had the other suggestions of my pamphlet been adopted, the subsequent disastrous war with the formidable New Zea-land chief, Heki, would have been prevented, and the land question, which afterwards occasioned an infinity of heart-burnings and a vast amount of ruin to individuals, would have been definitively settled within a comparatively short time and with the utmost facility. But Downing-street— like Solomon's *fool*—is generally too *wise in its own conceit* to avail itself of any amount of colonial experience; and the fatal results are sure to be realized, in due time, in in-dividual disappointment and ruin, if not in national defeat and disaster.

As soon as it was noised abroad in the colony that there was a movement in England for the colonization of New Zealand, the rage for speculation, which was then rampant in New South Wales, and could not be restrained even by the surges of the Pacific, extended itself to that group of islands; and numerous long-headed Australian colonists, either in their own persons or by approved agents, entered into treaties with the native chiefs for the purchase of im-mense tracts of land in the island, in order to steal a march upon Her Majesty's Government. It was in anticipation of something of this kind, which indeed had already commenced at the period of my visit, that I had been induced to urge upon Government the propriety of taking immediate possession of the whole group, and of asserting a right of pre-emption, on the part of the Crown, to all the lands held by the Aborigines. For, however unreasonable this may appear to certain would-be philan-thropists in England, and how much soever it may be decried in certain interested and suspicious quarters as an unwarrantable interference with the natural rights of the Aborigines, there is no other way in which the natives of uncivilized countries can be protected from the artifice and cupidity of Europeans, or in which justice can be done even to European colonists against one another.

The claims of the numerous purchasers of land from the natives of New Zealand came before the late Nominee Legislature of New South Wales, which had been authorised to make the requisite arrangements for the disposal of land in the islands, in the year 1840; and among others the claim of W. C. Wentworth, Esq., afterwards one of the Representatives of the City of Sydney in the late Legislative Council, and subsequently President of the Legislative Council under Responsible Government in 1861. Not satisfied, it seems, with being one of the largest speculators in land and stock in New South Wales, that gentleman had fixed his eye on a principality in New Zealand; and had duly purchased, from nine of the mere handful of natives who then inhabited the Middle Island, the whole or nearly the whole, of that island—a tract of country comprising twenty millions of acres! The bargain, or rather treaty, for the cession of this territory had been duly concluded between the high contracting parties— Mr. Wentworth and a few associates on the one part, and those sovereign and independent chiefs, E Toki, E Waru, E Piti, Rauparaha, Ka Witi, &c., on the other: the deed was drawn up in due form in the English and New Zealand languages; and the parchment was signed sealed, and delivered, in the presence of approved witnesses, by their High Mightinesses, the States of the Middle Island; to whom Mr. Wentworth had faithfully paid the stipulated number of English blankets (of the coarsest description), of Birmingham muskets (made to sell), and of kegs of gunpowder, besides a variety of other unsaleable articles from some warehouse in Sydney. Mr. Wentworth argued his claim in person before the Council, at great length and with great ability ; enlarging upon the rights of sovereign and independent nations, and especially of the chiefs aforesaid, with whom he had had the distinguished honour of making the aforesaid treaty ; proudly displaying his parchment with the signs manual and seals of the sovereign and independent chiefs aforesaid ; and concluding by asking nothing from the *generosity* or *charity*, but demanding everything from the *justice*, of England.

Sir George Gipps deserves the highest credit for the ability with which he exposed and set aside this peculiarly barefaced and impudent claim — setting forth at great length the practice of all European nations since the discovery of America, as well as of the United States of that country, in regard to the purchase and sale of the lands of the Aborigines; showing that the right of preemption was uniformly asserted by the colonizing power; exhibiting the injury and ruin that would inevitably result from a different practice ; pleading also the principle which his own immediate predecessor had established, and the Imperial Government had recognised, in the case of Port Phillip ; and concluding by literally overwhelming Mr. Wentworth and his notorious attempt to appropriate, for his own private benefit, the country which might otherwise become the happy home of myriads of his fellow countrymen from the United Kingdom, with a torrent of sarcasm which it is no marvel that that gentleman was never able either to forgive or to forget.* Mr. Wentworth was after-

---

* The following is an Extract from the very able speech of Sir George Gipps in the Legislative Council, on Thursday, 9th July, 1840, on the second reading of the Bill for appointing Commissioners to inquire into the claims to grants of land in New Zealand.

" I have not heard one reasonable and disinterested person object to the main purpose of this Bill. Of all the witnesses examined before the Committee of the House of Lords in 1838, no one was so wild as to say that all purchases from the natives of New Zealand were to be acknowledged : no one pretended, because the Narragunset Indians

wards the leader of the Opposition in the partially Repre
sentative Legislature which was subsequently established
in the colony, during the succeeding portion of the administration of Sir George Gipps; and as I deemed it my

sold Connecticut, as we have been told they did, for a certain number
of old coats and pairs of breeches, or because they sold Rhode Island
(as I find they did) for a pair of spectacles, that therefore Her Majesty
is bound to acknowledge as valid, purchases of a similar nature in New
Zealand. The witnesses whom I have alluded to all considered the
New Zealanders as minors or as wards of Chancery, incapable of
managing their own affairs; and therefore entitled to the same protection as the law of England affords to persons under similar and
analogous circumstances. To set aside a bargain on the ground of
fraud, or of the incapacity of one of the parties to understand the
nature of it, or his legal inability to execute it, is a proceeding certainly
not unknown to the law of England: nor is it in any way contrary to
the spirit of equity; the injustice would be in confirming any such
bargain; there would indeed be no excuse for Her Majesty's advisers,
if, by the exercise of her prerogative, she were to confirm lands to
persons who pretend to have purchased them at the rate of four
hundred acres for a penny; for that is, as near as I can calculate it,
the price paid, by Mr. Wentworth and his associates, for their twenty
millions of acres in the Middle Island.

"A great deal was said by this gentleman, in the course of his
address to the Council, of corruption and jobbery, as well as of the love
which men in office have for patronage. But, gentlemen, talk of
corruption! talk of jobbery! why if all the corruption which has
defiled England since the expulsion of the Stuarts, were gathered into
one heap, it would not make such a sum as this;—if all the jobs which
have been done since the days of Sir Robert Walpole were collected
into one job, they would not make so big a job as the one which Mr.
Wentworth asks me to lend a hand in perpetrating;—the job, that
is to say, of making to him a grant of twenty millions of acres, at the
rate of one hundred acres for a farthing! The Land Company of
New South Wales has been said to be a job: one million of acres at
eighteen pence an acre has been thought to be a pretty good job; but
it absolutely vanishes into nothing by the side of Mr. Wentworth's job.

"In the course of this gentleman's argument, he quoted largely
from Vattel and the Law of Nations, to prove the right of independent
people to sell their lands: and he piteously complained of the grievous

duty at the time to identify myself generally with that
Opposition, as a member of the Colonial Legislature, I
ascribed, in great simplicity, the part that was then taken
in it by Mr. Wentworth to the purest patriotism. From
the subsequent political tergiversation, however, of that

injustice which we should do to the New Zealanders, if we were to
deny them the same right; and the Council may recollect that when I
reminded him that he was here to maintain his own rights, and not
those of the New Zealanders, he replied, not inaptly, that, as his was
a derivative right, it was necessary for him to show that it had previously existed in the persons from whom he derived it; it was, in
fact, necessary for him to show that the right existed in the nine
savages, who were lately in Sydney, to sell the Middle Island, in
order to show his own right to purchase it from them at the rate of
four hundred acres for a penny!!

" Lastly, gentlemen, it has been said, that the principles on which
this Bill is founded are derived from the times of Cortez and Pizarro ;
times, when not only the rights of uncivilized nations, but the rights
also of humanity, were disregarded. To this I answer, that whatever
may be the changes (and thank Heaven they are many) which the
progress of religion and enlightenment have produced amongst us,
they are all in favour of the savage, and not against him. It would
be indeed the very height of hypocrisy in Her Majesty's Government
to abstain, or pretend to abstain, for religion's sake, from despoiling
these poor savages of their lands, and yet to allow them to be despoiled by individuals being subjects of Her Majesty. It is in the
spirit of that enlightenment which characterises the present age, that
the British Government is now about to interfere in the affairs of New
Zealand. That it interferes against its will, and only under the force
of circumstances, is evident from Lord Normanby's despatch; the
objects for which we go to New Zealand are clearly set forth in it, and
amongst the foremost is the noble one of rescuing a most interesting
race of men from that fate which contact with the nations of Christendom has hitherto invariably and unhappily brought upon the
uncivilized tribes of the earth.

" One of the gentlemen who appeared before you did not scruple to
avow at this table, and before this Council, that he can imagine no
motive Her Majesty's Ministers can have in desiring the acquisition of
New Zealand, but the increase of their own patronage. The same
gentleman is very probably also unable to imagine any other reason

gentleman, and especially from his turning his back upon himself as well as upon the people who had previously trusted and supported him, I have learned to ascribe it rather to his own disappointed ambition and thwarted cupidity."

I have deemed it expedient and necessary to include in this section the preceding rather lengthy extracts, which I trust the reader will not consider either tedious or irrelevant, for the double purpose of setting forth on the one hand those principles of equity and justice, on which alone a Government can be honestly set up and established by any Christian nation in countries inhabited by uncivilized tribes ;* and to enter my protest on the other against the continuance of the system which is now in pretty extensive operation in the Fiji Islands, on the part of certain long-headed individuals and Companies, having their head quarters principally in Melbourne, and professing to pur-chase from the natives, at remarkably convenient prices, large tracts of the finest land, which they expect to hold in

---

for the exercise of Her Majesty's prærogative than the oppression of her subjects. These, gentlemen, may be Mr. Wentworth's opinions : I will not insult you by supposing that they are yours. You, I hope, still believe that there is such a thing as public virtue : and that integrity is not utterly banished from the bosoms of men in office. To your hands, therefore, I commit this Bill. You will, I am sure, deal with it according to your consciences. and with that independence which you ought to exercise ; having a due regard for the honour of the Crown and the interests of the subject : whilst for myself, in respect to this occupation of New Zealand by Her Majesty, I may, I trust, be permitted to exclaim, as did the standard-bearer of the Tenth Legion, when Cæsar first took possession of Great Britain—'Et ego certe officium meum, Reipublicæ, atque Imperatori præstitero ;' fearless alike of what people may say or think of me, I will perform my duty to the queen and the public."

* They will also tend to throw a good deal of needful light on a somewhat interesting portion of Colonial history, which is just as little known in New Zealand as in New South Wales.

future absolutely as their own. These parties may not indeed be practising on so magnificent a scale as Mr. Wentworth and his associates, in 1840, by pretending to purchase from the natives so large an extent of territory as twenty millions of acres at the rate of one brass farthing for every hundred acres; but they are doing precisely the same thing, only on a smaller scale. Now no Government emanating either directly or indirectly from Great Britain, can ever tolerate such proceedings—can ever either relin-quish or surrender the right of pre-emption on the part of Government, in the case of all purchases of land from un-civilized tribes. This, I maintain, is absolutely necessary for the interests of humanity and justice, and for the protec-tion of the natives themselves. But there is another party who are also deeply interested in the case and on whose behalf I would urge my protest—I mean the humbler classes of the redundant population of Great Britain and Ireland; for if Mr. B. and his associates from Melbourne are allowed to purchase at their own convenient price, even moderate principalities from the natives and to hold them absolutely as their own, how would it be possible to create an Emigra-tion Fund for the transference of thousands and tens of thousands of these classes from their present cheerless habitations, to the happy homes that might otherwise await them in the beautiful isles of the Western Pacific?

It will be evident therefore that there is at this moment a peculiarly urgent necessity for the establishment of a Sovereign and Independent State on the shores of the Pacific; or in other words for Freedom and Independence for the Seven United Provinces of Australia.

SECTION IX.—THE FUTURE CAPITAL OF THE SEVEN UNITED PROVINCES OF AUSTRALIA.

About the middle of the 17th century, the detached and previously unconnected Colonies of New England, situated in the northern section of the present United States of America, finding it necessary to unite together for their common defence and protection, as well as for other general purposes, did so accordingly, and formed a body designated, "The United Colonies of New England," which was afterwards approved and recognized by King Charles II. But under the grinding despotism that subsequently prevailed, during the latter portion of the reign of that monarch, and under his successer, James II., this body fell into abeyance, and was never afterwards heard of. Its Head-quarters, however, was the City of Boston, in Massachusetts, which is situated in the extreme north of the present United States, although it was the natural centre and capital of the original New England Colonies. About a century thereafter, when various other colonies had been established much farther south, the celebrated Dr. Benjamin Franklin exerted himself very strenuously to form another and more comprehensive Union of the Colonies, for various important objects, including colonization in the western interior which they then held in common; and the place appointed for the meeting of the deputies who were chosen by the respective colonies to deliberate upon the basis of Union, was the City of Albany, in the Colony of New York, that is a long way to the south of New England altogether. *There* the deputies met accordingly in the year 1754, there being delegates present from the colonies so far to the south as Virginia and Maryland. But through the extravagant pretensions of the mother-country, which the promoters of the Union deemed utterly irreconcilable with the liberties of the colonies, this plan of Union also proved abortive. The next association of the kind was of a more permanent character and was not doomed, like the two that had preceded it, to suffer extinction from the obstructive policy of the mother-country. It was the famous Congress that eventually proclaimed the freedom and independence of the United States in the year 1776. That Congress was held

at Philadelphia, a city much farther to the southward than
the City of Albany; for the Colonies of North and South
Carolina, to the southward of Virginia, had in the mean
time joined the Congress, and their convenience had consequently to be consulted in fixing the place of meeting.
At length, when the independence of the country had been
secured, and the present Constitution definitively agreed to,
the seat of Government was finally transferred to the City
of Washington, still farther south than Philadelphia; as
the Colony of Georgia, the southernmost then in the group,
had in the interval joined the Union. Now, although
Victoria and the City of Melbourne would be the natural
centre and head-quarters for the National Government of
Free and Independent Australia, if there were no other
confederated provinces than those of New South Wales,
Victoria, South Australia, and Tasmania, it can no longer
be the centre of such Union or the proper seat for the
National Government, now that a series of additional provinces is either formed, or in process of formation, along
the whole line of the Pacific to Cape York. In short, as
the centre of Union had to be moved successively to the
warmer regions of the south in America, according as the
Union extended in that direction, from Boston to Washington; so would the centre of Union in Australia, even if
established in the first instance at Melbourne, have to be
ultimately moved to the warmer regions of the north, to
meet the claims of the northern provinces.

Melbourne is doubtless the largest and most commercial
city—the New York—of Australia; but the real city of
New York, although much the largest and most commercial
city of America, is not even the capital of the State to
which it gives its name, far less is it the capital of the
great American Union. The capital of the State of New
York is the city of Albany, which I have visited myself,
and which is situated up the Hudson River, a hundred and
thirty miles from New York; and the capital of the United

A A

States is the city of Washington, situated in the district of Columbia, between the States of Maryland and Virginia, far to the south.

Besides, the capital of the Australian Union must be on the Pacific, and not on Bass's Straits, or the great Southern Ocean. It is in the Pacific and the far North that our mission as a nation of the future properly lies. It is there, that we must earn our future laurels, through our promoting, to an indefinite extent, the heroic work of colonization. In short, the city of Sydney, which has the two very important advantages of being situated on the Pacific, the largest ocean, and of having one of the finest harbours in the world, is unquestionably the natural centre and must necessarily be the permanent head-quarters of the future Australian Empire.

Earnestly, however, as I desiderate a General Federation of the Australian colonies, and the establishment of a United Empire through such federation, I cannot conceal from myself that there are difficulties of a somewhat formidable character in the way—and when I recollect, as I have stated above, that there is no instance of a federal union of different States or Provinces having ever been effected among people of a Teutonic origin, except under the pressure of war from without, I confess I am not particularly sanguine, as to the accomplishment of this noble object very speedily. If a European war should occur, in which the mother-country should be one of the belligerents, I have no doubt it would be accomplished at once—from fear, at least, if not from affection. We have seen how M. Collas, the worthy Secretary of the French National Commission of 1849, informs us that England is the natural enemy of France, and adds—very considerately for us, Australian colonists—that France, whose navy, he tells us is as formidable as ours, would be quite ready, on the proclamation of war with that enemy, to attack the possessions of England all over the globe. Now if Victoria, with Mr.

Higinbotham's Navy, and her army of volunteers,—all to be paid for from her own funds, as becomes the veriest zealots for British connexion—is prepared for such a consummation, I am sorry to be obliged to confess that Sydney and the colonies on the Pacific are not. The fact is, we would rather be out of the war altogether, in the very safe and economical way of entire Freedom and Independence.

Nay, I have no doubt that the very suggestion I have made, that Sydney, being the fittest place for the capital of the future Australian Empire, should have that position on the realization of the Coming Event, will itself create what our brother Jonathan would call *a difficulty* in the case. The ancient Greeks devoutly believed that the island of Delphi was the centre of the earth; and the modern Victorians have an amiable weakness of a similar kind in regard to the city of Melbourne. But I have shown above that Melbourne neither is, nor ever can be, the centre of the Australian world.

Besides, Victoria is all for Protection, while New South Wales is all for Free Trade; and although the Victorian Ministry are supposed to be personally in favour of complete commercial freedom, it is alleged, on pretty good authority, that they are not free agents in the matter—especially in the prospect of a General Election and the pressure of an Anti-Immigration and Protectionist League. Tasmania and South Australia are ready, it is understood, to make concessions to Victoria in this matter, with a view to a Customs' Union and a General Federation; but New South Wales, in the persons of her delegates to the Intercolonial Conference in Melbourne—the Hon. Charles Cowper, Premier, and the Hon. Saul Samuel, Treasurer—stands nobly to her colours, on the principle of Free Trade and " No Surrender."

What then ? Are Melbourne and her two sister Colonies in the South, to form a separate interest with Melbourne as the capital on the principle of Protection with British connexion ? This is certainly one of the possibilities of the future; and so far from withstanding it on the part of New South Wales, I would even give Victoria as her dowry at parting the Riverine territory, with the Murrumbidgee for her boundary, as Lord John Russell proposed to do exactly thirty years since. I would do so for the following reasons : —1st., Because that portion of territory lies into Victoria and not into New South Wales. 2nd., Because New South Wales got it originally on false pretences, and it would be a mere act of justice to give it back; and 3rdly., Because New South Wales has virtually lost it already, from Victoria having engrossed and monopolized all its trade. But there is no disputing the point that the only capital for the Colonies on the Pacific, with their splendid prospects for the future, is the City of Sydney.

I have no doubt that, with a population increasing at the rate of a quarter of a million a year, and the earnest desire for an extensive emigration of the redundant classes of that population to which this state of things has given rise throughout the United Kingdom, the idea of the colonization of the multitude of the isles of the Western Pacific with a large portion of this redundant population, will be hailed with peculiar interest by numerous patriots and Christian men, including even statesmen, among our fellow-countrymen at home; especially as we are not asking two millions sterling for the purpose, from the rate-payers of England, like Mr. Torrens, M.P., recently from South Australia, but are proposing the arrangement on the principle of a mere mercantile speculation, which, if managed with common prudence, would pay itself. That the necessary funds for the purpose, even to the extent of Mr. Torrens' maximum, could be raised with perfect facility in London, on such security over the waste lands of these Islands as an Australian Federal Government on the Pacific could easily give, I can have no doubt whatever. And supposing all this to be practicable and nothing awanting to carry it into effect, but the assent of the Imperial authorities to the establishment of a Sovereign and Independent State on the shores of the Pacific, can any person suppose that, with myriads at home deeply interested in and earnestly awaiting THE COMING EVENT, any amount of pressure would not be brought upon these authorities from without, if it were at all needful, as I firmly believe it is not, to induce them to give their immediate assent to such a proposal? Let it be remembered that, besides New South Wales and Queensland, the actual colonies on the Pacific, there is a third, viz., Capricornia, all ready to be launched to the northward, and a fourth, Carpentaria, in prospect; while the coast-line of these colonies, extending from Cape Howe to Cape York, comprises not less than twenty-six degrees of latitude, or eighteen hundred English miles. Surely New South Wales, the oldest colony in the Australian group, and in reality the mother of all the rest—for what could any one of them have done without the fair start in stock and all the other materials for settlement with which New South Wales so liberally supplied them?—has a right to take the initiative in such a matter as this, and to act for herself; the consent of her big sister, Victoria, who is actually taller than her mother, and her sister colonies to the south, being neither asked for nor required.

Independently of the mercantile aspects—those of profit and loss—of the case, the planting of a British population, accompanied as it would doubtless be with the civilizing influences of education and religion, among the uncivilized tribes of the Western Pacific, would unquestionably be one of the noblest achievements of British philanthropy. It is only through a settlement of this kind—a settlement of people of British origin, of all ranks and conditions in society, mingling freely and familiarly with the inferior races—that the mass of the population in these regions will eventually rise to their proper level, or that an extensive influence for good can ever be exercised over them. The

famous settlement of Singapore, formed by Sir Stamford
Raffles, at the western extremity of the Indian Archipelago,
although successful enough in a commercial point of view,
has proved an utter failure in this far more important and
higher respect. The British residents of that settlement
are all merchant princes, who occupy the higher walks of
society exclusively, and never mingle with the inferior
population ; over whom therefore they exercise no influence
whatever. But let such a settlement as the future National
Government of Australia could easily form in each of the
three or four groups of the Western Pacific, be established
in these localities—consisting of people of British origin of
all grades of society, who would mingle freely with the
inferior races, and send forth their adventurous youth to
trade with them in the surrounding islands, to acquire their
languages and to establish friendly relations with them—and
the result would be very different and highly satisfactory.
"Rough whalers and brutal pirates," says Mr. Merivale,
on what authority I cannot tell, "have done more to
Europeanize the natives of Polynesia than the Missionaries."* I would place much greater reliance, however,
on the testimony of one who was likely to be much better
informed on the subject. "I want Missionaries," says
Captain Handy, of the American barque, *Belle,* himself a
Sperm Whaler in the Northern Pacific, but a Christian
man, and a worthy descendant of the old Puritans, "I
want Missionaries to be placed on every island of the
ocean; and I am willing to do what I can for the cause.
Whalers have been a curse to these Islands long enough,
and I am determined to do what I can for their good, so as
to have righteousness and justice established upon them."
And the first officer of the American captain's vessel added
sympathetically, "Whalers have done so much evil to the
people on these islands, that I will do anything I can for

---

* Merivale's *Rome under the Empire,* vol. iv. 390.

their good."* In one word, the colonization of the numerous isles of the Western Pacific with a British population, which, in all likelihood, would only be another missionary effort in another form, would be one of the greatest moral triumphs of the age.

SECTION X.—HOW AND WHERE IS THE INITIATIVE LIKELY TO BE TAKEN?

There are four classes of colonists whose approval of our entire political separation from the mother-country, and our attainment of the honour and dignity of a Sovereign and Independent State, is, for various reasons, somewhat doubtful, viz. :—1st., Public Functionaries and Government Officials; 2nd., Squatters; 3rd., Merchants; and 4th., Professional Men, of all the learned professions. But how or why any one of these classes should oppose such a measure—supposing that they should—I cannot conceive. In regard to

I. Public Functionaries; I would observe that as the Imperial Government has virtually left the decision of this great question to the colonists themselves, while the salaries of all public functionaries are now awarded by the votes of the representatives of the people, and will continue to be so equally under the proposed change, I cannot conceive how they should object to the measure, as it is not likely to affect them injuriously in any way, as far as their material interests are concerned.

II. Squatters. I would say precisely the same of this class as of the Public Functionaries; but as many of these gentlemen have no intention to remain in the country after they have amassed a sufficient amount of wealth to enable them to leave it with credit as men of wealth and fortune, it is natural that they should feel a little squeamish at the idea of their entire separation from the mother-country.

* *Morning Star Papers*, by the Rev. Dr. Damon, Honolulu, 1861.

III. Merchants. There is no class in these colonies so completely independent of the Local Government, as the merchants : there is none that has ever exerted itself so little for the cause of public freedom, and the rights of men. It was a maxim of the Ancient Greeks that every citizen should take an interest in the affairs of the State, and especially of the particular city to which he belonged, and should devote a regular portion of his time and attention to its concerns.* But our mercantile classes, with a very few honourable exceptions, actually pride themselves in taking no concern whatever in the government of the colony in which they are settled, and still less, if possible, in that of the city in which they are amassing their wealth. The fact is, these gentlemen are too much engrossed with the sordid pursuit of gain, to concern themselves in any way about the welfare and advancement of society in their adopted country, or to participate in those generous and noble feelings that honour and adorn humanity by proclaiming the sympathies of the individual with the common brotherhood of men.† Idolaters as they are, they worship one god, and one only ; and his name is Mammon.‡ He is the most exacting of all divinities and

---

* In a nation in which private existence was subordinate to that of the public, the industry employed in the increase of wealth could not gain the exclusive importance which it has among the moderns. With the ancients the *first* care of the citizen was for the state, the *next* for himself. As long as there is any higher object than the acquisition of money, the love of self cannot manifest itself so fully as when every other higher object is wanting.—*Heeren's Greece.*

† In colonies accumulation is nearly the only object of the capitalist : the desire to spend, which counteracts it to a certain extent in old countries, scarcely exists.—*Merivale's Lectures on Colonization*, vol. ii. p. 236.

‡   Mammon led them on ;
    Mammon, the least erected spirit that fell
    From heaven ; for even in heaven his looks and thoughts

the most intolerant. His worshippers must serve him day and night, with their bodies and souls; and they must offer their gifts on no altar but his own. Look at the men who have amassed large fortunes in the mercantile walks of life in these colonies, how few of them are there who have ever even attempted to do any permanent good with their money for their adopted country! How many of them, when they have acquired their supposed competency, pack up, and are off with the first ship to England, to make a show with the spoil, without ever supposing that they owe anything to the country that has enriched them, or in which God has given them power to get wealth ?* The association of any such idea as that of patriotism with the mercantile classes of these colonies is therefore absurd. They have no such feeling, and the country may sink or swim for all they care for it. In one word, as Lord Byron told the Modern Greeks, in one of his noble odes, when they were struggling for their freedom and independence with the Turks,

> Trust not for freedom to the Franks:
> They have a king who buys and sells.
> In native swords and native ranks,
> The only hope of courage dwells:

So would I say to the people of Australia, "Trust not for your freedom and independence to the colonial merchants. They will buy you and sell you again to the Government for half a per cent.; but they will never assist you in achieving your freedom and independence." In such circumstances, I should consider it a matter of very little

> Were always downward bent, admiring more
> The riches of heaven's pavement, trodden gold,
> Than aught, divine or holy, else enjoyed
> In vision beatific.
>   *Milton's Paradise Lost.*

* There was a very general complaint of precisely the same kind in America *before the Revolution.*

consequence whether these gentlemen should approve of Separation or not.

IV. Professional Men. These consist of ministers of religion, medical men and lawyers; and it may be taken as a general rule, which of course admits of individual exceptions, that all the three classes will be found pre-disposed against entire separation from the mother-country.

As a counterpoise, however, to the whole phalanx of public functionaries, squatters, merchants, and professional men—even supposing them, with their alleged anti-popular instincts and predilections, to be all opposed to the realization of the COMING EVENT, and determined to maintain things as they are, which I do not suppose is the case by any means, under the altered circumstances of the times—there are, on the other hand, the numerous class of colonial shopkeepers, general traders and employés; the mechanics and labourers of all descriptions; the free selectors, small farmers, or cultivators of the soil; and last, but not least in Australia, the miners,—whether they are mining for gold, for copper, or for coal. The advocates for things as they are, count only by units, tens, hundreds; but these advocates for things as they should be, who, I am quite sure, would rejoice in the advent of entire political freedom and national independence for their adopted country, count by thousands, tens of thousands, hundreds of thousands!

In one word, the colonial child—Young Australia—erewhile so ricketty in his constitution, and so stunted in his growth, from the strange mixtures with which his fond mother beyond seas was perpetually dosing him, under the old system of colonial *regime*—has at length, in the estimation of the whole civilized world, attained the form and stature of a man, and now stands forth before the nations in vigorous manhood and in robustest health. Is it not right, therefore, that he should be loosed from his mother's apronstrings, to which he was attached for a time by the ties of nature, during the helplessness of his childhood? Is it not right that his majority should be forthwith proclaimed, and universally acknowledged? "He is of age"—as the parents of the man who was born blind said of their son to the Jewish rulers;—"He is of age; ask him; he shall speak for himself." Yes! Put it to the vote of the Australian people themselves, and let the majority decide. How this may be done with propriety and with effect, will be seen in the sequel.

There is a remarkable peculiarity in the constitution of society in the Australian colonies, which is likely to have considerable influence in determining their future condition, but which has hitherto been seldom, if ever, adverted to— I mean the disproportionate size of their respective capitals, as compared with the whole extent and population of the different colonies. The inhabitants of the city of Sydney, for example, comprise at least one-fourth of the whole population of New South Wales*; and those of Melbourne bear the same proportion to the whole population of Victoria. Now there is no instance of a similar disproportion, in so far as my own researches extend, either in ancient or modern history. When Nehemiah, the governor of Judæa, under the Persian monarchs, went up to Jerusalem and found the city in a state of extreme desolation, he published an ordinance, requiring the rural population throughout the country to furnish one-tenth of their whole number for the permanent occupation and defence of the capital. It would seem, therefore, that in the opinion of that patriot governor, the proper proportion which the inhabitants of the capital of a country should bear to its entire population was one-tenth—a proportion which, it is worthy of remark, is considerably higher than that which the population of London, the largest capital of Europe, bears to the whole population of the United Kingdom.

* The population of Sydney and its suburbs is at present upwards of 120,000, while that of the whole colony is 483,000.

The following is a view of the proportion of the inhabitants in the different capitals of Europe as compared with that of their respective States, according to the Census and Estimates of 1851, for the *proportions* are doubtless the same still :—

STATES.	POPULATION.	CAPITALS.	POPULATION.	RATIO.
Great Britain and Ireland	27,019,578	London	1,873,676	or one in 14
France	35,400,486	Paris	900,000	" 39
Austria	37,662,486	Vienna	350,000	{ " 169
Austria, in Germany	12,006,000			" 34
Prussia	15,000,000	Berlin	290,000	" 51
Russia	62,257,700	Petersburg	500,000	" 124
Turkey, in Europe	12,200,000	Constantinople	600,000	" 20
Spain	13,000,000	Madrid	220,000	" 59
Portugal	3,412,500	Lisbon	270,000	" 12
Belgium	4,337,196	Brussels	120,000	" 36
Holland	3,414,374	Amsterdam	220,000	" 15
Denmark	2,000,000	Copenhagen	120,000	" 16
Sweden	3,100,000	Stockholm	80,000	" 38
Norway	1,200,000	Christiania	23,000	" 52
Naples	8,000,000	Naples	860,000	" 22
Papal States	2,250,000	Rome	160,000	" 16
Sardinia	4,001,132	Turin	120,000	" 33
Bavaria	4,440,327	Munich	100,000	" 44
Saxony	1,758,800	Dresden	80,000	" 21
Hanover	1,800,000	Hanover	30,000	" 60
Wirtemberg	1,700,000	Stuttgardt	38,000	" 44
Greece	900,000	Athens	20,000	" 45
Ionian Isles	200,000	Corfu	17,000	" 12
Switzerland	2,372,920	Berne	23,000 } 48,000	" 49
		Geneva	25,000	

It thus appears, that while the inhabitants of the cities

of Sydney and Melbourne are respectively one in four of the whole population of New South Wales and Victoria, the highest proportion which the inhabitants of any European capital bear to the whole population of the State or Kingdom to which it belongs is only one in twelve, as in Portugal and the Ionian Islands ; and that the proportion in the United Kingdom is not more than one in fourteen, while in France it is only one in thirty-nine. The population of the chief cities of the old American colonies appears to have borne a still smaller proportion to that of the respective colonies than that of the European capitals to their respective States. "The population of these [American] colonies" [at the Revolution], says the *Edinburgh Review*, "was less than 3,000,000; and their chief sea-ports, Boston, Newport, New York and Philadelphia, contained each from ten to twenty thousand inhabitants."*

"Towns increased so slowly," says Mr. Merivale, "that the largest in British America, Boston, had not more than 25,000 inhabitants when the revolutionary war broke out, 150 years after its foundation."† The same author makes a similar remark in regard to the chief cities of the present colonies of British America. "The cities are small, each having a slender neighbourhood to support it ; in fact, there are but three places deserving the name—Quebec, Montreal, and Halifax—in all British America."‡

In remarking that an opposite tendency—to a comparatively small extent however,—was exhibited in the Spanish colonies, Mr. Merivale attempts to assign its cause, as follows:—"It was this oligarchical character of society, together with the system of restrictions under which they lived, which produced the habit of the Spanish Creoles, especially in the mining districts, to congregate in cities,

---

* *Edinb. Rev.*, July, 1853. *Popular Education in the United States.*
† Merivale, vol. 1. p. 92.   ‡ Merivale, vol. 1, p. 106.

contrary to what has been already observed of the general spirit of modern colonists. * * * In this way the government may be said to have collected the people together artificially in towns."§

It will doubtless be alleged, that the amazing disproportion of the population of Sydney and Melbourne, as compared with that of the entire colonies of New South Wales and Victoria, has been owing entirely to the gold discovery, and to the extraordinary influx of population, which ensued upon that extraordinary event, into the chief cities of Australia. But this is by no means the fact; for the proportions I have given above are derived from the Census of 1851, which was taken in the month of March of that year, before the gold discovery was announced in either colony. Prior to that extraordinary event, as many as one-fourth of the inhabitants of each of these colonies respectively were cooped up in the colonial capital; which accordingly bore some resemblance to the strange animal in Van Dieman's Land, called " the devil," being all head and no body.

To what then is this extraordinary state of things, for which there seems to have been no precedent in the whole civilized world, either ancient or modern, to be ascribed? Why, to bad government exclusively—government from Downing-street, of the character of which, generally, I have given a few instances in the course of this work. This has been the whole and sole cause of the singular, the unprecedented, anomaly.

Had the people of these colonies been left to themselves, like the colonies of Ancient Greece —had they been left to the guidance and direction of such enlightened and patriotic men as they could easily have found among themselves—the population would have spread itself over the

§ *Lectures on Colonization and Colonies.* By Herman Merivale, A.M., vol. 1. p. 6.

country with great rapidity, and improvement would have gone on at a greatly accelerated rate, all over the territory. Forests would have been cleared away, land cultivated, and towns and villages planted in all directions; while the productions, and the wealth and general prosperity, of the country, would have increased beyond all present conception. But, in consequence of a whole series of measures, particularly in regard to the disposal of the public lands of the colonies—measures which I have no hesitation in saying were worthy of the inmates of a Lunatic Asylum—the population was prevented all along from spreading itself as it otherwise would have done, for its own great benefit, as well as for that of the colonies. And here we are, therefore, packed up in Sydney and Melbourne, in bodies of from a hundred and twenty to a hundred and fifty thousand each, like herrings in a barrel—elbowing each other in all directions; standing in each other's way; half of us doing little or nothing for the welfare and advancement of the country, and not a few of the other half merely helping them! To speak seriously, it is truly lamentable to think of the number of reputable and industrious families, who have been absolutely lost to society in this way, and been gradually absorbed in the population of these overgrown capitals—these immense wens on the body politic, as the late William Cobbett used, with much less propriety, to designate the city of London—to be employed in some petty huckstering concern in Sydney or Melbourne, who might, under a different system, have been dispersed over the whole face of the country, breathing its free air, raising the products peculiar to its soil and climate, rearing their delightful cottages along every navigable river or great road in the country, and forming everywhere that "bold yeomanry" who are "their country's pride." But it is one of the beautiful arrangements of Divine Providence that all great evils, in the political as well as in the physical world, contain the germs of their own remedy or cure. And it is remarkably so in the present instance. The cities of Sydney and Melbourne are now a great deal too large and too powerful to be controuled any longer by the powers that have so unwisely called them forth from political nonentity into such anomalous and formidable existence. The spirit, so long imprisoned, has got fairly out of the bottle at last, and already defies the conjurer. The people of these capitals have put away their childish things, and are now children no longer, but bearded men ; and as sure as they are so, they will take the initiative in deciding the important question of the day, which has been brought up for their decision by the Imperial Government itself, as to whether we are to continue for an indefinite period a series of dependent colonies, or to assume at once, with the entire concurrence and the best wishes of our mother-country, the high and highly influential position of a Sovereign and Independent State in the Southern Hemisphere.

In one word, if Paris is France, with less than one million of inhabitants to the whole thirty-five millions of the French empire, *a fortiori*, Sydney is New South Wales, and Melbourne is Victoria ; as these cities have each not less than a fourth part of the whole population of the country within their bounds. In such circumstances, they must, of necessity, take the initiative in fixing the future political condition of the country, whether that condition is to be one of humble dependence, or of manly freedom and national independence.* It is in these capitals respectively that the great question must be decided—that the battle of freedom and independence must be fought and won.

"In extreme danger," says M. Lamartine, " proximity

---

* C'est de la Metropole que partent toutes les impulsions qui ebranlent le peuple.—*Merle D'Aubigné, Histoire de la Reformation,* Tome iii. p. 471. It is from the Metropolis of the country that all those impulses issue that move the people.

constitutes a right. It belongs to that party of the people most approximated to public danger, first to provide against it. In such a case, the reach of the arm is the measure of power. A town then exercises the dictature of its position, relying upon ratification afterwards. Paris had exercised it several times before and after 1789. Fránce did not reproach her either for the 11th of July, the Tennis Court, or even for the 10th of August, when Paris had acquired for her, without consulting or waiting her, the Revolution, and the republic.

Besides, whatever may be the theories of abstract equality amongst the towns of an empire, these theories unfortunately yield to fact under exceptional circumstances; and that fact possesses its own right, for it is justified by its necessity. Without doubt those cities which are the seats of government are but members of the national body; but this member is the head. The capital of a nation exercises over its members an initiative power, that of leading and resolving, connected with the most energetic feelings, of which the head is the seat, in a nation as well as in an individual. Strict polemics may with reason contest this right; history cannot deny it."*

How then shall we ascertain the mind of Young Australia on the great question of the day, as to whether we, the Australian people, are still to remain, for an indefinite period, mere colonies of Britain, with all the inconveniences, the hazards, and the utter powerlessness for good under existing circumstances, which such a subordinate condition necessarily implies, or to assume at once, with the entire concurrence of Her Majesty's Government and the Imperial Parliament, the high and influential position of a Sovereign and Independent State? The question must now be limited to the four colonies, both present and prospective, on the Pacific, from Cape Howe

* Lamartine. *History of the Girondists*, vol. iii. p. 38, 39.

B B

to Cape York; viz., New South Wales, Queensland, Capricornia and Carpentaria.   For after the miserable result of the recent Intercolonial Conference, we can no longer presume to include the three Southern Colonies, on Bass' Straits and the Great Southern Ocean; viz., Victoria, Tasmania and South Australia, but must leave them, as God left Adam, to the freedom of his own will, with all their exploded theories of Protection and the blessedness of British connexion, till they come to a better mind. Perhaps, indeed, it is fitting that New South Wales, the oldest of the Australian Colonies, and the mother of all the rest, should take the initiative in this matter—especially with her commanding position on the Pacific, where particularly the necessity for immediate action lies.

How, then, I repeat it, shall we ascertain the mind of Young Australia on the great question of the day, as to whether we are to remain for an indefinite period a series of British colonies, with all the inconveniences and the hazards of such a condition, or to assume at once the position of a Sovereign and Independent State on the Pacific, with the City of Sydney for its capital ?   Shall we petition the Colonial Parliament on the subject to take our case into consideration, and to decide for us in the matter ? I think not; for that Parliament exists merely to administer the affairs of a particular colony under the British Crown— not to decide the larger question as to whether that colony shall, with others in a similar condition, assume the position of a Sovereign and Independent State. That larger question is for the Australian people themselves—for the electors of the different colonies proposed to be united—for the proceeding of which the Emperor, Louis Napoleon, has just set us so telling an example in France—in one word, for a *Plebiscitum*, or vote of the nation.   And in that proceeding the City of Sydney—containing as it does one fourth of the whole population of the great colony of which it is the head—must take the initiative; not however to coerce any of the other cities or towns of the colony so as to deprive them of their entire freedom of action in the case, but merely to set them the example. In one word, the case in question is pre-eminently a case for a *Plebiscitum*.

Section XI.—Results to be Anticipated from the Concession of Entire Freedom and Independence to the Australian Colonies on the Pacific Ocean.

Supposing, then, that the colonies on the Pacific Ocean—New South Wales, Queensland, and Capricornia including Carpentaria—were erected by the Imperial Government into a Sovereign and Independent State, on the principles and for the purposes I have stated above, what are the results to be anticipated from so mighty a change in the form of our political existence?

I. In the first place, " *a nation would be born in one day ;*" and while the whole civilized world would doubtless rejoice at the birth, the transition would infuse new life, with a vigour and energy unimagined before, into our whole social and political system. The change would work like magic in every direction, and would forthwith shew itself in an endless variety of ways. The boy would at once feel himself a man, and the young Samson would give early presage of the feats of strength and daring he is destined to exhibit on the great arena of national life.

Witness the wonderful enthusiasm of the whole French people, shortly after the proclamation of their First Republic in the year 1792, when their country was invaded by the Austrians, as described in the following glowing language of Lamartine.

"Men of every condition, of every fortune, of every age, presented themselves in crowds, in order to form the battalions which each department sent to the frontiers. * * Enthusiasm enrolled them, good-will disciplined

them, patriotic donations clothed, armed, paid, and maintained these children of the country.

"These volunteers received a route sheet to assemble at
the depôt designated by the minister of war, there to
receive equipment, instruction and organisation. They
marched off in groups, more or less numerous, to the sound
of the drum, to the strains of the patriotic hymn, accompanied to a great distance from their towns or their
villages, by mothers, brothers, sisters, and sweethearts,
who carried their knapsacks and arms, and who only
separated from them when fatigue had overcome not their
affection, but their powers.

"The inhabitants of the towns and boroughs which they
traversed came out to see them pass, and to offer them
bread and wine at the threshold of their houses. Disputes
arose in these billetting places, as to who should lodge them
as their own children. Patriotic societies went to meet
them, or to invite them to assist in the evenings at their
meetings. The president addressed them, the orators of
the club fraternized with them, and enflamed their courage
by the recital of military exploits, gathered from ancient
history. They taught them the hymns of the two Tyrtaei
of the Revolution,—the poets Lebrun and Chenier. They
made them drunk with the holy ardour of country, of
fanaticism and of liberty.

"Such were the elements of the army, which marched
in every direction from the centre towards the frontiers.
Dumouriez organized it while marching."*

"A vast population, influenced by a high degree of
excitement," says the late Chancellor of the Exchequer,
"is the most sublime of spectacles."†

And such a spectacle would doubtless be exhibited in
Australia as well as in France, if her national independence
were once conceded.

* Lamartine. *History of the Girondists*, vol. ii. p. 393, 395.
† *Alroy*, by D'Israeli.

" Hark !" says the eminent writer, last quoted, who has evidently studied human nature, and the history of mankind, to some purpose; "Hark! the people cheer! I love the people.— who are ever influenced by genuine and generous feelings, They cheer *as if they had once more gained a country.*"‡

II. *A befitting career would at once be thrown open to master-minds in every department, and to honourable ambition in every form.*

Those who could establish for themselves a high provincial reputation in any one of the provinces, would have a still higher and wider field opened up to them under the general or National Government. The Australian Legislature would be open to them, as senators, and members of the House of Representatives; and the highest offices of the country, including those of President and Vice-President, together with embassies to foreign states, would be within their reach. I say nothing of the Protectorates for the islands and the other offices that would necessarily be created, in the event of our attainment of Freedom and Independence, and that would be open in the first instance to all who had acquired colonial experience and were possessed of honourable ambition for such interesting and important spheres of action. In short, the maxim of the First Napoleon, *La carrière ouverte aux talens*, or, as it is quaintly translated by Carlyle, *The tools for those who can handle them*, would be fully realized in Australia; and the emigration of persons of the higher classes, from the mother-country, including all the liberal professions, would be great beyond all former precedent.

It has hitherto been a prodigious error in the colonial system of Great Britain, that it has held forth no suitable career in the colonies for persons of these classes in the mother-country; who have consequently been left to over-

‡ *Iskander*, by D'Israeli.

stock every profession, every branch of business above the condition of mere manual labour, so that, to use the felicitous expression of Mr. Wakefield, there is a *universal want of room* throughout the United Kingdom for all grades and phases of British gentility. It is from the numerous disappointed persons of these educated classes, that the humbler forms of dissatisfaction and disaffection usually obtain their leadership and their organization; and the consequent danger to society only becomes the greater, the longer the evil is allowed to exist, and the more numerous these classes become. Under the Grecian system of colonization, such unquiet spirits were from time to time drafted off, and disposed of in the colonies; where they became leaders of the people, and obtained those offices, and honours, and distinctions, from which they were virtually precluded at home. And so would it be under the system I propose. Hundreds and thousands of the disappointed, unquiet, and restless spirits that are always floating about on the surface of society at home—*cupidissimi novarum rerum*—would betake themselves to the United Provinces of Australia; where a new and highly promising field would be opened up to them—*a fair field and no favour*. The value of such an outlet to Great Britain, and its importance, in regard to the future stability of her institutions, are incalculable.

Even for the actual colonists, the change in this respect would be one of prodigious importance. Until yesterday, as it were, every respectable office, in connection with the different colonial governments, was hopelessly shut against the sons of the soil, as well as against British emigrants also, of whatever ability or talent, if without interest or connections at home. Indeed, the possession of superior ability of any kind was often a complete bar to admission into any office connected with Government in the colonies; as it served to cast a sort of invidious reflection upon the dull mediocrity around it.

Besides, the young Australians have generally but little chance of rising in the world as merchants, as they can have no *English Connections ;* and if they dislike going into the interior, to keep sheep and cattle, and are above taking a butcher's shop, or applying for a publican's licence, the only resource for them is to enter a solicitor's office—a branch of business which is consequently pretty well stocked already in the older colonies. No wonder, therefore, that the respectable classes in these colonies, especially those who have sons, should earnestly desire a thorough and entire change in our colonial relations. No wonder that the young Australians, whose attachment to their native land is intense, and whose opinion of its superiority to all others is universal, should already be learning and entering into the spirit of this Australian lay—

> " Sons of the soil, the die is cast !
> And our brothers are nailing their flag to the mast ;
> And their shout on the land, and their voice on the sea,
> Is, *The land of our birth is a land of the Free !"*

Writers on the colonies generally reproach them, and perhaps not undeservedly, with their inordinate love of money, as the characteristic and exclusive passion of all classes of their inhabitants. "Unfortunately," says Mr. Wakefield, "the ruling passion of individuals in our colonies is love of getting money."* But it is scarcely fair for our fellow-countrymen at home to reproach colonists generally with their money-making propensities, when, during the long period of Downing Street *regime,* they had closed every door of honourable ambition against us otherwise, through the bad system of government they had forced upon us, in the gratification of their own *lust* of empire. They meted out to the colonies precisely the same measure of injustice as they did to the Jews, whom they ridiculed and decried for their money-making pro-

* *A View of the Art of Colonization, &c.,* p. 101.

pensities, after they had shut up every other respectable and honourable walk of life against them. But let ability and desert of every kind have a fair field opened up for them—let the colonists know and feel that they *have* a country to labour for, and not a mere *Downing Street preserve for pitiful incapacity*—and the same generous and manly feelings will forthwith be developed, over the whole face of Australian society, as have uniformly characterized the birth of freedom and independence in every land.

The glorification of wealth, as the only object worthy of men's pursuit or ambition, was the necessary result of such institutions as were heretofore in exclusive existence under our past colonial system; and although it is therefore rather our misfortune than our fault, it had necessarily a debasing influence on the entire community. The circumstance of the late General Harrison, President of the United States, living in his own *log-cabin*, on the great bend of the Ohio river—or of the late President Polk dying worth only 25,000 dollars, that is, about £5,000—reminds us of the glorious days of old Rome, and of the real and not pretended contempt of riches for which her heroic people were so remarkable—

> " Privatus illis census erat brevis ;
> Commune magnum."

"The salaries of their public functionaries, and the estates of private individuals, were comparatively small; but the wealth and power of the State were proportionably great."* The creed of the Mussulman is, " There is no

* Curius Dentatus, having been presented by the Roman people with fifty acres of land, on account of the great ability and bravery he had exhibited in gaining a victory over Pyrrhus, king of Epirus, for which he had also been honoured with a triumph, declined receiving the gift, which he thought too great, and was content with the usual plebeian allotment of seven acres.—Columella, i. 3. (I think I am indebted for this illustration to Niebuhr, but I have omitted to mark

God but Allah, and Mahomet is his Prophet:" but the creed which was virtually taught by the institutions which prevailed until yesterday, as it were, in the Australian colonies, was, "There is no God but Mammon, and we are all his worshippers."

III. *A wonderful impulse would be given to the emigration of the humbler and working classes of the United Kingdom to Australia, as well as to the various groups of islands over which the proposed Australian protectorates would be established.* Australia, from its greatly superior climate and the better prospects it holds forth to emigrants generally, as well as from the more congenial character and origin of its actual population, would thenceforth in some considerable measure take the place of the United States; which, chiefly, if not exclusively, from their freer government, have hitherto monopolised by far the largest portion of British emigration. There are districts in the mother-country from which a National Government in Australia could, with the utmost facility, attract to this country a large emigration of the most valuable description.

For example, the county of Down, in the province of Ulster, in the North of Ireland, contains an area of 514,180 acres; which, according to a letter, published in the London *Morning Chronicle*, of the 29th of November, 1847, by the late W. Sharman Crawford, Esq.. M.P., was then occupied as follows (and the state of things at present is much the same as it was then) viz. :—

In farms of from   1 to   5 acres—in all 13,753 farms.
   do.   5 to 15 acres—in all 11,991 do.
   do.   15 to 30 acres—in all 3,865 do.
   do.   above 30 acres—in all 1,508 do.

the reference.) I wonder what this honest old Roman would have thought of *our* Mr. Wentworth—a patriot, like himself—claiming, from the late Sir George Gipps, Governor of New South Wales, the recognition of his *right* to the whole of the Middle Island of New

Now, as the county of Down affords a fair representation of the system which obtains generally in regard to the subdivision of land in the North of Ireland, it must be evident that that system has been allowed to proceed to an extent which is altogether incompatible with the permanent prosperity of the country, or the general advancement of its inhabitants. There is nothing similar to this minute subdivision of land in any part of Scotland. It may be possible, indeed, to extract a bare subsistence from such fragmentary farms as the greater number in this list; but it is utterly impossible that the general population of the province of Ulster can be maintained in a condition of comfort and comparative independence, such as is absolutely necessary for the general welfare and advancement, in connexion with such a minute subdivision of the land.

Emigration from all such localities in the United Kingdom would be a public benefit at home; while it could not fail to prove equally beneficial to the particular Australian province to which it might be directed. For, as it is well observed, by the late President Jackson, of the United States, " The wealth and strength of a country are its population, and the best part of that population are the cultivators of the soil."*

Under such efficient machinery, as it would be quite practicable for the National Government to create, there would very soon be a vast amount of emigration of the very best description from the United Kingdom to the Australian provinces; and a large portion of the mighty stream of population, that is now annually directed to the

Zealand, or about twenty millions of acres, under the notorious pretext of having purchased it, forsooth, for a few hatchets and blankets from a few of the natives ! It is impossible, from the nature of things, that genuine patriotism can co-exist in the same breast with such enormous greed.

* President Jackson's Message to Congress, Dec., 1832.

United States, would forthwith be diverted to Australia. I need scarcely add that Great Britain would derive material benefit from such a change of direction, in the stream of emigration setting out from her shores, as well as Australia, from the much better market which the same amount of population in the latter country affords for her produce and manufactures.*

IV. *All the other legitimate objects of Colonization would be realized to an indefinite extent.* When the first of the four legitimate objects of colonization has been secured in any instance by a colonizing country, in providing an eligible outlet for its redundant population, all the other three legitimate objects of colonization will also be attained in a greater or lesser degree, according to the capabilities of the country colonized, the variety and value of its productions, and the industry and energy of its inhabitants: in other words, a market of a constantly improving character will be created for the purchase and consumption of the manufactured goods of the mother-country; a field of, perhaps, boundless extent will be opened up for the growth of the raw produce required in those manufactures, as well as of other valuable goods and produce, and the trade of the mother-country will in the mean time be progressively and indefinitely extended.

---

* There is nothing more remarkable than the extreme ignorance that prevailed even among men of the highest intelligence otherwise, about the middle of last century, on the subject of emigration. They deprecated it as a national calamity; and one of Dean Tucker's arguments, in favour of a peaceful separation of Great Britain and her American colonies was the hope he entertained that emigration to America would thereby cease!

"Granting," he observes, "that emigrations are bad things in all respects—granting that they tend to diminish the number of your sailors, as well as of your manufacturers, yet how can you prevent this evil? And what remedy do you propose for curing the people of that madness which has seized them for emigration? I answer:

I have already noticed the impulse which the attainment of freedom and independence would give to emigration to Australia; but as the actual inhabitants of that country consume annually British goods and manufactures to the extent of £7 10s. per head of the entire population, it follows as a necessary consequence that a greatly increased emigration to that country will give a greatly increased impulse to the manufacturing industry of the mother country, and afford more extensive employment, and a higher rate of remuneration to the manufacturer and the operative—it will make trade brisker and will stimulate manufactures.

Now it is in this mutual interchange of products and good offices, and not in any domination that Great Britain exercises over us, that the real value of the Australian colonies to the mother-country consists; and whatever would promote and augment this interchange (as the freedom and independence of these colonies would unquestionably do to an indefinite extent) would only render Australia the more valuable to Great Britain, whether dependent or not.

In one word, it is quite in the power of Great Britain, by a single Act of grace (which, so far from implying any real sacrifice on her own part, would be productive of extraordinary and incalculable benefits to her people), to give birth to one of the mightiest Powers on earth, in

Even the remedy which hath been so often, and all along proposed, *A Total Separation from North America.* For most certain it is that, as soon as such a separation shall take place, a residence in the colonies will be no longer a desirable situation. Nay, it is much more probable that many of those who are already settled there, will wish to fly away, than that others should covet to go to them. * * * Under such circumstances, there is no reason to fear that many of our people will flock to North America."—Dean Tucker's *Humble Address Recommending Separation from America*, p. 68. Gloucester, 1774.

the Australian seas—a Power, as I have already observed, that would form the only formidable rival to the United States out of Europe. With a coast-line extending from Cape Howe to the Equator (including the island of New Guinea), and with whole groups of islands in the Western Pacific looking up to her National Government as their common parent and protector, where is there elsewhere on earth the prospect of so vast a power being called into existence, and within so short a period also, as that in which this entire *ideal* might be fully realized? It appears to me peculiarly desirable for Great Britain to have such a power in these regions bound to herself, as the one supposed would necessarily be, by the strongest ties, considering the vast ambition of our brother Jonathan. We are incomparably better situated in Australia for commanding the trade of the Eastern Seas, than the Americans are in California and the Oregon territory; and it must evidently be the highest interest of Britain that we should grow and prosper. The boundless extension of her own trade, and the happiness of myriads of her people, are indissolubly bound up with the freedom and independence of Australia. Why then should she imperil these mighty and substantial advantages for a mere empty and valueless possession—the mere whistle of a name? I cannot imagine anything either more interesting or more beautiful for the moralist, for the philanthropist, for the Christian man, than the strong and devoted attachment which would immediately spring up and ever afterwards subsist on the part of the Australian people towards Great Britain, if she were only to do us this one act of justice—to give us our freedom and independence.

V. *Annexation, and colonization, especially to the northward, would progress rapidly, and most beneficially both for Great Britain and for humanity.*

A National Government for the colonies on the Pacific Ocean would, I am confident, make immediate and energetic arrangements for the occupation and settlement of the great island of New Guinea, immediately to the northward of Cape York. Although that island, which is as large as all France, and probably as valuable as all the British West India islands together, could scarcely be colonized by any European power, without great expense and loss, it could be colonized with the utmost facility by our National Government, either from the Pacific coast, or from any of the settlements already formed at the head of the Gulf of Carpentaria. The valuable nutmeg tree is indigenous in New Guinea, as well as in the Molucca Islands; and its aborigines appear to be a decidedly improvable race, as compared with their congeners in Australia. Some of its tribes are agriculturists, in the interior, while others are fishermen and traders on the coast; and, like certain of the aboriginal tribes of the Archipelago far to the westward, they construct immense wooden buildings, in which all the families of a village live together, each however in its separate compartment as on board ship, the unmarried men having a separate house for themselves.

New Guinea would very soon become a province of the Australian Union, and would prove like the East and West Indies, to the adventurous youth of the southern provinces, who would there grow tropical productions by means of Aboriginal, Malayan, or Chinese labour.

Had the city of Sydney been like the ancient Grecian city Miletus, with her eighty or a hundred colonies, that is, free to engage in the heroic work of colonization, as it might seem conducive to her best interests and the welfare and advancement of her adventurous people to do, New Guinea would have been colonized, I believe successfully, a good many years since. There was a company formed in Sydney for the purpose,—and it was not the first attempt of the kind—of which I was invited to be one of the directors, within the last few years; but we were estopped at once from the want of that local authority which it was not competent for any mere colony either to assume or to impart, and without which the enterprise could not be undertaken either with propriety or with any hope of success. Not a few of our colonists at that time were willing to have contributed from their own funds for the success of the undertaking, and to have taken part themselves personally in the enterprise, fearing neither the climate nor the natives, and willing to bring all their colonial experience to bear upon it and to ensure its success. There is a very general impresssion also that the mountains of New Guinea abound in gold.

Besides, there is now a large and constantly increasing number of intelligent colonists from the West Indies in New South Wales and Victoria, who have been already inured to a Tropical climate, and who would willingly settle in New Guinea, to pursue the different agricultural operations to which they have been accustomed in such a climate, if a regular supply of cheap labour could be ensured to them. Now, as there are certain islands in the Indian Archipelago, inhabited by Malay Christians, with a redundant population, there would be no difficulty in getting any number of these people to settle as agricultural labourers for hire, under European superintendence, in any settlement in that island, from which their own islands are distant only a few days' sail. English schoolmasters, to be settled in the locality, under the patronage of the National Government, would teach the children of these people the English language and ideas, and thereby enable them to become the pioneers of our commerce and civilization in that extensive portion of the habitable globe. These Malay Christians, who are a very superior class of people, would thus be all amalgamated in due time with the general population of the new settlement, and would prove the means of inducing many others of their own race, from all the surrounding islands, to settle along with them, to be engaged as hired labourers in all the branches of Tropical agriculture under their European leaders.*

It would doubtless be undesirable, as well as impolitic in the highest degree, to promote the introduction and settlement of any of the inferior races of the East, or of the South Sea Islands, in the present Australian provinces; especially in the way in which they have been actually introduced already in considerable numbers into these provinces, to be employed as shepherds and stockmen in the interior: for it is morally impossible that in such a condition any measures for their gradual elevation in the scale of society could be brought to bear upon them. But it is hopeless to think of our ever getting a British population of the humbler classes, to form a regular and permanent labouring population, either on the northern coasts of Australia, or in the great island of New Guinea. Individuals of these classes—mechanics, shopkeepers, general dealers, and enterprising young men of all grades—will doubtless be attracted to these settlements from time to time from the southern provinces. But the inhabitants of British origin will constitute only a small proportion of the future population of these regions; which will consist in great

---

* The discovery of these Malay Christian islanders is one of the most interesting events of recent times. In the year 1824, if my memory serves me aright, the Dutch Government in the Archipelago commissioned a sloop of war, under the command of a competent naval officer, to visit certain remote islands to the eastward, with which there was a tradition of their having had relations of some kind more than seventy years before, but which had during that long interval been entirely lost sight of. The islands in question are situated far to the eastward, near Timorlaoet, and the one on which the officers of the expedition landed was called Kissa. A large portion of the inhabitants of that island were Christians, whose forefathers had been converted from heathenism through the zealous labours of Dutch Presbyterian Missionaries from Amboyna at least a century before, and who during their long period of isolation had retained the know-

measure of an amalgam of Malays and Chinese. Britons will form, from the first, however, the natural aristocracy of the country—the aristocracy of mind; and their interest and duty, in accordance with such judicious measures as might be adopted for the purpose by the National Government, will be to elevate the inferior population, whether consisting of Aborigines, of Malays, or of Chinese, to their own higher level, through the gradual prevalence of our language, our laws and our religion, by means of a European education, and the extension of equal rights and privileges to all. In short, under the system I propose, the future inhabitants of European race in these northern regions would form a grand mission of civilization for the elevation of all the inferior races; and it cannot be denied that these regions form at this moment one of the noblest fields for such a purpose on the face of the earth.

"On reviewing the history of the Greek colonies," observes the late Sir George Lewis, in whose sentiments I entirely concur, "the conquests of Alexander and of the Romans, and the settlements of the modern European nations in Asia, Africa, America, and Australia, it will be seen that the advancement of mankind is to be expected rather from the

ledge of the truth and the profession and practice of Christianity. Their church, built of stone, was ninety feet in length, and their teacher, as they called their pastor, on learning that there was a Dutch minister on board, the Rev. Mr. Kam, from Amboyna, met him with his people on the beach and marched up with him in procession to their church, singing the Twenty-fourth Psalm by the way. One of the natives of Kissa happened to be in Sydney in the year 1843, as man-servant to a gentleman who had been travelling in the Archipelago, and was examined as a witness before a Select Committee of the Legislative Council of which I was a member. Being greatly struck with the man's name, which was Shadrach, I questioned him on the subject and found that he had two brothers or other near relatives who were called respectively, Meshach and Abednego; the old Puritan practice of giving Scripture names to their children being still cherished among them.

C c

diffusion of civilised nations than from the improvement of barbarous or half-civilized tribes. The promotion of successful colonization is, therefore, one of the best means of advancing and diffusing civilization, and raising the general condition of mankind; and whoever can devise or carry into execution any effectual means for facilitating and improving it, is among the greatest benefactors of his race. But *there is nothing in the colonial relation which implies that the colony must be a dependency of the Mother-country; nor generally is it expedient that such a relation should exist, even in the case of a newly-founded Settlement.*"*

VI. The cause of education, morals, and religion would advance and prosper. I am strongly of opinion that the freedom and independence of the Australian provinces on the Pacific would give a wonderful impulse to the cause of popular education throughout these provinces; if, indeed, anything of the kind should be deemed necessary, after what has already been done in this most important matter, both in New South Wales and Queensland. In the new States of America large appropriations of the public lands are uniformly made by Congress for general education from the very first; and these school-lands are placed under able and vigilant trustees, who realise the largest possible revenue obtainable from them, for the particular object of their destination; it being the general belief of men of intelligence and public spirit in the United States, that the republican institutions of the country could not be sustained, if the people were not generally a well-educated people. The proportion set apart for the support of education in the new States is every 36th allotment; and it is an interesting fact, as illustrative of the effect which republican institutions have upon a people, in inducing them to support institutions for education, that the State of Connecticut,

* *Essay on Government Dependencies.* By George Cornewall Lewis, Esq., p. 235.

having had a portion of waste land in the State of Ohio, somewhat larger than the whole kingdom of Holland, assigned to it after the Revolution, in lieu of certain claims for territory to the westward which it agreed to relinquish for the public benefit, nobly resolved to set apart the whole of this princely domain for the support of education.

I am persuaded that liberal appropriations would in like manner be made by any popular government in Australia for education of all kinds—for common schools, for academies, for colleges, and for universities—and that a noble field would thus be opened up for emigrants of standing and ability in all the liberal professions, and especially in all departments connected with the education of youth. That education should become popular in any country, it is absolutely necessary that its professors should be respected; and this very desirable consummation can only be arrived at by giving them salaries that will place them on the same level with other respectable men. The Rector of a public academy or high school in the city of Boston, in Massachusetts, receives as high a salary from the public as the Governor of the State.*

I am equally confident that the triumphs of Christianity, in its purest forms, would be rapid, signal, and extensive under the flag of entire freedom and national independence in Australia. The recent Australian colonial system, of supporting all forms of religion equally from the Treasury of the State, which was happily abolished after a great struggle in New South Wales, in the year 1862, was essentially latitudinarian and infidel in its character, and therefore necessarily irreligious and demoralising in its

* "It was a happy and memorable feature in the character of the American colonists, and especially of the people of New England, that the work of tuition, in all its branches, was highly honoured among them, and that no civil functionary was regarded with more respect, or crowned with more distinguished praise, than a diligent and conscientious schoolmaster.—Grahame, iii. 845.

tendency. It would never be permitted to subsist again under the reign of freedom and independence. There would then be a fair field for all, and no favour for any ; and as the truth is great, it would ultimately prevail. At the same time it is one of the profoundest mysteries in the history of man, that the progressive landing of 50,000 British criminals on the shores of Australia should have been the first in that series of events which is evidently destined, in the counsels of Eternity, to issue in the occupation and settlement, the civilization and christianization of a large portion of the southern hemisphere. It reminds us, at all events, that *God's thoughts are not our thoughts, neither are our ways His ways. For as the heavens are higher than the earth, so are His ways higher than our ways, and His thoughts than our thoughts.**

Australia is at this moment one of the most important centres of moral and Christian influence on the face of the globe. It possesses this character in a degree incomparably higher than the United States of America. The forty millions of the Mahometan and Pagan inhabitants of the Indian Archipelago, whom Christian Europe has left almost entirely uncared for these three centuries, are now within a few days' sail of our actual settlements on the Gulf of Carpentaria. New Guinea, one of the largest islands in the world, is at our door; *and the multitude of the isles* of the Western Pacific are close upon our seaboard, while China looms in the distance from the northern extremity of the land. There is clearly, therefore, no part of the habitable globe on which it is of more importance at this moment to plant a thoroughly Christian people than the shores of Australia, and the islands of the Western Pacific. With half a million of such people—and there would be no difficulty in finding them—Australia would have a moral machinery 'to bring to bear upon the

* *Isaiah,* lv. 8, 9.

heathenism of the earth, unsurpassed by that of any other Christian country of equal population in the world. I confess I entertain the highest hopes of my adopted country in this important particular. I believe it is destined, in the councils of Infinite Wisdom, to be the seat of one of the first of the Christian nations of the earth; and that while *the number of its* Christian people *will yet be as the sand of the sea which cannot be measured or numbered, it shall come to pass that in the place where it was said unto them, Ye are not my people, there it shall be said unto them, Ye are the sons of the living God.**

* *Hosea*, i. 10.

THE END.

APPENDIX.

[Additional Extracts from the pamphlet entitled "New Zealand in 1839, or Four Letters to the Right Honourable Earl Durham, on the Colonization of that Island, &c.," intended to set forth the principles on which the colonization of any country inhabited by uncivilized tribes should be conducted by a Christian government—with a special reference to what is actually going on at present in the Fiji Islands, as well as to what is absolutely necessary at this moment, for the cause of justice and of humanity, in that very interesting and important group.]

"In these circumstances,"—that is, after the Bill for the Colonization of New Zealand had been thrown out by the House of Commons in the year 1838, and while the Colonial office was strongly opposed to the measure in 1839—"the New Zealand Land Company has been formed to effect the original object of the Association of 1837, without the sanction of an Act of Parliament at all, and entirely on the principle of a Joint Stock speculation. For this purpose the Company have acquired titles to certain large tracts of land in various parts of the island; the said land having been previously held by private individuals, on deeds of sale from the natives, but since disposed of by these individuals to the Company; and the Company propose to resell this land to intending emigrants or capitalists at the rate of one pound per acre, and to allow the purchasers three-fourths of their purchase-money in the conveyance of industrious emigrants of the humbler classes of society to New Zealand; the remainder of the purchase-money to be appropriated for the payment of the cost price of the land, and the maintenance of the general establishment of the Company.

"But whether the Company should succeed in disposing of a large portion of their land or not, the mere existence of such a Company will produce an immediate and powerful effect in New Zealand and the Australian colonies, whenever the fact comes to be generally known, and will exert a reflex and superlatively evil influence on the unfortunate New Zealanders. The fact, which the existence and operations of the Company will sufficiently proclaim, of its being practicable to purchase land in that island, perhaps even at a penny an acre to-day, and sell it at a pound to-morrow, will immediately excite the cupidity of a whole host of speculators and adventurers in these regions ; and the scramble for land in New Zealand, which is at present active and unprincipled enough, will consequently be increased tenfold, and be generally characterized by a total disregard of all moral principle, and of the rights of humanity. * So far from discountenancing such procedure, the formation and acts of the Company will only give it character and respectability; as the titles to all the land which the Company have purchased in the island are merely the titles of individuals who, in all probability, have been despoiling the natives in precisely the same manner. The march of injustice and oppression, of demoralization and extinction, on the part of the Europeans towards the unfortunate natives, will thus be prodigiously accelerated, and the consummation which has been already realized in Van Dieman's Land, will perhaps ere long be realized also in New Zealand—I mean the complete extermination of the aboriginal race. We are accustomed to talk, my Lord, with virtuous indignation and abhorrence, of the brutal atrocities of Cortez and Pizarro, and of the gaol-gang of Spanish ruffians that followed these bandit chiefs in Mexico

---

* As was sufficiently obvious in the Wentworth claim of 1840.

and Peru; but we forget that even in the nineteenth century we have ourselves, as a civilized and colonizing nation, been acting over again the same bloody tragedy on a different field. Why, my Lord, it has only taken the same period of time—about thirty short years—te exterminate the aborigines of Van Dieman's Land, under the mild sway of Britain, that it took to exterminate the aborigines of Hispaniola, under the iron rod of Ferdinand and Isabella.

"Let the Company, therefore, lend their influence and support towards the maintenance of Her Majesty's undoubted right of pre-emption, in all cases, both past and future. The establishment of this principle will be of incalculable advantage to the New Zealanders; and not only to the New Zealanders, but to all persons whatsoever, in this country, who are about to embark in any way in the New Zealand colonization scheme.

"For this purpose, let the Company make a voluntary and entire surrender of their native titles to Her Majesty's Government;—to be adjudicated upon individually by a temporary Board, like the Court of Claims in New South Wales, to be appointed for the purpose by the Government, on the understanding and condition that the Company shall have the right of pre-emption from the Government, at the minimum price of crown-land to be established in the island, deducting the full amount the Company may have already paid for their lands, either to the natives, or to individual Europeans. The moral influence of such an example would be salutary in the highest degree, in New Zealand, as far as the actual European population of the island are concerned, and would strengthen the hands of the Government exceedingly, at the outset of the Colony, in carrying out the simple but most important principle of Her Majesty's right of pre-emption in all cases, as regards the aborigines and their lands."

* * * * * * *

"It is one of the beautiful arrangements of that beneficent providence which governs the world, that the interest
and the duty, both of individuals and of nations, are
generally conjoined; insomuch that in discharging the
one, the other is materially advanced. It is the bounden
duty of the British Government, for example, to interfere
at the present moment for the protection and preservation
of the natives of New Zealand by the establishment of a
British Colony, founded and conducted on equitable and
Christian principles, on their coasts.

*   *   *   *   *   *   *

"The grounds on which the Bill for the Colonization
of New Zealand was successfully opposed in the last session
of Parliament, were, that the establishment of a British
Colony in that island would necessarily be effected on
infidel and not on Christian principles; that the rights of
the natives would consequently be sacrificed and themselves
speedily exterminated; and that these natives, being a
Sovereign and Independent people, advancing rapidly in
civilization and christianization, the British Government
had no right to interfere with them in the manner proposed.
In direct opposition, however, to such ideas, I am confident,
my Lord, that a British Colony could, with the utmost
facility, be both established and conducted in New Zealand
on Christian and philanthropic principles, and that such a
colony would not only afford the requisite protection to the
natives, and the requisite security for the maintenance of
their rights, but would form a most desirable *point d'appui*
and centre of action for missionary labour among the
aborigines.

*   *   *   *   *   *   *

"It is acknowledged also as a maxim or first principle of
the law of nations, that if the new country so discovered
is inhabited, and under a government of any kind, the
mere discovery of it by a civilized nation, (while it still
gives such a nation a right to colonize it, if it is susceptible

of colonization, in preference to all other civilized nations,) confers on that nation no right of sovereignty over it—no right of property to a single inch of its territory. In the celebrated case of the Cherokee Nation against the State of Georgia, tried before the Supreme Court of the United States in the year 1832, the late eminent Chief Justice Marshall, in his admirable summing up of the argument on both sides, laid down this equitable principle as having been the principle on which the British Government had uniformly acted towards the Indians in the colonization of America, previous to the war of American independence; and proved incontestibly that as the American Governments had merely inherited British rights by the event of that war, they could have no right of property whatever upon the territory of a free and independent Indian nation.

"In fact this equitable principle seems to have regulated the transactions of the more respectable civilized nations with semi-barbarous tribes from the remotest times. Whether we believe the story, handed down to us from antiquity, of the bullock's hide cut into a thong of great length for the purpose of measuring off the piece of land which had been previously purchased by Queen Dido, from the natives of Northern Africa, for the erection of the city of Carthage, or not, the very fact that such a story was told and credited by the ancients sufficiently apprises us of the principles on which the merchant-princes of Tyre and Sidon were known to regulate their intercourse with uncivilized men; for instead of seizing it by force of arms, and thereby exciting a war that would in all probability have laid waste the country and ruined their own commerce, the Phœnicians evidently purchased from the native chief of the district, at a certain fixed price, the piece of land they had selected in his territory as the site of their trading factory of Carthage.

Referring to the right of Her Majesty to colonize New Zealand as a dependency of New South Wales, which the writer had successfully suggested as the only way of getting out of the difficulty of the time —

"The Royal Commission of 1787, appointing Captain Phillip, R.N. to be Captain-General and Governor-in-chief in and over the territory of New South Wales and its dependencies, included all the discoveries of Captain . Cook in the Southern Pacific; the said territory and its dependencies being described in that Commission as extending "from Cape York (the extremity of the coast to the northward), in the latitude of 11 deg. 37 min. South, to the South Cape, (the southern extremity of the coast,) in the latitude of 43 deg. 30 min. South; and inland to the westward as far as 135 deg. of East longitude, *comprehending all the islands adjacent in the Pacific Ocean, within the latitudes of the above-mentioned capes.*"

"If it should be urged, however, that this description could not be supposed to include islands so far to the eastward of New Holland as New Zealand, I beg to reply, my Lord, that it was not only supposed to do so, but that it really did include such islands; the island, called Norfolk island, situated to the northward of New Zealand, on the same meridian, being actually colonized by Captain Phillip, in virtue of his Commission above quoted, as a part of the territory of New South Wales and its dependencies. Nay, shortly after the commencement of the present century, the British Government had it seriously under their consideration to appoint a Lieutenant-Governor of New Zealand, as a subordinate penal settlement and dependency of New South Wales, on a representation, pointing out the propriety of such an appointment, by Lieutenant-Colonel Foveaux, of the New South Wales corps. Happily, indeed, for New Zealand, that recommendation was not acted on; but so lately as the close of the government of the late Major-General Macquarie, in the year 1820, that island was still regarded, not theoretically but practically, as a dependency of New South Wales, and within the

limits of the government of that Colony; for when the
Rev. Mr. Butler was about to proceed to New Zealand, as
Superintendent of the Church Mission in that island, he
was actually created a Justice of the Peace for the territory
of New South Wales and its dependencies, by Governor
Macquarie, and authorised to exercise his functions in that
capacity in New Zealand."

Referring to the case of the adventurers from Van
Dieman's Land taking possession of Port Phillip in 1835—

"Now, I conceive, my Lord, that the case of all purchases of land from the natives of New Zealand is a case
precisely similar; and the interests of humanity, as well
as of Her Majesty's Government generally, demand that
Her Majesty shall not suffer the Royal prerogative to be
invaded by individual and unwarranted speculation in that
island, any more than it was allowed to be invaded in a
similar manner on the South coast of New Holland. By
maintaining the Royal prerogative in the case of New Zealand, as it was maintained at Port Phillip, Her Majesty
will reserve to herself the salutary and important right of
revising every alleged purchase of land. in that island—
will retain the power of confirming honest men in their
possessions, and of obliging persons of a different description to restore to the natives, or to the Government on their
behalf, the land they have acquired dishonestly—and will
thus establish a precedent of most beneficial operation for
the aborigines of every uncivilized country in the South Seas
having relations with British subjects in all time coming.

"In regard to the assumption of the sovereignty of New
Zealand, on the part of Her Majesty, considered as distinct
from the right to colonize the island on the terms I have
mentioned, I am aware of no other principle on which
such a measure could be justified than that of sheer necessity; a principle which, your Lordship is aware, however,
is superior to law, or rather which creates a law for itself.
It is absolutely necessary, on the one hand, that a regular

and energetic Government should be established forthwith
in that island; but the native chiefs are utterly incapable,
on the other, of forming such a Government of themselves;
being altogether destitute of the intelligence, virtue, and
energy of character that would be indispensably requisite
to sustain a republic, and too jealous of each other to allow
any one of their number to exercise authority as lord paramount over the rest. But if the sovereignty of the island
were at once assumed by Her Majesty, and exercised, as it
would undoubtedly be, for the protection of the natives
from European aggression, for the preservation of peace
between their different tribes, and for the promotion of
their intellectual and moral advancement, there is no room
to doubt, from all I have heard of the New Zealanders in
all parts of the island for the last sixteen years, that such
an event would be universally hailed by the natives and
most cheerfully acquiesced in. The New Zealanders are
uniformly desirous that Europeans should settle among
them; and so untutored are they in regard to the ideas of
civilized men on the points of national independence and
sovereignty, that they have often represented it as a singular
instance of bad taste, as well as of partiality, on the part of
the British Government, that the Sovereign of Great
Britain should have sent a Governor for so inferior a race
as the black natives of New South Wales, and none for
them.

"I beg therefore most respectfully to suggest that Her
Majesty should be advised forthwith to assume the sovereignty of New Zealand, for the general purposes of
colonization from the mother country, as well as for the
protection and preservation of its aboriginal inhabitants;
such colonization to be effected on the principles on which
the colony of South Australia has recently been established, but with a special reference to the superior intellectual
condition and general prospects of the aboriginal race. If
an Act of the Imperial Parliament could be obtained for

such a purpose, it would doubtless be highly desirable; but it appears to me that under the original Act of Parliament authorising the King in Council to form a Colony on the east coast of New Holland, including within its jurisdiction the adjacent islands of the Pacific Ocean, Her Majesty is fully authorised to take immediate steps, if she shall think fit, for the colonization of New Zealand, without the sanction of a new Act of Parliament at all.*

"Supposing, therefore, that it should be determined on the part of Her Majesty's Government to colonize New Zealand, or to speak more properly, to throw open that island for colonization, I would earnestly recommend that the following general principles should be acknowledged and established as the fundamental principles of the undertaking:—

"1.—That the land in all the islands constituting the New Zealand group —including Chatham Island, the Auckland Islands, Norfolk Island, and Lord Howe's Island —belongs to the aborigines of these islands respectively; and that no part of that land shall be settled by European colonists without the express consent of the natives, and without having been previously purchased from the natives at what they consider a fair and adequate price.

"2.—That all private purchases of land from the natives whether past or future, shall be utterly disallowed, as an infringement of Her Majesty's undoubted right of pre-emption; the Government, or Commissioners acting on their behalf, to be the sole purchasers from the natives, and a Board of Protectors of the aborigines to ascertain beforehand, and to certify to that effect in every particular case, that in all such purchases, the interests and feelings and wishes of the natives have been duly consulted.

"3.—That the land so purchased from the natives shall be sold by the said Commissioners at not less than a certain

---

* Which was done accordingly.

fixed price per acre, and that the proceeds of such sales shall be appropriated in the following manner, viz. :

" 1st. Towards the payment of the original price of the land as purchased from the natives.

" 2nd. Towards the payment of the salaries of the Board of Protectors of the aborigines; that that Board may be alike independent of the European colonists and of the Local Government.

" 3rd. Towards the support of schools and other kindred institutions for promoting the intellectual and moral advancement of the natives.

" 4th. Towards the encouragement and support of voluntary emigration from Great Britain and Ireland.

" It is extremely gratifying to observe that the generous and philanthropic policy I have thus advocated, in regard to the aborigines of New Zealand, has found supporters, in the highest and most influential quarters, in regard to another most interesting race of aborigines, in the United States of America. The General Government of the United States, as your Lordship is well aware, allows no private individual, nor even a Sovereign State, to acquire land from the Indians in any way; the right of acquiring such land being vested by the Constitution in the Supreme Government exclusively. The land so acquired, whether by purchase, by exchange, or by the extinction of native titles in any other way, is sold thereafter by the General Government at a certain fixed price—about five shillings per acre—and the proceeds of such sales are thrown into the Public Treasury of the United States. In his Report to the President, however, of November 25, 1832, the American Secretary at War strongly recommends that in future the revenue, (amounting recently to four millions sterling per annum) arising from such sales, should be appropriated exclusively towards the general improvement of the aborigines.

"It cannot be doubted," observes the philanthropic Secretary, in the Report referred to, "that a course, so, consistent with the dictates of justice, and so honourable to the national character, would be approved by public sentiment. Should we hereafter discard all pecuniary advantage in our purchases from the Indians, and confine ourselves to the great objects of their removal and establishment, and *take care that the proceeds of the cessions are applied to their benefit*, and in the most salutary manner, we should go far towards discharging the great moral debt which has come down to us as an inheritance from the earliest periods of our history, and which has been unfortunately increased during successive generations by circumstances beyond our control. *This policy would not be less wise than just*. The time has passed away, if it ever existed, when a revenue derived from such a source was necessary to the Government. The remnant of our aboriginal race may well look for the *full value*, and that usefully applied, of the remnant of those *immense possessions* which have passed from them to us, and left no substantial evidences of permanent advantage to them."

"In the event of the colonization of New Zealand, I conceive, my Lord, there would be no necessity for a body of military to protect the colonists. If many hundred Europeans can live at present in perfect safety among the New Zealanders in all parts of the island, even when pursuing a species of traffic that reduces the unfortunate natives to absolute beggary in their own land, it must be evident that as many thousand Europeans would stand in still less need of military protection, especially when living together in concentrated communities, and all their intercourse with the natives conducted on the principles of impartial justice and enlightened Christianity. The protection of one or two ships of war, to be employed in surveying the coast, and in establishing a friendly intercourse with the native tribes at a distance from the principal settlement, would be all the protection which the colonists would require from the mother-country.

"Much of the beneficial influence to be hoped for from European colonization in New Zealand, as far as the natives are concerned, would depend on the number and concentration of the colonists, and on the moral and educational machinery with which they should be attended from their first landing on the island. The settlement of a few straggling European adventurers among the uncivilized aborigines of any country is always unfavourable to the moral welfare of both parties. It would therefore be of importance to the New Zealanders to prevent such dispersion, and to induce the Europeans settling in the island to concentrate themselves in suitable localities.* In a pastoral country like New South Wales, this would doubtless be both absurd and impracticable; but in a maritime and agricultural country, like the northern parts of New Zealand, it would be comparatively easy. Besides, the Government Commissioners, and Board of Protectors, would have it fully in their power to prevent any European colonist from acquiring property in land wherever his settlement might be deemed likely to prove unfavourable ,to the natives.

* The Local Government of the British Colony of Massachusetts passed an ordinance, shortly after the foundation of the Colony in the 17th century, prohibiting the formation of any new settlement within the Colonial territory, unless there should be thirty families associated in the enterprise, and unless these families should bind themselves to support a minister of religion and a schoolmaster within their limits. And to prevent such scenes of surprise and massacre as have occurred so often in late years in the case of solitary families in New Zealand, their fastnesses in these out-settlements were regularly loop-holed for defence against the Indians of the period—who, I firmly believe, were precisely of the same race and origin as the Maories of New Zealand. I published a work on this subject, now long out of print, in the year 1834, entitled *View of the Origin and Migrations of the Polynesian Nation*; *demonstrating their original discovery and progressive settlement of the*

"In the prospect, therefore, of the colonization of New Zealand, on such principles as those I have taken the liberty to suggest to your Lordship and the public, it becomes a question of importance, what is to be done with these parties, and with all the other Europeans who have acquired land in that island, by alleged purchase from the natives ? Are their titles to be held good in all cases, and are the British Government to become a party to the iniquitous bargains they have notoriously concluded in many instances, and to the wholesale injustice and oppression they have avowedly perpetrated on the defenceless natives ?

*　　*　　*　　*　　*　　*　　*

"For my own part, knowing that there are reputable men in New Zealand, who have acquired the lands they occupy by fair and honourable means, and who have greatly improved these lands by the erection of valuable buildings, while there are others whose regularly drawn deeds in the English and New Zealand languages, give them no title in equity to the lands they lay claim to, I would respectfully recommend that, in the event of the colonization of New Zealand, and the assertion of Her Majesty's right of preemption in all cases whether past or future, a Board should be appointed, like the Court of Claims in New South Wales, with full power to decide definitively, in all cases of

Continent of America. The idea was suggested by a violent gale of westerly wind of a whole month's duration, which I experienced in the year 1830, immediately after writing the verses at page 380 of this volume, and which carried our good ship right across the Pacific to Cape Horn. For if such a gale, which usually rises suddenly in the Pacific, had caught some unfortunate canoe on the coast of Easter Island in latitude 27° 5' South—a case which has occurred hundreds of times elsewhere in the Pacific—it must have carried it without fail to the American land, and in all likelihood landed the first inhabitants of that continent somewhere near Copiapo, in the States of Chili. Easter Island is only 1800 miles from the American land; and such voyages, originating either in accident from sudden gales, or from the

land claimed on the ground of purchase from the natives ; and that that Board should be instructed to lay it down as a general principle that no such Deeds as I have mentioned should be regarded as a valid title to land, but that each case should be decided upon on its own individual merits, and that according as it should appear that the natives had or had not been fairly treated, and that an adequate consideration had or had not been given, the holder of the native Deed should either receive a Deed of grant from the Crown for such part of the land he claimed as he should be found fairly entitled to, or should merely have the right of pre-emption within a certain period at the Government minimum price. By this means the rights of honest men would be secured, while the Government would have ample means of doing justice to those natives who have been wrongfully despoiled of their lands by unprincipled Europeans.

"Such, my Lord, was the general impression produced upon my own mind by my short visit to New Zealand in the months of January and February last. While that impression was strong and vivid, I committed my ideas on the subject to writing, a few days after we had lost sight of the island, while our vessel was pursuing her homeward course across the Pacific ; and with only a few unimportant alterations, the preceding pages have been printed as they were then written. In writing these pages, I was, therefore,

fortune of war compelliug the vanquished to take to sea, rather than remain to be butchered on land by the conquerors, have been frequent in the Pacific in all past ages. Besides, Captain Cook shews us that the inhabitants of Easter Island, from the wonderful remains of their colossal architecture, must, in some distant age, have been a comparatively civilized people. At all events, the Indo-American civilization was decidedly Polynesian in its type. And that type was derived from the earliest period in the history of mankind, when the order of the day in architecture was the pyramidal and colossal style of Egypt. That style was carried out in Polynesia, and was afterwards re-produced in Peru and Mexico.

entirely unconnected with either of the parties who, I knew, had been at issue in England, on the New Zealand question; I had no private interest to serve in the matter; I had no motive to induce me to write but a sincere desire to subserve the cause of humanity, and to promote the interests and extension of the British empire. On touching at Pernambuco in the course of my voyage home, I was fortunate enough to obtain a copy of your Lordship's Report on the affairs of Canada, which had then just arrived from England in the Brazils; and on my arrival in London, I was induced, from my perusal of that admirable Report, and from the fact of your Lordship's having subsequently become the Governor of a Company established for the colonization of New Zealand, to address these letters to your Lordship.

JOHN L. SHERRIFF, WYNYARD SQUARE, SYDNEY.